The Twelfth Cross

Melanie Hodges

Copyright © 2024 Melanie Hodges
All rights reserved

For Valerie who first introduced me to Eleanor and her crosses.

And for my husband, David, without whose support this novel would not exist.

Map Section

PART I

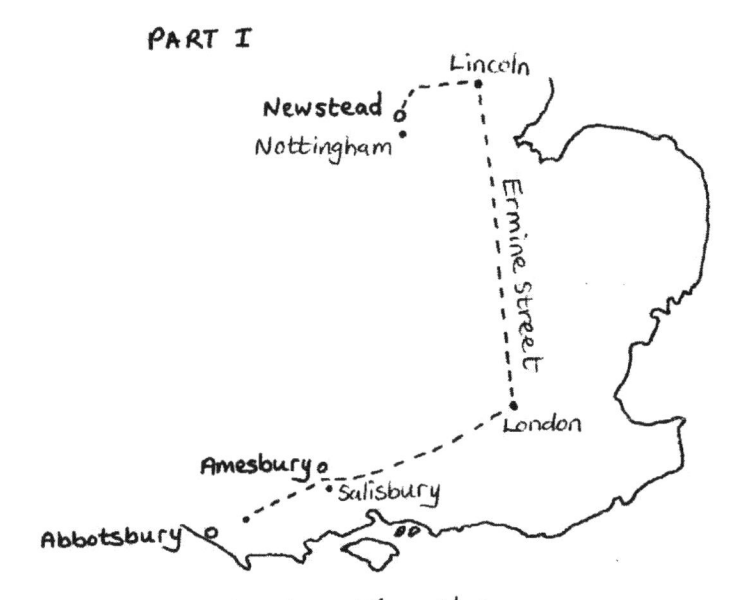

Brother Clément's journey
Abbotsbury to Newstead via Amesbury

PART I

Journeys of the Royal Court

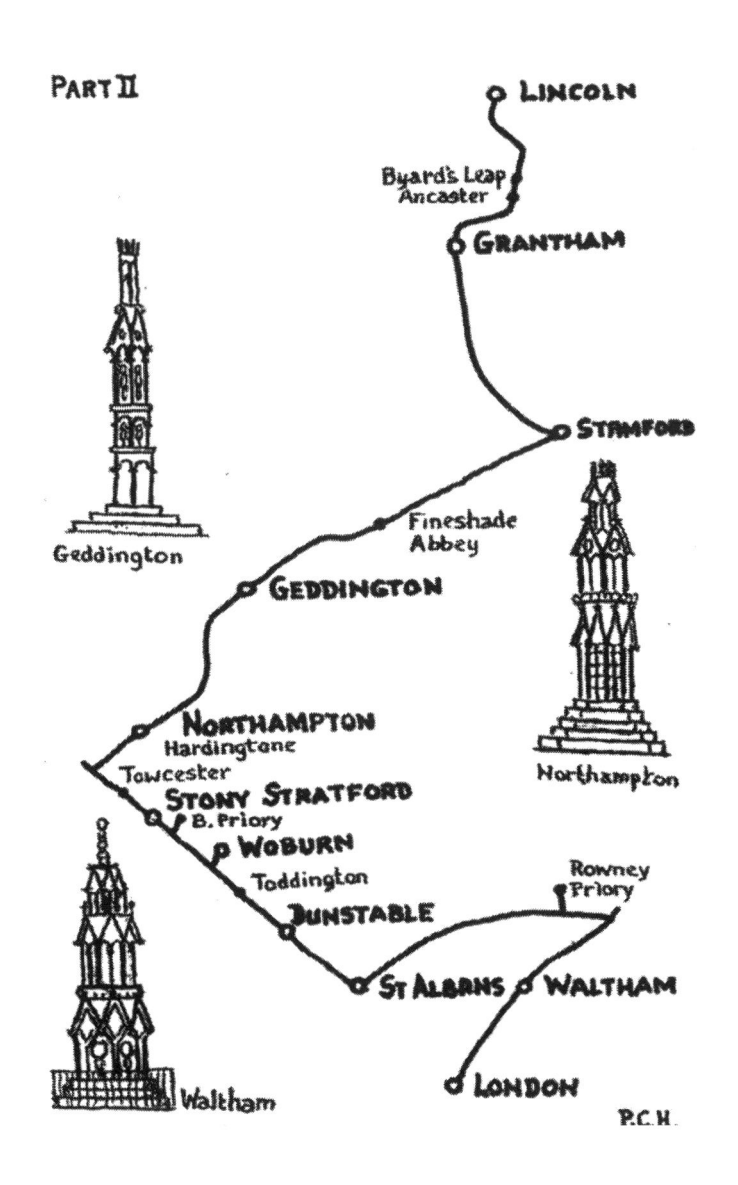

PART II

LINCOLN
Byard's Leap
Ancaster
GRANTHAM
STAMFORD
Fineshade Abbey
GEDDINGTON
Geddington
NORTHAMPTON
Hardingstone
Towcester
STONY STRATFORD
B. Priory
WOBURN
Toddington
DUNSTABLE
Rowney Priory
ST ALBANS
WALTHAM
Northampton
Waltham
LONDON
P.C.H.

PART III LONDON

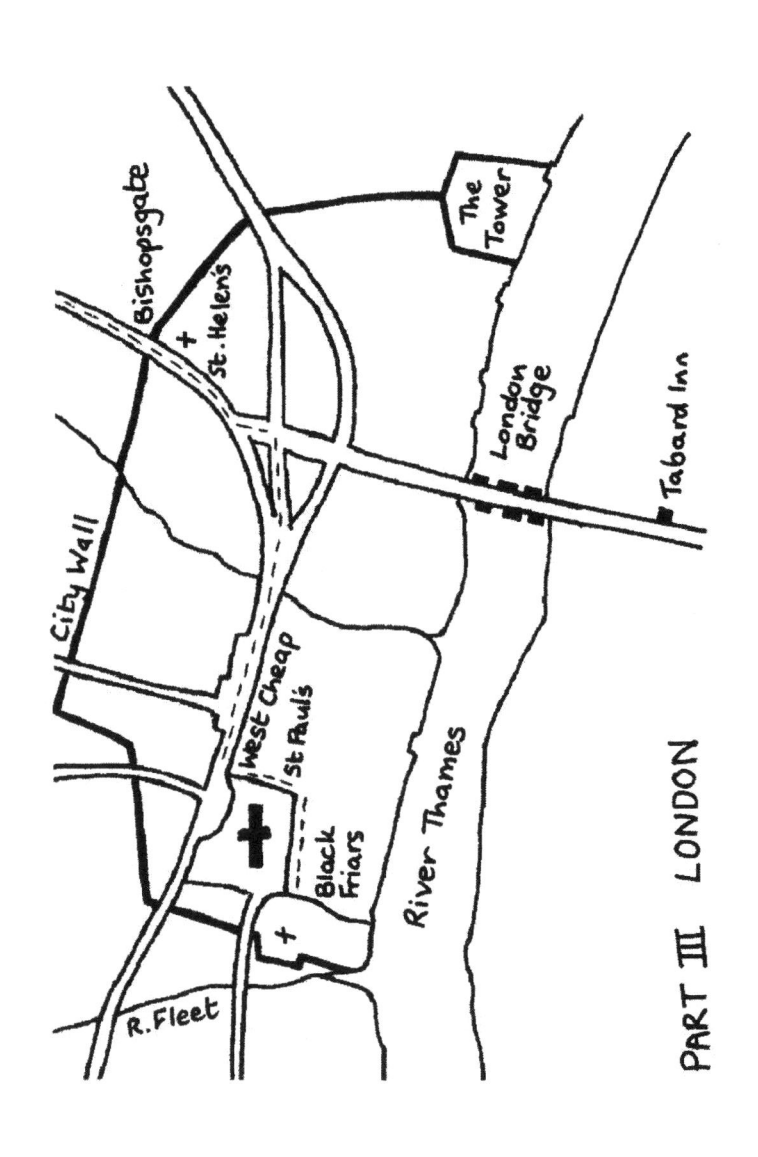

PART III
LUDGATE TO WESTMINSTER

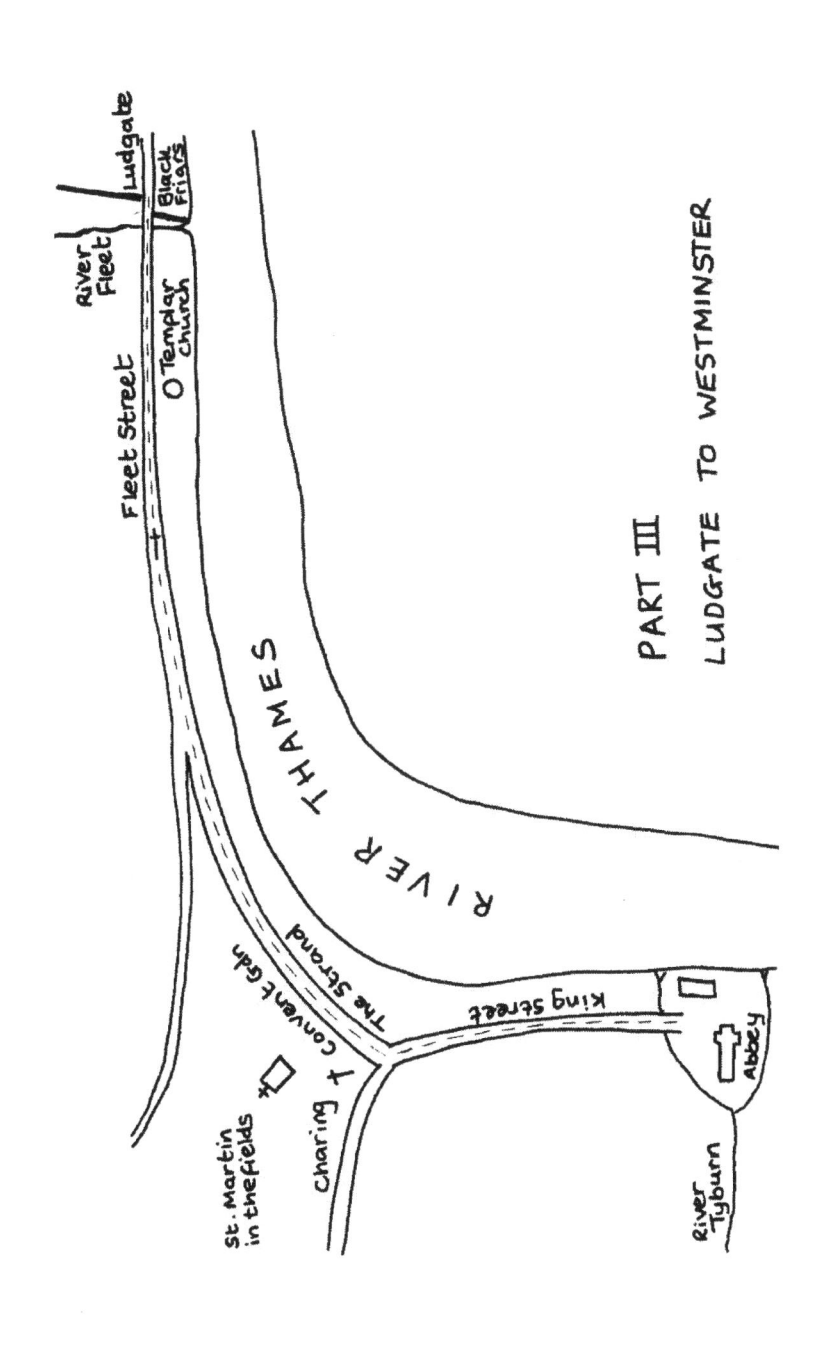

Part I

The Ammonite Curse

PART I

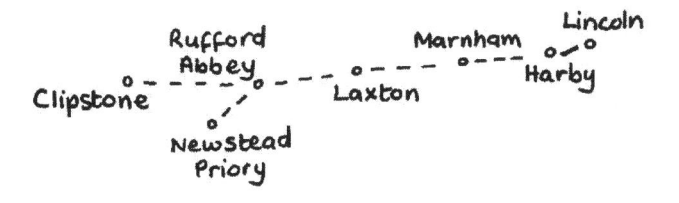

Brother Clément's journey
Abbotsbury to Newstead via Amesbury

PART II

Journeys of the Royal Court

Prologue

Easter 1315, Abbotsbury, Dorsetshire

A traveller stopped to roll his shoulders, and dislodged the heavy leather pack on his back. The tools of his trade emitted a distinct metallic clang. He set the pack straight, rubbed his temples and pursued his path downhill through a wooded gully and across a stream. He skirted the edge of a hillock where sheep grazed on lush grass, sprouting from strangely reddish earth. The man shuddered at a memory it stirred, of blood-drenched soil beneath the body of a guard. His hand moved to the pommel of the slender knife hanging from his belt. He quickened his step.

Ahead lay a longer, flatter stretch of track with water meadows on his left and beyond them a dense reedbed. That must be the end of the lagoon I could see from the ridge, he thought. I have to pass beyond it to reach the shore. At last, he arrived at a steep, stony bank, the final hurdle of his arduous journey to find his quarry. He paused for breath, recalling how he had last seen Brother Clément, five and twenty years ago, down the shaft of his crossbow.

The man scrambled up and over the bank of stones and spotted the monk down by the water, standing alone, staring out to sea. The traveller called to him but his voice was drowned by the roar of the surf and the rasp of shingle hauled away by ebbing waves. He approached and tapped the monk on the shoulder. Clément spun round.

∞

Twenty-five years earlier, 4th September 1290, Abbotsbury, Dorsetshire

Brother Clément tripped over a piece of driftwood and plunged headfirst down the steep bank of pebbles towards the sea. Time expanded and he had a sensation of flying before the ground rose to meet him. A jet of pain shot up his arm as he fell on the stones. For a few moments, he lay as he landed, sprawled on the shore, waiting for his wits to return. As his pounding heart settled, he listened to the thud and rush of his blood, echoed by the rhythmic roar of breakers crashing on the shingle. He had never seen waves from this angle before, rising in a pure green curve to pounce predator-like on the pebbles and drag them, crackling, away to the deep.

Clément sat up gingerly, leaning on his unhurt arm; the other was starting to throb but he felt no pain elsewhere. A little way offshore, a patch of sea suddenly blazed beneath a break in the clouds. At this glimpse of glory, the monk's mind lifted and flew like a homing pigeon to Queen Eleanor. What was she doing at that moment? Was she perchance reading one of the manuscripts he had copied for her; her golden skin touching the vellum his own hand had brushed as his quill formed the letters? He wondered if she had noticed the length of his absence from her court – now twenty-four days. Did she even spare him a thought? Probably not. He knew well enough that her very being revolved around King Edward. How often Clément had seen her eyes light up at the sound of his voice. He had even occasionally glimpsed private loving looks exchanged between them amidst the crowded royal court. So why should the queen think of her absent scribe when she was in the company of her lord?

"Brother Clément! Are you injured?" called Brother Mark, labouring along the stony shore. He knelt beside Clément.

"Only my wrist is hurt, Mark. It struck a rock as I landed."

"Which wrist, brother?"

"The left, God be praised. I will still be able to write."

"Can you move it at all?" Clément turned his hand palm up, wincing. He was surprised to see three small parallel grazes on the heel of his hand, oozing blood. He searched around for the rock he had hit and studied it.

"Look at this shape in the rock, brother. It is like a snail's shell," he said to Mark.

Mark glanced at it, distractedly. "Never mind the stone! Your wrist may be broken; we must get you to the infirmary."

Clément lifted the rock with his good hand to try its weight. Not too heavy. Mark raised his eyebrows, but seeing the determined look in Clément's grey eyes, he picked up the rock for him. The young brother helped his companion up, taking care not to disturb his left arm which Clément held across his chest. They turned their backs on the sea and set off at a careful pace uphill towards the Abbey of Saint Peter at Abbotsbury.

"Judging by your reaction, Mark, I take it this is not the first time you have seen a patterned rock like this. As we walk, would you tell me what you know about such stones? It will at least take my mind off my throbbing wrist."

"I know little; only that stones like this are not uncommon on these shores. Brother Anselm once told me he collected them when he was a lad. For all I know, he may still have them," said Mark.

"But it is against our Rule to keep personal possessions," said Clément.

"Exceptions can be made at the abbot's discretion, for objects of study. Perhaps these stones are such an exception. You may ask Anselm yourself if he is in the infirmary when we arrive."

Chapter 1

4th September Current year, Lincoln Cathedral

Daniel leaned over the horizontal mirror reflecting the cathedral's ceiling. He gazed down at the elegant arches soaring high above, and caught a glimpse of a hand just before it slammed into the back of his head, flattening his face against the mirror. Daniel slithered sideways, squirming free of Jim's grip, and instinctively raised his arm to ward off the next blow. His bag dropped out of his hand but he didn't dare pick it up. He didn't look at their faces or at his bag, not wanting to draw their attention to it. He stood slightly aloof, eyes lowered in the region of their stomachs.

"Sorry, Geek, didn't see you there," Jim said. Daniel stole a glance at Jim and noticed that he too avoided eye contact. It struck Daniel that, being so short, there were few people Jim could look in the eye, without 'looking up to them.' But he compensated for his small stature by always appearing with his henchmen: a thin girl with long, dark hair and a blond boy who towered over them all.

Daniel clenched his teeth. "My name's Dan," he said.

"What was that, Geek?"

"Just, my name – it's Dan."

"No, Geek. I'm Daniel: James Daniel Thompson. Those names are taken. Your name's Geek, or if you really don't like it, we could change it to Nerd or ... Turd! Ha!" Jim laughed at his own rhyme. Daniel drooped a little and said nothing. "So where's your angel dress today?" Jim said. "You could put it on and sing to us while we traipse round this boring old dump." Ed grinned and Natalie tittered. Daniel remained silent until Jim said, "Well?"

"I only wear choir robes for singing in the choir, at services. That's what choir robes are for, funnily enough." Daniel regretted the note of sarcasm as soon as the words escaped his lips.

"Let's see what's in Geek's bag shall we, Nat?" Jim said. Natalie picked up the bag, opened it and rummaged around.

"Chocolate, pencil case, books and what have we here? A letter from Mummy!

"Give it here," said Jim. He snatched the letter.

"That's private!" Daniel snarled. Jim snorted and the others laughed outright.

"Nothing's private," said Jim. "Haven't you got that yet, Geek? I thought you were supposed to be clever. Now, let's be reasonable. You want mummy's letter back and I don't want to do my history essay. So, I reckon we have the makings of a deal. My history essay done by Friday and you get your precious letter back. No essay, no letter. Or maybe I will give it back - after I've read it out in the common room!"

Shrieks of laughter erupted from Natalie and Ed, attracting the attention of a blue-robed verger, who shushed them. Jim and his mates slouched off. Natalie slung Daniel's bag under a monument as she went, so he would have to crawl under to retrieve it. He waited until they were well out of kicking distance before he knelt to reach it. The chocolate was gone, no surprise there, but the books and even the pencil case were still there. It could have been worse.

Daniel shouldered his bag and resumed his stroll around the cathedral, trying to refocus his mind. It was strangely comforting to tread on the stone floor worn smooth over the last nine centuries. Countless others had walked here, just like him, with their problems and anxieties. If these pillars could talk, what secrets they could unlock.

This trip was the first history lesson of term. Their assignment was to find something of interest in the cathedral and then research it for an essay. Daniel now had two essays to write in a week. It shouldn't be too difficult. He already knew a lot about the cathedral and was here most days. He had become a Lincoln chorister a year ago, joining the cathedral school in year 9. As well as singing in the choir, Daniel often hung out here in his free time. Sometimes he helped out in the café. The cathedral had become a sanctuary where he could escape the attention of Jim and his friends. They would never dream of darkening the doors of a church. Until today.

The fact that his refuge had been violated bothered him far more than the actual incident. He tried to banish it to the back of his mind. Suddenly he ducked, startled by a noise above his head. A pigeon clapped its wings and flew up and up into the tower. He watched until it disappeared into a nook high above.

Daniel found himself at the far end of the cathedral below the great east window. He stopped in front of a large stone medieval tomb. On top of it, carved in darker stone, lay the statue of a woman, her crowned head resting on two cushions and her long, wavy hair cascading over her neck and shoulders. He read the notice.

Eleanor of Castile, Queen Consort of Edward I, died November 28th 1290 at Harby, near Lincoln. Her viscera are interred here. Her body was carried in stages to London where the rest of her body is buried in Westminster Abbey.

Daniel wondered what viscera meant. This might be promising material for an essay. He slipped his phone out of his pocket and took a photo of the notice and the queen's statue. He walked right around the coffin. Along the bottom on each side were vivid coats of arms; three different shields in a repeating pattern. He took a picture of the first one – three standing golden lions on a bright red background. That one probably represented England. The other two shields were unfamiliar. One had three diagonal blue stripes on a brown background, edged with red. Daniel preferred the last one. It was divided into four quarters: two showed a striking black lion on a white background and the others had a gold castle on a red background. Perhaps these were the shields of Castile, wherever that was. He would Google it later.

His eye was drawn back to the queen's marble statue. Eleanor of Castile. He had never heard of her. She looked quite young, maybe around his mum's age. Her face was attractive and serene, with very even features. Daniel wondered if she was that perfect-looking in real life or if the sculptor had felt obliged to portray her that way. What was she really like? And how did she die? Hopefully he would be able to find out.

Daniel still had to find an idea for another essay. Near to Queen Eleanor's tomb lay another, even older. This one had a man's statue lying on it. Daniel walked round to the other side and spotted the sign about it.

Saint Hugh, Bishop of Lincoln, died in London, November 1200. His body was brought back in stages to be buried here in the cathedral he served.

It struck Daniel as an odd coincidence: two medieval characters who died in the same century, lying here side by side; one whose corpse was carried from London to Lincoln for burial and the other, the same journey in reverse. Daniel was still snapping photos of the tombs when Miss Hetherington came to round up the troops to walk back to school.

Chapter 2

4th September 1290, Abbotsbury, Dorsetshire

The two monks made an odd sight as they walked through the gatehouse of the Abbey of Saint Peter and across the great court towards the infirmary. The young novice, Mark, moderated his long stride to support Brother Clément, his senior by some ten years. Clément was a little below the middle height and slight of frame. Intelligent, pale grey eyes shone out from his otherwise unremarkable face. Brother Simon, taking the air at the infirmary door, observed pain in those grey eyes and saw how Clément cradled his arm.

"What has befallen you, brother? Come within and let me look at you." He bustled Clément into a cell separate from the main infirmary where his regular patients lay, and helped him onto the cot.

"I fear my wrist may be broken, Simon. I took a fall down the bank on the shore and my hand struck a rock."

"Well then," said the infirmarer, "let us get to work on you and see if your diagnosis is correct." He poked his head out of the door and summoned his assistant, before gently probing Clément's hand, wrist and arm. However tenderly he was handled, Clément could not help wincing with the pain. Brother Anselm glided into the small room. Without looking up, Simon instructed him, "Measure out a dose of poppy juice; Clément is in pain."

Anselm left the room as softly as he had entered a moment before. He returned with a small glass phial in one hand and a cup in the other. He gave the poppy juice to Clément and stepped back fixing his eyes on Brother Simon, content to await further instruction or merely to watch and learn as the infirmarer went about his work as skilfully as a master craftsman plies his trade.

"You also have a surface wound, I see," Brother Simon said.

"Yes," replied Clément, "but it's nothing to trouble about."

"Anselm, see these grazes are cleansed. Even small wounds can fester and turn bad. And I will set about making a poultice for the wrist. It is not broken, Clément, just badly sprained. And fortunately for you, being a scribe, it is your left. I take it you are right-handed?"

"Indeed, I am, else you would have heard me lamenting bitterly; for I value my craft as I see you do yours." Simon raised his eyes to Clément's face and acknowledged the compliment with half a smile.

"All crafts are valuable to God and happy is the man who discovers his gift and works at it with his strength," he said.

"Amen to that," agreed Clément.

During this exchange, the silent Brother Anselm had once more left the room and returned, this time with a small bowl of warm water and some soft cloths. Clément smiled at the contrast between the infirmarer and his assistant: Simon clucking over his charges like a mother hen and Anselm gliding between them as silently as an owl. The two men discharged their duties with equal care and efficiency but their manner in doing so could not be more different.

Anselm lifted Clément's hand and began to bathe it.

"Brother Mark, do you have the rock we brought from the beach?" Clément asked.

Mark, who had been standing aside all this time, retrieved the stone from the folds of his habit and placed it in Clément's good hand.

"Mark told me that you might be able to answer my questions about the curious pattern," Clément said to Anselm. "It is as if a shell has become embedded in the rock."

Anselm's soft green eyes lit up at the sight of the stone. "Indeed, brother, I have a small collection of stones like this, along with other curiosities I have found on the shore. I am permitted to study them. This one is a fine specimen. You are fortunate to have stumbled upon it."

"It felt more painful than fortunate, Brother Anselm," said Clément, wryly. "But do you know what it is?"

"I cannot say with certainty but I will gladly share with you what I have learned thus far."

"Brother Anselm," Simon interrupted, "please recall, that your first duty is to tend our patient's wounds, not to lecture him on the study of rocks."

"Yes, brother," said Anselm, lowering his eyes and resuming his task. Clément squeezed his hand and when Anselm looked up, gave him a conspiratorial wink. Anselm's face broke into such an appealing impish grin that Clément caught a glimpse of the carefree boy who spent his days scouring the seashore for treasures washed up by the tide.

Later, after the service of Vespers, Clément and Anselm made their way up a winding stone staircase. Anselm unlocked a heavy door, for the library within housed many valuable books, some of them chained to their shelves for safekeeping. Despite his familiarity with the room and the fact that some of the manuscripts were the result of his own painstaking copying, Clément always felt a sense of reverence here, subtly different to his sense of the holy in church. This one chamber connected him to a treasury of learning from across the globe and down the centuries.

"How does your work here progress?" Anselm said. "I understand you are transcribing a work of Hildegarde of Bingen for the queen?"

"I completed it today, praise God. I took a walk on the shore to celebrate and this happened," Clément said, with a glance at his bandaged wrist. "I hope it will not delay my return. I am most eager to present the manuscript to her grace. I believe that she too will be deeply impressed by Abbess Hildegarde's visions and learning."

Evening light slanted through the windows of the now deserted library. Anselm crossed to a table in the far corner, reached up to a high shelf and lifted down a small wooden chest.

"This is where I keep my treasures," said Anselm, setting the box upon the table and opening it. Inside, Clément saw an assortment of stones of various sizes and colours, unlike any he had seen before. Some were smooth and bore the imprint of fern-like leaves. Others were shell-shaped like the stone that had grazed his hand earlier in the day. Anselm watched with satisfaction as a look of wonder lit up Clément's face.

"What are they, brother?"

"I cannot be sure but my study of ancient texts led me to Xenophon. He speculated that long ago the shells and bodies of dead creatures rotted away and the space they had occupied was filled in with particles that gradually solidified into stone. This seems a logical explanation to me. Some call them figured shells but locally they are known as snakestones because many, such as yours, are coiled like serpents. Do you see this one here?" Anselm pointed to a smooth stone with distinct many-hued segments, spiralling inwards.

"May I?" said Clément, picking it up to examine it. "It's fascinating. What is it?"

"It is the same kind as the one embedded in your rock, but this is the inside. It has been split in half and polished." Anselm beamed. He seldom had the opportunity to display his collection and he relished Clément's admiration. Clément pondered them for some moments in silence; then he said,

"Anselm, if my stone were split in half and polished, do you think it would be like this one?"

"Yes, I believe so."

"Would it not make a fine gift, even for the queen? The court jeweller is highly skilled. I'm sure he could split it. Yes, I will show it to the queen and if it pleases her, her goldsmith can fashion it into a pendant."

"A splendid idea, Clément. In that case, you must take this one with you, to show her what the inside may look like. And also," he rummaged in the chest, "this small one, for the jeweller to practise upon." Anselm placed the stones into Clément's hand and would not hear of taking them back.

"I thank you for your generosity, brother. It gladdens my heart to think that I will be able to present her grace with such a gift."

Chapter 3

4th September 1290, Abbotsbury, Dorsetshire

Brother Simon insisted that Clément rest his wrist for a couple of days before undertaking his long journey to rejoin the royal court, currently touring the Midlands.

On the third day after his accident, immediately after the service of Prime Brother Clément and a groom, Michael, checked their saddle bags for the last time. Clément's luggage contained the precious manuscript, carefully wrapped in layers of cloth. In the leather scrip, dangling from his belt were the snakestones, including the one he had found, which Anselm had carefully chiselled from its rock. Michael's saddlebag contained food for the first couple of days of their journey. After that, they would have to rely on the hospitality of other abbeys and priories which lay on their route, and in between them, on the kindness of strangers. Satisfied that all was safely stowed, they said their final goodbyes, mounted their mules and set out. As they reached the gatehouse, Brother Simon ran up, puffing and panting, and handed Clément a small glass phial.

"Some poppy juice for the pain, Clément. But do not use it while you are riding, it will make you too drowsy," he said.

"I may not need it; my wrist does not pain me much."

"Believe me, Clément, when you have been in the saddle a few hours, your injury will make itself felt."

"I thank you, Brother Simon, for this and all your kindness," said Clément.

"God speed."

They progressed well enough for the first few hours, their mules plodding up and down the country paths. But towards the end of the morning, Clément's wrist began to throb with the constant jolting. He was glad to turn aside at midday at the church of Saint Mary at Melbury and enjoy a light meal with the priest there. Late in the afternoon, they reached the king's highway at Ilchester and now Clément hoped the way would be smoother and his wrist would not trouble him as much.

Clément made a detour in order to spend the third night of their journey at Amesbury Priory, where the young Princess Mary lived, as a companion to her grandmother, the prioress. He hoped to carry back their greeting to the queen. Clément was aware that news of King Edward's mother was unlikely to bring much pleasure to his mistress; relations between the two Queen Eleanors were cordial but not close. However, his patroness would be delighted to hear news of her daughter. In the morning, Clément therefore sought an audience with the prioress and, once the necessary civilities were exchanged, he begged leave to call on Mary, if she could be excused from her lessons.

Mary fairly skipped across the courtyard towards the unexpected visitor, though her excitement visibly dimmed on seeing merely an unassuming young monk.

"My lady, you will not remember me; I am Brother Clément, a scribe in your mother's household."

"Oh yes," Mary replied, "the one with the remarkably fine hand, I recollect." Clément flushed with pleasure. "How are my parents?" Mary said.

"When last I saw them, they were both well and in fine spirits," he replied.

"Truly? Has my mother recovered from the strain of Margaret's wedding? She was so exhausted by it all when I came away; I have been worried for her." Clément looked at her searchingly and decided to honour her frankness with a candid reply.

"The queen has not yet recovered her full vigour, but she was quite well when I parted from her, some four weeks ago. I have been in Abbotsbury, copying a manuscript for her and now I am en route north to rejoin the court."

"What manuscript have you copied? May I see it? I like writing too. I have been excused lessons until High Mass. May I detain you that long or must you resume your journey?" Clément smiled at the child's talkativeness. He did not wonder at it, since she was obliged to pass much of her time in silence here in the convent. Her request left him feeling torn between his duty to return to the queen as quickly as possible and the opportunity to indulge Mary's pleasure in the novelty of his visit. Looking into her bright brown eyes, he found he could not resist them.

"If it will please you, I will go and fetch the manuscript directly."

"I will wait for you in the cloisters, brother," Mary said, beaming. She made her way to the colonnaded quadrangle beside the priory church. After looking both ways to check she was alone, she raced all the way around, laughing. Next, she walked around it slowly, looking towards the garden at its unroofed centre. This was one of her favourite pastimes; noticing the subtle changes of view as she passed each stone arch, watching the play of sunlight on the grass and observing the priory buildings from ever-changing angles. She often wondered whether this was part of the master mason's purpose for the structure. Beyond providing a covered walkway connecting different areas of the priory, did he intend a lesson here: that each step we take may bring a fresh perspective on the familiar, if we take the trouble to open our eyes and look?

On his return, Clément carefully removed the protective wrappings from the document and laid it on a stone bench.

"This is the Scivias of Abbess Hildegarde of Bingen." Mary knelt down beside it to look.

"How marvellous! I have never before seen a book by a woman," she said.

"Hildegarde was a remarkably gifted woman. God blessed her with visions throughout her life, from the age of three. These she wrote down, as well as works on philosophy, medicine and natural history. She was also a prolific composer of music."

"How marvellous!" Mary repeated. "And you have copied it so beautifully. I am glad my mother will be able to read her book. Shall we go into the garden?" she said, abruptly changing the subject. "There are still some glorious roses in bloom."

In the priory garden, Mary skittered from one flower to the next, beckoning Clément to look at this one and to smell that one.

"You have inherited your mother's love of gardens, I see," Clément observed.

"Yes, but these are a sad showing compared to the ones at King's Langley. My mother made them so beautiful. And the water gardens! Did you ever see them? I had such happy times playing there with my brothers and sisters." Clément watched Mary's eyes take on a wistful look as she recalled her earlier childhood. To her it must seem long ago, he reflected; she was now about twelve years old, and it must be five years, if not six, since she had joined the priory. She had been here for half of her young life. The bell for mass startled them out of their reveries. Mary smiled at Clément; he in turn bowed his head and they parted.

The rest of the journey passed without incident. Careful night-time use of the poppy juice made the riding manageable for Clément and finally, he arrived at Newstead Priory in the county of Nottinghamshire, where the royal court was installed.

Chapter 4

11ᵗʰ September Current year, Lincoln Minster School

"Hand in your essays and settle down quickly," said Miss Hetherington in a no-nonsense but cheerful voice.

Daniel approached her desk sheepishly and said in a low tone, "I'm sorry, Miss, but I haven't finished mine yet."

"Did you say something, Daniel?" Miss Hetherington said, looking up from her screen.

"Yes, Miss."

"Well, speak up. I can't hear if you mumble."

"I haven't finished it yet," Daniel said, "I've done about two thirds but I fell asleep before I got to the end!"

"What do you mean, you fell asleep? Are you ill? You look all right to me, a bit flushed perhaps."

The class had fallen completely silent and Daniel could feel the gaze of his classmates boring into the small of his back. "I had some other homework to finish first, and by the time that was done, I was shattered – look." Daniel held up his paper and pointed to a wavy line of ink trailing off from an incomplete sentence.

"I see." Miss Hetherington cast an awkward glance around the room. "This is most out of character, Daniel, but I can't make exceptions. You will have to stay after class and complete your essay in detention at break time." Daniel hesitated, but said nothing more. The teacher dismissed him, "Off you go now, find your seat."

Daniel turned and flung himself into his chair, his eyes glued to the floor. The silence had broken and now the kids were muttering their amazement that 'Geek' hadn't finished his homework. At this point, Jim stood up, walked to the teacher's desk and threw his essay onto the pile with a flourish.

"Well, this morning is full of surprises," said Miss Hetherington, appearing slightly flustered. "Please open your textbooks at page 157." As Jim swaggered back to his place, he smirked at Daniel, who managed to raise his head and glare back.

At the end of the lesson, Daniel was glad to remain in class and finish his essay under the protective and slightly concerned gaze of Miss Hetherington. She fetched a coffee and then began marking the essays. Jim's was on the top of her pile. Daniel stole a few glances at her. She raised an eyebrow a couple of times and even shot him an anxious look. But she passed on to the next essay without comment. When the bell rang for the end of break, Daniel was on his final sentence, 'and in this way, King Edward's love for Queen Eleanor was immortalised.' He hurried over to the desk.

"I haven't had time to read it through but I've finished it at least."

"Hmm. Don't let it happen again, Daniel. Are you sure everything is all right?"

"Yes, Miss. More or less," he answered evasively and sped off to maths.

∞

"Did you see his face when he had to confess he hadn't done his homework?" Jim said to anyone who cared to listen in the dining hall.

"I swear there were smudges on his essay where he'd dribbled in his sleep!" said Natalie. Silence fell as Daniel entered the room.

"Has Geek done his det then?" Jim taunted. Yet Daniel detected a trace of concern on Jim's face. Was he wondering if Daniel had spilled any beans in his cosy tête-à-tête in the history room with Miss Hetherington? Daniel decided to make him sweat a little while there was safety in numbers. Damn the consequences.

"Yeah. That's all sorted, thanks, Jim," he said smugly. Daniel walked straight past, pulled out a chair and sat down at a nearby table. One of the good things about this school is the food, he thought as he tucked into his steaming shepherds' pie.

Jim stood up, knocking over his chair. "What's that supposed to mean?" he said.

"That I finished my essay." Daniel replied as calmly as he could. Don't let them see it's getting to you, he told himself.

Jim leaned over Daniel's dinner and said into his face, "That better be all."

"What else could it mean?" Daniel asked innocently.

"Come on," Jim said to Natalie and Ed with a jerk of his head. Natalie looked longingly at her chocolate mousse but got up obediently with Ed and they loped out of the hall with Jim. Daniel breathed a sigh of relief and sat back to enjoy his meal. He liked Tuesdays. He didn't have any classes with Jim for the rest of the day and after lessons he had choir till supper. There was only dorm time but that was ages away and he would cross that bridge when he came to it.

∞

In the cathedral choir stalls, Daniel lost himself in the music. The melody rose and fell, and he was carried along with it, like a ship on the swell of a tumultuous sea. Singing timeless words, in this ancient sacred place, gave him a sense of belonging to an unbroken line of worshippers reaching back across the centuries. He could be anyone, at any time in the last thousand years. For Daniel, choir practice was a cocoon: solid and reassuring; the only time he didn't feel homesick.

In the common room, meanwhile, Jim was the one sweating for once.

"Do you think Geek told her?" he said.

"I dunno," said Ed.

"I'm sure he didn't, Jim," said Natalie reassuringly, "he's too smart for that."

"Maybe. But I'm gonna teach him a lesson just to make sure. You still got that letter in your bag, Nat?"

"Geek's letter from mummy?" She rifled through her bag. "Yeah, here it is."

"Well, I said I'd return it and I'm a man of my word, so I will give it back - shredded." Ed and Natalie snorted with laughter.

"How will you shred the letter, Jim?" said Ed.

"With a paper shredder, thicko."

"Yeah. But we haven't got one, have we?"

Jim shrugged. "There's one in the resources' room."

"That room's always locked," Ed persisted, "How are you gonna get the key?"

"Natalie will be able to sweet talk Mr. Charles, won't you, Nat?" Jim said.

"Okay, I'm on it," said Natalie, glad of any excuse to put off doing her homework. She took the letter, slipped it inside a bundle of old papers and made her way down to the administrator's office. On the way, she stopped, leant on the cool wall, and read Daniel's letter.

Dear Daniel,

How has this week been for you, love? I'm fine and so was Dad last time I spoke to him, which was Tuesday, I think. Grandpa had another fall yesterday. He was on the floor from mid-afternoon until I got back from work. I got a bit cross with him – I couldn't help it. The silly man lay there for hours when he could have pressed his emergency button. Guess what he said when I asked him why. 'Because it wasn't an emergency. I was okay, just stuck on the floor. I knew you'd be back soon so I just got as comfy as I could and had a nap.' Honestly, Daniel, what can I do with him? I'll ask the doctor to try to talk some sense into him, because he doesn't listen to a word I say.

Anyhow, that's enough of my worries. How is everything at your end? Are you still getting on well with your roommate? Are you managing all the homework on top of choir practice? Remember Dad and I want to be involved in your school life and you can ring us any time.

That's all for now, love. I'll ring you on Saturday.

Love, Mum

Natalie blinked back tears. Her mum had never written to her. She'd never thought about it until now. She got quite a few texts: Maisie's got a new tooth, Maisie did a wee on the potty, Maisie misses her big sister, Maisie this, Maisie that. But this handwritten letter was something else – a little piece of home. Daniel's mum had sat down at a table, thinking about him and penned those words.

And she was about to shred them. She stuffed the letter back into the middle of her papers and walked off.

"Good afternoon, Mr. Charles. How are you today?" Natalie said, with a smile.

"Hello. Natalie, isn't it? I'm fine thank you. What are you after?"

"Me? I just want to shred my draft history essay. It's so bad. Please may I use the paper shredder?"

It was an odd request but he couldn't see any harm in it. "I'll come and open the room for you," said Mr. Charles, all too aware that Natalie was not to be trusted with any item of school property. He stood inside the door and watched over her shoulder, as the shredder gobbled the pages and spewed them out in tatters.

When Natalie returned to the common room, Jim grabbed the slithers of paper and stuffed them in his pocket, ready for the moment of maximum impact. He didn't have long to wait. Daniel returned from choir looking relaxed, settled into a chair and pulled his homework out of his bag.

Jim stalked over. "Hey, Geek. Thanks again for the history essay," he said, smiling. "Here's your letter as promised." He produced the shreds from his pocket, as if pulling a rabbit out of a hat, and deposited them on Daniel's maths book.

Daniel clenched his fists and fought back the tears that threatened. He blocked out the titters of a few students who liked to keep on the right side of Jim and his cronies. If he had looked up, he would have seen most of the kids look away, suddenly engrossed in their homework or the social media feed on their phone. Several exchanged covert glances or text messages, sympathising with Daniel but equally unwilling to stand up to Jim.

Later that night Daniel's roommate, Stephen, said,

"You've got to tell someone, Dan. He can't get away with this. Why didn't you speak to Miss Hetherington in your history detention while you had the chance? She must have suspected that essay wasn't Jim's work."

"I know, but it didn't feel right. I want to stand up to it in my own way and show Jim I'm stronger than he thinks."

"But Dan, he's walking all over you," said Stephen.

Daniel felt his face redden, and was glad the lights were out. "I know it looks that way," he said, "but Jim's afraid as well. Scared I'll snitch on him. That gives me a kind of power over him too. And besides, it might just make it worse."

"How could it get any worse?"

"Believe me, it could."

Stephen thought for a moment, "Yeah, I guess it could. All the more reason to get it sorted now. I bet the teachers would love an excuse to get rid of Jim."

"Well, it's not going to be through me, not at the moment anyway."

Several hours later Daniel lay wide awake, glowering with resentment, at Jim for destroying his letter and at life in general. He could hear his dad's voice in his head, 'Don't let the sun go down on your anger. Put things right before you go to bed or you won't be able to sleep.' Well, that part was certainly right. But he had no idea how to get rid of the anger raging inside him. Perhaps Stephen was right and he should tell Miss Hetherington. But what could the school do anyway? Put Jim under 24-hour surveillance? Jim was crafty. He knew how to charm the teachers and keep in their good books. Even Miss Hetherington might not believe Daniel. But how could he deal with this anger, simmering away beneath the surface, threatening to boil over at any moment? If it had been just Jim, he'd have taken him on any day. But Jim took care never to appear alone or vulnerable. There must be some way Daniel could prove himself against Jim, some contest apart from geekiness that he could win.

And what about his mum's letter? Daniel hadn't even opened it. He'd been saving it for later when he was safely in his room. He'd have to write back of course. Could he get away with, 'Thanks for your letter, it came on Thursday,' with no further reference to it? Usually mum asked loads of questions and he answered them in his reply. He'd have to wing it. He'd write a seemingly rushed letter saying he had to go to something important, choir practice; his mum would understand. He started composing the letter in his head. That was not the way to get to sleep. Finally, he gave in, turned on his lamp and crept quietly out of bed to rummage in his rucksack for paper and pen. He didn't want to wake Stephen, whose deep contented breaths were wafting over from the bed on the other side of the room. Daniel scribbled down the letter and then sank back onto his pillow. He reached for his phone, put his earbuds in and eventually drifted off.

Chapter 5

13ᵗʰ September 1290, Newstead Priory, Lincolnshire

"Is her grace at leisure to see me now?" the scribe asked, stepping tentatively into the royal chamber.

"You may enter, Clément. And where have you been all this time, may I ask? We expected you days ago," said Queen Eleanor, lifting her merry eyes to the face of her most devoted servant. The slim, dark-robed monk stepped forward and held out the manuscript he had copied for her.

"Your Grace, the Scivias of Saint Hildegarde of Bingen." As he reached forward, the queen's eye fell on the binding on his wrist.

"But, Clément, what has befallen you on the road? An accident? You were not attacked, surely?"

Clément retracted his arm, his colour mounting; dismayed that he should have alarmed the queen, yet thrilled by her concern.

"Merely an absentminded slip, your Grace, entirely my own fault. I beg you not to regard it."

"But has it been properly tended, Clément? I can summon my physician."

"I thank you for your concern," he said, glowing inwardly, "but I received excellent care from the infirmarer at my abbey and it mends well. I hardly need this dressing any longer but Brother Simon instructed me to wear it for a month and so I do."

"That is well. But will you give me your word that you will inform me if anything seems amiss with your arm?"

"Madam, you do me too much honour; I give you my word."

"Good, I thank you, Clément, for the manuscript. I am in need of diversion. The king is much occupied at present." There was a note of dismissal in her voice but Clément said,

"Your Grace, by your leave, I have two more gifts to offer. The first is a greeting from your daughter, Mary, and from her grace, the king's mother. I took the liberty of breaking my journey at Amesbury that I might see them and bring back their news." The queen's dark eyes lit up.

"Oh Clément, how kind of you. And how is Mary? Has she grown since July? Does she attend to her lessons?"

"She is in blooming health. She has indeed grown and is almost as tall as your grace, I believe. I found her charming and she took a great interest in the manuscript."

"And my husband's mother?" Eleanor inquired.

"She is in her usual robust health, your Grace. And now the last gift - a curious object I found on the seashore. May I?" The queen smiled her acquiescence and Clément delved into the pockets of his habit and drew out the sand-coloured stone. He tipped it into her delicate, outstretched hand, resisting the impulse to linger at the touch. The stone fitted snugly in her palm. Her ladies-in-waiting crowded around her to get a better view.

Queen Eleanor studied the stone carefully, running a finger over its ridges, round and round the spiral till she touched its centre. She turned it over to see if it looked the same on both sides; it did. It was no thicker than a man's thumb.

"Surely, Clément, this has been carved. For it is of stone, with the appearance of a shell. A craftsman must have dropped it."

"When I found it, your Grace, it was embedded in a larger rock. Brother Anselm, the infirmarer's assistant, carefully chiselled it out. He is knowledgeable about such stones." The queen listened with keen intelligence as Clément related Xenophon's theory. He concluded, "I believe these stones are a marvel of nature, praise be to God."

"Amen," she said, "Pray, tell me how you discovered it."

Gratified by her interest, Clément launched into a brief account, ending, "It seems that these so-called figured shells are abundant on the shores in that region, near the mouth of the River Char, especially in winter or after a storm."

"It is a fascinating gift, Clément, I thank you. However, it does not quite make up for the length of your absence from my court and I forbid you to leave my side for so long in the future." The scribe flushed with pleasure at his queen's gracious words.

"With your permission, madam, I would like to ask your jeweller to polish the stone and mount it as a pendant. Brother Anselm gave me another to show you; this one has been split in half and the inner surface polished."

Queen Eleanor took the proffered stone and examined it. "Yes, I see now. I can imagine a worm-like creature coiled here when it was a hollow shell. As you said, brother, it is a marvel, a beautiful marvel." She handed both stones back to her scribe almost grudgingly.

Emboldened by her evident pleasure, Clément said, "In the southwest, these particular figured shells are called snakestones and are believed to ward off snake bites. Forgive me if I overreach myself, but I have heard tell that in the Holy Land, my lord the king was bitten by a venomous snake and that your Grace saved his life by sucking out the poison. It came to my mind that this may have a bearing on your Grace's ailments. Perhaps there may be some benefit in wearing the snakestone as a talisman?"

The queen's laugh trilled like a peal of high-cast bells, "Is that tale still circulating after all this time, Clément? How gratifying. I must admit that we took no steps to quash the rumour as it served to counter certain prevailing hostile tendencies towards me." She laughed again, "Well, I earnestly hope that if the king had been bitten by a serpent, I would have done my heroic duty. But thankfully the occasion did not arise. Though he was once wounded by an assassin's blade. That story is true." Her face clouded momentarily at the memory. "Yes, Clément, I approve your scheme. Take the stone to Derian. Now leave me; I am weary and must rest before my lord returns."

Chapter 6

14th September 1290, Newstead Priory, Lincolnshire

The jeweller, Derian Scand, was bowed over his work as Clément entered. He did not look up. The scribe cleared his throat noisily. Derian continued steadily polishing the stone. Clément, sensing animosity in the air, greeted the jeweller in an extra cheery tone,

"Good morrow, Master Goldsmith. How does your work proceed?"

"Hmph" grunted Derian, scowling. At last he looked up, fixing his dark blue eyes on Clément's earnest, grey ones. Clément lowered his gaze. "I told you it would take me some days, scribe. Why do you come harassing me after only one?"

"Oh, master," cried Clément, "you mistake me. I come purely out of interest, to see how the appearance of the stone alters as you work upon it."

Derian leant back slightly so that the stone on his small workbench was revealed, "There," he said, "satisfied?" The stone lay in two halves; one had been slightly damaged by the operation of splitting it. But the other was even more intricate and delicately coloured than the one Brother Anselm had given him.

Clément gasped and was momentarily overcome. "The stone is even more of a wonder than I realised – gem-like. Glory be to God for the riches of his creation!" Derian leaned forward over his work with a finality that clearly dismissed the scribe. Clément bade him good day and hurried from the room.

Derian grimaced. "Yes, run off and tell your queen, worm. Monks and priests," he muttered under his breath, "I hate the lot of them. But this one, this scribe, grates on me like the keel of a boat hauled over the stones. His adoration for the queen is written all over his puny face. Why do these lads go into the church if they cannot do without the love of women? It makes for nothing but trouble. Parading around piously, pretending to serve the Almighty, while inside they're burning for lack of love."

As Derian anticipated, Clément trotted off to inform the queen of the exciting development. Approaching her chamber, he heard her chattering in Spanish and laughing with her ladies-in-waiting. He paused on the threshold to listen, savouring the sound of her voice when she was at ease, the weight of the crown briefly forgotten; a lady, enjoying a jest with her attendants. In another life, he might have shared such a carefree moment with her. But not in this life, not ever. His fate, he knew only too well, was to love from a distance, faithfully and silently. As he lifted his hand to knock, the door opened and one of the ladies almost rushed into his arms. She jumped back, startled.

"Brother Clément! Are you spying on us?" she scolded, pretending to be affronted. Peals of giggles rang from within the chamber and Clément flushed deeply.

"Not at all, m...mistress," he stammered, aware of his hot face and that they were amusing themselves at his expense. "I was about to knock when you took the door away from my hand."

"Enter, faithful scribe," called the queen's amused voice from within. Clément stepped back to allow the young woman to pass; Carlita, he thought her name was. She looked barely older than a child, he observed, as she swept past him, head held high. He folded his hands back into his copious black sleeves and then stepped into the radiance of the queen's presence.

"Good morning, Brother Clément. What brings you to my chamber at this early hour?"

"Forgive the intrusion, your Grace, but I come straight from your jeweller with an interesting development to report."

"Speak on, Clément, you have my attention."

"Master Scand has succeeded in splitting the stone into two halves and the inner side, now showing, is wonderfully smooth, with many subtle shades of colour."

"Your news pleases me, Clément. If I have time, I will pay him a visit to see for myself. Does Derian say when the pendant will be ready?"

"No, my lady. He has never worked on such a stone before and is proceeding in the dark, as it were. He does not take kindly to being rushed."

"Nor to his queen, as I am given to understand," Queen Eleanor said, her dark eyes glinting with mischief.

"My lady! I am sure he is your faithful servant!"

"As am I, but he does not have to like me to serve faithfully, does he?"

"It pains me to hear you speak thus of any of your subjects, my Queen."

"Dear Clément, only a foolish queen would pay no heed to how she is regarded by her subjects. I know full well that many of our people, though most loyal, do not enjoy having a Spanish princess on the throne of their beloved England. Nor do they take kindly to some of my land acquisitions. But I have borne the king many children and for this, they honour me, in their way. I am content." Clément bowed his acquiescence and began to withdraw. "Not so hasty, Clément. I require you to take a letter for me." Clément bowed again and walked to a small table set near the window, where ink, quill and parchment lay ready.

Chapter 7

September 14th Current year, Lincoln Minster School

Daniel switched on his desk lamp, picked up his pencil case and took out a highlighter pen and a pencil. A book he had ordered about Eleanor of Castile had arrived. Finding her tomb and writing his essay had piqued his interest in this obscure medieval queen. He had done some online research but there was so much information, some of it contradictory, that he decided a book by an expert would be a better option. He looked for a date on the inside page. 1990. Surely that was before the internet was widely available and research became a series of mouse clicks. For the author of this book, research must have been a labour of love, travelling to historical sites and consulting archives.

The family trees showed that both Queen Eleanor and her husband Edward I were descended from William the Conqueror. Edward was born in 1239 and Eleanor's birth year was around 1241. She was known as Eleanor of Castile to distinguish her from multiple medieval Queen Eleanors including Edward's mother, Eleanor of Provence. Daniel raised his eyebrows and drew a big exclamation mark in the margin by the part about their marriage, arranged by their families. Their wedding took place in August 1254 when Prince Edward was 15 and Eleanor only 12 years old! He couldn't get his head around the thought of their being married at around his own age. He read on.

Eleanor's arrival in England rendered her instantly unpopular, apparently, because she brought a large entourage with her. Why would people dislike her for that? He thought about the royal family today. Maybe it was because all her servants and ladies-in-waiting would be kept at taxpayers' expense? To counter this unpopularity, Edward's father, Henry III, gave Eleanor gifts to offer at churches on her journey to London and a gold buckle for the shrine of Edward the Confessor at Westminster Abbey. The alarm on Daniel's mobile made him jump. Time for choir.

He grabbed a piece of paper that had fallen out of the book when he opened it; a delivery note, he assumed. He was about to use it as a bookmark, then did a double-take. There was handwriting on it. Not just any handwriting, but his mum's! How on earth? He stared at the familiar blue pen strokes. It was the stolen letter, supposedly shredded by Jim. How had it got into the new book he'd just unwrapped? He glanced at his phone. He would have to run to make it to Evensong on time. The mystery of the letter would have to wait.

Chapter 8

15th September 1290, Newstead Priory, Lincolnshire

Clément refrained from visiting the jeweller the next day, but managed to collar his apprentice as he ran out on an errand. They made a comical pair as they stepped across the sunlit courtyard together, the diminutive monk trotting to keep pace with Warin's loping strides. When Clément inquired after the snakestone pendant, the young man puffed out his chest and announced that Queen Eleanor herself had crossed their threshold to see it.

"Did she seem pleased?" Clément asked.

"Yes, I believe so," replied the wiry lad, "though it was hard to tell since few words were exchanged between my master and her grace."

"Was the queen affronted by your master's manner?" asked Clément, alarmed.

"No, Derian values his position too much to be uncivil to her face, but the air was cool, if you catch my meaning." Clément wrestled with the urge to defend his mistress' reputation, but fearing that the words of an obscure French monk might do more harm than good, he retreated. Unable to think of a reason to visit his patroness, he returned alone to his cell and resumed his work. The air was growing chilly now as late summer faded to autumn. Clément dragged the blanket from his truckle bed onto his knees and picked up his quill. For the next hour or more Clément was intent on his writing, as quill scratched parchment, producing a perfect copy of the text in front of him. When the bell rang for high mass, it startled him. He surveyed his morning's labour briefly, but today not even his self-critical eye could find fault. He rose, smiling, shook out the blanket, laid it carefully back on his bed and left the room.

Clément crossed the courtyard at a brisk pace, trying to keep his mind off the remote possibility that Queen Eleanor might be attending the service too. She was not known for her devotion to the offices of the church. The more he tried to keep his mind on heaven, the more it strayed to earth. Clément passed through the door of the church and bowed his guilty head towards the Lord on the cross.

"Christ have mercy," he muttered. And then he saw her and his heart danced. Eleanor was kneeling between two of her ladies-in-waiting, hands clasped in prayer. Her hair was modestly covered, with just one or two auburn waves escaping their confinement and tumbling over her shoulder. When it caught him off-guard, the sight of even the back of her head robbed his legs of their strength most ludicrously, while his heart and soul seemed to rise on the wings of a dove. Clément tore his eyes away, found a place to stand, and with a heroic effort, rallied his attention to the mass. His love for God was deep and reverent. His zeal was caught up and carried along on the words of the litany.

After mass, Clément waited to make his reverence to the queen, who acknowledged him with a slight inclination of her head as she swept by, ablaze in a gown of deep terracotta.

∞

16th September 1290, Newstead Priory, Lincolnshire

Derian Scand sat hunched over his workbench, not working but thinking. Did he dare? Was it worth the risk? Although he hated the queen, he both admired and feared the king. Edward was a true monarch, strong and intractable. If you valued your life, you made every effort to keep on his right side. Derian glanced down again at the curse he had composed. He recited it once more to ensure he had memorised the wording exactly. Then he tossed the parchment into the brazier and watched it shrivel and burn.

Who would possibly suspect him? In fact, why would anyone suspect foul play at all? The queen was often sick with fever, picked up in the east when she accompanied the king on crusade. She had followed him everywhere, like a puppy, instead of staying behind and caring for her children, like any woman should, even a queen. And then, there was that ridiculous story about her saving the king's life, sucking out the venom when he was bitten by a snake. It was clearly a tale they had put about to enhance Eleanor's sorry reputation. She had hardly endeared herself to her subjects - amassing good English land for her dower at every opportunity; half of the wealthiest towns in the land. Where would it end? Maybe it would end here, and soon.

Derian tipped some drops of polish onto his cloth and took up the curious pendant. He stroked the stone lovingly with his rag, over and over, round and round, muttering quietly but distinctly,

"Cursed be this mysterious stone
And cursed the neck on which it hangs;
Cursed the queen who wears the crown,
Beguiles the king and steals our land.
Let this stone bring her nought
But sickness, pain and death!"

So spoke Derian as he polished the stone, pouring into it his hatred like a poison, making his fine workmanship an abomination. He repeated the chant again and again as he continued burnishing the stone which grew ever brighter and more beguiling in his hands. Every so often he paused to add another few drops of polish from the phial.

He was so engrossed that he did not hear his apprentice return from his errand and enter the workshop cautiously, expecting the customary scolding. Warin stood on the threshold, listening intently, aghast at the abominable words he heard. He knew Derian to be a harsh and exacting master, scathing and intolerant of weakness or folly in others. But what he witnessed here was of a different order: a venomous, calculated loathing, full of intent to harm and destroy. Appalled, Warin retreated silently and fled across the courtyard and out through the priory gates. Where he was heading, he neither knew nor cared, as long as it took him away from the chilling words of his master. He ran and ran, attempting to blot out from his mind the secret evil he had unwittingly stumbled upon. But however much distance he put between himself and Derian, the fateful curse rang on in his ears. Finally exhausted, he threw himself on the ground and wept.

Derian continued polishing the stone, working until long after the bell sounded for compline, the last office of the day. Finally, when it would absorb no more ointment, he set it down carefully on the bench, admiring his handiwork. The stone gleamed and its subtle colours were captivating. Derian's glance fell on the other half of the stone, lying discarded on the bench. It looked dull beside its twin. Now a second evil scheme presented itself to his devious mind; one stone, two birds. He rubbed his tired eyes; he could ill afford more candles. He would polish the other half of the stone in the morning. With this satisfying thought, he stoppered the phial and went wearily to his cot.

Chapter 9

17th September 1290, Newstead Priory, Lincolnshire

Warin woke shivering in the dark. He sat up stiffly and gave his limbs a vigorous rub. Why was he outside beneath a tree instead of lying snug in his cot? Reality flooded back into his mind, and with it, questions. What was he to do? He had long known Derian to be a cruel master but this was something quite different - attempted murder. No, worse even than that; it was treason. But what could he do about it? Who would take the word of a scatter-brained apprentice against that of the court goldsmith? Derian was not well liked, it was true but he was valued as an excellent craftsman. If Warin accused him without proof, he himself would most likely rot in prison; or worse, if Derian got hold of him. And besides, Derian was his kinsman, his father's cousin. To accuse him of treason would bring shame on his whole family. No, he could not do it. But neither could he return and pretend nothing had happened. How could he continue working for such a monster?

But if he could not bring the evil to light, he could yet try to prevent it! He could steal the pendant and hide it, so it could not be given to the queen. Warin's heart quaked at the very idea but nevertheless he resolved to do it. He leapt up but his legs collapsed beneath him, stiff and weary from his panicked flight. He chafed them for a minute and then looked around to try to get his bearings. It was still full dark with only the faintest moon obscured by clouds. His heart sank as he realised he would have to wait until first light. He wrapped himself in his cloak as best he could and slumped back down against the foot of a large tree.

Warin woke again even colder than before. Now he could see the trees around him. He stretched his sore limbs and slowly got up. He had no idea where he was. In his alarm the previous night he had fled like a startled deer with no thought of how he would get back. All around were trees but about a hundred yards to his right there seemed to be a clearing. He headed towards it. The ground rose in a gentle slope. As he drew nearer the clearing, he could smell smoke and on gaining the top of the ridge he could see it swirling upwards from a dwelling about half a mile away. He would make for there and ask for directions back to Newstead. He trotted down the hill and a few minutes later he came across a dark-haired maid drawing water from a well.

"Good morrow, mistress. If you please, can you direct me to Newstead Priory by the shortest route?"

"Lost, are we?" said the maid, teasing. Warin felt a crimson blush sweep up his neck to redden the tips of his ears.

"Yes," he stammered. "I suppose I am."

"I heard the king and the whole court are at Newstead. What can you be wanting with the court?"

Warin drew himself up to his full height,

"I am apprentice to the court goldsmith; and I must return without delay."

"My, my, a goldsmith. Have you any trinket for a pretty maid?"

"I truly am in a fearful hurry. Please give me the directions."

"Oh well," she sighed, sorry not to be able to prolong an encounter which seemed so promising. She turned and pointed, "You see that tall hill to the southwest. Head for the brow of that hill and you will be able to see it from there."

"My thanks, mistress," Warin headed off at a trot but called over his shoulder. "I am sorry I have no trinket for you, pretty maid."

∞

Clément rose in a daze at the sound of the Matins bell and staggered sleepily to the silent chapel. Although he was a monk, he was on loan to the queen's household, along with a number of precious manuscripts which he was charged to copy for her grace. He could be recalled to his abbey at any moment but he chose not to think about that. He missed the fellowship of his brothers at the monastery of Saint Peter, though there were one or two without whom he could quite happily live. He had vowed to the abbot that he would keep the offices of the church, alone if need be, and so far he had kept his vow, rising just after midnight for Matins to greet each new day in God's presence and begin it with his praises.

Clément rubbed his eyes and pulled his cowl over his tonsured head to ward off the autumn chill. Mortify the body to purify the soul, he told himself. And how his soul needed purification. He knelt on the cold chapel floor and immersed himself in the office.

At the next bell, for Prime, Derian rose, not to offer afresh his soul to God, but to finish his deadly work. He kicked Warin's cot to rouse him. Though it was still dark, the way the cot skidded away from his foot told him that there was no one sleeping in it.

"Warin, are you up early for once? Get the brazier going? I have work to finish." He made his way over to his workbench, groped for his tinder box and lit the lamp. "Warin! Where is the fool boy?" No matter, he would pay for it later.

Derian sat down and took up the unpolished half of the stone. He conjured up a mental picture of Brother Clément, pathetically smitten with the foreign queen. He allowed hatred to well up until it filled his being, overflowed and the curse took shape in his mind,

> "Cursed be this mysterious stone
> And cursed the neck on which it hangs.
> Cursed be the worm-faced scribe
> Who put this stone into my hand.
> Let this stone bring him nought
> But sickness, pain and death."

In a trance-like state, Derian polished the stone again and again, chanting the dread words.

An hour later, Warin walked as calmly as he could through the gatehouse of Newstead Priory. The king and his knights were congregating in the forecourt for a hunt. Though clad in plain, practical hunting gear, King Edward drew the eye, the tallest man on the tallest horse, striking and erect. But Warin dared not linger. He turned aside from the grander apartments and made for the goldsmith's quarters along the south east corner of the enclosure. Once he came within sight of it, he glanced round warily. Usually blundering, he now trod delicately and almost noiselessly towards the threshold. He paused there, listening intently. Hearing nothing, he pushed open the door.

"So, you deign to put in an appearance do you, you good for nothing bag of bones." Warin raised his arms to ward off the inevitable blow. Too late. Derian struck him full on the side of his face.

"Where the devil have you been?"

"Forgive me, Master, I went for a walk in the evening and somehow lost my way. I slept in the woods. I found my way back as soon as it was light."

"Liar! You've been dallying with some girl in a hayloft, you mean, though I don't know who would be fool enough to have you."

"No, Master. I swear, I was lost. I slept in a wood. Feel how damp my cloak is."

"What do I care for your cloak? Get the brazier lit. My hands are numb with cold. Then take a message to that fool monk. Tell him our mistress' stone is ready." Warin stood stock still, for which Derian clouted him again.

Warin's hands trembled so much that it took him far longer than usual to light the coals. Derian stood watching him every moment. As soon as the brazier was lit, he had no choice but to leave on his errand. He dragged his heels across the great court, not even looking up at the riders still assembling for the hunt. So it was that he almost collided with Brother Clément.

"Ah, Warin, I am on my way to see your master." Warin's mind flailed around for some excuse but found none and he merely replied,

"And I to bring you a message. He bade me tell you that the stone is ready."

"Ah good, splendid. But what happened to your face, Warin? It looks bruised and sore."

"It's nothing, Brother Clément." He turned away slightly.

"Is this your master's work?" Warin's silence was answer enough. "For shame! That hands which fashion such fine jewellery should also leave these marks!" Clément exclaimed. He sighed helplessly, knowing there was little he could do. Such treatment of apprentices was not uncommon. Warin shrugged.

"Do not fret, brother. I am used to it. It troubles me little." Warin lagged beside the monk with an anxious heart. He racked his brain for a subtle way to prevent Clément from collecting the cursed stone and giving it to the queen. He had only spoken to Brother Clément once or twice before. Should he confide in him? He knew that now was his only chance to act but he could not think clearly. The queen's life might be in danger, forsooth! He willed himself to speak out and damn the consequences. But he was no hero. Inwardly he lamented his pitiable cowardice while leading Clément nearer and nearer to the cursed gift.

Chapter 10

17th September 1290, Newstead Priory, Lincolnshire

Before any reasonable plan presented itself to Warin's frantic mind, Clément reached and entered the workshop.

"Master Derian, I thank you for your message." His eyes alighted on the pair of stone pendants, one strung on a fine gold chain and the other on a simple leather cord. "And I commend your workmanship," he said heartily. "May I?" Derian nodded his approval and Clément gingerly lifted the gold-strung pendant to examine it closely. Words temporarily failed him. He was awestruck by the complexity of the pattern and the countless subtle sandy colours. At length, he whispered, "It is indeed fit for a queen."

"So it is," Derian stated. "Then make haste and present it to her grace with my compliments."

"That I will and most eagerly, Master Goldsmith. I thank you."

"But before you go," Derian added, almost absentmindedly, "there is the other half of the stone; the twin of the queen's pendant, as it were. By rights, it belongs to you, since you discovered it."

"But, Master Derian, I would not presume."

"Here," Derian insisted, "you keep the other half. I have strung it on this leather cord for you. It will look well next to your cross. It is a wonder of God, is it not?" Derian picked up the leather cord and handed it to Clément.

"Why thank you. But this one too is polished. I must be in your debt for your labour."

"On the contrary, I am in your debt for bringing this marvel to me. It was a pleasure to work on it. And besides, I am amply recompensed by our mistress." Clément accepted the unexpected gift from Derian's hand and stowed it in the folds of his habit. He left the outbuilding, his plain face radiant with the two-fold joy of the gifts - one received and one to give. Watching him hurry away, Derian stood at the workshop door, his face also gleaming, with malevolent satisfaction at the two-fold prospect of being rid of the foreign queen and her bothersome scribe. Behind him, Warin slumped onto a bench with his head in his hands.

Clément hesitated a moment, as always, before the queen's chamber, savouring the anticipation of being in her royal presence. He knocked. One of the ladies in waiting opened the door and ushered him in. Though bursting to announce his news, Clément waited meekly for the queen to speak first. At length she bade him come. He made his obeisance and approached; his face exultant.

"I see you have good news, Clément," said the queen.

"Indeed, your Grace, I am this moment come from Master Derian's workshop where I have collected your pendant. It is even more wondrous than we anticipated."

"Come, Clément; do not tease. Show me my gift." Clément drew his hands from within his habit and presented the pendant to the queen with a bow. She held it in her open hand and examined it for a long moment. Seeing its intricacy, she carried it to the window. She tilted it this way and that until the light fell fully on its translucent swirls. The deep brown of the larger outermost segments soon faded to greenish bronze, and as the tear-shaped sections spiralled inwards, diminishing in size, their colour gradually lightened to tawny saffron. "I have never seen an object so—" she searched for the right word, "enthralling. Its shape draws you in almost as if it would entrap you in its coils. Perhaps that is how the long-lost creature hunted its prey." Clément flushed with pleasure as he observed her reaction.

"It is exquisite, Clément. I am 'enchanté.' Help me to put it on and we shall see how it looks." The monk was too taken aback to demur. Queen Eleanor turned her back on him and lifted her hair, revealing her slender neck. It was a moment of intoxicating pleasure for Clément, whose hands shook as they encircled the queen's olive-skinned throat. This moment would cost him hours of penance, but he would not have swapped it for the world.

The queen spun round with a flourish. "Does it look well?" she said. Clément, against his better judgement, fixed his eyes on the queen's chest, where the stone lay snugly on her bare skin.

"It looks well, my lady, though even this is eclipsed by your Grace's own beauty."

"Fie, Clément, you flatter me! My beauty's days are long gone. I have borne the king sixteen children; God rest in peace those who have gone ahead to heaven." At this the queen, Clément and all her ladies crossed themselves. "Alas, even royal status cannot prevent the wear and tear of life, travel and childbearing. But I thank you for your compliment and even more for your gift. I will treasure it and, above all, I hope it will please the king." Eleanor's thoughtfulness towards her husband shamed Clément. She well deserved her nickname, "Eleanor, The Faithful." In their many years of marriage, she had hardly been parted from King Edward, travelling all over Christendom, even to the Holy Land itself. The king returned Eleanor's affection in kind. He, who could have any woman in the kingdom, had eyes only for his wife.

The queen's attendants gathered around her, admiring the new adornment in their singsong voices. Clément said quietly,

"Shall I withdraw, my lady?"

"Yes, Clément, but how goes your work?"

"It comes along. I endeavour to work all the daylight hours, but these are diminishing now as autumn draws on."

"Indeed, Clément. When the darkest days come, apply to my steward for extra candles. I would not have you strain your eyes."

"I thank you, your Grace." Clément left the chamber and walked solitarily back to his simple cell. There he withdrew the leather-strung pendant from his pocket and tied it around his bony neck. The thought that its twin lay at that moment upon the queen's throat thrilled him immeasurably. At length, he forced himself to be calm, sat at his small writing desk and took up his quill.

Chapter 11

18th September 1290, Lincolnshire

Clément plodded along on his mule, Bessie, as the royal court removed to Rufford Abbey, some miles northeast of Newstead. As Bessie bumped along, he complained about the itinerant lifestyle of the court to Warin, who was walking alongside him to keep out of the way of his master. Since he had overheard Derian cursing the stone pendant, he could hardly bear to be near the jeweller. Warin's ineffectual anger had now settled into a profound antipathy. So he relished the prospect of the journey because his master would have no need of him until they arrived at Rufford. He attached himself to Clément, hoping to discover whether the queen had actually put on the pendant.

"You see, lad," Clément was saying, "the constant travelling leaves me frustrated. I so often lose the hours with the best light for working. We are hardly ever settled in one place for as much as a week before we move on yet again."

"My master says so too. For his work, he has even more need of a well-lit room than you, brother." Warin said, "But just think how many sights we see! No, I say it's a grand life we lead, travelling the length and breadth of England with the royal court. And if I am footsore or wet through on our journeys, I say to myself, 'Only think of what your brothers and sisters would say, not to mention that odious neighbour, William the Tanner. If they could but see me now, they would be green with envy. How they would wish to change places – to see our noble King Edward and his knights any day of the week; to see the towns and cities of England and the wide open spaces between, filled with forests, rivers and hills.' Whenever I start to grow used to such privileges, Clément, I remind myself not to lose the wonder of it all."

"Indeed, my lad, you are right. I am humbled by your zeal for court life. I too must endeavour to cherish, as you say, the wonder of it all." Clément felt chastened by this wisdom from the apprentice, his junior by a dozen years or so, for the lad could not be above sixteen. He turned towards him in appreciation. It was the first time he had looked properly at Warin that day. He was shocked by the change in the boy's appearance in the last twenty-four hours. The purple bruises on his face and dark rings under his eyes accentuated the pallor of his complexion.

"Warin, my lad, you look wretched. Are you feeling unwell?" Clément reined Bessie in and swung down from the saddle. He felt Warin's forehead. There was no fever. "Here, you should ride. You must be sickening with something. I can walk well enough."

"There is nothing amiss with me, I assure you. I have been somewhat anxious, that's all. Not able to sleep."

Clément frowned. "Has your master's treatment of you grown even harsher?"

"No, it is not that. I am anxious for the queen's health," Warin said.

"For the queen? The queen is in fine health, or was when I saw her yesterday. Why should you be worrying your head about the queen?" Warin looked at his feet and wrung his hands.

"I am, um, worried about that pendant you gave her. I mean, we do not really know what it is, do we? It could be harmful. It could be cursed." Clément put his arm around Warin's shoulder.

"Come now, lad, what has put that idea in your head? The stone is a marvel of God; I myself found it on the seashore."

"I just have a bad feeling about it. Did the queen put it on?"

"Yes, she tried it on as soon as I presented it to her. It pleased her greatly." Clément recalled only too vividly the sight of the pendant gracing the queen's neck. He blushed. "And I am myself wearing the twin of the queen's pendant around my neck. If there were anything amiss with it, I would feel it too. But I am perfectly well, as you can see." Clément cast around for some way to distract Warin from his childish worries.

"Have you heard the story of the miraculous cross of Waltham?"

"No, brother, but are you sure the queen is well?"

"Perfectly sure. This is the tale I am copying for her grace at the moment. The legend was written down over a hundred years ago by a canon of the Abbey of Waltham. But the origins of the tale go back to the reign of Cnut the Dane."

"How long ago was that?" asked Warin.

"Ah, now there you have me. I do not have the date at my fingertips but let us work it out together." His eyes drifted upwards as he made the calculation. "It is now some 220 years since the accession of William of Normandy." He threw a nervous glance at Warin, who was of Saxon stock, while Clément was French. King William was still a sore point for many Saxons, who called him, 'the Conqueror.' But he need not have worried.

Warin said, "And before William came Harold, who was never crowned and before him, Saint Edward."

"Well done, Warin. And I believe our king's namesake reigned for just over 20 years and Cnut preceded him."

"So, your tale is from roughly 250 years ago. Pray, go on, brother." Clément remounted Bessie again as it was clear that Warin would not consent to ride. He settled himself to tell the story, pleased to have piqued the boy's interest.

"In the village of Montacute in the West Country lived a blacksmith; a trustworthy, good-hearted fellow. One night he dreamt of a graceful figure bathed in light who gave him a message from God. He was to ask the priest to gather the villagers together for a time of prayer and fasting and then lead them to the top of a nearby hill where they should dig for a buried cross.

"On waking, he dismissed it as just a dream. But when he had the same dream again, he told his wife about it. She did not believe in it, so he did nothing. Soon afterward, he had the dream a third time but this time the messenger gripped his arm. When he woke up, his arm showed marks of the fingernails from his dream. He got up in a fright, hurried to the priest and gave him the message, showing him the prints of the fingernails." Clément paused for dramatic effect.

"Did the priest believe in the dream?" asked Warin, "What happened next?"

"The priest summoned the villagers and told them of the vision. They fasted and prayed in the church all day and the following morning, they went in procession behind the smith, singing hymns as they walked up the hill. At the top, they dug a deep hole. They unearthed a large stone, cracked across the centre. The blacksmith heaved it up and underneath he found a figure of Christ on the cross beautifully carved in black flint."

"Just as the angel foretold, for it must have been an angel," said Warin in a hushed tone.

"Yes, certainly. The figure of Christ carried a smaller cross in his right hand and a bell in his left. The villagers were overjoyed. Being afraid to touch such holy things, they covered them with a tent and took turns to keep watch while a messenger was sent to Tovi, the lord of the village. Tovi was a marshal in Cnut's army and the king's closest friend. He set out for Montacute straight away and when he arrived, he knelt before the cross and gave thanks to God."

"He was not a pagan, then, though he served the Danish king?"

"No, for Cnut himself was a Christian. Tovi decided that the smaller cross should be placed in the village church but the larger one should be installed somewhere grander. He put it on a wagon drawn by twelve red oxen and twelve white cows."

"That's a lot of cattle to pull one wagon!" said Warin.

"The priest prayed that God would reveal where the cross was to be taken. Tovi named aloud the great churches of Canterbury, Winchester, Glastonbury and London but the cart stood as if rooted to the ground. No matter how hard the oxen pulled they could not shift it. Tovi prayed and named all the other important churches he could think of, then many ordinary ones. The cart remained motionless. At last, Tovi recalled a little hunting lodge he had begun to build in the forest at Waltham, a richly wooded spot on the banks of the river Lee, northeast of London. As soon as he spoke the name Waltham, the cart began to move, almost as if the wagon was pushing the oxen, instead of the oxen pulling it. Many of the villagers chose to follow and as the cross was transported through the country, people were cured of diseases. When they reached Waltham, sixty-six of the villagers stayed and settled there, founding the town. Tovi had a church built to house the cross. He also had some jewelled ornaments made for the figure of Christ upon it. But when a craftsman attempted to fix these onto the body with a nail, blood gushed from the flint."

Warin blew out a long, marvelling breath. "What a miracle!" he said.

"Amen," said Clément. "Tovi and his wife remained devoted to the cross for the rest of their lives and dedicated many riches to the church."

Clément paused and wriggled his feet out of the stirrups to stretch his stiff legs. His mule, Bessie, promptly turned her head to see what he was up to and bumped his outstretched foot. Clément wobbled and lost his balance. Warin lunged and shot out a steadying hand as Clément flung himself forward, his arms around Bessie's neck.

Warin chuckled, and said, "Next time you want to stretch your legs, brother, I suggest you get off and walk for a while."

"Yes, I think I will do so now." He dismounted and sighed with relief as he planted his feet on the good earth. Clément picked up Bessie's lead rein and fell into step beside his young friend, who said,

"And what of the miraculous cross? Is it still there at Waltham?"

"Yes, but I have more to tell; after Tovi died, King Edward the Confessor gave the church at Waltham to his heir, Earl Harold, who rebuilt and decorated it. He visited Waltham frequently, donating many valuables." Clément turned to Warin, "You know the fate of Earl Harold?"

"He that was killed at Hastings?"

"The same. But perhaps you do not know that on his way south from his victory at Stamford Bridge, he broke his journey at Waltham to pray at the holy cross for victory over William, Duke of Normandy. While Harold was praying, the figure of Christ on the cross, who had always looked upwards, bowed his head and looked down sadly on Harold."

"Another miracle!" whispered Warin.

"Indeed; a prophetic one. The canons, who looked after the church, took it to be a bad omen for the coming battle. They chose two of their brothers to accompany Harold to the battle and if the worst should happen, to bring back his body. This they did and he was buried at Waltham."

"And the cross?" said Warin. "You said it is still there at Waltham. Have you seen it?"

"Yes, I have been twice to Waltham with the court. And now that you travel with the king's household, you are likely to see the cross for yourself someday. It is believed to have worked many miracles; I should say rather that God worked many miracles in the presence of the cross. For God is the author of all such wonders; we should never forget that, lest we become worshippers of idols. And now I must rest my voice for I have talked so much, my throat is sore." Engrossed in his storytelling, Clément had paid little attention to the road. Now he looked ahead towards a steady incline. "Ah, I think we are nearly there, Warin. Run ahead to the top of the slope and see if you can spot the tower of the abbey church."

"I hope you are right, for my stomach is grumbling. I want my dinner!" said Warin, grinning over his shoulder as he trotted away.

It was mid-afternoon when Clément rode in at the gatehouse of Rufford Abbey. He eased himself out of the saddle and stood nursing his stiff limbs until a groom came and led Bessie away to the stables. They had missed dinner but bread and cheese was laid out for them in the guest hall. Clément was familiar with the abbey and was glad to be shown to a guest cell he had occupied before. He unpacked his few belongings from his saddle roll and set the tools of his trade on the writing desk: a horn of ink, his quill and his knife. He usually held the knife in his left hand while he was working, ready to sharpen his quill or scratch out a blot or mistake from the vellum but today his bandaged wrist ached from being jostled on the journey, so he laid his knife on the desk.

He worked at his copying until the bell sounded for supper. Clément decided to join the monks in the refectory rather than the rest of the court in the guest hall. But on the threshold, he hesitated, curiously reluctant to blot the sea of flowing white Cistercian robes with his own Benedictine black. Seeing him there, the brothers nearest the door ushered him in and gestured their silent welcome, since their strict rule allowed no mealtime conversation. They were generous hosts, passing him dish after dish of fish and vegetables. and Clément tucked into his meal eagerly. Clearly the brothers had gathered a good harvest and now was the season to rejoice in and savour God's bounty.

The queen did not attend Vespers that evening, nor any offices of the church the next day. As she did not send for Clément, he worked alone in his cell on the manuscript he was copying for her.

Chapter 12

20th September 1290, The King's Houses at Clipstone, Nottinghamshire

The next day Clément packed his tools, shouldered his saddle roll once more and made his way to the bustling courtyard where the royal party was assembling to move on to Clipstone Palace. There, the king and his advisors were to make the arrangements necessary to host the Michaelmas Parliament in a few weeks' time. As soon as Clément had mounted Bessie and ridden through the gates, Warin ran up from behind, tugged his sleeve and said,

"Have you heard, brother, that the queen has been taken ill?" Clément spun round, alarmed.

"I have not. Is it serious? Tell me all that you know, I beg."

"I overheard a groom say the queen would not need her horse. She is to rest in her carriage for the whole journey, rather than riding beside the king for part of it, as is her custom. What is more, I had it from a chambermaid that the queen's physician has been sent for and a courier dispatched to Lincoln to purchase medicines."

"I fear it may be the onset of the queen's winter ailment," said Clément. "She is often beset by fever and coughs in the winter months. But not usually as early as September."

"But the pendant, Brother Clément, what if the queen's illness has something to do with the stone?" said Warin.

"Now, lad, don't jump to any rash conclusions. Remember that I wear half of the stone too and I feel perfectly well, apart from a little soreness in my throat, which I put down to talking too much while riding yesterday. Besides, the weather has turned chilly rather suddenly."

"Yes; but I think the queen has been in her bed the whole time we were at Rufford."

"I wish I had been told. I would have been praying for her recovery." Clément spurred Bessie on, eager to reach Clipstone. There he could visit the queen and find out for himself how she truly was. He felt some concern for her, but he could see that Warin was truly agitated.

"Today it is your turn to tell a story, Warin; your own story. Where do you come from and how did you come to be apprenticed to the court goldsmith?"

"Certainly not through any deserving or desire of mine," Warin said. "My father is cousin to Derian. When the court last came to Winchester for the parliament, Derian visited us; for we live not far from the city, in the village of Fordingbridge. I think my father must have helped Derian out of some scrape or other. Derian took me on because he was indebted to my father in some way; but the nature of the debt they kept secret. When the court moved on, I went with them and I have been driving my master out of his wits ever since."

"If you had your choice, what would you do instead?" Clément asked.

"I would be with the horses in the king's stables." Warin let out a long sigh, "But my father would think me going down in the world if I were to have my wish. He longs for me to become a master craftsman but I fear that sooner or later I must disappoint him. And what about you, brother, how have you come to this life? You are a monk and by rights you belong behind the walls of a monastery."

"In the providence of God, the queen happened to see some lettering I had done at a time when she needed a scribe. She admired my work and asked leave of my abbot for me to join her entourage as one of her personal scribes. It does me good to be reminded that by rights I should be there, at the abbey of Saint Peter at Abbotsbury. It should stop me griping about this endless journeying. If I were there, I would likely be hankering after a bit of travel and adventure. I suppose it is part of our nature to grow accustomed to our circumstances, however blessed, and grumble about them instead of seeing the good."

"Aye, it is human nature, but that doesn't make it right."

"No, it does not. And I am grateful to you for reminding me." They went along for some minutes in silence until Warin said,

"Is the queen truly as learned as people say?"

"What do they say?"

"That she reads many books and writes well and speaks a dozen languages."

"Perhaps not a dozen," said Clément chuckling, "but let me see: Spanish, of course, is her native tongue; she learned Latin and Greek for her education and French and English once she married the king. How many is that?"

"Five. And do you speak all those languages too?"

"All except Spanish; French is my native tongue."

"I never quite believed that Queen Eleanor could be so clever because she is so beautiful," the apprentice said.

"Fie, Warin. Can a woman not be beautiful and intelligent? If my lady heard you say this, she would soon put you in your place. She is indeed blessed by God with mental agility as well as physical beauty, but it also requires great diligence to become as learnéd as she. The queen has applied herself and worked hard, as should we all, whatever our natural talents; as should you in your apprenticeship."

"But I have no natural talent for fine craftsmanship," Warin grumbled. "I am clumsy and in no way suited to such delicate work. My fingers will not do what my mind commands. But give me a horse and a brush and I'm your man." At this point Warin was called to help free one of the carts which had become stuck in the mud. Clément ambled along in solitude, trying now to view the journey as a treat and not a burden. At least the day was dry, though overcast.

Clément was still feeling uneasy about the queen's health when they arrived at the King's Houses at Clipstone. He intended to call on her chamber as soon as she might have settled in. But by this time his sore throat had worsened and his head had started to throb. He tried to continue his work but his eyelids began to droop. At last, he gave in and rose from his stool. As he crossed the small room to reach his bed, he was surprised how leaden his legs felt. He lay down on his cot to have a rest before supper.

When he woke, it was full dark. He got up quickly, ashamed of having slept during the time of work but as he rose, his head swam and he was forced to lie back down. The next time he came to, he was shivering violently and his robes were drenched with sweat. Again, he tried to rise but fell back in a faint.

Chapter 13

20th September Current year, Lincoln Minster School

Daniel was struggling to focus in Computer Science. He felt weird; he couldn't tell whether he was hot or cold or both at once. And he could feel his skin prickling. He tried to concentrate but his mind was all over the place. And staring at the screen didn't help. When Mr. Brock's round of the room brought him to Daniel, his spreadsheet was still blank.

"Is there a problem, Daniel?"

"Sorry, sir. I'm not feeling well. I can't seem to focus." Mr. Brock looked at his face, then put his hand near Daniel's forehead.

"You're burning up. You'd better go to the medical room." Glancing around he said, "Ethan, go along to the medical room with Daniel. We don't want him keeling over on the way. But mind you come straight back."

"Yes, sir."

∞

Later Daniel heard the door handle and forced his eyes to open.

"Blimey, you look rough," said Stephen. "How are you feeling?"

"Rough."

"You left your bag in class," Stephen said, slinging it near the foot of Daniel's bed.

"Thanks."

"Do you need anything?"

"No, matron dosed me up with Lemsip. It was foul but I suppose it works. I just need to sleep."

"Okay, I'll go and do my homework in the common room. Bad luck for missing the fireworks."

"What? Oh yeah." It was school birthday. Every year the same - a procession and special assembly in the morning, birthday cake at lunchtime and fireworks to round it off. "I think I'll live," he said.

"See you later."

It was past ten and the fireworks rattled out like gunfire. Inside, Daniel was smouldering like the bonfire on the school field. He'd got up and dragged his chair to the window to watch the fireworks. It didn't take long to discover that fireworks and flu were not a great combination. Before collapsing back into bed, he decided to pack his bag for the next day in the hope that he'd be well enough. That was when he realised his money was gone. All that work in the holidays for the elderly people in the village and now there was precisely nothing to show for it. He was livid. He'd been so careful not to leave any money in his room, always carrying it with him in his blazer pocket or his bag, and now Jim had managed to steal it from his bag while he was ill. He wanted some of that money for bus fares. He was planning a trip, once a free Saturday came up, to find the location of the first Eleanor Cross, the Lincoln one. He could probably walk it but it was quite a long way, and he might not manage it in between choir practice and Evensong. Stephen would lend him some cash, but if he told his roommate his money had been nicked, he'd start going on about telling a teacher again. Daniel still felt that now wasn't the right time. The situation had taken an interesting turn and he wanted to see how events would play out.

When his mum's letter mysteriously appeared in his new book, Daniel guessed that either Ed or Natalie had gone to the pigeon holes, opened his parcel, slipped the letter into the book and re-sealed the parcel. Easy enough to do on the sly; most kids checked their pigeonholes regularly for post. But the key point was that one of them, Ed or Natalie, had gone behind Jim's back. They had dared to give Jim a bunch of shredded paper that wasn't his mum's letter. Daniel hoped that somehow this small act of rebellion might signal the beginning of the end of the bullying. The next time he'd seen them, he deliberately made eye contact first with Natalie, then Ed, searching for some glimmer of conspiracy. Both their faces were inscrutably blank. He learned nothing, except perhaps an inkling that maybe Ed and Natalie were not just accomplices but also victims of Jim's intimidation.

What perplexed Daniel most was why any of them succumbed to the treatment Jim dished out, to victims and accomplices alike. Why didn't Ed thump him? Jim was small and Ed was built like a truck. Why didn't Natalie outsmart him? Jim wasn't thick; but Natalie's mind was sharper, more agile. Once or twice Daniel had noticed her holding back, waiting for Jim's more plodding intelligence to catch up. But why? What hold did Jim have over them? And over Daniel himself? Jim was good-looking, for sure, and cool; always flush with money and the latest gear: trainers, phones, game consoles. Whatever the latest on-trend item was, Jim had it first and everybody knew it. Was his power nothing more than money and looks? Was it really so depressingly shallow? No, there was also some other assertive quality that Daniel couldn't quite pin down. Charisma, maybe? Self-confidence or at least, bravado that masqueraded as confidence?

Chapter 14

20th September 1290, The King's Houses at Clipstone, Nottinghamshire

Fortunately for Clément, Warin was watchful in his anxiety over Derian's curse. When the scribe did not appear at supper that evening, Warin went to look in on him. He found him out of his senses with a fever. He rushed to find someone to help and, in his hurry of spirits, took a couple of wrong turns in this maze of a building. As he rounded a corner, he ran headlong into the chaplain.

"Come now, lad, what's the hurry?" The chaplain said, regaining his balance, "You nearly had us both off our feet."

"Forgive me, Father. My friend is ill; he has a raging fever. I must fetch help. But now I have lost my way, clumsy oaf that I am." The chaplain held up a hand to stop him gabbling on.

"Your care for your friend does you credit," he said kindly. "My name is Father David and I am chaplain here. Will you bring me to your friend? Between us, we will see what we can do to help him."

"Oh, thank you, Father David. Brother Clément asked to be lodged near the chapel."

"Ah yes; I believe I caught sight of him earlier. This way, my lad." As David led the way, Warin said,

"Brother Clément is the queen's scribe."

"And your name, friend?"

"Warin."

"Are you also a scribe?

"Me? No!" Warin laughed, "I cannot read. I am apprenticed to the queen's jeweller."

"Ah, so you are another kind of craftsman, gifted in a different way with your hands."

"My master is, but I fear I will never be like him."

"Patience, friend. You are young; you have years to learn. Here we are." David knocked on a door on the left and entered. He felt Clément's forehead and listened to his breathing. "You are right, Warin. His fever is high. We must try to get it down. Agatha in the kitchen has some skill with herbs. I will ask her to make a draught and fetch some water. You can collect some cold stones, large as you can find, from outside. We will put them around Clément in his cot. They will also help bring down the fever. Don't look so agitated, boy. He is quite young and usually in good health, is he not?"

"Yes, I think so," said Warin.

"Well then, with God's help and a little care from us, he will mend."

Warin fetched stones as quickly as he could and then returned to Clément's chamber.

"Brother Clément," he whispered. The monk did not open his eyes. Warin shook him gently. No response. Warin lifted the folds at the neck of Clément's black tunic and saw the snakestone pendant lying there. He slid his knife from his belt, slit the leather cord and started to pull the cord slowly from Clément's neck.

"What are you doing there, boy?" said Father David from the doorway. Warin froze. In two strides the chaplain was upon him. He spun Warin round and saw the knife in one hand and the pendant in the other. David tightened his grip on Warin's collar. "Thief!"

"N-no!" Warin stammered, "It is not theft."

"Not theft? I have caught you in the act of stealing from a holy brother who lies helpless with fever!" Tears started into Warin's frantic eyes.

"I beg you to hear me, Father. The queen's life is in jeopardy; please listen to me for her sake." David planted his considerable bulk between Warin and the doorway and said, "Far be it from me to deny any man his say."

Warin took a long breath and tried to gather his thoughts.

"As I told you, I am apprentice to the court goldsmith. A week ago, this good brother," he gestured at the unconscious form in the bed, "returned from a journey with a gift for the queen." He held up the pendant for David to see. "It was this stone here, though this is but half of it. It is a curiosity. Clément presented it to the queen and she had him take it to my master to be polished and set as a pendant. Five nights ago, when the court was at Newstead Priory, I happened upon my master polishing the stone, repeating some words over and over as he worked. This was strange. My master always works in silence and berates me for speaking at all. I crept closer to hear what he was saying. It was a curse! He was repeating it over and over and I listened until I could make it all out."

"Do you recall the words, Warin?" Father David asked.

"They have haunted me since that moment. They go round in my head like bees round a hive."

"Could you repeat them to me?"

"But if I say them aloud, will not I be adding to the curse?"

"No, Warin, not if you mean no harm." In a faltering tone, Warin recited,

"Cursed be this mysterious stone
And cursed the neck on which it hangs;
Cursed the queen who wears the crown,
Beguiles the king and steals our land.
Let this stone bring her nought
But sickness, pain and death!"

And then he blurted out, "I should have spoken out right away but I was in terror of my master. He uses me harshly. And also, he is my kinsman. I didn't know what to do. I tried to steal the pendant before it ever reached her grace but I was too late. Oh, what have I done?" Warin buried his face in his hands and wept.

"So, you believe this brother's illness to be caused by the curse on the stone? Why is Clément wearing the stone instead of the queen? And why is her grace's life in danger if the stone is here?" Warin lifted his despairing eyes to David's.

"The stone has two halves, almost identical. The queen wears the other half threaded on a golden chain. It must be removed. There is no time to lose. Her grace fell ill a few days ago and now Clément is suffering the same symptoms. Queen Eleanor is in peril!"

"This is a grave matter indeed, if it is true. And I believe you. However, we cannot march into the queen's chamber and demand that her jewellery be removed. And for all we know, she may not be wearing it anyway. I must think and possibly consult the authorities."

Half an hour later, David sent a kitchen boy to watch over Clément and invited Warin to his own quarters. Here in private he asked Warin to repeat his tale of the curse. The chaplain listened gravely and then sat for some minutes in silence, pondering. At length he said,

"This is a delicate situation. Lives may be at stake; we must tread carefully. Are you certain you are not mistaken about the goldsmith's words, Warin?"

"Yes, Father. I did have to strain to hear, but Derian repeated the same words so often, I know I am not mistaken."

"If we go to the king, I fear that not only the goldsmith's life will be threatened but also yours, Warin," the chaplain said gravely. "The king is just and fair but he will brook no threat to his beloved wife. If this stone has indeed harmed her, his wrath would be terrible and may fall on any involved, perhaps even poor Clément. The queen is unwell. We have no way of knowing the cause. Nevertheless, we must do what we can to counter the curse. Firstly, we must ensure that the pendant is removed. I myself will go to her grace's chamber and ask to be admitted to pray for her recovery. If she still wears it, I will endeavour to have the pendant removed. You, Warin, go back to your master and betray no hint of what you know. Try to behave in your usual way. Do you think you can do that?"

Warin drew himself up tall. "I will do my best, Father."

"The queen's own physician is attending her but you and I must do all we can for Clément. It may be that there is no power in this curse. The illnesses could be coincidence. Let us hope and pray that they are."

Chapter 15

20th September 1290, The King's Houses at Clipstone, Nottinghamshire

The chaplain knelt to pray at the queen's bedside. After some moments he rose and said to her attendants,

"I observe that the queen wears an unusual pendant. There is a monk, the queen's scribe, who wears the other half of this stone. I happen to know that he too has fallen ill. It is probably unconnected, but as a precaution, might I suggest the pendant be removed from the queen's person?" Three of Queen Eleanor's ladies-in-waiting surged forward from the edges of the chamber; the first to reach her mistress undid the gold clasp, grabbed the pendant, and threw it down in disgust. "I thank you," said Father David. "May I take it away to examine it?" He glanced around the room and chose to interpret the blank looks as consent. He stooped, picked up the necklace by the chain, taking care not to touch the stone, and dropped it into the leather pouch hanging from his belt. Then he knelt again and resumed his prayers, saying silently,

"In the name of Jesus Christ, I hereby break and cast out any and all evil curses or incantations that have been placed upon this daughter of God. Heavenly Father, I beseech You to bind and cast away any and all sorcery and evil powers that have been summoned against her grace. I plead the blood of Jesus, shed on the cross, which has defeated the powers of hell."

Father David was tempted to ask God to revisit the curse on the man who laid it. But an inner voice whispered to him Christ's words, to love our enemies and pray for those who persecute us. Somewhat reluctantly he added,

"And I pray for the one who laid the curse. May he repent the wicked acts of his past and henceforth embrace your way of love and compassion. Lord, have mercy; Christ, have mercy." The chaplain prayed steadfastly on throughout the long, cold hours of the night, hardly disturbed by the occasional ministrations of servants who built up the fire or the succession of ladies-in-waiting who took turns, hour by hour, to watch over the queen.

When the bell rang for Prime, he leaned towards the queen and said in her ear,

"Your Grace, I do assure you that you will remain in my prayers day and night." Queen Eleanor's lips curled in a small smile and she inclined her head slightly to thank him.

After breakfast, Father David returned to his cell near the chapel and tipped the queen's pendant out onto his desk. He had never seen an object quite like this before. It was beautiful; but his rudimentary knowledge of plants and herbs was sufficient to warn him that beautiful things could be deadly. He wished to try to lift the curse from the pendant as he had from the queen but this was an object, not a person. He was unsure how to proceed. He would have liked to consult the wisdom of others but in this case, discretion was paramount. He placed the pendant in a wooden coffer, locked it and carried it to his oratory. The tiny anteroom was furnished with a large cross and a small prayer-desk. Father David knelt, holding the chest containing the cursed stone. In one brief prayer, for he was exhausted, he offered the problem to God and sought his counsel. Then he rose from his knees and, setting the chest on his prie-dieu, made his way to his bed at last.

The chaplain woke before noon with a conviction of his next step and a robust sense of purpose. First, he walked along to Brother Clément's cell to see how he did. The scribe's fever had broken and he felt well enough to sip a little broth. Next Father David visited the royal apartment to ask after the queen. He received welcome news; overnight her fever too had abated and she had improved during the morning. He also learned that, bowing to her physician's advice, the queen had consented to remain here to rest and recover, when the king and his retinue travelled west. The king would return in a few weeks for the Michaelmas Parliament.

Father David sent a kitchen boy to find Warin. Shortly afterwards the young apprentice appeared looking anxious.

"Sit down, Warin, and take your ease. I have welcome news; both Brother Clément and the queen fare much better. I hope, by God's grace, that the crisis is past." Warin perched on a bench by the small brazier that took the chill off the room. The chaplain was dismayed to observe that the tidings about Clément and the queen did little to ease the boy's anxiety. He pressed on with his plan and said, "Do you still have the pendant you cut from Brother Clément's neck?" Warin nodded, reached into his pocket and pulled out a folded rag, loosely tied with a leather thong.

"Good," said the priest. He fetched the box containing the queen's pendant, unlocked it and said, "Drop it in here with its twin." Warin untied his little bundle and did so. The chaplain sat at his desk and said, "Be so good as to recite the curse as you did last evening, so I can write it down. I wish to compose a blessing which mirrors it." Warin reluctantly repeated it, line by line, as the chaplain scratched away with his quill. When he was satisfied that he had it word-perfect, Father David said, "You go and sit with Brother Clément and I will fetch you in due course."

An hour later found Warin and Father David kneeling together in the chaplain's closet-like private chapel. Their hands rested on the chest containing the cursed pendants and they prayed,

> *"Blessed be this mysterious stone*
> *And blessed the neck on which it hangs;*
> *Blessed the queen who wears the crown,*
> *Loves the king and serves our land.*
> *Let this stone bring the bearer*
> *Blessing, now and forever!"*

They repeated the blessing twelve times. And afterwards Warin said,

"Do you truly believe our prayers can break the power of the curse, Father?"

"Yes, I do; for God's power is greater than the powers of evil."

"So, Brother Clément and the queen will make a full recovery?"

"If the curse was indeed the cause of their illness, then yes, I believe so. But sickness is part of the ordinary course of life. We are all subject to the frailty of the flesh." The chaplain's joints underlined this lesson as he rose from his knees. "For our part, we have done all we can, and now we may rest easy in our minds." Father David hoped Warin would take these last words to heart. By involving the lad in lifting the curse, he hoped to ease Warin's torment at his own involvement in the strange events.

That afternoon, the chaplain looked in on Clément from time to time and gave him a strengthening draught of herbs. In the evening Father David found him sitting up in bed. Before the chaplain could congratulate him on his recovery, Clément said,

"Do you have news of the queen, Father? Does she fare any better?"

"She has been quite unwell, brother, with a high fever like yourself. But the worst is over and she is recovering."

"I must go to her," said Clément. He started to get up but David placed his hands firmly on Clément's shoulders and eased him back against his pillows.

"The queen is well tended by her physician. What would she want with you? You might go and infect her with your own malady." This last argument persuaded Clément. He would rather die than cause the queen any harm.

Towards evening Warin appeared at the entrance to Clément's cell and studied his friend,

"You look much better, Brother Clément. Your colour has returned."

"Yes, I am, Warin, I thank you. Though I am a little distressed in mind. I seem to have lost the beautiful pendant your master gave me. The cord must somehow have severed. I wish I could get up and look for it, but Father David insists I keep to my bed at least for today."

"Father David has your pendant, ready to be returned to you."

"That is good news indeed. How did he come by it?"

"I gave it to him. I cut it from your neck, while you were out of your wits with fever."

"I understand you not; you took it from me?"

"Yes, but with only your well-being in mind. I could not get it out of my head that of all the people in the court, only you and the queen had been taken ill with sore throat and fever. Only you and the queen wore that stone. I feared it may have some evil property. When I confided my concerns to Father David, he agreed that, as a precaution, both pendants should be removed and so it was done."

"And both her grace and myself are better today! Oh, curse the day I found the stone! I have brought ill upon the queen! God forgive me."

"Calm yourself, brother," Warin said, instantly regretting his words. "It may be pure coincidence. Most likely it is. The pendants were removed only as a precaution. And even if they were the cause of the illness, no blame could attach to you. You gave the queen a beautiful gift in all innocence. If it caused her any harm, it was all unwitting on your part."

Warin looked down at the monk in his bed. The healthier tint in his cheeks had blenched and his hands gripped the edge of his blanket. Thankfully Father David had sworn Warin to secrecy about Derian's curse. Poor Clément was distressed enough that he had even given the necklace to the queen. The chaplain was right, passing on knowledge of the curse would give it power. Keeping it secret was akin to depriving a fire of air. It would wane and die. Warin wished Clément would forget all about the pendant. But the scribe said,

"I would like to have the snakestone back, if I may."

"Naturally; it is your property. I will fetch it directly." Warin left the room to find Father David, and returned within a quarter of the hour.

"Father David also had the queen's pendant," Warin said. "May I give it to you for safekeeping until her grace is fully recovered?"

"Indeed you may," Clément replied. Warin handed them over, thankful at least that Father David had replaced the curse with a blessing.

"But do not put it on, I beg; just in case. I must leave you now, for Derian expects me. Be at peace. The queen's health improves."

"Off you go then, lad; do not keep your master waiting."

Chapter 16

23rd September Current year, Lincoln Minster School

Days passed with no further trouble from Jim. Most of the students were hanging out outside enjoying the bright, chilly autumn sunshine. As usual Daniel was inside, researching Queen Eleanor, his latest historical obsession, whose internal organs were buried in the cathedral. He was reading on his phone about the Eleanor Crosses. Daniel jumped as his phone sprang into life, ringing and vibrating.

"Hey, Mum."

"Hello, love. How are you?"

"I'm good. I was just thinking about you actually."

"Uh oh, that sounds ominous."

"I've been reading up about this medieval queen, Eleanor."

"Eleanor of Aquitaine? Nasty piece of work she was."

"No, not her. Eleanor of Castile, Edward I's wife," Daniel said.

"Oh, what about her?"

"Well, I found her tomb in the cathedral but it only contains her internal organs."

"Urgh. Isn't history delightful?" Mum said.

"She died near Lincoln. Her body had to be taken to London so she could be buried in Westminster Abbey. So, she was embalmed here; that's why her innards are here. Anyway, they went to London in twelve stages and at each place, Edward later had a cross built in her memory."

"Oh, the Eleanor crosses; yes, it rings a bell now," Mum said. "It's quite a romantic story, isn't it? What's this got to do with me?"

"One of the crosses is in Geddington, near Stamford. I wondered if we could drive there on the way home at half term."

"I've never heard of Geddington. Isn't there a cross in Lincoln?"

"No, it was destroyed in the civil war. But Geddington's not far, I looked it up," Daniel said.

"Alright then. If it's not too much of a detour."

"Great. How are things at home?"

"Oh, you know. Same old same old. Mrs. Osborne had a stroke. I went to see her in hospital today."

"How's Hadrian?"

"Driving Dad mad. He's been digging holes in the lawn again."

"Oh dear," said Daniel, a big grin spreading over his face. He could just picture his dog scratching away at the lawn with his front paws to get at the dark, soft soil underneath, snuffling away with his muzzle until it smelled right and then eating a few mouthfuls. But it started to make him feel homesick so he changed the subject. "I came top in a French test today."

"Well done, darling. Is everything else okay at school?"

"Yeah."

"How's Stephen? Are you two getting on alright?"

"Yeah, he's good. How's Dad, apart from mad at Hadrian."

"Oh, you know Dad; he's never here. Always worrying about someone or other in the parish. Or shut in his study preparing his sermon. So, he's fine."

"Right. I have to go, Mum. I have choir practice soon."

"Okay, love. You take care. And I'll call you next weekend."

"Yep, bye Mum." Daniel ended the call, the usual mixture of comfort and homesickness welling up in him. He always looked forward to speaking to Mum but somehow it was always a let-down. And he hadn't asked about Grandad, because he didn't want to hear the latest instalment of the catalogue of woes about being old. He felt guilty but not guilty enough to wish he had asked.

∞

11ᵗʰ October Current year, Lincoln Minster School

Daniel trotted up the corridor whistling the melody of the hymn they'd sung at Evensong. He opened the door of his room and stopped dead. It looked like a bomb site. Most of his belongings were strewn on the floor. Damn. He had loads of homework and now he'd have to spend hours sorting through all this to work out what was missing. What a waste of time. He checked the clock. Crap. Stephen would be back from rugby practice any minute now.

He launched himself into the turmoil and started scooping up the debris onto his bed. It looked like it was only his stuff, thank God. Stephen would go straight to the housemaster if any of his gear had been touched. He spotted his wallet poking out from under the bed and stooped down to retrieve it. As expected, it was empty. There hadn't been much in it since Jim had already cleaned him out twice this term. As he straightened up, Stephen walked in.

"What the hell?"

"Don't worry; they haven't touched anything of yours."

"Dan, you have got to report it this time. This is beyond a joke."

"There's nothing missing really. A fiver and a box of chocolates."

"That's not the point, Dan. It's intimidation."

"What makes me laugh," said Daniel, playing it down, "is that if they had two brain cells to rub together, they'd realise that the way to get to me would be to steal my books or my homework, not cash and chocolate."

"What about your phone? You had it on you, right?"

"I forgot about that," Daniel said, slapping his blazer pockets.

"Damn, my mum's going to kill me if I've lost it." He dropped on to all fours and started rifling through the pile on the floor.

"You haven't lost it, Dan. It's been stolen!"

"Same difference. I haven't got it any more. That's the point."

"No it isn't, Dan. For God's sake, when are you going face up to what's going on here? If you don't tell them in the morning, I will." Stephen picked up his towel and went out, slamming the door.

Daniel picked up the last of his books and slumped down at his desk. Stephen might cool off but he knew what would happen tomorrow night anyway. His mum would call and not be able to get through. So, the following morning she'd ring the school office and then it would all come out. But events proved otherwise.

The next morning a notice was given out that a phone had been found. Anyone missing it should report to Mr. Hampson at break. Daniel saw Jim smirk – it was obviously his then and presumably smashed. After Geography, Daniel went along to the staff room.

"It was found down a lavatory in the boys' bathroom in the science block."

"Oh, right, it must have fallen out of my pocket." Mr. Hampson scrutinised Daniel's face. "You're sure there was no unpleasantness involved then, Daniel?"

"No, sir. Just my clumsiness. I was in those toilets yesterday afternoon. I don't suppose you know if it still works, do you, sir?"

"It's been disinfected, so let's find out," he said, handing over the device. Daniel pressed the power button and sighed with relief as it buzzed in his hand. He keyed in the password and the menu popped up. He grinned.

"It seems to be fine, sir. Thank you. I thought my mum was going to kill me."

"Try keeping it in your blazer pocket. You might not be so lucky next time, young man."

"Yes, sir."

Daniel walked away smiling. He could picture Jim, Natalie and Ed trying all evening to crack his password, putting in all the usual stuff then chucking his phone down the loo when they gave up. They wouldn't guess his password in a million years; an obscure history date, as usual. He hurried off to Religious Studies, leaving his phone screen on so Jim would see it when he walked in. He wanted to show them that they'd tried to get at him and failed. He wasn't too bothered about the break-in to his room and now he had his phone back in working order. Daniel decided to take this one as a mini victory over Jim, rather than the other way round. Maybe he was just telling himself what he wanted to hear. Whatever. Even though he knew Jim was probably already plotting the next incident, Daniel couldn't help feeling smug about this one for the rest of the day.

Chapter 17

23rd September – 13th October 1290, The King's Houses at Clipstone, Nottinghamshire

During the time the king was away, the queen's health waxed and waned. She hated to be inactive but for three weeks Queen Eleanor did not leave her chamber. Occasionally she sent for Clément to read to her or to play chess if she was well enough to sit up. Clément was now able to give her a better game, after studying a chess manual he copied for her earlier in the year. One day after she had tired of their game, she bade Clément to write a letter at her dictation.

"Speaking of letters," the queen said, "I have received one from Mary, at Amesbury. She remarks on what pleasure she had from your visit."

Clément's eyes brightened at the thought of Eleanor's young daughter. "I trust the princess thrives," he said.

The queen laughed, though a flicker of sadness passed over her face. "She is in good health, but thriving is hardly a word I would apply to Mary in her cloistered life. She submits to it with good grace, but I doubt she will ever feel it as a true vocation. How I regret that I ever gave my consent. She was just six years old at the time. But her father and grandmother were set upon it and I could not dissuade them. However, I contrive to bring her to court as often as I can, which is some consolation to us both. Now, to our letter. Please begin in the usual way."

Clément took up his quill, dipped it in the inkhorn and wrote, '*Eleanor, by God's grace Queen of England, Lady of Ireland and Duchess of Acquitane.*'

Derian Scand and his apprentice also remained at Clipstone, along with others who belonged more properly to the queen's household than the king's. Warin did his best to behave normally in front of his master, but in his anxiety, he was clumsier and more forgetful than usual, which resulted in yet more blows and bruises. Whenever he could be spared from the workshop, Warin loitered near the queen's chambers to glean what news of her he could overhear. As he dallied there one day, he heard calls at the outer gate and watched it swing open to reveal the king and his retinue riding into the courtyard.

From that moment, the enclave was jolted out of its lull and energised to capacity, as the royal court made preparations to celebrate the feast of Martinmas and host the autumn parliament. Every healthy pair of limbs, including Warin's, was enrolled to fetch and carry. He threw himself into the menial work with gusto, delighted to be busy and out of Derian's reach. And when word went round that the queen's health had rallied on being reunited with her husband, he dared at last to breathe easily and hope that the threat of Derian's curse lay behind them.

∞

Over the next few days, Warin wore out Derian's patience asking if there were messages to take or items to fetch. The jeweller caught him with a clout on the ear,

"Do you take me for a fool, boy? I know you just want to gawp at the new arrivals for the parliament. But as it happens, you can fetch me something: news. Find out who arrives today. As the queen does not need me at present, it maybe I can pick up some work among the visitors."

Warin slipped out into the chill air of a bright autumn morning to find the great court bustling with activity. All manner of servants came and went, their arms piled with baggage. It felt to Warin like a holiday, and he meant to enjoy it. He stationed himself by the stable block nearest the gatehouse. From there he had an excellent view of the newcomers and could follow the grooms into the stables and find out their masters' names. As the morning wore on, he found that his help to feed and water the horses unlocked the tongues of the grooms. Soon Warin was able to report back to Derian that Humphrey, Earl of Hereford, would be unlikely to want any jewellery for his wife but may well be tempted by a trinket for his latest mistress, who had recently borne him a son.

Later that evening Derian returned to his workshop having called on Earl Humphrey. He slumped down onto his bench, rubbing his temples. Ever since he had cursed the snakestone he had been plagued with headaches. He despised himself for being so weak. But now he did not know which he most feared: success or failure. If he succeeded, the queen would die. He had been sure that it would serve England to rid her of a woman so unworthy to sit on the throne. But now he had witnessed at first hand how downcast the king had been when his wife fell ill. He would never understand how Edward, the epitome of a king, could dote on that foreigner but that he doted on her was not in doubt. Too late to undo his curse, Derian wondered how Edward would fare without Eleanor by his side.

"Pour me some ale, boy," he shouted. Warin knew better than to delay. Derian took a slug of his ale and snarled, "Well? Aren't you going to ask me how I fared?"

"Yes, master, I was just waiting for you to take your ease; you seemed preoccupied. Did you have success?"

"Yes and no. Humphrey of Hereford would like a gift for his mistress but only of enamel as befits her place. A mere trinket, unworthy of my attention. So, you can undertake that."

"But, master, I am not skilled enough yet. What if—?"

"I know. You will never be skilled enough for royalty. That much is plain to see, but at least your blunder will only be adorning the neck of some hussy."

"Yes, master."

"You can start tomorrow at first light."

∞

27th October 1290, The King's Houses, Clipstone, Nottinghamshire

The parliament began. The nobles gathered in the great hall of the palace and the king strode in among their bowed heads and took his seat on the dais with the Lord Chancellor at his side.

The main topics under discussion were a proposed new crusade to the holy land and the imminent arrival of Margaret of Norway in

Scotland, to take up her role as queen there, child though she was. This was a happy prospect for King Edward since she was Prince Edward's bride-to-be. When the children's marriage eventually took place, he would realise his ambition to annex Scotland, with never a drop of blood shed. The proceedings dragged on through the morning until a messenger arrived with dire news. Young Margaret had died on the journey, throwing the Scottish succession into confusion. It was full dark before the king returned to his chamber. He threw his cloak onto a stool and said to the nearest servant,

"Send to the queen and tell her to expect me presently. We should be able to have half an hour of peace before dinner is served."

"Yes, your Grace."

Edward was drying his face with a towel when the servant returned and said with a quiver in his voice,

"Your Grace, the queen has been taken ill again."

"What?" Edward barked. "When? Why wasn't I informed?"

"Lady Isabella thought it best not to disturb the parliament, your Grace."

"Damn the parliament. My wife is Queen of England!" He pushed the servant aside and strode out of the room. He marched unannounced into the queen's chamber and addressed her ladies in waiting in a voice quivering with anger.

"From this moment, if there is any change in my wife's health you will inform me immediately." He waved away their apologies and sat on the edge of Eleanor's bed.

"My heart, they didn't tell me you were ill again. How is it with you now?" Eleanor turned her head towards him and smiled weakly.

"I am better for seeing you, my love. You have had a trying day, with the report of poor young Margaret."

"Indeed, but Eleanor, tell me how you do."

"I am weak and slightly feverish. Peter says I must not speak much. It brings on the coughing."

"Very well. I will do the talking; I will tell you of the parliament. It may send you to sleep, though with today's news it was livelier than usual, as you can imagine." Eleanor smiled and squeezed her husband's hand.

Chapter 18

27th October Current year, Lincolnshire

Mum was nattering away as they drove home for half term. Daniel relaxed, enjoying the prospect of two weeks without watching his back.

"Start looking out for the sign, love. We need to turn off the main road soon."

"Mum, chill, the SatNav will tell you."

"I know, but I don't trust it any more. Last week it sent me to Edgware via Timbuktu and I was fifteen minutes late for giving a lecture."

"Well, we're not in any hurry today, are we?"

"No, I suppose not, love. But I'm tired; I don't want to make our journey home any longer than necessary."

"Okay, okay; I'm looking for the sign." They spotted the sign at same the moment the SatNav intoned its instruction. Mum turned off towards Geddington on a wide country road and Daniel watched sloping fields drift by, dotted with sheep. Mist hovered over patches of lower ground despite the golden sunshine. The road began to descend and they passed a Geddington village sign.

"I hope we'll be able to find the cross after all this," said Mum. They rounded a bend and Mum's words died on her lips. The road opened out into a kind of small village square, dominated by a monument in the centre. Surrounding the square were quaint old houses, some of them thatched.

"Yeah, I hope we'll be able to find it," Daniel said. Mum shot him a withering glance and pulled up in front of the church on their right. Daniel grabbed his scarf as they left the car; there was a nip in the air.

They gazed up at the cross towering over them, mounted on a plinth of steps.

"Impressive," said Mum, "though it's not really a cross, is it?"

"No, I think it used to have a cross at the top." Daniel replied. The sand-coloured obelisk was three-sided and covered in intricate carving. About half way up each side a weathered statue of Queen Eleanor stood in a niche.

"Somehow it's not what I expected," mused Mum, shielding her eyes from the sun.

"You were expecting a cross," stated Daniel simply.

"Not just that. It doesn't look .... English."

"You're right. I read that the architect for this one was Spanish, like Eleanor."

"Weren't all twelve crosses exactly the same?" asked Mum.

"No, my book said that several different masons worked on them. The payments were recorded in royal records."

"How many of them are still standing?" said Mum.

"Only three. The others either collapsed or were pulled down in the civil war."

"Shame. It's rather romantic, isn't it, for a king to build twelve beautiful crosses to commemorate his wife. It makes me think of the Taj Mahal in India. Well done, Daniel. It was worth the detour. Have you got all the photos you want?"

"Yes, but I'd like to have a look in the churchyard. There used to be a royal palace there. That's why they stopped here overnight."

"Okay. I'll try to find somewhere we can have a cup of tea. Meet you back here in fifteen minutes or so?"

A while later they were heading off to a teashop. "You'll love the bridge," said Mum. "It looks really old and there's a ford next to it."

"I think my book said the bridge was built in 1250. So, the royal party would have crossed it when they left."

"How was the church?"

"Good; there are still some bits surviving from 950 AD," said Daniel.

"Gosh. We must bring dad here some time. He'd love it."

"There's a funny little carving of a jester behind the altar, possibly based on the fool who entertained King Edward and Queen Eleanor when they visited the palace here. But there's nothing left of the palace; just a special door into the church that used to connect to it. It's called the King's Door and only the royal family used it." They walked across the narrow stone bridge, Daniel peering over the side at the ford.

"Watch your back!" said Mum, and they squeezed into triangular niches as a van edged past.

"Look, this car's heading for the ford. Can we go through it, Mum?"

"We're not coming this way." Beside the bridge, the car descended to the river, splashed through the shallow water, and came up the other side.

"But just for fun, Mum, please."

"All right, then. After I've had a cuppa," she said. "It's hard to imagine there being a palace here, isn't it? It's such a tiny place."

"It was a hunting lodge, rather than what we think of as a palace. But still pretty extensive. I'm glad the village has stayed like this, unspoilt." Daniel said.

"Me too. And I'll be even gladder when I'm tucking in to some coffee cake." True to her word, before they left Geddington, Mum drove, slightly apprehensively, down to the ford. On the way she drove through at a snail's pace but after turning round she put her foot down and they sped through, sending up a great bow wave in each direction, both of them giggling.

∞

3rd November Current year, Lincoln Minster School

"Alright Dan?" said Stephen, dragging his bag through the door.

"Yeah; you?"

"Yeah. How was half term? Did you go away?" He pushed the door shut with his foot and flopped down on his bed.

"No, Dad was too busy. But it was fine; I like being at home in Abbotsbury. What about you?" said Daniel.

"We went to my mum's place in France. It wasn't really a holiday because we're still doing it up. I sanded some of the floors with a machine. That was fun. Then I painted my room."

"Sounds like hard work."

"Yeah, but my mum's partner paid me for the sanding. What did you get up to?"

"Not much. I went for lots of walks with Hadrian. I don't think he gets enough exercise when I'm away."

"What's that round your neck?" asked Stephen. Daniel pulled a black cord over his head and held it out for Stephen to see the pendant.

"Cool, a fossil. Where did you buy it?"

"I didn't. I sort of nicked it."

"This I have got to hear," Stephen said kicking off his shoes and lying back on his bed.

"It wasn't really stealing; I got it from a dead person." Daniel said.

"What the hell?"

"It's not as cool as it sounds. There's an archaeological dig going on in the grounds of the old abbey near my house. So I went along most days to watch or to help when they'd let me. They found a medieval coffin with a skeleton in. They reckon it was probably some abbot from the monastery."

"Was that fossil in the coffin then?" Stephen asked.

"Yeah, it was lying near the skull - he must have been wearing it around his neck. There was a big silver cross as well. The archaeologists were so intent on the cross and the bones that they didn't spot this. It was covered in mud and stuff, so it wasn't obvious. It just happened to catch my eye. They all went off to the pub to have lunch—"

"So, you just helped yourself! I can't believe it, Dan. You, nicking something! You're usually such a goody-goody." Stephen said, leaning over and giving him a friendly punch on the arm.

"Don't you start, Stephen; I get enough of that from the others."

"Only kidding. But I still can't get my head round it. Daniel Templeton - grave robber!" Stephen collapsed into giggles, his breaking voice squeaking and scratching.

"It's no big deal. It didn't belong to anyone, did it? Not anyone alive. Just some dead monk and he doesn't need it anymore."

"I s'pose not. So, you're wearing something that's been hanging around the neck of a skeleton for hundreds of years."

"Yeah. Awesome, isn't it?"

"No. It's completely gross."

"Oh, come on. I gave it a wipe. It had this hole in it, so it must have been hanging on some kind of cord that rotted away, probably leather. So, I got this black cord and here it is."

"It still creeps me out," Stephen said.

"But if you think about it – this ammonite was only hanging round that dead guy's neck for a tiny fraction of its existence. Before that, it must have been stuck in a cliff or in a rock at the bottom of the sea for millions of years. And before that, it was swimming around in the ocean."

"I guess it is kind of awesome when you put it like that."

"I wonder who he was though," said Daniel.

"Who?"

"The bloke in the coffin."

Chapter 19

13th November 1290, The King's Houses at Clipstone, Nottinghamshire

The parliament session lasted above three weeks and all that time the queen remained in her chamber. Some days she was able to rise and sit for a while. Occasionally she sent for Brother Clément for him to take down a letter or to see his progress on the manuscript. One afternoon he read her the story of the miraculous cross of Waltham. But Clément's usual delight at being in the queen's presence was tarnished by his concern for her health. Her complexion lacked its customary golden glow and her eyes had lost their sparkle. She spoke little, for fear of provoking a coughing fit. The lion's share of the king's time was necessarily occupied by the parliament discussions or private meetings with barons; yet Edward spent every moment he could spare at Eleanor's side. Clément observed her efforts to rally and be more animated whenever her husband was present. But as soon as he left her, the queen sagged and sank back on her pillows.

Warin had developed the habit of calling in on Brother Clément whenever Derian could spare him. And although the monk was now fully recovered, he kept up the practice. Today he found the scribe writing at a tiny table by a window. Clément smiled at his friend and laid aside his quill.

"I hope you feel as hale as you look, brother," Warin said, pulling up a stool. He glanced over the sheet Clément was filling with his fine, even script. He could not read, but he admired the beauty of the writing.

"I do feel well, I thank you, my lad," he replied, reflecting that his young friend did not look well. Once he was over the worst of his own illness, Clément had noticed with dismay that Warin's appearance had lost its youthful vitality. For some days, he had worried that the lad had caught his ailment and was sickening but as time went on, he grew neither better nor worse.

Warin had always been cowed in the presence of his master, Derian, for reasons Clément now understood; but until recently, Clément had often seen him striding about the court on an errand, stopping to pass the time of day with a kitchen boy or share a joke with a groom. Now he went doggedly about his master's business, with his head down. He often sought out Clément and asked after the queen with touching anxiety. He seemed to be still worrying about the stone pendant, but why? Even if it did have some ill effect, Warin had played no part in it. And in any case, Warin knew that as soon as Clément had recovered fully from his illness, he had tied the snakestone around his neck once more, in order to see if it made him ill again. It did not. In Warin's fretting for Eleanor, however, there seemed to be something more that the scribe could not tease out of him.

"And how are you faring, my young friend? You look a little troubled," Clément said.

"Do I? No, I am well, I assure you." Casting around for a different topic of conversation, he said, "I believe you have never told me how you came to be a monk in the first place. Was it a life of your own choosing?"

"No, it was not. But, in time and by God's grace, it has come to be my true vocation. My father died when I was but a babe. I was the youngest of my mother's children by him, with two older brothers and a sister." He stared, unseeing, out of the little window. "I recall little of that life, except playing with them in the fields by day and huddling around a fire in the evenings. They are happy memories, I thank God. Many are not so fortunate. But my mother could not afford to keep us all and I was given to God as a young boy."

Warin eyed his friend with compassion. He had struggled with the separation from his family when he began his apprenticeship. He could not imagine being sent away as a small boy, though it was not uncommon.

"Of my mother I have but few recollections," Clément continued. "A warm loving face, though often sad; long, dark wavy hair and soft skin. Much later she married again and had other children, half-siblings whom I have never met."

"You could almost be describing the queen, brother," said Warin. The likeness of the two women had never before crossed Clément's mind but now it struck him like a blow. For some minutes he contemplated it, while a rogue tear wet his cheek. Eventually he cleared his throat and said,

"You are right, Warin. I had not realised. But my mother's eyes were green or perhaps hazel, whereas the queen's are deep brown."

∞

The parliament broke up and the barons rode out in every direction back to their manors and castles. At Clipstone, the king gathered his closest advisors as well as the queen's physician, Peter of Portugal. Edward had intended to journey north to Scotland with the whole royal court when the parliament ended but on the physician's advice, this plan needed to be revised.

"Peter informs me, and indeed I can see for myself, that the queen is not fit at present to travel to Scotland. So, we need to discuss what to do."

"My lord, though it will pain you to be parted from your wife while she is unwell, it is imperative that you proceed as planned to Scotland. You need to make your presence felt. And make sure of your allies," said Lord Burnell.

"You could go, Robert, as my ambassador."

"Of course, I am willing, but I feel strongly that your presence is required." The king glanced round at the others: Otto de Grandisson, Lord William de Leyburn and Sir Phillip de Willoughby.

"Do you agree with Robert?" They all nodded their assent. The king grimaced and continued, "And what about the queen, Peter? Should she stay here at Clipstone? Should we send her back to Westminster?"

"Not Westminster; not yet. She is too weak for such a journey. I think we might try to reach Lincoln though, your Grace. The Dominican brothers there could aid me in caring for her and I would have ready access to the best herbs and medicines."

"Lincoln: yes, indeed that would serve. The city is better connected than here. It would be more convenient for sending messages and for me to travel back to keep the feast of Christmas."

Edward and Eleanor were dismayed. In thirty years of marriage, they had hardly ever been parted but there seemed no other solution. With the succession of the Scottish throne in contention, the king's presence was required. They resigned themselves to a period apart.

The queen's physician insisted that on the journey to Lincoln, each day's travelling should be kept to a minimum and the queen should have a whole day's rest before the next stage. So the journey was made in short stages. A good number of courtiers were sent ahead to Lincoln, to give news of the king's imminent arrival and the queen's needs. The royal party were to travel with minimal staff as they would have to stay some nights at local manor houses. When a message arrived for Clément that he was to travel ahead of the royal party to Lincoln, he was distraught. He went immediately to Eleanor's quarters and asked her to plead with the king to allow him to remain with her.

"Your Grace, I know there will be little room but I am happy to bed down with the servants on any hall floor." So it was agreed.

The first phase of their journey took them only from Clipstone back to the Cistercian Abbey of Rufford. After a day's rest, they set off for Laxton, where they stayed at the manor of Adam de Everingham. The Lord of Laxton was away for his schooling, being a boy of eleven years, but the royal party were warmly received by his mother, Alice.

∞

17th November 1290, Manor of Laxton, Nottinghamshire

In the early morning winter sun, King Edward stood on the walls of Laxton Castle, looking east. It had a commanding view, high on a hill above the village on its plateau.

"Look, Robert," he said, pointing. "You can just make out the cathedral towers. There is Lincoln."

"You have good sight, my lord," replied Robert Burnell, shielding his eyes from the low sun.

"How far do you reckon it is?" the king said.

"About twenty miles, sire."

"If only I could carry Eleanor with me on Bayard. One day's hard riding and we would be there." Robert stamped his feet and blew on his frozen fingers.

"There's the Trent to cross, Your Grace. You would need the Bayard of legend, not your own trusty horse, to leap the river and cover the distance without wearying her grace." But Edward was not listening.

"One day's ride! Then she could be comfortably settled and recover her strength. She could remain there till spring if it takes that long."

"Your Grace," Robert said gently, "the physician said we should prepare ourselves."

"Damn the physician! What does he know? No more than I, I warrant. What good has he done her thus far? Eleanor has a strong constitution, Robert. And she has overcome this ailment many times, as you know. She will rally. I know she will." Edward gripped the parapet. "She must. I cannot do without her."

After another rest day, the court set out once more, this time for the Chaworths' manor at Marnham, near the western bank of the river Trent. The following day while the queen rested, half the party went ahead; it was a laborious business getting carts and riders across on the ferry. Each rest day the king hoped Eleanor would rally, but each time his hopes were dashed. One more day's travelling brought them to the manor of Richard de Weston at Harby. Here Edward's spirits brightened for the end was in sight. They were a stone's throw from Lincoln and the king had convinced himself that there, comfortable and well cared for, the queen's recovery would begin.

Chapter 20

20th November Current Year, Lincoln Minster School

Ed grabbed a crisp packet with his litter picker and dropped it into the black bin liner Natalie held open. They had been given litter picking as detention for locking a Year 7 in the resources room.

"Do you ever wonder why Jim hates Daniel so much, Nat?" said Ed.

"Same reason I hate him I suppose," Nat replied.

"What's your reason then?"

"He reminds me of my big brother, such a goody-goody, always top of the class. Every time I see him, I want to punch him."

"Who – Daniel or your brother?"

"Both!" Natalie laughed.

"You're clever as well, Nat,"

"Not clever enough," she spat.

"Not clever enough for what?" Ed said, flicking a pile of damp autumn leaves with his litter picker.

"For my parents."

"Oh."

"If you'd just study a little harder, Natalie darling," she said, mimicking her mum's patronising whine, "you could be top of the class like your brother."

"Oh," repeated Ed. "Do you think you would, like, be top of the class if you tried a bit harder?"

"Ed!" Natalie thumped him.

"What was that for?" he said, retaliating with a gentle shove.

"For sounding like my stepdad."

"Oh, sorry." Ed dropped a coke can into the bag and said, "It's just as well I haven't got your parents. I usually follow stuff pretty well in class but once I'm on my own, my brain just gets in a muddle. Even if I studied 24/7, I'd still be lucky to get to the middle of the class."

"I'm usually in the top ten but that isn't good enough for them."

"My mum's always going on about how Gran and Grandpa are making sacrifices to pay for my education," Ed said, "But I wish they'd just spend their money on holidays or something. I'd be perfectly happy to go to the school down the road with all my mates from primary school." There was a long pause which would have been awkward, like this whole conversation, if Jim had been there; but as usual, he'd managed to wriggle out of detention. On their own, Ed and Natalie were more chilled; they could chat or argue or beat each other up without any angst.

"What do you want to do when you leave school?" asked Natalie.

"Dunno," shrugged Ed. "I like the idea of making things, but I'm useless at product design. I'm too clumsy."

"What stuff do you enjoy doing?" asked Natalie.

"Swear you won't tell anyone?" said Ed, eyeballing her.

"Course," said Natalie, suddenly all ears.

"Horse riding," said Ed.

"Why don't you want anyone to know that? I thought it was going to be much juicier."

"People think it's girlie. At least, my dad thinks it is."

"Ugh!" Natalie exploded, flinging the bin bag on the ground. "Crap like that does my head in. Horses are for girls, right? So, what about jockeys? What about knights, for God's sake?"

"Knights, yeah, I'll have to remember that one, in case it comes up again with my dad. But it won't; I had to give up riding. Gran used to pay for it but now she's paying school fees everything else has stopped. I wish I could tell her I'd much rather live at home and go horse riding every week."

"Why don't you tell her?"

"Mum would kill me. She says Gran's giving me the chance to make something of my life. But I'm pretty sure plenty of other people make something of their lives without going to boarding school."

"Yeah. Still, I'm glad you're here, you great, clumsy thicko!" Natalie snatched up the bin bag and sprinted out of Ed's reach though she knew full well he'd never hurt her. It creased her up that Jim used Ed to intimidate other kids. He looked the part but he wouldn't hurt a fly. She, on the other hand, did not object to taking out her angst on other people.

Chapter 21

22nd November 1290, Manor of Harby, Nottinghamshire

The king strode into the cramped bedchamber and dismissed his wife's attendants with an impatient gesture. He pushed the door shut behind them, leant upon it and took a long, slow breath. Having composed his features, he turned to scrutinise his wife, propped on pillows in the bed, eyes closed. He searched for any sign of improvement, but saw only Eleanor's pallid face contrasting shockingly with the red lions of England on the bedclothes. A mere two paces brought him to her side and he sat gently by his queen.

Eleanor opened her eyes and attempted a smile. The king reached for her hand as she visibly gathered herself to speak.

"Edward, I would not have you lonely; I give you my blessing to marry again."

"God's blood! Do not speak so, dearest. I forbid it. How could I ever look at another woman?"

"Edward, my own, do not deny me my say when time may be short. I am sorry to give you pain but we must consider the future. The needs of the kingdom come before your own wishes, in this as in all matters. If a marriage alliance becomes necessary, undertake it with my blessing and try to be happy."

"How can you imagine me happy with another?"

"At least try not to resent another woman because she is not me. If this comes to pass, please give her, whoever she may be, the chance to please you, for your own sake as well as hers."

"Eleanor, spend your energy on getting better, I beg you. Do not let your thoughts flow this way. However weak you feel, fight against it, for my sake and for our children."

The chamber door opened and the physician entered followed by an assistant carrying the tools of their trade and a couple of the queen's ladies. Peter of Portugal acknowledged the king with a bow,

"Your Grace, forgive me. May I minister to the queen?" Edward turned back to his wife and whispered,

"Fight it, Eleanor; remember," and withdrew without another word.

∞

Clément knocked timidly at the door of the manor where the royal party was installed. Otto de Grandisson, a knight of the king's close acquaintance, opened the door.

"Yes? Brother Clément, is it? What is your will?"

"My lord, I humbly beg leave of the king and queen to admit me to the queen's chamber to pray for her. May I enter and kneel quietly to keep vigil in some corner?"

"Wait here," Otto said. "I will ask, but I must warn you the king is already vexed at how many are squeezed into the poor space. He does not allow all her ladies to enter at once but makes them take turns." Clément was left wringing his hands on the threshold. Otto knocked at the door of the solar which was opened by Robert Burnell.

"My lord, the scribe, Clément, is without and is anxious to keep a vigil of prayer in the queen's chamber. Would you entreat the king to admit him?"

Burnell sniggered. "I believe that young monk loves the queen almost as much as does the king. I will ask but I hold little hope for him." He turned on his heel and left the room. Moments later Burnell re-entered with the hint of a smile on his comely face. "By all means, let him come. The king desires her grace to be upheld in prayer by all who wish her well."

"And so she is! But I am pleased for Clément. He is in a sad way, poor fellow."

When Clément beheld the queen, he almost cried out. Her cherished face was rendered almost unrecognisable; its warm, golden complexion now ashen. Her brown eyes, usually dancing with laughter, stared up at him from gaunt sockets. And her profusion of chestnut hair lay lifeless on the pillow. It was only because she lay in the royal bed, surrounded by her attendants that Clément even recognised his mistress. A single tear trickled down his cheek. Beyond doubt Death had stamped the queen with his pallid mark; it would take nothing short of a miracle to wrest her from his icy grip. So, Clément must get to work. Did he not believe in the God of miracles? Even now, if God willed her to live, she would live. The monk slid himself into a nook near the window and sank to his knees. Helpless but not hopeless, he held out empty hands before his Lord and implored him to breathe life back into the queen's earthly body. Or if that was not his will, to welcome her into eternal life.

Presently the king entered. Ignoring the gaggle of people who made their reverence to him, he pulled up a chair, sat down beside his wife and took her hand. Eleanor painstakingly turned her head towards him and attempted to smile.

"Edward, my dearest love." The king pulled his chair yet closer and leaned over to hear her faint, rasping whisper.

"Don't tire yourself by speaking, my heart. You must rest and regain your strength."

"It's too late for that, my husband."

"No, do not give in, I implore you. You must fight it, Eleanor."

"Do you remember the day we met, Edward?"

"Of course."

"You were the most handsome young man I had ever seen – and the future king of England. I fell for you in an instant. And I was just a twelve-year-old girl in braids. What must you have thought of me?"

"You were pretty enough. But, God forgive me, I was far too taken up with my own importance to pay much attention to you. It was my duty as the prince to marry as my father saw fit and he chose you. Little did I dream of the happiness we would share."

"So my lord, when did you begin to think of me as more than a young girl in braids?" Eleanor asked teasingly.

"Though it was less than a year later that I returned to wed you, I saw immediately that you were greatly changed."

"Yes, my ladies had worked hard with me, helping me grow from girl to woman. And I wanted to be a woman in your eyes; I wanted you to admire me as I admired you."

"Well, my dear, in this scheme you succeeded. When we stood before the altar, you spoke the marriage vows with such feeling and gazed at me so intensely with those deep, brown eyes. I think that that was the moment you cast your spell over me."

"Are you calling me a witch, husband?"

"Aye, my love, for you bewitched me. You stole my heart that day and entwined it with yours." The king's voice faltered but he continued, "And if your heart stops beating, I believe that mine will too."

"Hush, my love. Do not let the darkness steal the moments we still have together. Let us be thankful. We have shared more happiness than most people can dream of." The king lifted Eleanor's hand to his lips and held it there for a long moment. "Edward, do not be bitter when I am gone," the queen continued. "We have been blessed with a lifetime of joy. Try to be glad and remember the countless pleasures we have shared."

"But you cannot understand. You are reconciled to leaving this life but I will be left alone in a cold, empty world."

"I can feel your pain. I felt it before, remember? When the assassin's poisoned blade wounded you at Acre. I thought I was losing you."

"Yes, and I don't remember much bravery or acceptance on your part! I believe you had to be removed from my bedside because your weeping and wailing was such a distraction to the physician cutting away the infected flesh."

Eleanor smiled. "Yes, but we were still in the first flush of our love. We had not grown old together then." Here the queen was racked by coughs. A lady in waiting rushed forward and gave her some syrup.

"I am still in the first flush of love, my heart. That is why I cannot bear for you to leave me." The queen's eyelids began to droop. "I should leave; I am tiring you." The king said.

"No, Edward, stay a few moments longer, until I sleep." She closed her eyes. The king sat by her side, lost in a maze of memories. When Eleanor's wheezing breaths had settled into a regular pattern, he dragged himself away to attend to state business.

Chapter 22

23rd November 1290, Manor of Harby, Nottinghamshire

When the king entered his wife's bedchamber early the next morning, he discerned a slight improvement.

"Eleanor, my love, how have you slept? How do you feel?"

"A little improved, my lord; somewhat more like myself. I think I will try to sit up." A lady-in-waiting approached but Edward waved her away. He gently lifted his wife with one hand and scooped the pillows behind her with the other. Eleanor gazed at him with such tenderness that tears started into the eyes of Brother Clément, who still knelt in his corner. Edward strode to the door and bellowed,

"Summon the physician!" Some minutes later, Peter of Portugal bustled in, looking anxious. "Good news, I think, Peter," said the king cheerfully. "Examine my wife and tell me your opinion. I think she looks somewhat better. And she herself confirms it. What do you say? If you agree, we will waste no time and repair to Lincoln where the queen will be more comfortable and the rest of us housed more suitably. It is a shambles here." Peter of Portugal took his time examining the queen, while the king paced up and down. "Well, man, what do you say?"

"The queen does seem somewhat better. But I advise caution. To move her grace so soon might well bring on a relapse. I recommend waiting for twenty-four hours to ensure that this progress is lasting."

"But," began the king and then thought better of it. "Oh, very well; I must take your advice. We must not risk it if you think it might endanger the queen." Peter nodded his approval.

"But I will make plans to move tomorrow so that all may be done swiftly. Does that satisfy you?"

"Yes, your Grace." Peter turned back to the queen. "My lady, will you take some broth?"

"Yes, Peter. And a little wine." One of the ladies left to fetch broth while another poured wine and held it to Eleanor's lips. "Thank you, Alice. Now would you fetch Brother Clément?"

"I am here, my lady," said Clément, rising stiffly.

The king turned on his heels. "Are you still here, brother? You should take rest and refreshment."

"My only desire is to remain here to pray for the queen and be nearby if she requires my services," the scribe said.

"I thank you for your prayers, Clément," said the queen, "But I wish you to take your ease now while I am feeling better."

"Yes, your Grace, but you just called for me."

"All I wanted was for you to send to Lincoln for fresh parchment. I may wish to dictate some letters if I feel strong enough this afternoon."

"Yes, my lady."

"I will see to the parchment," said the king, "Let's send this good brother to his rest." Clément was dismissed. He went out into the solar where Robert Burnell and Otto de Grandisson sat by the fire talking in low voices. They looked up to see Clément swaying a little on his feet. Otto was up in an instant and half led, half carried Clément to the bench he had just vacated.

"Come, brother, you need to rest. And when did you last eat?"

"I know not."

"You, boy, fetch bread and mead," Robert called to a scullion.

"Forgive me, my lords. I do not wish to trouble you."

"Nonsense, brother. How does the queen fare this morning? Is there any change?" said Otto.

"She is somewhat improved, my lords, God be praised." Robert Burnell let out a long sighing breath and glanced at Otto whose shoulders visibly relaxed. The boy returned with food and drink for Clément. When he had finished, Otto said,

"You should sleep now."

"Where may I sleep, my lord? I think I am meant to have quarters in Lincoln but I do not wish to leave."

"You are in no state either to ride or walk there," said Robert, "No, you must stay. The queen values you and we are no fools; we know you only wish to be here. Take your rest here in the solar, if you will. There's a good fire. Lay yourself down as comfortably as you may. The king and queen occupy the only bedchambers here. The rest of us make do with whatever space we can find." Clément fetched his travelling cloak from the hall below and came back quietly into the solar. He crept into a corner, lay down and slept immediately.

∞

"Brother," said a lady-in-waiting, tentatively nudging Clément's shoulder, "if you are rested, the queen bids you come to take a letter." Clément awoke with a jolt and sent the fire irons clattering across the hearth in his haste to rise. "Be at ease, my lady will await your leisure." She withdrew to the doorway and averted her eyes as Clément stood and gave himself a moment for the blood to flow back into his limbs. He removed his cloak, ran his hands through the unruly hair below his tonsure and picked up his scrip containing quill, knife and a few scraps of vellum.

"Does her grace truly feel well enough to turn her mind to business?"

"Yes, and I believe she deems the business urgent." Clément followed the woman back to the chamber set aside for the queen's use. The inadequacy of the accommodation distressed him: the room was of moderate size but the ceiling was low and the windows draughty. At least the king always travelled with his own portable bed. Clément had marvelled the first time he saw it dismantled in a matter of minutes by the king's attendants and packed neatly into its own leather bags, ready to be resurrected at the court's next staging post.

In this bed, Queen Eleanor was well propped up in a semi-reclined position. Clément was delighted to see her smile as he approached and paid his reverence. He waited patiently for her to speak first, which she did, somewhat hoarsely.

"There are letters I must write, Clément."

"Yes, my lady, and I rejoice to see you recovered enough to think on them."

"I cannot speak much. I will tell you the essence and leave you to fill in the formalities."

"Of course, your Grace; do not strain yourself, I beg."

"What day is it, Clément? I have lost track."

"It is the feast of Saint Clément, my lady," he said with a half-smile.

"Ah. And were you named for him because you were born on this day?"

"I was, my Queen, and also in the first year of the papacy of our most recent Pope Clément."

"Then may God and Saint Clément bless you on your birthday."

"With all my heart I thank you, but please waste no more words on me. Save your strength, your Grace."

"Indeed. The letters: I wish to inform several minor lords that after my death, an inquiry will be undertaken into my property dealings – no, pray do not object, Clément," the queen said, seeing his mouth open. "I must set my affairs in order and have no time to waste on protestations." A fit of coughing racked the queen's slender frame, underlining her sentiments. One of Eleanor's ladies administered a soothing draught. Clément sat mute, eyes lowered, waiting for the queen to be able to speak again. Eventually she continued, "The inquest will ascertain whether any sin was committed. If it was, reparation and penance will be offered. If these lords bear any grievance, they are to write to my steward and their complaint will be heard. You will find a list of their names on the desk. Pray, compose a letter, then read it over to me." Clément withdrew to a desk which had been placed for him by the window, though the winter light was already beginning to fade. He drafted the letter in the tiniest imaginable writing on his scraps of vellum. He read it over to the queen and she made a couple of alterations.

"That is enough for today, Clément," Eleanor said. "Take parchment to copy these and have them sent without delay. Now you have the letters in hand, I can be at peace. I came without dowry to my marriage and King Henry could not afford to grant me lands. I needed to provide for myself in case I was widowed. But I fear that my agents were over-zealous in their acquisition of land for my estate. And I did not always scrutinise matters as keenly as I should."

"Yes, your Grace. Have no fear; the letters will be sent forthwith." Clément rose to withdraw but the queen raised a hand,

"Stay a while, brother. As I rest, would you tell me the story of your saint?" She closed her eyes.

"As you wish, my lady."

He drew up a stool to her bedside and thought over the story he had heard many times from his mother. "Clément of Rome was consecrated as priest by the Apostle Peter himself. And in time, after Peter's martyrdom, he succeeded him as bishop of Rome. Under the Roman

Emperor Trajan, Clément was imprisoned. Like Saint Paul, this did not prevent him spreading the good news of our Lord Jesus, for he continued to preach to the Roman guards and his fellow prisoners. Trajan was furious and sentenced him to death. Clément was tied to an anchor and cast into the sea. A sad ending; but a fitting one, I feel. For does not Scripture describe our hope in Christ as an anchor for the soul? Saint Clément was propelled by an actual anchor into the glory of God's presence; but Christ had gone before him to prepare the way, as he has for each of us, when our time comes."

Brother Clément paused. The queen did not stir; she must be asleep. He longed to remain by her side but he gathered up the tools of his trade and left in search of a quiet corner where he could copy the letters. Before settling to his work, he decided to take a turn around the courtyard to refresh himself.

Descending the steps from the manor, Clément saw a tall, proud-looking woman ride in at the gate, wearing the white-edged black cowl of a nun. She was Edward's mother, Eleanor of Provence, whom he had last seen at Amesbury where she was prioress, having taken the veil after the death of her husband, King Henry. Clément's eyes were arrested, however, by the girl riding demurely behind her, whom he recognised as Princess Mary. It was only two months since he had last seen her, and Clément was taken aback by the change. In that short time she had grown from girl to young woman and, moreover, into her mother's likeness. Her merry dark eyes glinted and a wisp of chestnut hair escaped from her nun's wimple. Brother Clément knew her to be twelve years of age but she could easily pass for sixteen. The riders halted and grooms hurried forward to help them dismount. A messenger rushed past Clément to announce their arrival to the king.

Clément reached the bottom of the steps and stood aside. A moment later Edward strode out to greet his mother and daughter and lead them inside. Mary followed behind as was seemly; her movements were lithe and her hungry eyes roved around her new surroundings. When her eyes fell on Clément, she flashed a conspiratorial smile at him. This glance alone confirmed his suspicion that the contemplative life was not for her. After all, she was Edward and Eleanor's daughter. She was made for activity and adventure. Clément pitied her but there was no help for it. Like himself, she had been given to God as a child. He knew himself to be fortunate; he had grown into his vocation. Convent life brought delight, as well as discipline to those truly called to it. But in Clément's view, it was a travesty to impose it on any against their will or too young to know their own mind. The royal party passed on up the hall steps and out of Clément's sight.

Chapter 23

28th November 1290, Manor of Harby, Nottinghamshire

Bishop Oliver had heard the queen's confession and administered the last rites. Now with the king sitting on her right, she was bidding farewell to her household, one by one. The queen whispered in her lady's ear. Carlita scanned the room until her eyes hit upon Clément.

"The queen asks for you, Brother Clément. Come forward." Clément approached the royal bed and bent his head towards the queen, who whispered hoarsely,

"You have served me faithfully, brother, and many times I have been glad of your company and conversation." Clément mutely grasped the queen's outstretched hand. At his touch, she whimpered, "Clément, I am fearful. I do believe but now my time draws near, what if there is no life to come, what if there is only darkness?" The queen's distress galvanised the scribe and he said vehemently,

"If that were so, your Grace, then rejoice that in this life you have truly lived and loved. But take heart, for if it is true, as we believe, then you are about to enter into Life and Love. Trust in Christ, my lady. Remember his words on the eve of his own death, 'Do not let your hearts be troubled. Trust in God; trust also in me. In my Father's house are many rooms. I am going to prepare a place for you.' My dear Lady, trust in the Lord who has gone before you and even now awaits you in His glory." The queen remained silent for several long minutes, meditating on Clément's words. Then with a slight press of his hand, she whispered,

"Thank you, Clément." She released his hand and Clément knew that he had exchanged his last words with her. He withdrew to a quiet corner and sank to his knees to pray for the queen's soul.

Next the queen spoke to Otto de Grandisson, the king's close friend and a great favourite with Eleanor.

"I have a request to make of you, Otto."

"My lady, whatever you ask, if it be in my power, it shall be done."

"Do not agree until you have heard. It is no small thing I charge you with. My soul is heavy and I am afraid. When you reach the Holy Land to prepare for the crusade, I would have you pray for my soul on the mount of our Lord's crucifixion."

"I would do anything to ease your soul, my lady. I will set out as soon as the king gives me leave."

"God bless you, Otto," she said. Otto lifted the queen's pale hand to his lips and then withdrew. Edward leaned forward and kissed his wife tenderly on her forehead, her cheek and her lips.

"I can't let you go, Eleanor. God must not take you from me. I can't bear it."

"My dearest love, king of my heart, we must bear it. Be strong. I am going to our little ones, dear Alphonso and Henry and John."

"No, Eleanor, rally and stay to mother our children yet living."

"I fear I cannot, my love; my strength is spent. I charge you to care for our children. In your grief for me, do not bar them from your heart. Comfort them and let them comfort you. Edward, I thank God for every happy recollection of our love. I have been the most beloved of women."

"And I the most loved of men."

"Let my children come forward."

Eleanor shared some parting words with her daughters; the eldest, Eleanora, then Joan and Margaret, both recently married. They kissed her and withdrew as the younger children, Mary, Elizabeth and young Edward approached. Her strength was visibly failing now and she could only say to Edward,

"You will be king. Imitate your father." They each stooped to kiss her limp hand and withdrew.

King Edward knelt by his wife's side and held her hand and her gaze for a few minutes more until she lost consciousness. Over the next half hour, the queen's breathing grew fainter and fainter until with a last outward breath she gave up her life to God.

Everyone in the room crossed themselves and silently committed the queen's soul to God. Then one or two of her ladies began whimpering. Prince Edward and Princess Elizabeth stood bewildered and forgotten. King Edward sat motionless by Eleanor's side. He said quietly,

"Leave us."

"But your Grace," began Robert Burnell.

"Leave us," the king growled. Silently everyone withdrew and left the king alone with his grief. Clément went straight to the little church where he threw himself down on the chill stone floor to pour out his soul to God and pray for his departed queen.

When he was alone with her, Edward climbed onto the bed next to Eleanor. Her skin was already losing its warmth.

"Oh my love, my queen, my heart. How can I do without you? Always you have been by my side. In all my days as king, I have faced nothing alone. This life of constant travel mattered not to me, because you were with me and you were my home. Now I have no home, nor ever will have. God's blood!"

The room grew cold. Eventually, still cradling his wife's corpse in his arms, Edward fell into a troubled sleep. A servant entered and made up the fire in the grate. Another came and brought food and wine, but they lay untouched.

All night, Edward lay on the bed with his dead wife, grieving; and all night, Clément lay on the floor of the church, praying. In the morning, Clément knew he should ride to the friary at Lincoln where he was meant to be lodged. But he didn't want to be away from the queen. He went back into the manor house, found a bench, wrapped himself in his cloak and tried to sleep. He did not sleep. He felt he would never sleep again, nor eat, nor do any of the things that until now seemed normal. The sun had gone out of his life and he was left alone in chill darkness.

Clément's hands felt inside his scrip for a small cloth bag. His fingers loosened the drawstring, reached inside and closed over the queen's ill-fated pendant. He drew it out, threaded it alongside his own snakestone and replaced the fine gold chain in the bag. He had to know if there was any harm in it. If he remained well, his guilt would be assuaged. If not, he would rightly share the queen's fate. What did it matter now?

Besides, the pendant was a link to Eleanor. He could still see it, hanging at her slender, olive throat and the happy glint in her eye as she admired it. This inward sight of her at last brought the tears. Clément buried his head in the folds of his black habit and wept.

Chapter 24

1st December 1290, Manor of Harby, Nottinghamshire

Robert Burnell rode in at the gatehouse of the de Weston manor shortly after Prime on the second day after the queen's death. He dismounted, tossed the reins to a groom, and strode across the courtyard. He ran up the stone steps leading to the hall, crossed this and entered the solar beyond, where he hoped to find the king. As he entered, Otto de Grandisson looked up from his seat by the brazier where he was warming his hands. Otto read the question in his friend's face,

"No; the king has not emerged. He's still closeted in there with the queen, God rest her."

"Has he eaten?"

"No; servants have taken in fresh food every few hours but it lays untouched," Otto said.

"Has he spoken?"

"Only to order me from the room." With a groan of frustration, Robert sank down heavily in a chair opposite his friend.

"What are we to do, Otto? We cannot stand by and watch Edward go to pieces like this."

"Nor can we command him how to behave. Yet, even in the wake of his loss, he is the king. It falls to us to coax him back to the realities of his kingdom."

"The first reality is the queen's body," Burnell said bluntly. "The corpse must be laid out - today. He must tear himself away. The Dominican friars of Lincoln are sending a small party here at noon for the purpose." A grave silence ensued while both men considered their delicate conundrum. At length Burnell said, "Might we ask Bishop Oliver to accompany the friars? He could appeal to the king with the authority of the church."

"A good thought. May I ride to the bishop's palace to make the request? My horse is in sore need of exercise," said Otto, eager to escape the confines of the house of mourning.

"Yes; and in the meantime, I will try what I may with the king, though I am likely to get my head bitten off for my pains," replied Robert with a grim smile.

As Otto passed through the hall, all heads turned towards him, but his countenance remained blank. The servants knew how to interpret that blankness. The king remained unresponsive. As soon as Otto had left, they started to talk amongst themselves. Until this point, Clément's thoughts had been wrapped up in his own grief and in praying for the queen's soul. Now the needs of others forced themselves into his consciousness. He heard servants saying that the king had not spoken or eaten since Queen Eleanor died. Clément got up and made his way to the hall door and down the steps to the courtyard.

He pulled his cloak tightly around him against the biting cold. He crossed the courtyard and left the manor enclosure behind. Clément needed a quiet place for thought and prayer, but he was so tired, he knew that if he went to the church, his weariness might overtake him. The outdoor chill would keep him wakeful. He knew that ahead of him, due east, lay Lincoln with its awe-inspiring cathedral. He found an eastward path between the strips of tilled earth and prayed as he walked. He interceded for the king: that he would be given comfort and the strength to carry on and to take up the burden of ruling alone. He prayed that the Lord Chancellor and the king's other advisors might discern how best to approach and encourage the king. He prayed for arrangements for the royal funeral. It pained him deeply to form in his mind the words 'bury' and 'funeral' in relation to the queen, but for the king's sake, he bore it. All kinds of decisions must be made. Would the queen be buried at Lincoln or might the king want to take her to Westminster, where his father was interred by the shrine of Saint Edward? As he framed this last thought, an image floated into his mind of a monument he had seen some years ago. It hovered at the edges of his memory – an impressive cross by the side of a road. What was the story behind it? He cast himself back in his thoughts.

Clément had been travelling with the king and queen in Gascony, France. It was his first major journey with the royal household and he was still rather awe-struck. Though he had exchanged but a few stammering words with the queen, he had already fallen under her spell. They had been travelling in France when they saw the great cross. A groom had told him the tale. When King Louis died in Tunisia on his way to the Crusade, his body was brought back to France for burial; later, great crosses were erected to mark the stages of the route of his funeral cortege. Clément felt at the time what a fitting memorial they made to a much-admired and saintly king. He stopped in his tracks as a thought struck him; how fine it would be if the queen could be commemorated with memorial crosses. They would serve as a prompt for people to pray for her soul as it passed through purgatory. They would ensure that her name lived on from generation to generation. And in the here and now, the idea might rouse the king – a grand project to engage his mind during these first shocking days of grief.

As these thoughts cascaded into Clément's mind, it seemed to him that they had been planted there by God. He turned on his heel and began to hurry back. He must gain an audience with Robert Burnell. If the king would listen to anyone, it would be him. As the manor came into view, Clément slowed, then halted. What right had he, a mere scribe, to make such a suggestion to the Chancellor? Now that the queen was gone, by rights he no longer even belonged in the royal household. But even as these doubts assailed him, the idea of the memorial crosses impressed itself on his mind with the persistence of a dripping tap. He paced up and down in a state of extreme agitation. At last, he recalled the conviction he had felt that the idea was from God; after all, it had come to him while he was praying for the king. How if this was the seed of an answer to his prayers? He drew himself up tall and headed for the gatehouse.

Chapter 25

1st December 1290, Manor of Harby, Nottinghamshire

As Clément approached the hall, Lord Burnell emerged and descended the steps, calling for his horse. Clément thanked providence and advanced to meet him.

"My lord," he said, "might I have a word?" Robert Burnell looked at him rather absently,

"Brother Clément, is it? I suppose you are wondering what is to become of you, now your mistress is no longer with us. I am afraid I have rather more pressing matters to attend to at present."

"I realise that, my lord. It is about those pressing matters that I wish to speak." Burnell merely raised an eyebrow. Clément swallowed hard and continued,

"My lord, when I travelled to Gascony with the court, between Saint-Denis and Paris, I saw a great cross." A groom appeared leading Burnell's horse.

"Come to the point, brother, I beg."

"This monument commemorated the venerable King Louis who died far from home. A number of crosses were built to mark the route of his cortege back from North Africa. I am sure the king would have seen them on his many travels."

"Most likely. But what exactly is your point?"

"If the queen is to be carried to Westminster for burial, the king might wish to consider erecting such monuments in her memory. They would remind people to pray for her soul. And the planning and design of them might help to lift the king out of his current state of withdrawal." Clément noticed the Chancellor look at him with more focussed attention.

"It is a good thought." He paused, contemplating. "You did well to bring it to me."

"My lord, I believe it may be from God for it came into my mind while I was praying."

"Thank you, brother," he said, dismissing Clément. And to the groom he said,

"I won't be needing my horse at present."

Robert Burnell paced up and down the solar until Otto returned from Lincoln and said,

"Bishop Oliver will come."

"Good," Burnell replied. "You know the queen's scribe, Clément?"

"Yes, what of him."

"He came to me with an idea, which might serve our need."

"Oh?" Robert briefly conveyed Clément's idea.

"Yes," Otto said, staring into the flames as he warmed his hands at the hearth. "I recall looking at such a cross outside Paris, when I returned from the holy land almost twenty years ago. I dare say the king will remember it too. I agree, Robert, this could be what he needs; a cause to set his mind on, not ignoring his grief, but channelling it." A servant entered the room bearing a tray and placed a jug and two goblets on the table.

"I thank you," said Robert, crossing the room and pouring the wine. He passed his friend a cup, raised his own and said,

"To the king's health!"

"The king's health," replied Otto. They sat down and drank. "The first hurdle is how to entreat the king to listen to our suggestion."

Behind Otto, the door opened and the king appeared, looking haggard and pale. The two men sprang up.

"Your Grace," said Burnell, bowing low, "I offer my deepest condolences."

"And I mine," echoed de Grandisson.

"I thank you," said the king hoarsely. They led him to a seat and called for food and more wine. The king ate and drank mechanically. Presently Otto gave Robert a look which said, here's our chance.

"My lord," Burnell began, "I was just recalling to Otto here that you told me once of some fine monuments you saw in France erected in memory of King Louis. I believe they marked places where his funeral procession passed on the way back to Paris." The king remained impassive. Burnell pressed on, "You told me how passers-by were thus reminded of the venerable king's life and exhorted to pray for his soul. If the queen's body," Burnell saw Edward flinch, but continued bravely, "forgive me, my lord. If the queen is to be carried back to Westminster, might your Grace consider the possibility of planning similar monuments?" Burnell fell silent, fearing the king's anger if he persisted. For a long time, the king stared at the wall, occasionally sipping his wine.

"My lord, plans must be made. It is becoming urgent," Otto ventured. The king answered wearily,

"Yes, I know, gentlemen. Summon my sergeants to meet here in two hours. Now leave me." Edward sat mute for several more minutes, though a careful observer would have seen his mind firing back to life behind his weary eyes. He summoned a servant and said,

"Bring ink and parchment."

At the appointed time, the court sergeants arrived. They were responsible for organising the king's travel plans. The king beckoned them to draw chairs to the table. He said,

"At first light tomorrow, we remove to Lincoln where the queen will be," he cleared his throat, "taken care of by the Dominican brothers. We will have two days in Lincoln to devise plans for our journey south. It is my wish that the queen be borne in procession with all dignity and ceremony to Westminster. The route should enable the greatest number of people to pay their respects. I wish for her soul's passage to be eased by many prayers, vigils and masses. I also intend to set up, as soon as may be, a monument in each town where her body rests overnight. There will be twelve crosses to honour my wife's devotion to me and to England. God willing, the monuments will also prompt prayers for her soul. Gentlemen, you have one day to consider these matters. Tomorrow we shall reconvene in Lincoln to make our preparations."

After Prime the following day, the royal party crowded into the courtyard of the de Weston Manor to take their leave. As Richard de Weston and his lady bade farewell to the king, Edward managed to observe the necessary courtesies but it was all too evident that his heart and mind were elsewhere. And little wonder; ten days ago, the de Westons had welcomed the royal couple to their home, but only the king departed their manor living.

Chapter 26

1ˢᵗ December Current Year, Lincoln Minster School

Daniel was ill again. Pounding head, shivers, earache, the works. At least his throat wasn't too sore. He didn't want to miss many choir practices as they had just started rehearsing for Christmas and he had a chance of being chosen for a solo. He had been lying in bed puzzling over how to get some money. He had still not managed to make the bus journey to see the site of the Lincoln Eleanor Cross. Over half term at home, he had been too occupied with the dig at the abbey ruins to manage any odd jobs to earn cash.

When Daniel woke up, his nose was blocked and he was shivering again. Damn! He'd fallen asleep. He dragged himself to matron's office for more medicine. Half an hour later he was dosed up and feeling half human again. While the caffeine kick lasted, Daniel set his mind to work on his financial setback. Why didn't he have any money? Because Jim was always nicking it? What could he do about it? He couldn't think of anything. Nothing at all. Except... nick it back. Nick it back. Nick it back! The idea was both terrifying and liberating. He had to do it right now while his mind was still clear and his courage was up. Where would Jim be now? He checked his phone – 14.30. Rugby practice. Jim and Ed's room was on the floor above Daniel's. Would it be locked? Daniel and Stephen had been neurotic about locking their room since the break-in. Given half a chance, Jim would be in there again trouncing his stuff and stealing whatever he liked. But Daniel could only hope that Jim was so confident of his reputation that he felt he no need to lock his door. And maybe Ed was too stupid to remember or even to be responsible for a key.

Daniel left his room, stopping in the corridor to look both ways, as if he could already be caught in the act, betrayed by his own guilty intentions. Guilty? He was only intending to reclaim his own possessions, for goodness' sake. It certainly wasn't stealing. Why hadn't he thought of this before? It was only now that he really wanted money for something that he cared it had been stolen. But more than that, this was an opportunity to stand up to Jim and his mates. There would be hell to pay, of course. But, what the heck, there'd be hell to pay anyway.

Daniel padded in his socks along the corridor and up the stairs to the second floor. At the top of the stairs, he peeped round the corner, feeling like James Bond. Still on a slight high from the flu medicine, the adrenalin was now pumping him into a state of excitement and nervous tension bordering on hysteria. He felt invincible. The coast was clear. Daniel tiptoed along the corridor to Jim's room. He looked left and right again and then gingerly turned the door handle. The door didn't open. Damn. It's locked. But then he remembered that his own door stuck sometimes. He wedged his knee on the door and shoved. He fell into the room and shut the door behind him. Now he had no way of knowing if at any moment Jim was about to walk in. He rubbed his sweaty palms on his trousers.

Daniel glanced around the room. There was no money just lying around. He stood upright and forced himself to take several deep breaths. He began to look intelligently around again. My room's more or less the same as this, he thought. Where do I keep my money? Top drawer of the bedside table. He wrenched open the drawer and rifled through its contents: scraps of paper, old, sticky sweet wrappers; ugh, it was disgusting. But no money. What if Jim kept his money on him all the time? No. Keep calm. He wouldn't carry all of it around. Daniel opened the next drawer down and searched more methodically. A shriek of laughter bounced off the walls of the corridor. He froze. There was nowhere to hide. Just like his own room; there were drawers under the bed, a tiny wardrobe, every last inch was used. You couldn't even hide behind the door unless you wanted your face smashed in when it opened. Daniel started to shake uncontrollably. Crap. Don't let Jim see me like this, please God. The footsteps drew nearer, paused and then passed by. Daniel remained motionless for a few moments while he calmed down.

Still trembling slightly, Daniel fumbled in the bottom drawer of the cabinet. His hands hit on what could be a wallet. He pulled it out. It was a wallet. He yanked it open, grabbed a tenner, shoved the wallet back in the drawer, rammed the drawer shut and made for the door. He paused to listen for sounds out in the corridor. His own blood was still pumping so furiously that it was difficult to hear external sounds. All seemed quiet. Daniel opened the door a crack. He could still hear nothing. He stuck his head out and looked both ways. Then he fled along the passage back to the stairs. He started to charge down three at a time. Suddenly Jim, Ed and Natalie appeared round the corner at the bottom of the stairs and started to ascend. Daniel froze again. They looked up instinctively as if they smelt him – their prey.

"Well, well; what's Geek doing on our floor, Ed?" said Jim.

"Ugh, you're sweating like a pig. What have you been up to?" said Natalie.

"I'm ill. I was sleep-walking."

"Don't come near me then. I don't want your lurgy," said Natalie. Daniel said nothing; he held his head high and proceeded down the stairs in as dignified a manner as he could manage. He reached the stair on which the others stood blocking his path.

"Excuse me, please," said Daniel.

"Ooh, excuse me please, is it?" jeered Jim. "No, you get out of our way, Geek."

Daniel duly pressed himself into the wall and they shoved past him three abreast, squashing him still further into the wall – slightly winding him – though he had been holding his breath anyway.

They were gone. Round the corner, laughing, at him no doubt. He didn't care. He had nicked back his own money. Down on his own corridor he uncharacteristically whooped with triumph and then high-fived his door which fell open.

"Hey! What's with the cheering, mate? I thought you had flu," said Stephen.

"Yeah, I'm a bit high on the medicine. But I've just kind of got my own back on Jim."

"Tell me more!" Stephen said grinning. Daniel filled him in on his heroic exploit and Stephen slapped him on the back. "Good for you, Dan. It's a good first step. Next time wait for me, I'll be your look-out. So, what's next in your plan?"

"Er. I don't know. There isn't a plan. I just wanted my money back. I need it for something. But it does feel great to have stood up to him. Even if he doesn't notice the money's missing because he's loaded, I know I did it and I suppose that's what matters."

Chapter 27

2nd December 1290, Lincoln

The sombre procession entered Lincoln through the ancient arch which formed the northern gate of the city. The cobbled streets were lined with onlookers wishing to pay their last respects to the queen and offer silent support to the king. As Clément had not been privy to the plans for this journey, he was unsure of their exact destination. The cortege turned northeast and skirted the high northern wall of the cathedral precincts. Of course, he thought, we go to the Dominicans - the order most favoured by the queen. And before long they passed through a simple gateway and were greeted by the prior. Here the cortege halted and prayers were said. Then the queen was carried into the church and laid in the mortuary chapel. More prayers were said.

The king exchanged a few words with the prior, insisting that the queen's body should at no time be left alone. Then Edward abruptly tore himself away, pain etched on every line of his face. Clément wondered whether the king would lodge with the bishop at his palace south of the cathedral or with his friend de Lacy at the castle. He hoped the king would be with the sheriff for he certainly needed the companionship of his closer friends at this time. Clément, at any rate, had no intention of leaving the queen's side. He sought out the hospitaller and asked leave to stay in the guest hall. Later he would join the friars as they kept vigil over the queen's body through the night.

Elsewhere in the priory, Carlita, lady-in-waiting to the late queen, perused Derian's works in progress as she smoothed her hair and dress.

"Who is this dainty silver one for?" she said, looking over her shoulder at Derian, still stretched out on his cot.

"That's just a template, a design I was working up to show his grace. A possible Christmas gift for the queen. But there will be no more gifts for her. Has anything been said to you, of what's to become of us all, now she's gone to her rest?"

"No, nothing official as yet, but the other ladies assume that her grace's household will be dispersed after the funeral at Westminster." She fingered the pendant, tracing its swirls. "You will never lack work, your skill is enough to speak for you, let alone your experience as court goldsmith. The king will probably retain you but if not, any of his barons would leap at the chance to boast of having the queen's jeweller in his employ." Carlita perched herself prettily on a wooden stool. "I have nothing to recommend me for a new position, either here at court or in any other household. My needlework wants precision, my voice is mediocre and my accent foreign. I was fortunate that her grace had a fondness for me; I reminded her of her young daughter, Mary, who was given to God as a child."

"Come now, Letty, don't pout; it spoils your features. And you may have need of them, now more than ever. You must not give way to despair or underestimate your charms. A pretty face and a winsome smile may carry a woman far in this world. And you are mistress of more arts than you know. You have certainly charmed enough trinkets out of me. Here is one more for your collection." He plucked the pendant from the bench and strung it on a thread-fine silver chain that he whipped from his pocket with a flourish "By now you must have enough set by to keep you comfortable for some little time to come."

This was true. The sporadic liaison between these two self-interested creatures had yielded treasure to each. Derian had gleaned titbits of information and gossip of a private nature to be unearthed and used if ever he saw a chance to turn them to his own advantage. For her part, Carlita had collected a little trove of jewels; items that did not quite meet Derian's exacting standards. He dangled the pendant in front of her.

"This one bears a holy pattern - I copied it from an ancient cross in a churchyard."

∞

At Lincoln Castle, the king paced relentlessly up and down his royal apartments. It was one of the few places he had never stayed with the queen and for this one night he needed to be free from visualising her in every nook and cranny of his surroundings. He had hoped he could banish her from his thoughts just while he knew her body was being embalmed. Folly – he now realised. Eleanor had been his constant love and companion these six and thirty years. No power on earth could for one moment erase her from his mind.

He could not help but picture the cut of the blade that slit open Eleanor's dear olive skin, always so warm, so soft. He felt every movement of the blade as if it sliced his own flesh. He clutched his head, it was unendurable, this violation of his wife's body by strangers. It is necessary, he told himself over and over. She is the queen; she must be carried in state to London and buried at Westminster near my father, and the shrine of Edward, the blessed Confessor. It is necessary; the corrupting course of nature must be held at bay for at least the duration of the journey and the funeral. God's blood, then why does it hurt so? It is necessary; her precious body, the sole object of his passion, must be lacerated, organs removed, cavities filled with barley. Sickened and faint, he thumped the stone wall. Relishing the physical pain, he drew his arm back to repeat the act. But he checked himself; this would not do, the responsibility of the crown reasserted itself and he stormed from the room, shouting,

"Saddle my horse!"

∞

There was no stopping the tears of Brother Clément, who knelt clutching the altar rail of the church of the black friars. His mind also was beset by gruesome images of the desecration of Eleanor's royal person, now taking place in the mortuary chapel not fifty yards from him, shielded by a screen. He wept and prayed and prayed and wept, crossing himself over and over, never pausing in his violent torrent of grief to listen for the whisper of comfort or feel the touch of peace which fell in answer to his fervent prayers.

Chapter 28

2nd December Current Year, Lincoln Minster School

"Listen to this, Stephen – 'The Queen's Embalming,'" Daniel said.

"The queen's what?"

"Embalming; what they do to dead bodies to stop them decaying before they're buried."

"Urgh, gross! What, like Egyptian mummies?" Stephen said.

"I guess so, may be not so thorough. The Egyptians preserved bodies for thousands of years. Malteser?" he said. He reached across the gap between their beds and offered the packet to his room-mate. Stephen stuffed a few in his mouth and asked,

"How do they actually do it?"

"That's what I'm trying to work out. It says here, 'Payment was recorded for eight gallons of barley to place in the queen's body.'"

Stephen munched his Maltesers thoughtfully, "How on earth do you get all that barley inside someone's body?" he said. "There's no room."

"I think they take out all the soft bits that decay quickly and then stuff the space with the barley."

"That's disgusting. I don't want to think about it. Read it in your head." Stephen turned back to his laptop and tried to focus on his maths assignment, but a few minutes later he said, "Which bits did they take out then?"

"I thought you didn't want to know," Daniel said, laughing. Stephen shrugged his shoulders. Daniel turned a page. "It says here "the heart and viscera were removed."

"What's viscera?"

"I don't know – the other internal organs, I suppose."

"What, like liver and kidneys and stuff?" Stephen said.

"Your guess is as good as mine."

"I'll google it," Stephen saved his homework and opened a new tab. "What shall I put in – embalming?"

"Yeah, okay. Maybe medieval embalming," Daniel said. He leant back on his pillows and popped another Malteser in his mouth.

"I hope there aren't any pictures." Stephen said.

"That makes a change. I thought you only looked at the pictures."

"Ha ha," said Stephen. "How do you spell medieval?" Stephen typed it into the search engine and scanned down the list of websites. "Science Museum; that might be good." Daniel stood up and looked over Stephen's shoulder at the screen.

Daniel skimmed down a page entitled, 'Preserving the body.'

"Quite interesting but not really what we're looking for. Try a different site," he said.

"How can you have read all that? I've only just got past the title!" said Stephen. Daniel looked at his friend.

"I haven't read it all. I just scanned it for keywords. If you read the whole page on every website you land on, you'll never get anywhere."

"That must be my problem." Stephen tapped back to Google.

"Try this one, 'Political Effigies – Dead Media Archive,'" Daniel suggested. They looked at the page. Stephen said,

"I'm not even going to start reading all that. I'll scan the pictures and you do the text."

"Yeah, that sounds fair," Daniel elbowed Stephen in the shoulder. They concentrated on the screen. After a while, Daniel said, "This is great stuff. I'll come back to it later. Can you send me the link?"

"Where does it say which bits were taken out?" said Stephen.

"It doesn't. It's totally irrelevant, but fascinating anyway. I'll look at it another time."

"Blimey, Dan. No wonder they call you Geek."

"Don't you start."

"I'm not. It's just, you know, most kids only do research on a need-to-know basis, not because they find it interesting."

"So what?"

"So nothing."

"Go back to Google then." After a few more fruitless attempts, they deleted "medieval" from the search and just looked under embalming, ending up as usual on Wikipedia.

"Sanitization, presentation and preservation of a corpse; this is more like it," said Daniel. Again he skimmed the page but gleaned little extra information.

"I've had enough," said Stephen, "Let's go for it and look on images."

Daniel stuffed the last few Maltesers in his mouth absentmindedly. "Urgh!" Daniel turned away from the screen and then crashed back onto his bed.

"Holy crap!" said Stephen, slamming his laptop shut. "Are you okay, Dan? You've gone completely white."

"I shouldn't have eaten those chocolates. Don't show me any more images."

"No fear. I wouldn't look at that again if you paid me,' Stephen said.

Daniel had an idea, "Try putting 'diagram' in the search. That should be safer."

"Are you sure?" Stephen said, lifting the screen again.

"It's up to you. I'm not looking until you tell me it's safe."

"You trust me then?" Stephen said.

"No, but if you show me anything gross, I'll chuck up my chocolate all over your bed."

"Point taken. Okay, here goes." While Stephen searched, Daniel lay back, trying to block the last images from his mind. Stephen began sniggering.

"What's so funny?" Daniel asked.

"Nothing. Just 'bits,' if you know what I mean. It's still not specific enough. I'm changing it to 'viscera diagram.'"

"Watch out," said Daniel.

"This is more like it. It's safe to look, unless you're even more of a wimp than I thought."

"Oi," said Daniel, lobbing a pillow at Stephen's head.

"Mind the laptop, Dan," Stephen said, batting the pillow aside, laughing.

They looked at the screen. It showed a simplified diagram from the neck down to the lower stomach. Daniel stared at it for quite a while; he was better with words than pictures.

"Lungs, liver, colon, stomach and other smaller bits," he said. "So it sounds as if practically everything inside was removed except bones and they packed out the corpse with barley to keep the shape. In the book it mentions incense as well, presumably to cover the smell. Then the body was wrapped in cloth."

"What like a mummy, in bandages?"

"No idea. Ugh, horrible history. All that was done to Queen Eleanor's body, 730 odd years ago today - December 2nd." Daniel paused and looked down at his middle, "It's weird to think of what's under our skin, isn't it?"

"Yeah, skeletons and squishy bits. It's kind of freaky, isn't it? That's all we are, at the end of the day."

"Mm. My Dad would say that we're more than that - because we have a soul. And that we're designed to live forever in heaven."

"Do you think he's right?"

"I'm not completely sure. But I guess I do think people are more than just bones and muscles and stuff. More substantial or something. When my grandma died last year, it didn't seem possible that she just didn't exist anymore."

"Yeah, I know what you mean. I felt the same when my cousin died; that he couldn't have just stopped. He was only twenty-two." There was a slightly awkward silence while both boys thought about it, not really having anything else to say but also not wanting to be the one to change the subject. Finally, Daniel moved and Stephen said,

"I'd better get on with my maths."

Chapter 29

4th December 1290, Lincoln

Early in the morning, Clément stood up stiffly after his cold vigil kneeling on the cathedral's stone floor. He had spent the night praying with many other monks and nuns by the body of the queen, who lay on an open bier on the high altar, wearing her crown and majestic flowing robes. Clément filed out behind the Dominican friars and followed them back to their priory to sing the office of Prime.

Afterwards, Clément watched a closed coffin being carried with all dignity by six friars from the mortuary chapel. Tears welled up as he realised that the casket contained the queen's viscera. The cortege halted in the frosty courtyard to be arranged with Bishop Oliver preceding the coffin and the highest-ranking men falling in behind it. King Edward was grim-faced, as if he were about to do battle with his deadliest foe rather than bury his wife. But, Clément reflected, there was not so much difference. Edward faced mankind's arch-enemy, death; not his own, but that of one whose life he had cherished more than his own.

The king was accompanied by Henry Lacy, Earl of Lincoln and constable of the castle. Lacy was Edward's staunch ally and had been a favourite of the queen. He was cut from the same cloth as Edward, tall, soldier-like and doggedly loyal. They were followed by the elder princesses, Eleanora and Joan. Clément shivered as he took his lowly place towards the back of the procession. They walked at a slow pace through the friary gate and along the narrow street towards the cathedral. Entering through the great west door, the procession made its way up the nave and almost filled the enormous church. Clément was among the last to enter, so perhaps only he saw how the sun suddenly blazed through the stained glass of the high windows and lit up the floor and slender columns in a myriad of delicate, dancing hues. The colours reached deep into Clément's grief-wrung soul and shone a glimmer of light there.

At the head of the nave, the cortege skirted the high altar and proceeded onwards towards the east end of the cathedral, the new Angel Choir, so called because of the many angels carved into the vaulted ceiling. Ten years ago the king and queen had presided over its opening. Clément stole a glance at the king; his face was an icy mask.

With the customary words of burial, Bishop Oliver committed Queen Eleanor's soul to God. Incense burners were waved, prayers were said and with ghastly finality, this first partial funeral was abruptly over. They moved in procession back to the high altar where the bier bearing the queen's body was raised and carried to the south door.

Clément lingered; he might never be in this place again. For what did his own future hold but a return to the static, cloistered life he had contentedly accepted, before the unimaginable experience of the royal court? He returned to the Angel Choir and offered yet more prayers for Eleanor's soul at the shrine of her neighbour-in-burial, Saint Hugh, the bishop who had built this glorious church. Clément was comfortable praying near the gentle saint – a fellow Frenchman. As he prayed, a vivid image formed in his mind of Saint Hugh standing at the threshold of heaven, arms outstretched. Towards him walked Eleanor, not a queen now, merely a child of God returning to her Father. Hugh welcomed her with a warm embrace and the vision faded. Clément was lost in wonder and prayed that this might be not merely a picture from his imagination but a true glimpse of heaven.

He rose from his knees comforted, for the first time since the queen's death. Realising he was now alone in the cathedral; he hurried out to catch up with the cortege. Clément emerged into a morning washed clean by a heavy snowfall. Momentarily blinded by the whiteness, he felt as if he had stepped back into his heavenly vision. Reality soon dawned, however, and he made his way, walking downhill as briskly as he could, in a light-drenched world where the only sound was the crump and creak of fresh-fallen snow beneath his shoes.

Clément caught up with the cortege as it passed east of the bishop's palace. It proceeded steeply downhill towards the crossing of the river Witham. Beyond the mourners who lined the street, Clément could see mile after mile of snow-laden landscape, dazzling in the sunshine. They reached the bottom of the hill and crossed the river by a stone bridge leading to a broad straight road through the suburb of Wigford. All was eerily quiet in this usually bustling place. Even the horses' hooves were virtually silent on the fresh snow, as they passed potters, timber-workers and shopkeepers standing in front of their workshops and booths to pay their respects. The cortege proceeded past the White Friars and the priest of St Botolph's before his church, past rich folk in front of fine stone houses and the poor by their shacks; distinctions of rank irrelevant in the face of death, which spares none, whether royalty, nobility, clergy or laity.

Leaving the town behind them, they followed the road, built in ancient times by the Romans, until it was joined by another from the east. Here the procession halted. Clément observed the king in earnest conversation with Robert Burnell and others. Perhaps they were discussing the route. He was not privy to their plans, accustomed to following where others led. Now he saw Bishop Oliver step forward to the queen's bier. Clément crept forward into earshot. The Chancellor said,

"In the name of the king, I hereby proclaim that at this place, in due course, a great cross will be erected in memory of her grace, Queen Eleanor, and also in each of the eleven further towns where the queen's body will rest overnight, during her passage to London." The bishop sprinkled holy water over the ground around the bier and offered a prayer.

God be praised, thought Clément; the king has taken up the suggestion of the memorial crosses. And for a moment his heart rose above the leaden desolation of grief. The cortege passed on but again Clément lingered. He lay down in the snow on the ground where the cross would one day stand. He stretched out his arms in the shape of the cross and praised God for answering his humble prayer. He offered thanks for the twelve monuments that would stand as perpetual memorials to his queen.

Chapter 30

4th December Current Year, Lincoln

Daniel managed to get the front double seat on the top deck to himself. He made himself at home and settled down to enjoy the ride. He loved sitting above the driver, scraping along the overgrown trees and careering bluntly round bends. He grinned; Jim and his mates had followed him to the bus stop but he had outrun them. They had no idea where he was heading; surely they wouldn't bother to wait for another bus to follow him. But that was where he was mistaken. Back at the bus stop, Jim was arguing with Ed.

"Well, I'm gonna wait and get the next bus, with or without you two. I want to know what the slimy turd's up to. I bet he has a geeky little girlfriend and he's going off to meet her in some library." Jim roared with laughter at his own wit. Ed and Natalie joined in half-heartedly.

"Alright, we'll come," said Natalie, who was the spokesman of the pair. "But will we have enough money left for MacDonald's when we get back?"

"Yeah, probably," said Jim, relieved that he didn't have to go alone.

"Here it comes," said Ed. A bus pulled up and they got on.

Daniel's bus jolted to a halt at a bus stop and brought him back to reality. He peered out of the steamed-up window. There was a park on the left. He jumped up and charged down the stairs; he'd been daydreaming as usual and this was his stop. He reached the bottom just as the new passengers were trying to come up.

"Sorry, sorry, excuse me," he said as he barged through them. He jumped off the bus as the doors began to close. Daniel pulled up his hood. He wanted to consult his book but it was raining so hard that it would be soaked in seconds. He peered around looking for shelter. He spotted an ugly concrete building that was probably toilets about a hundred metres to his left. He ran to the gents, which stank, and pulled his Queen Eleanor book out of his rucksack. He tried to breathe through his mouth to shut out the smell but then he could almost taste the stench. The site of the Lincoln cross was thought to be at the foot of a road now called Cross o' Cliff Hill. Daniel brought up the map on his phone. It was about three hundred metres south of here. He braved the rain and started walking briskly. As he passed the bus stop, a bus drew up and spilt Jim and his two friends onto the wet pavement. Ed and Natalie were moaning about the rain.

"Oi, Geek!" Jim called after Daniel.

Without looking around, Daniel broke into a run. It wasn't far now but there was a busy road to cross. He paused at the kerb and dived across through the first gap in the traffic. He could see the road sign, 'Cross o' Cliff Hill,' in front of some black railings and a tall hedge, which screened a large house from the road. This was it. What with the rain, the traffic and Jim, it was hard to imagine an Eleanor Cross here, like the one at Geddington. He glanced behind him to see Jim and his cronies still waiting to cross the road. He'd have to start running again but he loitered for another moment and took one step forward...

∞

... A blast of cold air stung Daniel's face and he squinted, eyes dazzled by the sudden brightness of sunlight reflecting off snow. He lifted his hand to screen his eyes and then opened them properly again. All he saw was an open, snowy landscape. The railings, road sign, hedge and house had vanished. In their place were Christmas-card-fir-trees dusted with snow. He spun round. The road and traffic had also disappeared. Daniel's mind began to race, searching for a rational explanation. A moment ago he was by a busy road in rain-soaked Lincoln. He had taken only one step forward and here he was in the snow.

He looked down. At his feet lay a figure sprawled in the snow, arms spread wide as if making a snow-angel, except that he was face down. In fact, Daniel was treading on the edge of his black cloak. He took a step back and forced his bewildered mind to focus. He must be dead, Daniel thought; no one in their right mind would lie down like that in the snow. He had never seen a corpse before.

Part II

The Unlikely Pilgrims

PART II

Lincoln
Byard's Leap
Ancaster
Grantham
Stamford
Fineshade Abbey
Geddington
Geddington
Northampton
Hardingstone
Towcester
Stony Stratford
B. Priory
Woburn
Toddington
Dunstable
Rowney Priory
St Albans
Waltham
London

Northampton

Waltham

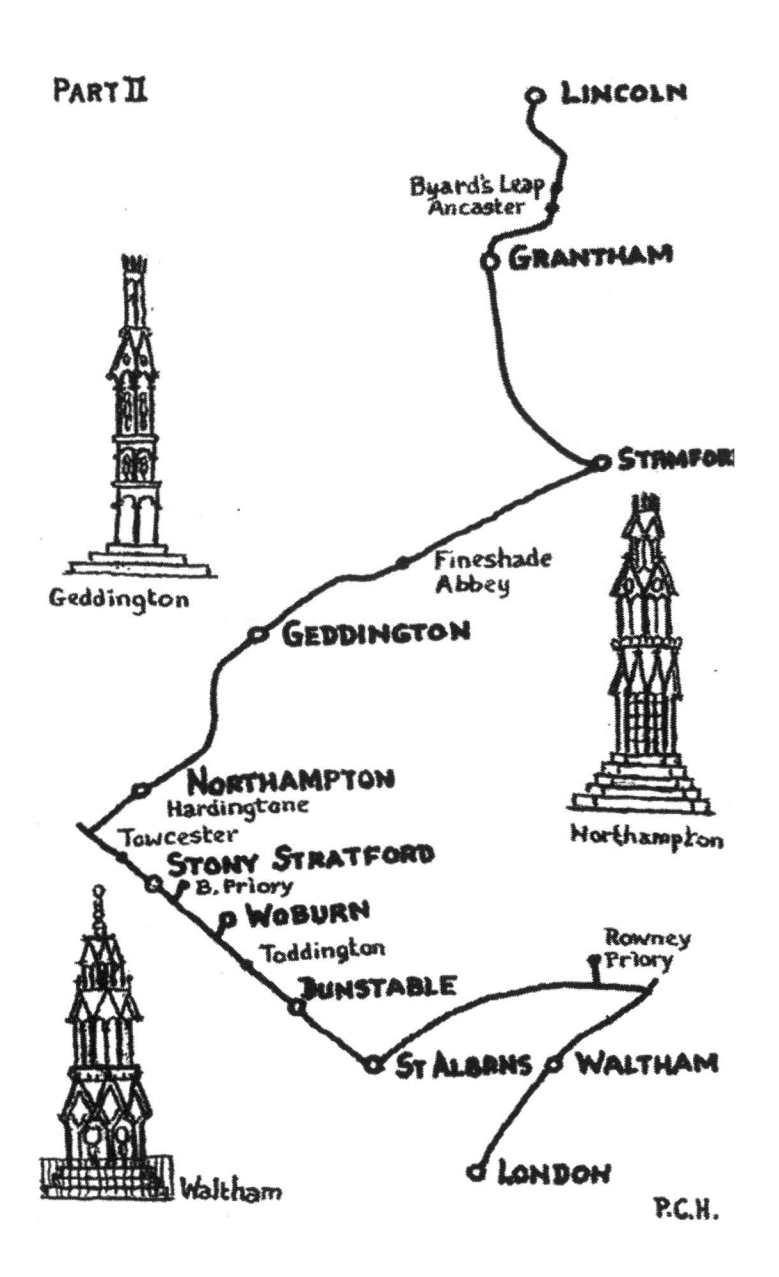

P.C.H.

Chapter 31

4th December, Lincoln

On the other side of the road, Daniel's pursuers stopped dead. He had vanished.

"What the hell?" said Jim. As he spoke, a gap opened in the traffic and the three friends bolted across the road. They stood on the street corner, gaping stupidly. The spot was deserted; Jim took one step more, then blundered into Daniel, who in turn collapsed onto the prone figure in the snow.

"Sorry, I'm sorry," Daniel stammered, rolling off the body beneath him. With a gasp, the dark-robed figure rose up from the ground. Beneath a black hood, an ashen face gazed at them with far-away eyes. Daniel and Jim backed away from him, aghast. The man shuddered and seemed to recollect himself. He stood up straight, brushed away the snow that clung to his dishevelled robe, and scanned the horizon.

"Forgive me," the man said distractedly. He fixed on some distant objects, dark against the snow, and set off at a stumbling run towards them.

"What the hell was that?" said Jim.

"I don't know. A monk, maybe? I thought it was a dead body lying in the snow," Daniel said. "I fell on it when you crashed into me, then it got up!"

A second later Natalie and Ed appeared out of nowhere and stood dumbstruck. Moments passed then everyone started talking at once.

"What the hell have you done, Geek?" Jim said, "Is this your idea of a joke?" Daniel laughed and said,

"Yeah. It's a great trick, isn't it? Changing the weather and making roads and buildings disappear."

"If it's not you, what is it? Where's everything gone?"

"I don't know, do I? I'm as confused as you are. One moment everything was normal, the next moment it was like this," Daniel said, with a vague gesture at the snowy vista.

"Look over there, in the distance," Natalie said, screening her eyes and pointing in the direction the dark-robed figure had run. "There are some people. Let's go and ask them."

"I'm not sure. They're strangers and we've no idea where we are," said Daniel. "Let's have a look around first. At least let's watch them for a bit before we speak to them."

"What do you mean look around? There's nothing here except snow." Jim said.

"There are some trees," said Ed pointing over their shoulders to where the park had been moments ago.

"And some sheds or garages up that way," Natalie said, pointing uphill to their left. As they looked, a horse-drawn cart appeared at the crest of the hill and rolled towards them silently over the snowy ground.

"What the hell?" said Jim again. "A horse and cart?"

"I'm going to ask the driver where we are," said Natalie, stomping off up the hill. Daniel was beginning to have an inkling, but he kept his thoughts to himself and followed her.

"Um, excuse me," called Natalie towards the cart, "we're a bit lost, me and my friends. Where are we exactly?"

"Good morrow, my lady. Lost your way? It's easy to lose the road in this snow. Well, this here is the meeting of the two ancient ways. To the north, of course, is the city of Lincoln, whence you have come, I dare say. To the south," he said, gesturing, "lies Bracebridge, not far. Whither are you bound?"

"You what?" said Natalie, turning to Daniel, "What's he on about? Why's he talking like that?" Daniel stepped forward and addressed the cart driver,

"Pray forgive my companion, sir, the cold has affected her wits. I thank you for your help and we bid you good day." The cart rattled away as Natalie stared at Daniel, along with Jim and Ed who had caught up in time to hear Daniel address the man. Jim grabbed Daniel by the sleeve and Ed instinctively stepped up, close to his face,

"What the hell was that all about?" Jim said, "Why were you talking like that? I'll have you for this, if you're trying to get one over on me."

"Keep your voice down!" Daniel said firmly. Under his breath, he added, "If you want to keep your head attached to your body, for God's sake shut up until we're on our own." Jim let go of Daniel's sleeve but otherwise stood his ground.

"I don't get it. Where are we?" Ed said, to nobody in particular.

"I think the bloke said Lincoln but how can it be? Everything's completely different," Natalie said.

They walked off the road into the cover of trees.

"You'd better come up with a frigging good explanation, Geek," said Jim. "Where the hell are we?"

"I have a bad feeling that the question is not where we are, but when. I think we're still near Lincoln, but not in the 21st century." That took the wind out of Jim's sails. Daniel watched their bemused expressions as the others tried to process the information.

"What? Like Doctor Who and the Tardis – time travel and all that crap? You expect me to believe that?" Jim said, "When a Dalek appears and exterminates you, maybe then I'll believe you." Then turning to the others, "This must be some kind of reality TV prank. Look for hidden cameras. Geek's trying to get his own back on me somehow and I'm not falling for it."

Daniel burst out laughing. "You've got a vivid imagination, Jim, if you think I could come up with all this. Look, I have no idea how or why we've ended up here, but if I'm right, I suggest you let me do the talking and we might just get out of this alive."

"What, what do you mean, Daniel?" said Natalie, her voice quivering.

"If we have gone back in time and they catch on that we are from the future, we could end up being arrested or worse."

"He's just pulling our legs, isn't he, Jim?" said Ed looking to Jim for reassurance.

"Let's put it to the test, shall we," said Jim, starting to run after the cart, calling out,

"Yeah, yeah, you had us there for a while. Hilarious; but we've sussed it now. You can take your fancy dress off. Show us the cameras."

Chapter 32

4th December, Lincoln

Daniel launched himself after Jim and as they reached the cart he yanked him back, saying to the driver,
"Forgive my friend, he's also a mite touched in the head. Come now, James, you need to rest." He pulled a struggling Jim back to the others, surprised by his own audacity. "You haven't listened to a word I've said, have you? We've gone back in time, whether we like it or not. And as you haven't got the faintest idea how to behave, keep your mouth shut or we'll all end up dead." Jim looked to Natalie and Ed for support but they kept their eyes on the ground. Daniel began again in a more conciliatory tone, "Look, I don't have a clue how it happened but we are still near Lincoln. Look behind you, there's the cathedral. We didn't actually move; our surroundings changed but we stayed in the same spot." They turned round. In the distance, on the summit of a hill, was a cathedral dominating the landscape; and a little to its left, much lower, was a castle.

"How can we be in Lincoln, you moron? I know what Lincoln looks like and this isn't it," said Jim.

"You know what Lincoln looks like now, Jim. But if I'm right and we've travelled in time, not space, Lincoln would still be here, but different." Jim scowled and turned to Natalie and Ed,

"Don't listen to Geek - he's gone mad," he said, then emphasising each word, "There is no such thing as time travel!"

"That's exactly what I would have said until ten minutes ago," Daniel protested, "But I can't find any other rational explanation."

"Rational! How can it be rational to say we've gone back in time? It's got to be some kind of trick."

"Hey, it could be a movie set," suggested Natalie, stamping her cold feet and slapping her arms to keep some life in them. "They sometimes film historical stuff at Lincoln. Maybe that bloke was in character."

"Yeah. That's more like it, good one Nat," said Jim approvingly.

"Maybe, but I still don't get how everything else disappeared," Ed said. He stared at the outline of the cathedral on the horizon. "And that cathedral doesn't look quite right. It's similar but the shape's different somehow."

"Yes, you're right, Ed. It's not tall enough," Daniel said. "The minster was built after the Battle of Hastings, but it was much smaller. It was added to over the years; I've got a book about it. If we have gone back in time, from what I remember about the cathedral, I'd guess that we're sometime in the medieval period."

"What's that in English, Geek?" Jim asked.

"Roughly speaking 1000-1500AD."

"Great. That means sod all to me."

"Sometime between William the Conqueror and Henry VIII, if that helps?"

Natalie took her mobile out of her back pocket.

"We can test it," she said. "If we've gone back in time, there'll be no signal right?"

"Who are you calling?" Jim said.

"You; is your volume up?"

"Yeah." They stood listening. Nothing.

"So, there's no mobiles, no TV or anything?" said Ed.

"Hang on, maybe there's just no signal here," said Jim.

"There's nothing electrical; it's before the industrial revolution so they haven't even invented steam engines yet," said Daniel.

Jim put his mobile back in his pocket. "It's the bloody dark ages. They must be idiots and savages. We've got to get home."

"Calm down, Jim. They're not savages or idiots. Look at the cathedral! They built it without any machinery. But you're right to be scared; we are in danger. They won't understand that we've come from the future, any more than we understand it. But unfortunately in the Middle Ages they tended to put anything they didn't understand down to witchcraft. We mustn't speak to anybody until we have a plan."

"Supposing Daniel's right; we must have stumbled on some kind of time portal thing," Natalie said. "If we retrace our steps exactly, surely we can just get back the way we came." They spent the next half hour walking around in circles, attempting to reverse whatever had happened. It ended in a row with Jim, Natalie and Ed all blaming someone else for the fact that it wasn't working. Finally Daniel said,

"Right, we've given that a good try. Let's try something else."

"Like what?"

"How about heading back to town to see what it looks like there?"

"There won't be any buses. How are we going to get there?" Ed said.

"We'll have to walk," Daniel said.

"Walk! But it's miles!"

"Only about two; if we get a move on it won't take long."

"But I'm freezing," said Natalie forlornly, fighting back tears.

"Come on," Ed said, putting his arm around her, "we'll warm up a bit if we walk fast."

"I think I've got a pair of gloves in my bag," Daniel said, rummaging. "Yes, and a hat as well. Here Natalie." He held them out. Natalie grimaced but took them and put them on.

For half a mile, there was little to see except snowy countryside, and the cathedral looming in the distance on the summit of a hill. It was at once both comforting and disconcerting.

"We need to find out what year it is. We'll have to ask someone," said Natalie.

"No!" said Daniel firmly. "We have to think of some other way. What has dates on?"

"Newspapers; did they have newspapers then?" Ed said.

"Not if we're in the Middle Ages. Printing wasn't invented 'til the 1400s."

"How on earth do you remember all this stuff?" Ed said, impressed.

"I'm interested in it, so I remember. You probably know who played in the FA Cup final this year and what the score was. I don't have a clue because I'm not interested in football; I'm interested in history."

"Graves!" exclaimed Natalie out of the blue.

Chapter 33

4th December, Lincoln

Daniel stared at Natalie.
"Graves - they have dates on!" she said.
"Brilliant! Let's find a graveyard and look for a recent grave."
"Great!" said Jim, sarcastically. "Let's walk around in the snow for hours looking for a graveyard."
"It won't be hard; there were churches all over the place in the Middle Ages. We'll keep heading back towards the city and stop at the first church we come to."
They quickened their pace and soon saw some wooden huts straggling at each side of the broad, straight road. Daniel tried not to get distracted by the fact that he was walking along the medieval route of the Roman road, Ermine Street. There was nothing to see beneath his feet anyway but snow, slightly compacted and rutted along the cart tracks. Before long they came to a plain-looking stone church on the right. Stepping into the churchyard, Daniel felt the change under his feet from compacted to virgin snow. So the snowfall must be pretty fresh, he thought; strange that it was so well-trodden on the road.
They split up and started looking at the graves, brushing off the dusting of snow which clung limpet-like to even the vertical surfaces.
"There's some writing but I can't understand it," said Natalie.
"It's probably Latin," said Daniel, "and the dates will probably be in Roman numerals. You know: M is a thousand, C is a hundred?" The others looked at him blankly. "You just look for a headstone that looks fairly new and I'll try to work out the date." They meandered around the

wintry graveyard, their hands going from numb to stinging with cold from touching the frozen snow and stone.

"Here's one that looks new," Natalie said, brushing off the snow. Daniel and the others hurried over and peered at the carving on the headstone.

"MCCXC. One thousand, two hundred and ninety. Blimey, 1290 - or thereabouts. I suppose the grave could be from last year but it looks pretty new," Daniel said.

"Oh my God, are you telling us that we're in the year 1290? That's over ...um..." there was a pause while Jim slowly counted the centuries. Natalie and Daniel got there way ahead of him but kept quiet. "Seven hundred years ago! How on earth can we have travelled back seven hundred years? It didn't feel like we went anywhere. It just happened."

"We didn't go anywhere physically, though, did we? We were still in the same spot outside Lincoln, but suddenly everything around us looked different. Although we call it time travel, it's not really 'travelling,'" Daniel said, signing speech marks in the air, "in the sense that we usually mean. It's another dimension, not space."

"I don't get it," said Ed.

"We haven't 'gone' anywhere, Ed," said Natalie emphatically, "we just slipped back through time somehow."

"Why does it matter what year it is? All we need to know is how to get back," Ed said.

"Yeah, Geek," agreed Jim. "You think you're so clever with your talk of dimensions but that's all rubbish if we can't get back,"

"Stop saying 'if'!" Natalie screeched, making the boys jump. "What do you mean 'if'? We have to get back! We can't stay here! There's no electricity! That means no phones, no computers, no music, no TV, not to mention our mums and dads!" She dissolved into tears and Jim and Ed shuffled about awkwardly muttering that of course they'd get back. Eventually, Daniel put his arm around Natalie and tried to reassure her.

"We're going to figure it out, Natalie. We need to stay calm and work together." Natalie shrugged Daniel's arm aside and rubbed her eyes, instantly regretting her outburst. "I need the loo," she said. "What do they do for toilets around here?"

Now it was Daniel who shifted around awkwardly, trying to think of the least bad way to break the news.

"Um, er, I don't think they really have what we'd call toilets. And definitely not public ones."

"I'll have to knock on someone's door and ask to use theirs then. I don't care."

"That may not be a good idea, Natalie," Daniel said. "Only the rich people would have anything like a toilet and you can't just go strolling up to a manor house and ask to use the privy. We have to keep a low profile, while we figure things out."

"What do you suggest then? It's all right for you blokes, isn't it? Any old place will do for you. But what about me?" Natalie said.

"You'll have to go behind a bush, Nat." said Ed practically, "You must have done it before."

"Actually I haven't done it before and I don't intend to now. I'll wait." Natalie said and folded her arms, though it was really her legs she wanted to cross.

Daniel perched on a headstone and tried to think.

"What were you doing on that street corner anyway, Geek? There was nothing there," Jim said.

"Oh. There used to be a big cross there, a monument to a queen who died near Lincoln. I was looking for the spot. I wrote about it in my history essay; the one we had to write about the Minster. She's buried there. Well, her innards are at least. The rest of her is in London."

"Ugh. That's gross!" said Ed. "Why did they take her guts out?"

"The king wanted her to be buried in Westminster Abbey. But she died near Lincoln. Her body was embalmed so it would last the journey to London for her funeral."

"Huh? It only takes a few hours to get to London," Ed said.

"Not in 1290. The fastest way to travel was on horseback but a royal funeral procession had to go much more slowly."

"Did you say 1290? That's now. Did this queen die in 1290?" asked Natalie.

"Yes."

"So that's this year that we think we're in, right?"

"Yes," said Daniel.

"And you were looking for something to do with her." Daniel stared at Natalie, willing her to go on. "Maybe there's a connection - with this queen, whoever she was."

"Queen Eleanor, Edward I's wife," said Daniel, starting to get excited. "She died on November 28th but then they faffed about with her body and her funeral in the Minster wasn't until around December 4th."

"That's today!" said Natalie emphatically.

"So what?" said Ed, not keeping up, "What are you two on about?"

"Yes! Either it's a massive coincidence or there's some kind of link, a reason for why we ended up here," said Daniel.

"It's a long shot but this Queen Eleanor thing is the only clue we have. We should at least think about it," said Natalie. Daniel and Ed nodded their agreement, but Jim expressed his view by saying,

"I need to pee," and stumped off towards the churchyard wall. Daniel, Natalie and Ed followed him with their eyes for a moment and then politely turned and faced the other way.

"Aargh!" Their heads shot back towards Jim, stumbling towards them, fumbling with his flies, his face aghast.

Chapter 34

4th December 1290, Lincoln

"A witch! There's a witch over there. She was watching me doing it! She's spying on us."

"Calm down, Jim," said Daniel, looking over at the old crone staring at them from just beyond the graveyard wall.

"What makes you think she's a witch?"

"She looks like one. She's all bent over and her teeth are crooked. She must be."

"Get a grip, Jim. Now who's being medieval? She's probably just old and poor."

"Whatever she is, she's coming over," said Ed.

"Right, try not to look scared and let me do the talking," said Daniel with only a slight quiver in his voice. He took a few paces towards the old crone and said, "Good day to you, lady."

The old woman began wheezing and whistling through her teeth or rather the gaps where her teeth should have been. Daniel stood rooted, unsure if she was having some kind of seizure, torn between offering assistance and running away. Then with a snort, she stopped and said,

"Lady, is it? I know not whence you hail, to be calling me 'lady.' And a good day to you, my lord." She curtseyed with a flourish and strained her bent neck to look up at them. Now Daniel caught the gleam in her eye and realised she was laughing at him. He was flummoxed as to what to say, but the "witch" spoke again. "I think you are in need of some help."

"Um, yes, we are. We were wondering..." But she cut him off, lifting a gnarled finger to her lips,

"Come. Safer to talk indoors." She turned and scurried away, reminding Daniel of Mrs. Tiggywinkle. Even if she'd been able to stand upright, she would have been far smaller than Jim, but as it was, she was tiny.

Though wizened and aged, the woman was surprisingly agile. She was fast disappearing around the side of the church. The other three looked to Daniel for a lead. With a shrug of his shoulders, he said,

"So much for keeping a low profile. But at least she's unlikely to snitch on us; seeing as she looks like a witch herself. Come on," and with a nervous chuckle, he jogged forwards to catch up with her.

Daniel rounded the church just in time to see the "witch" exit the rear of the churchyard through a rickety gate. Here she paused for them all to catch up, her hazel eyes glinting with light reflecting off the snow.

"I don't like that twinkle in her eye," said Jim, "What's she getting so excited about?"

"I guess it must be that her evil plan is working and she's luring us into her trap!" said Daniel.

"It's no joke," squeaked Natalie. "What if it is a trap?"

"Look, Natalie, there's four of us and only about half of her," said Ed. "What d'you think she's going to do? Shove us in a cage and fatten us up for eating?" Daniel shot him an admiring look and trotted on. Jim persisted,

"What if there are more of them, like her? Or if she can use magic?"

"She's a little old lady," Daniel said. "She's taking a far greater risk, inviting four complete strangers into her home, if that's where she's taking us. For now, we'll have to go with the flow, unless you've got a better idea." With these last words, Daniel turned round and for once looked Jim straight in the eye. For the split second before Jim lowered his gaze, what he saw there was pure, unmasked fear. Unbidden, a feeling of compassion for Jim awoke in Daniel. Gently now he groped for the most tactful words and said,

"If you don't feel right about this, Jim, you can wait for us here. Just keep your head down." Jim looked back at the deserted graveyard, hesitated for a moment, and then said grumpily,

"No, I'll come. We need to stick together, right?"

They followed the "witch" down a path between snow-laden

hedgerows. Daniel figured they were heading southeast because in the gaps he could still make out the cathedral over his left shoulder. Suddenly the old lady turned sharp right and disappeared between clumps of bushes. If he hadn't seen her turn in, Daniel would have thought she'd vanished into thin air, in much the same way as the four of them had vanished from Cross o'Cliff Hill a couple of hours earlier.

When he reached the gap through which the "witch" had gone, he started to have misgivings himself. Before him lay a tunnel-like path, overhung on both sides with rambling hedges, leading to the door of a tumbledown hovel. Behind the hovel loomed a wood. Daniel paused and gulped. His new-found role as leader of this unlikely group required him to make instant decisions affecting them all. By nature he would shrink from this responsibility, but here he realised there was no option. Though confused, at least his passion for history gave him some clues to work with. The others were not only bewildered but almost as helpless as babies. He mustered his most confident swagger and walked into the tunnel, willing the others to follow. There was no sign of the witch as he reached the end of the overgrown path. But the door to the hovel stood ajar. With a tentative knock, he stooped and entered.

Chapter 35

4th December 1290, Lincoln

The transition from sunlit snow to the gloomy interior of the hut left Daniel blind. A bony hand gripped his wrist and he gasped. From outside he heard Natalie call,

"Daniel!" and then Ed came crashing through the doorway, bowling Daniel and the witch like skittles over the earth floor. Daniel scrambled onto his hands and knees with a mouthful of what felt like straw. His eyes were beginning to adjust to the gloom but Ed was still blind.

"It's all right, Ed," he blurted before the lumbering lad could do any more damage. "I was just startled by the darkness. Stand still and in a minute, you'll be able to see." Daniel stood up and offered to help the old crone but she waved him away and clambered to her feet with the aid of a wooden stool.

"What's going on in there? Ed? Daniel?" came Natalie's anxious voice from outside.

"It's okay, Natalie; it's just really dark in here. It gave me a shock, and then Ed came charging in and sent us flying. Wait there with Jim for a minute, there's not much room." Then turning to the witch, "Are you okay? I'm so sorry we knocked you over."

"What is okay?" the witch said in a croaky singsong voice.

"Are you hurt?"

"No, not hurt. Okay is hurt?"

"No, um, okay is not hurt; okay is good."

"You are too old to speak such nonsense, lad."

"I'm sorry. My language is different to yours. Have you any light?"

With swift, deft movements the witch laid her hands on tinder-box and candle stub, and in a moment the hut was dimly lit. A single glance showed Daniel her one-roomed home. On the left-hand side of the door behind him, a tatty curtain screened off one section, presumably the sleeping quarters. In front of him, a large metal cooking pot hung over the barely glowing embers of a fire. It was lucky he hadn't been a couple of paces further forward when Ed collided with him, as his head would probably have struck the jagged edge of the stone hearth. The witch must have flung herself to one side as she fell, no doubt aware of the location of every item in her sparsely furnished home.

Daniel felt Ed's large hand trembling on his shoulder,

"She is a witch, Dan; Jim was right. Look at the cauldron! It's straight out of a fairy tale," he whispered. Ed's eyes flitted to the ceiling of the square room and he added, "And bats! There are bats hanging from the roof! I'm getting out of here." Daniel spun around and grabbed the back of Ed's shirt before he reached the door.

"They're bunches of herbs, Ed, not bats. Calm down. And everyone in this time would have a cooking pot like that. She's no more a witch than your granny. Don't go putting the wind up Jim and Natalie; they're scared enough as it is." When Daniel felt Ed relax slightly, he let go of his shirt and turned back to the 'witch.' She was scrutinizing them with an amused yet piercing look.

"I saw you," she said in a decided tone. Daniel humoured her, wondering if she was a bit dotty.

"Yes," he replied, speaking slowly and loudly, in the unfortunate tone his Dad reserved for communicating with foreigners. "You saw us in the churchyard."

"No. Before that. I saw you. You came like a spirit. First you," poking her knobbly finger right at Daniel's nose so he went cross-eyed, "then the small one, then the maid and him," now pointing over Daniel's shoulder at Ed.

"Ah," said Daniel nervously, desperately racking his brain for some kind of plausible explanation, knowing full well that there was none. She had seen them when they appeared out of thin air. "Ah," he repeated.

"Blessed Jesus and all his saints, I said to myself, you have sent your angels to carry me out of this wicked world and up to my dear dead husband," the old woman said. "But no; you began quarrelling and shouting, and I said to myself, they are not heavenly angels. They have come from the other place to carry me out of this beautiful world and drag me down to my wretched dead husband. But no; you looked frightened. They are not wicked devils, I said to myself, they must be spirits of restless souls sent by my rotten dead husband to torment me in this weary world. But no..."

Daniel interrupted, torn between crying and laughing, but unwilling to let Ed listen to any more of the woman's outlandish guesses about their sudden appearance.

"We're not any of those beings, as you see. We are flesh and blood like you. Is that why you grabbed my wrist when I came in?" Daniel said, pointing from her to his wrist. She nodded. "We are just children," he said. "We came here from, um, another place, far away. We don't understand how it happened." He held out his hands, "All we want is to go back; but we don't know how." On this last word, his voice faltered and he was suddenly fighting back tears.

Any suspicions the old woman may have been harbouring about them vanished as she watched Daniel battle to master himself in front of his companion. Her maternal instinct urged her to comfort this vulnerable boy-on-the-cusp-of-manhood. But common sense restrained her; that would not help his struggle for composure. She stood aloof, softening only her eyes in an attempt to communicate the sympathy she felt.

"I am Aerlene," she said.

"I'm Daniel and this is Ed."

"Where are the others?"

"They're just outside," he gestured over his shoulder, "shall I call them?"

"Yes, bring them." Daniel went to fetch Natalie and Jim who were stamping around in the frozen ground.

"She's called Aerlene and she's been watching us ever since we appeared here so she's pretty freaked out. She thought we were angels or demons or ghosts but I think I've convinced her we're just normal kids. I'm pretty sure she's harmless so we need to get as much information from her as we can."

"She'd better have a hot drink and some food for us. I don't know which is worse: freezing our butts off or starving to death," said Jim.

"Oh, and don't freak out at the cauldron, it's just a standard cooking pot in these times," Daniel added. "And the stuff hanging from the ceiling is just herbs."

Jim and Natalie followed him back into the hut. Ed was sitting on a wooden stool by the fire, which Aerlene was poking, coaxing the glowing logs into a blaze. Ed looked up and gave a nervous grin. The old woman soon wiped that off his face; she jabbed towards him with her poker saying,

"Get up! Stand up for the girl!" Then she thrust a bucket into his hand. "Go, fetch water."

"Okay, okay," Ed said scrambling to his feet while warding off the blows, "Where's the tap?"

"I don't think there's a tap, Ed," said Dan.

"Oh. Where is the water?" Ed asked the old woman. She looked at him as if he was a complete moron.

"Where is the well?" said Daniel, trying to help. Now he received the moron look.

"Fools! Well is frozen! Bring snow," she said. In a completely different tone of voice, she said to Natalie, "Come, my dear, sit here and warm your hands."

"Oh, er, thanks," said Natalie, perching on the hard stool, longing for her lovely sofa at home. Daniel introduced Jim and Natalie to Aerlene. She started to manoeuvre a heavy wooden chest from the edge of the room towards the fire. Daniel offered his services and the old lady stepped away to give him room. He tugged at the chest. It didn't budge. He flushed scarlet, put his back into it and heaved. It still hardly moved.

"What, not as strong as the little old lady, Geek?" jeered Jim laughing, relieved to see something here that Daniel didn't excel at. Aerlene pushed Daniel aside and gestured for Jim to help. He couldn't shift it either. Aerlene snorted with laughter and hauled the chest over to the hearth.

"Sit," she said. The boys obeyed and an awkward silence fell, as Aerlene bustled around them preparing the best meal she could muster from her meagre resources.

There was already a dark liquid bubbling in the bottom of the cauldron but Aerlene added herbs from her supplies hanging from the ceiling and some things which Dan assumed to be vegetables though they looked weirdly misshapen. Ed reappeared and deposited the bucket of snow by the hearth, rubbing his frozen hands. Daniel gave up his seat by the fire to Ed, before the old woman could brandish her poker again. Aerlene added some handfuls of snow to the steaming cauldron. Next, she started cutting what looked like a dark brown brick into slices. These she handed round to the children. Jim, Ed and Natalie just stared at it but Daniel bit into it.

"Good bread, yes?" said Aerlene, eager to please her strange visitors. "Oh yes, very good. Thank you," said Daniel. Natalie took a tentative nibble and barely disguised her disgust. But Ed was so famished he'd have eaten anything.

Aerlene ladled out the contents of the cauldron into four wooden bowls. Dan scooped some of the broth into his mouth. The predominant flavour was mushroom, which he didn't like, but at least it was hot. After the shock of the first taste, it improved. Daniel smiled appreciatively and said,

"It's good, hearty broth, Aerlene, thank you. Which herbs did you use?" Thankfully she launched into her culinary tips and kept her focus on Daniel, as he intended, so she missed the disgusted looks the others exchanged as they tasted the pottage.

Chapter 36

4th December 1290, Lincoln

Once they had eaten, Aerlene reached out and touched Daniel's coat, rubbing the fabric between her fingers and said, "How is this made? Is it warm?"

"Yes, thanks, it's nice and warm. I'm not sure how it's made. My mother bought it for me."

"Get up, get up," Aerlene said, gesturing to Natalie and Jim, who were sitting on the wooden chest. They sprang up, confused and a little scared. Aerlene opened the chest and pulled out some woven wool leggings. She held them up to Ed's legs and said, "Yes, good. Put them on."

"Er, thanks. But I'm happy with my own trousers."

"Go on, Ed," said Daniel. If we're stuck here for now, we've got to try to blend in. At the moment, everything about us is wrong – our clothes, the way we act, the way we speak."

"Ed, for Edward? Like the king?" interrupted Aerlene. It took Daniel a moment to register.

"Yes, that's right, like the king," he smiled.

"A fine name," said Aerlene.

"At least I've got something right," said Ed, taking the trousers from Aerlene's wrinkled hand. He hesitated, glancing round the shack for somewhere private to change his trousers.

Daniel said to Aerlene,

"These belong to your family? Surely you need them?"

"No, my husband and son died last winter, God rest their souls. They have no need of clothes where they are." Her eyes took on a far-away look, not sad exactly, but wistful. Daniel left a respectful pause, then said,

"I'm sorry for your loss. But I think these clothes are still of much value to you. We have no money to pay you."

"Speak for yourself," said Jim. "I've got money. Ask her how much."

"I don't think your money is of any use to her, Jim," Daniel said. Aerlene must have followed the gist of their exchange, for she said,

"I set the clothes by to sell in winter when my stores run out. But I will get a better price for these." She touched Ed's jeans. "They are new, and very fine," she said. She shook the leggings in Ed's hand. "Put these on." Ed raised his eyebrows at Dan and flushed crimson.

"Am I meant to just strip, here, right in front of Nat?"

"Unless you want to go outside in the snow," said Dan. Jim snorted but Natalie turned away, saying,

"I won't look. Ugh, as if I'd want to."

Ed put them on. They were a bit tight around the waist and bottom, but they had some give in them. Jim howled with laughter. Aerlene promptly rummaged in her chest again and with a flourish held out a smaller pair for him.

"No way," said Jim, folding his arms, "I'm staying as I am." Daniel fixed him with a firm stare and said,

"You can't; you'll put us all in danger." The atmosphere in the room prickled. Jim looked to Ed and Natalie to back him up but they avoided his glare. Daniel added in a cheerier tone,

"Come on, Jim. We'll all look as daft as each other by the time Aerlene's finished with us." There was a tense pause. Then Jim snatched the trousers and they all looked elsewhere while he changed. Nobody ventured a comment. Aerlene handed cotton undershirts to Ed and Jim. They weren't so bad, a kind of tee shirt shape but in coarse, non-stretchy fabric.

"This isn't going to keep us very warm," said Ed, pulling it over his head.

"I think it might be a kind of vest," said Daniel. Now Aerlene was handing the boys a long, baggy shirt in a natural stone colour, like the undershirt. Next came a belt, leather, with a sheath for a knife and a small leather bag dangling from it. Daniel suddenly realised that they needed to know what all these items were called. He pointed to the shirt,

"Shirt?" he said.

"Cotte," replied Aerlene. He repeated the word to himself.

"Trousers?" Daniel continued.

"Hose," said Aerlene.

"Hose?" laughed Ed, "that's what you water the garden with." Daniel tried to think of a way to explain the joke to Aerlene but gave up.

"Okay, trousers are called hose. Let's try to remember."

Now Aerlene brought out two, short dresses. Natalie started to reach for one.

"Not you, them," said Aerlene, surprised.

"You're having a laugh," said Jim. "I am not wearing a dress!"

"It's just a tunic - like a long waistcoat. Look, Jim, it's freezing out there. We need all the clothes we can get. And everyone else will be wearing the same stuff. These clothes give us a chance to blend in." Ed slipped his tunic over his head and grinned,

"It's like what a knight has under his chainmail. Come on, Jim. You're not going to look any worse than me."

"If that's supposed to make me feel better, it's not working. You look a complete prat." He grabbed the tunic and put it on, scowling.

"It fits well," Daniel said. Aerlene was picking up the clothes the boys had dropped on the floor and feeling them, stroking her wizened cheeks with the luxurious material. She turned one inside out to look at the seams.

"What is this?" she said, pointing at the label.

"It's called a label. It tells you what material it's made of and how to wash it."

"You can read?" Aerlene asked, impressed.

"Yes; where we come from everybody goes to school and learns to read," Daniel replied. Aerlene raised her bushy eyebrows at Natalie,

"Everybody? Maids too?"

"Maids?" Natalie said, just about keeping up. "Is that girls?"

"Yes," Daniel replied.

"Yes, of course, maids as well. Why wouldn't we go to school?" she said.

Lastly, with a flourish, Aerlene produced thick cloaks and leather ankle boots, the costliest items in her chest. She must have been better off when her husband was alive, Daniel thought.

"Cloak?" he said.

"Mantle," Aerlene replied.

Jim's boots were a couple of sizes too big and Ed's pinched a little; they both longed to have their trainers back. Aerlene stood back and nodded approvingly. But her chest now stood empty. Daniel thanked Aerlene warmly. She was being very generous with her meagre possessions.

"What about me? I suppose I'll have to borrow one of her dresses."

"She may not have any others," said Daniel, and in a whisper, "she's really poor." Natalie opened her mouth to argue that no one could have just one outfit. But she thought again. What did she know about Aerlene's life?

Aerlene looked at Daniel and Natalie and then at the empty chest. She said,

"Wait here," went through the door and was gone.

Chapter 37

4th December 1290, Lincoln

"What a stinky old hag!" said Jim as soon as the door closed on them. It was true. There was an all-pervasive smell of stale sweat in the little house and particularly on Aerlene. But the bunches of herbs hanging from the ceiling and the rushes on the floor went some way towards masking it.

"She's just fed us and given you two a whole set of clothes each, Jim. Can't you see how poor she is?" Daniel's voice cracked with exasperation.

"Yeah," said Natalie, "It's really kind of her to help us when she's got so little herself. I can't imagine living here. How on earth does she cope?"

"I guess it's what she's used to," said Ed practically.

"I've been thinking," said Daniel, "You remember that large group of wagons we saw in the distance when we arrived?" The others nodded. "Well, if this is the exact date of Queen Eleanor's funeral, that could have been the back of the funeral cortege."

"The what?" said Jim, "Speak English, Geek."

"The procession to London. You remember how our Queen Elizabeth died in Scotland at Balmoral and her body was brought back to London for her state funeral at Westminster Abbey, well it's the same kind of thing. Like I told you before, the queen who died was the wife of Edward I. You know, the one who's known as the Hammer of the Scots?" By the blank looks on their faces, that clearly meant nothing to the others. "Anyway, I don't think he's hammered them yet. He was married to Eleanor of Castile, that's in Spain. They had a long and happy marriage and lots of children though quite a few of them died."

"Died of what?" asked Natalie.

"I don't know. The death rate was much higher in those days, especially for children. Anyway, Edward and Eleanor travelled all over the place including to the Middle East and somewhere Eleanor picked up an illness. She had bouts of it off and on for a few years but always recovered. This time she didn't. They were on their way up north to Scotland and she was taken ill on the journey and died at Harby, near Lincoln. That was about a week ago, like I told you, and since then her body has been embalmed and—"

"What, like an Egyptian mummy?"

"A bit. At least, it's been preserved because they have to travel back to London so she can have a state funeral at Westminster Abbey."

"The same Westminster Abbey that's in London now?"

"Yes. It's changed a bit since then but essentially it's the same building."

"Whoa. That's pretty cool," said Ed. Jim shot him a withering look and he shut up.

"They must have had a funeral for her innards in Lincoln Minster this morning and now they're heading for Grantham," Daniel said.

"That's so gross. How do you know all this stuff? You're like a walking history book," said Natalie.

"Because he's a sad little nerd who hasn't got anything better to do than read all day," said Jim.

"Seeing as we've landed up in 1290 somehow, it's just as well one of us is a bit clued up, isn't it?" said Natalie.

"We wouldn't have ended up here at all if he hadn't been snooping around looking for some non-existent cross," retorted Jim.

"And us three wouldn't have ended up here if we hadn't been chasing him, would we?" said Natalie.

"Look, this is getting us nowhere," said Daniel. "We're here and we don't know why or how. We need to focus on how to get back. That's all that matters. And in the meantime, we've got to be careful to stay out of trouble."

"Right. Get on with the story then," said Ed.

"I've told you most of what I know. The rest is background. Later I think we need to try to catch up with that big group we saw in the distance when we arrived here, the queen's funeral cortege. But before that, we need to come up with a cover story for who we are and what we're doing here. I need to think."

Daniel sat down and stared into the fire. He felt they needed to join the cortege as the connection with Queen Eleanor was the only clue to go on. But how could they do that without arousing suspicion? They needed a believable reason to be travelling to London. Business? It was clear that they didn't have anything with them to trade. Visiting family? Possibly. Why else could they be travelling? A pilgrimage! That might just work. Loads of people made pilgrimages in the Middle Ages. Where could they be travelling from and to? It had to be somewhere in London so they could remain with the cortege all the way. Daniel guessed the main attraction in London for pilgrims would be Westminster Abbey. That was perfect - exactly where the cortege itself was headed. So, all he had to figure out now was where they should claim to come from. It should probably be abroad, he mused, as everything about them would appear foreign and strange. But it couldn't be anywhere King Edward and his court had been, because they would easily be tripped up. That ruled out most of Europe and the Middle East. They clearly didn't come from Africa or the East. So, what did that leave? Scandinavia? That was a possibility. He knew next to nothing about Scandinavia. It would be best to choose somewhere one of them had been so that they could answer any questions that were asked.

"Have any of you been on holiday to Scandinavia?" Daniel asked.

"What?" said Jim in his most scathing tone. "What on earth has that got to do with anything?" Daniel told them about his pilgrimage idea.

"I think we need to claim to be foreigners because our language and behaviour will seem to be foreign to the people in 1290. But it has to be somewhere we know a bit about in case they ask questions. Where have you been on holiday?"

"Mallorca, Las Vegas, France. Those any good for your precious plan," said Jim.

"It can't be anywhere in Europe because King Edward and his close companions have been all over Europe. It would be easy to discover we're lying. America hasn't been discovered yet by Europeans. What about you two?"

"I've only been to America and Europe," said Natalie.

"I've been to France, but that's no good. Just places in Britain apart from that: Wales, Yorkshire and some Scottish Islands," said Ed.

"Scottish islands. That might work."

"They're all part of Britain, though," said Ed.

"They are now," Daniel replied, "but I think some of them used to belong to Norway at some time."

"Oh yeah. That rings a bell. I think we heard something about that when we went there. I wish I could remember."

"Which islands did you visit, Ed?"

"The Orkneys and the Shetlands."

"What were they like? Tell us everything you can remember," said Daniel.

"Er, freezing cold, windy and there was nothing to do. Except bird watching, which my mum likes."

"What else? Try to remember. If we're going to pretend we come from there, we need as much info as you can give us."

"Um, it stayed light a long time. We went in the summer holiday last year. It didn't get pitch dark at all, like Norway, land of the midnight sun and all that."

"Good, anything else? What did the people sound like? Could you understand them?"

"You must be kidding. I could only pick up the odd word. They've got their own dialect but even when they were trying to speak English to us, I could only make out a couple of words."

"That sounds about right then. If we're lucky, no one we meet will ever have been there, so they won't know any different. What did the landscape look like?"

"Fairly boring: flat, no trees, lots of farmers' fields. I can't remember much else."

"What about the beaches? There must be beaches if it's an island," said Natalie.

"It's not just one island. There are loads of them. Some don't have any people. The beaches are lovely to look at but it was too cold to enjoy them and do normal beach holiday stuff." Ed paused and added, "There's a lot of sky. It just seems enormous there and you notice it much more than here."

"So, we've got cold and windy weather even in summer, fields, fairly flat landscape, attractive beaches, no trees, big sky, longer daylight. That's a good start. If any of us think of more questions, we'll ask."

Chapter 38

4th December 1290, Lincoln

A gust of freezing air swept through the opening door and Aerlene returned, carrying a bundle. She tipped the bundle into the chest, looking very pleased with herself; then extracted a woollen garment.

"From my brother," she said, handing it to Natalie.

"Turn round then," Natalie said to the boys. When she let them look, Daniel did a double take. In the long woollen dress, Natalie looked a different person; softer and timeless. Aerlene reached up and pulled something woollen over Natalie's head. It covered her head and shoulders, like a hood and shawl in one. Ed and Jim sniggered. Natalie stuck her tongue out at them.

"That looks cosy," said Daniel.

"Yeah, it's warm," Natalie replied, "But itchy."

"What's this called?" Daniel asked Aerlene.

"Cowl." She gave Natalie some boots and handed Daniel a bundle of clothes like Ed and Jim's. It was only now, undressing, that Daniel realised his ammonite pendant was missing. He had a quick look on the floor but as this was covered in rushes, he was unlikely to find it unless he trod on it. He either had to make a fuss or let it go. He quickly put the clothes on, muttering the names of the unfamiliar garments to himself.

Straightening up, Daniel said, "Aerlene, did you see the king pass by today?"

"Yes," she replied. "Sad, sad king. How he loved his Spanish Queen." Aerlene shuffled around them and scooped their discarded clothes from the floor. She folded them with utmost care and stowed them in the chest. Ed and Natalie pitched in and helped her. Daniel watched, pondering how much to tell this kind-hearted woman who had aided them so unquestioningly. At length, he said to Aerlene,

"We need to catch up with the king's party and travel with them to London. I believe the court will stop at Grantham this evening. Do you know how we could reach there?"

"To London? No, no - it is too far; not safe for you younglings!" Aerlene protested.

"That's why we need to catch up with the cortege," Daniel said. "We hope to travel under the king's protection."

Aerlene was silent for a few moments. "Wait here," she said and once again hurried out of the door.

"I think I'd better get rid of my rucksack," said Daniel. "It looks way too modern."

"What's in it?" said Ed. "What if we need the stuff?"

"Um, a book about Queen Eleanor, some money,"

"Hey, you nicked that money from my room!" said Jim, squaring up to Daniel.

"Yes, money that was mine in the first place," Daniel said, meeting his gaze.

Natalie patted Daniel's bag, "What else have you got in here?" she said, trying to break the tension.

He opened it, "Map of Lincoln, phone, bottle of water and some chocolate."

"Let's have the chocolate," pleaded Natalie.

"No, not yet. We need to save it until we really need it." Daniel felt inside his cloak for pockets. He found one and slid the book in, hoping it was deep enough. It was.

"Have you got deep pockets in your cloak, Ed?" Daniel asked.

Ed groped around, "Yeah."

"Here, put the map in it and keep it out of sight. We mustn't get any of our own stuff out unless we're completely alone. We'll keep our phones for when we get back, but we should turn them off."

"They could be useful if we get separated," said Ed.

Natalie rolled her eyes. "And where do you think we're going to get signal, in 12 flipping 90?"

"Oh yeah," said Ed, reddening. "I can't help it. I'm just used to it."

"Yeah, we all are," said Natalie, giving Ed a friendly thump.

"Let's put our phones in the leather purse things on our belts."

Daniel added his rucksack to the pile of their clothes in the chest as Aerlene walked in. She picked it up and turned it over in her hands, marvelling. Daniel showed her how to zip it up. She clapped her hands like a delighted child. Daniel said, "Zip."

Aerlene undid the zip saying, "Zip." She laughed and did it again, saying, "Zzzziiippp!" Then she put it back in the chest, suddenly serious again.

"My brother will take you; you must leave now or it will be dark before you reach Grantham," she stated simply.

"Thank you for all your help," said Daniel. Ed and Natalie mumbled their thanks too and they all looked around at Jim. He was oblivious; earbuds in, jerking his head in time to his music.

Before anyone could stop her, Aerlene pulled an earbud from Jim's ear and stuck it in her own. She shrieked and yanked it out again.

"Put it away, Jim," Daniel said.

"Quit telling me what to do, Geek, or—" said Jim.

"Or what exactly, Jim?" They stared at each other across the small room.

Aerlene looked at one, then the other, and said, "Foolish boys," and promptly cuffed them each round the ear. There was a moment of tense silence, then Natalie sniggered, and they all laughed. Aerlene pointed at Jim's phone and said,

"Keep all strange things hidden, in your scrip."

"Scrip?" said Daniel. She pointed to the little leather bag dangling from his belt, then herded them all out of the door into the snow.

They headed past the church. On the road in front of it was a small pony and cart.

"My brother, Aldred," said Aerlene. They introduced themselves quickly. Aerlene pressed a blanket into Natalie's hands and gestured for her to get up at the front with Aldred. The three boys climbed into the back of the cart and made themselves as comfortable as they could. Aldred flicked the reins; the pony took the strain and the cart creaked forward over the snow.

Chapter 39

4th December 1290, Lincolnshire

They headed south, the cathedral behind them, back down the road they had walked up a couple of hours ago. They were soon back at the spot they had arrived at. Jim suddenly jumped down from the cart.

"What are you doing?" shouted Daniel.

"If we leave here, we might never get back. There must be some kind of time portal. We just need to find it!" He started pacing frantically round and round the spot, muttering under his breath. Aldred brought the pony to a halt and looked around, raising his eyes at Daniel.

"Sorry, we'll just be a minute. He lost something earlier.' He and Natalie climbed down.

"It's no use, Jim," she said gently. "We've tried that already and it didn't work."

"Maybe we didn't try hard enough. We need to stay here and keep searching."

"All right," Daniel relented, "we'll have another go for a few minutes but we can't keep Aldred waiting longer than that." Ed jumped down from the cart as well and they walked round and round, crisscrossing each other's paths, churning the snow into filthy slush, trying to cover every centimetre of the area. Daniel looked out for his ammonite pendant but found nothing. After a few minutes Aldred, bemused, began turning his pony and cart around to go back the way he had come. Daniel ran over,

"No, no, please. We're coming now."

"Come on, we have to go," Natalie said to Jim. "We have to accept we can't get back the same way we came."

"You can't be sure. We don't know anything for sure."

"We know that if we stay here on our own, we'll freeze or starve," said Daniel, with quiet authority.

"That doesn't mean we should go chasing after some flipping dead queen! It's madness."

"I know it seems crazy but the link with Queen Eleanor is all we've got to go on."

"Well, I'm staying here. And you two should too," Jim said, glaring at Ed and Natalie, "if you know what's good for you."

"Come on, mate," said Ed. "You know we can't just stay here in the middle of nowhere. What would we do when it gets dark?"

Without a word, Aldred stepped down from the cart, strode over to Jim, picked him up and slung him over his shoulder, then dropped him in the back of the cart. He climbed up front, gave Natalie a hand up, and flicked the reins. Ed and Daniel scrambled on board as the cart rattled away. Jim sat hugging his knees and staring back at Lincoln long after it vanished from view.

The snowy landscape trundled by mile after chilly mile. When she could bear the tense silence no more, Natalie said,

"Let's go over our cover story again."

"Good idea," said Ed, "I'm worried I'm going to say something stupid and give us away."

"Okay. You two recap what we've got so far," Daniel said.

Ed kicked off, "We say we're from the Orkney islands, where it's cold, windy, dark all day in winter, and light all night in summer. We're going on a pilgrimage to Westminster Abbey and we're asking to travel with the queen's funeral procession thing for protection."

"Yeah, that's all we've got so far," said Daniel.

"I don't really know what a pilgrimage is," said Ed.

"Oh, it's a journey that has a spiritual purpose; usually to a religious site like a saint's shrine or something," said Daniel.

"I still don't get it," said Ed. "What's the point?"

"Um, I guess people believed that if they prayed at a holy site, their prayers were more likely to be answered."

"Seems a bit stupid to me," said Natalie. "I don't know if I believe in God or not, but if he does exist, then he's everywhere isn't he, so why would it be better to pray in one place than another?"

"I'm not sure really, I think there were other aspects to it. The journey itself was a chance to step away from ordinary life and learn more about yourself."

"Sounds like an excuse for a holiday to me," said Jim. The others were so glad to hear him speak at last that they all agreed over-enthusiastically.

"Yeah, that's exactly right. It was a holiday for them too."

"So what's the supposed spiritual purpose of our journey?" asked Natalie.

"We need to think of one," said Daniel.

They were passing a small hamlet. One or two people were going about their work in the grounds of a small stone manor house set back from the road on their left. And beyond that, a sandy-coloured church stood out from the snow like a decoration on a Christmas cake.

"What could be the point of a pilgrimage to Westminster Abbey?" mused Daniel.

"Is that the one where King Charles was crowned?" asked Natalie. "I watched it on the telly."

"Yes," Daniel said, "that's the one."

"Can we stick to the point?" said Jim. "I thought we were meant to be coming up with a plan."

"Yep, you're right. Have any of you been to Westminster Abbey?" said Daniel. They all looked blank. "Okay. I went a couple of years ago. Had a guided tour. Nearly all our kings and queens were crowned there and most are buried there as well. But a lot of what I saw was later than 1290. I need to strip away all the newer stuff and try to imagine it how it was then. Give me a few minutes."

In his head, Daniel glanced up at the elaborate, eroded stone carvings of saints and gargoyles on the high west front of Westminster Abbey, then stepped through the arched entrance. The air was cool and still, abruptly remote from the London street, a few metres behind him, bristling with tourists. He tingled with a sense of excited awe he sometimes felt in Lincoln Cathedral; an intangible connection with all the lives which had flowed in and out of the ancient walls over the years, decades and centuries.

In his mind's eye, he re-walked the tour he had been on, discarding everything he'd seen that had been added since 1290. The great church shrank, and emptied itself of Poets' Corner, the tomb of the Unknown Soldier and most of its royal tombs. Bright paintings appeared on the walls and pillars, bringing Bible stories to life, showing him the delights of heaven, and warning him of the horrors of hell. In his mind, he wandered up and down until he came to the heart of the abbey - the high, tiered, green and gold tomb of Edward the Confessor, the last Saxon king of England. This was it! The shrine of a pious king from an era that many in 1290 would look back to as a golden age, before the Normans came and conquered.

"I've got it!" Daniel said. "We can be making our pilgrimage to the shrine of Edward the Confessor."

"Who's he?" said Jim.

"He was the last Saxon king of England before William the Conqueror. You know, 1066?"

"Rings a bell," said Ed.

"Ha! Geek's got his history knickers in a twist," Jim crowed. "Everyone knows Harold was king in 1066. He was killed at the Battle of Hastings with an arrow in his eye."

"Yeah, even I know that," said Ed. Daniel took a deep breath.

"Yes, that's right. Harold was king, but only for a few months, and he was never actually crowned. William thought he had just as good a claim to the throne as Harold, so he invaded and you know the rest."

"What I don't get," said Natalie, "is how the king in 1290 can be Edward the First if there had already been another King Edward before."

"Good point; the numbers weren't used until later when it got confusing with so many kings with the same names, like all the Henrys. But they only counted the kings and queens who came after 1066."

"We're getting off the point again," said Jim.

"Sorry, just wondered," said Natalie. Jim rolled his eyes. They all looked at Daniel.

"So, we're travelling to London to visit Edward the Confessor's shrine at Westminster. That's good. But we need more details in our cover story. We come from the Orkney Islands but who are we and why are we going on pilgrimage now?"

A thought-filled silence. The cart bumped over an unseen obstacle beneath the snow. Daniel looked up; the cart was slowing. The pony's breath made steamy clouds in the wintry air as it strained to pull its load uphill.

"The road rises steeply here, friend. Is this a route you know well?" Daniel said to Aldred.

"Yes, I often pass this way. The High Dyke - a very ancient road. Most times a good, dry road, though utterly exposed to the wind. But no roads are good in this snow. At least it is frozen over so the cart does not sink but it may start to slide as we go on up."

Daniel had heard of the High Dyke; it ran along the route of the Roman road, Ermine Street. After a few minutes, the road levelled out onto a ridge, and the land dropped away sharply on the right. On the other side, Daniel could just make out sheep standing forlorn and dirty-looking in the pristine snow.

Natalie broke the silence, saying hesitantly,

"As Daniel's the only one who knows the history stuff, he'll need to do most of the talking. If any of us three open our big mouths, we're bound to put our foot in it."

"Speak for yourself," said Jim.

"No, really, Jim. It could be life or death, or getting back home or not. So," she hesitated again, "I think we should pretend that he's the master and we're his servants."

Chapter 40

4th December 1290, Lincolnshire

"No way! Absolutely no way!" said Jim.

"No, I don't think that would work either, though I see what you're getting at, Natalie," Daniel said. "Look at your hands."

"You what?" said Jim.

"If you were servants, your hands would be rough and probably red and sore in this weather." Jim and Natalie looked at their hands. Soft skin, cleanish nails; not servants' hands. Ed's were a bit more workmanlike. "Well, maybe Ed could get away with it." Ed just shrugged, happy to follow whoever took the lead. He said,

"What sort of servants would they have? I'd have to understand what to do, wouldn't I, at least the gist of it?" Ed asked.

"Um, I don't really know but I'm guessing a party of travellers would have a couple of men-at-arms for protection," said Daniel.

"Like bodyguards?" said Natalie.

"Yes, kind of. And grooms to look after the horses."

"I'm quite good with horses," said Ed, warming. "I could maybe get away with that. My uncle in Essex has a couple of horses and when I stay there in the holidays, I help out; you know - mucking out stables, brushing, filling up their water, all that stuff."

"Urgh," said Jim.

"I like horses. And they seem to like me," said Ed.

"Okay, that's a start," said Daniel. "That leaves us three."

"I suppose you're going to be 'Lord Daniel of Orkney,' Jim said in a posh accent. Daniel laughed.

"That sounds pretty good to me," said Natalie.

"Oh, for God's sake, I was kidding, Nat."

"I know, but seriously, I think it sounds good." All eyes fixed on Daniel. He coloured. "Well?" said Natalie.

"I don't know," he stammered, "Maybe? It does have a kind of ring to it. But it doesn't seem fair."

"It's not about being fair, it's about keeping out of trouble until we get home. So, Lord Daniel of Orkney and his groom, Edward," said Ed.

"Named after the king," chipped in Natalie, laughing despite the look Jim was stabbing her with.

"What about you two?" said Ed.

"My cousins?" Daniel suggested. "Then we don't have to look alike or have exactly the same social status, but you wouldn't be servants, just companions."

"I'm in," said Natalie. "Jim?"

"Whatever," he shrugged.

"Kids our age wouldn't be travelling all that way alone, would they?" said Natalie.

"No, you're right. We need to think of a reason why we got separated from the rest of our party," said Daniel.

"Byard's Leap," said Aldred emphatically, making all four of them jump. "You like a good tale?" he continued, looking over his shoulder at the boys.

"Yes, of course, sir. We love a good story, don't we?" said Daniel, elbowing Ed in the ribs. Ed nodded enthusiastically.

"This village here is called Byard's Leap. A curious name - and I can tell you how it came by it. When my grandfather's grandfather was a lad, not much bigger than you, a wicked crone lived in these parts who went by the name of Old Meg. The villagers went in fear of her and her evil doings. One year she cursed the crops and they withered. All the villagers went hungry that winter and some of their young'uns died. They went to Old Meg's cave in the woods and pleaded with her to leave but she just laughed at them. Most of the villagers were too afraid of her witchcraft to try to force her out but an old soldier stepped forward boldly and vowed he would kill her by driving a sword through her heart. He chose the best horse for his task by throwing a stone into the village pond where all the horses were drinking. The horse that reacted the fastest was called Blind Byard, for he couldn't see."

Aldred cast a look over his shoulder to make sure he still had a captive audience. "The soldier rode to the witch's hut and called her out but she said she was eating and he would have to wait. Then she crept up behind Blind Byard and sank her long nails into his rump. He sprang into a gallop and from his gallop into a leap of sixty feet. Somehow the soldier stayed on Byard's back and managed to rein in the horse just as they reached the village pond. The hag had pursued them and when she caught up, the soldier turned and thrust his sword into her heart. She fell into the pond and died. And from that day to this, this place has been known as Byard's Leap after that magical horse. I named my pony here 'Byard' after that horse, but he don't leap, not as I have ever seen." This last statement tickled Aldred and from the cart the children watched his shoulders bounce as he enjoyed his own wit.

"A very good story," said Natalie, feeling that some thanks were necessary.

"How much longer is this going to take? I can't feel my hands or feet," said Jim.

"I've no idea," Daniel admitted. "The cortege had a good head start while we were at Aerlene's. But at least we haven't had to walk."

"Walk? No one could walk this far!" Natalie exclaimed. Daniel suppressed a smile. So, the others didn't realise that joining the cortege meant they would be walking to London over the next twelve days. He toyed with spelling it out to them but in the end, he decided that the best approach was to drip-feed them that kind of information on a need-to-know basis. He gazed around at the high plateau they were bumping over. The cart was no limousine but thank God they hadn't had to walk this leg of the journey at least. As far as he could see in any direction white clouds hung foggily above the white ground. They would never have found their way in this whiteout. And getting lost in these conditions could easily prove fatal.

Chapter 41

4ᵗʰ December 1290, Lincolnshire

"Ancaster," said Aldred, making them all jump again. Ahead lay a sturdy wall, encircling a town. In a few minutes, they trundled under an arch through a gate in the wall, manned by a sentry who nodded to Aldred and waved them through.

"Has the king passed this way?" Daniel enquired.

"Yes, my lord. His grace stopped for an hour's rest here at midday." The sentry announced proudly.

The name Ancaster rang a bell in Daniel's head but he couldn't think why. He certainly hadn't been there before but he knew he'd written the name - he could picture the word in his own handwriting. It was a neat little town and by the look of it, seemed to be thriving. As they passed the church on their right, the elusive memory surfaced. He'd mentioned the town in his essay for Jim about Saint Hugh, the bishop of Lincoln, who had died in London in the year 1200. Yes, his body had been brought back to be buried in Lincoln Cathedral. His cortege had stopped at Ancaster on the final night of their journey.

Daniel looked over at Jim. He looked cold, sullen and withdrawn. Twenty-four hours ago his feelings about Jim had been a tangled mixture of hatred and fear. He clenched his fists as those feelings resurfaced. In their bizarre situation, whatever lay ahead of them would test them all and reveal their true colours. At the moment, Jim seemed the weakest, full of anger, thrashing around for someone to blame; the most likely person to do something stupid and land them all in danger. But time would tell what Jim was made of and Daniel too, for that matter. So far

Ed appeared to be coping the best - able to go with the flow as long as someone else took responsibility and told him what to do. But what about Natalie? She was more calculating. Although she had come close to panicking a couple of times, she had mastered herself.

Another stone arch slid past overhead and they were out into open country again. The icy road cut its way through a broad snowy wilderness, broken here and there by a grove of trees. The dead straight road was now undulating rather than level. There was no sign of the cortege, apart from deep ruts in the snowy road.

"I wonder what the time is," Natalie said. "What if we don't catch up before it gets dark? Where will we sleep?"

"I reckon it's two of the clock," said Aldred, with a quick dart of his eyes at the sky. "Never fret, lass, we shall reach Grantham afore dark. And the king will go no farther this day."

"And what about you, Aldred? Will you stop overnight at Grantham? You cannot drive back in the dark in this snow?" Daniel asked.

"Byard knows the way; he will take me safe home, day or night, summer or winter."

Daniel hoped Aldred's confidence in his old pony was justified. He certainly hoped they would all be somewhere safe and warm by nightfall. But in the meantime, there was nothing he could do but trust Aldred's knowledge of their route and watch the pale, silent fields slip by.

They took a right turn. After a cluster of small houses, the road dropped, steeply at first, then more gently into a wooded valley. At the bottom of the hill, they crossed a river on a stone bridge, turned left and rounded a bend. Suddenly there ahead of them was the cortege. There were covered carts almost as far as the eye could see, and in front of the carts, large groups on foot. In the distance, at the front of the procession, there were horsemen.

"Blimey, Dan. Is this what you were expecting?" said Ed. Daniel wasn't sure whether to trust his voice. His heart had begun to race and pound.

"Er, something like this, but maybe not quite so many people and carts and everything. I guess it is the king, so there's bound to be a lot of stuff."

"Reckon this is as far as I go," said Aldred. He drew the pony to a halt and stepped down. "Bide there a moment, lass, while I find me legs." He stamped around for a moment slapping his legs to get the blood flowing again. Natalie eyed the ground uneasily. The road had been turned to filthy slush by the passage of hoofs, wheels and feet. She was in no hurry to step down into that.

Daniel jumped down from the back of the cart, and shook hands with Aldred to thank him and wish him well for the return journey. Ed watched him and did the same. Aldred handed Natalie down. Daniel noticed that she appreciated this old-fashioned attention but was less impressed by the old-fashioned mud she stepped into. All eyes turned on Jim, still slumped in the back of the cart. Eventually, with a face like thunder, he slid himself down into the mud and glared at Daniel.

Aldred turned the pony and cart around, and they all watched until he disappeared back around the bend in the road. He was gone. Daniel wondered if any others would be as willing to help them as Aldred and his sister had been. They would soon find out. It would be hard to keep Jim and the others onside much longer if they remained as cold and hungry as he felt right now.

Ed and Daniel stamped around in the slush and shook their arms to get the life back into them while Jim and Natalie stood shivering. They were all staring towards six covered carts, drawn by mules, rumbling slowly away, about fifty metres ahead. It looked surreal - like a wagon train in a cowboy film, weirdly set in an English winter rather than the scorching heat of the American Midwest.

Daniel said, "Come on then," and set off, his legs leaden and his stomach churning. He inwardly rehearsed their cover story and with every step he took, it sounded more ludicrous in his own head. He felt like a condemned man walking towards the hangman's noose.

As the gap closed, the leader of the final wagon looked over his shoulder and spotted them. He inclined his head slightly by way of greeting and then turned back and continued his trudging. He seemed scarcely better dressed against the biting cold than themselves. Daniel took a deep breath of frosty air, stood up straight and stepped forward to address the man,

"Good morrow, friend." The man stopped, turned to face them, and looked hard at Daniel; whatever he thought inwardly, he maintained a blank, resigned look, impossible to read.

"Good morrow," he said hesitantly, as if unsure of the correct form of address.

"Am I right in thinking that this is the funeral cortege of the late queen?" said Daniel, a little too loudly in his effort to overcome his nerves.

"Aye; though we are merely the baggage train. Way up yonder," he said, pointing, "goes the king attended by his knights and sundry churchmen in royal procession." Thankfully the man asked nothing of Daniel and his companions, though he raised a curious eyebrow. Daniel decided to satisfy the man's unspoken interest and take the opportunity to practise his story on a person of little importance.

"We are pilgrims, friend, bound for Westminster Abbey. I go there to pray for the souls of my late parents. And to ask for wisdom as I take up my father's estate and duties. North of Lincoln, I and my companions were set upon by thieves. We three escaped because, being young, we outran our pursuers." The man's face remained inscrutable. But he responded courteously enough.

"Sorry I am to hear your tale, my lord." Daniel had no idea if the man believed his "tale" but he pressed on,

"We were told in Lincoln the sad account of the queen's death. I wish to pay my respects. Even so far north we heard much of Queen Eleanor's beauty and her devotion to the king."

"Indeed, my lord, no man could ask for a more faithful wife. And his Grace takes her death very hard. They say," he continued, leaning towards Daniel, and speaking in a confidential tone, "that for three days and nights after she died, he never left her side. His attendants were going frantic. But I forget myself." He straightened up again and said formally, "If you desire to pay your respects, my lord, you should seek audience with the Lord Chancellor, Lord Robert Burnell. He has the ear of the king."

"My thanks, friend."

"I could send my lad on ahead with a message if I may know your name, my lord."

"My name is Daniel of Orkney."

Daniel returned to the others. Bowing flamboyantly, Jim said,

"My name is Daniel of Orkney. Yes, my lord; no, my lord; three bags full my lord." He turned to Natalie and Ed and said, "Who does he think he is, right?" But the others merely shrugged.

They followed the wagons in uneasy silence until a rider approached and reined in beside them.

"Who might you be, young sir? How is it that we did not see your party approach and here you are, unannounced, at the rear of the royal train?"

"Royal what?" said Jim aloud, "I can't see any train."

"Peace, cousin James," said Daniel firmly. He took a deep breath, turned to the stranger with a small bow and said,

"My lord, I beg you will forgive the suddenness of our arrival and our tardiness in introducing ourselves. I am Daniel of Orkney. We are lately come from the isles of Orkney in the far north. Do you know them?"

The man raised his eyebrows. "No, sir, I have not had that pleasure. A long journey indeed! It must be above five hundred miles. What, may I ask, is the purpose of your journey?"

"It is indeed far, my lord, and we are weary of the road. I am under oath to make a pilgrimage to the shrine of the blessed Saint Edward the Confessor, to pray for the souls of my late parents. But on the road, our party was attacked and robbed. We came in a pitiable state to Lincoln where we heard of the queen's untimely death. We four, uninjured, have come to offer our condolences to the king. And to beg his grace's permission to travel with the cortege, having lost our escort."

The knight inclined his head in acknowledgment. "I will bear your condolences to his grace. I regret the king does not admit visitors at present. He is in deep mourning, as you will understand."

"My thanks, lord," said Daniel.

"Pardon me, sir, but your accent and speech are curious, unlike any Scotsman I've heard."

"You are right, sir. We are a race apart - not Scottish by descent but Norwegian and by this time not Norwegian either. Our speech is our own. Many find the accent difficult to understand, but you, my lord, have comprehended me admirably. Good day to you." This time Daniel inclined his head and began to withdraw, motioning for the other three to follow him.

"Oh, I get it now," said Jim. "Look, at him, you two. Geek is getting such a kick out of all this. Somehow we end up God knows where, but don't panic, because His Royal Geekiness, Lord Daniel of Geekland will ride in and save the day! Look at him - he's loving it!" He grabbed Daniel by the scruff of the neck and eyeballed him. But Ed elbowed the two of them apart and jerked his head towards the horseman riding away, but still in sight.

"Yes," said Daniel, "I happen to love history and by some freak, we've ended up in it. But I want to get back home as much as you. And right now, I haven't the foggiest idea how to 'save the day' so my brain's working overtime trying to figure out what to do. But you wouldn't understand that, would you? You must have a brain in there somewhere but it's in sleep mode." Jim threw himself at Daniel but Ed, by far the strongest of them, stepped in between them.

"Calm down, guys. Whatever's going on, bashing each other's brains out isn't going to help."

"Yeah," added Natalie. "Ed's right, we need to calm down and work out a plan." Jim scowled but said nothing. It was clear that Ed and Natalie were transferring their allegiance to Daniel. And he didn't know how to stop them.

Chapter 42

4th December 1290, Lincolnshire

They tramped along miserably at a discreet distance from the last wagon for another half an hour or so. Then they spotted a rider on a fine, black horse cantering down the convoy of wagons towards them.

"Uh oh; he looks important," said Daniel.

"This is suicide," Jim wailed. "They're never going to buy our stupid story. Let's make a run for it while we can." He was so terrified, Daniel felt sorry for him.

"Try to keep calm and follow my lead. Here goes."

"Just hold your head up high and act proud," whispered Natalie encouragingly.

The rider slowed his horse to a walk, then a halt, right in front of them. Daniel bowed his head slightly towards the man and the others copied the action.

"I understand you are Lord Daniel of Orkney," he said rather dryly. "My name is Robert Burnell, Lord Chancellor. The king has heard of your plight and invites you to join our procession. I will find a horse for you. I am given to understand that you lost your own mounts."

"Lord Burnell, please convey our heartfelt thanks to the king for his goodness," Daniel said, bowing his head, hoping the interview was over. But the Chancellor continued,

"We had not heard that there are masterless men roaming so close to the city of Lincoln. Did you report your trouble to the sheriff at the castle?"

"No, my lord, I regret that we did not. We were in a state of confusion.

When we heard about the cortege, we made haste to join you as soon as we could, to seek your protection for the remainder of our journey, knowing that you also are bound for Westminster."

"I marvel that you undertook such a pilgrimage at your tender age and moreover that you wish to continue having lost your escort," he said, somewhat condescendingly.

"I made a sacred vow to pray for the souls of my late parents at the shrine of Edward the Confessor. My father died on that saint's day. I confess I now have misgivings about the wisdom of my undertaking, but I am under oath."

"Indeed, my lord," said Robert, torn between admiration and scorn. "You did what seemed right in the circumstances. It is all that is required of any man. I will see to it that a messenger rides back to Lincoln to the sheriff. We break our journey tonight at Grantham. You may find hospitality at the Franciscan Friary. The king is indisposed at present but if you wish to pay your respects to the queen, her body will lie this night before the altar of Saint Wulfram's Church."

"I thank you, Lord Burnell, for your kind reception. Please pass on my deepest condolences to his grace. We will trouble you no further."

"God be with you," Burnell said, as he wheeled his horse round and spurred it to a trot. Just before he passed out of sight, he turned and called, "I will send provisions. You must be hungry."

"My thanks, my lord," Daniel called back, raising his right arm.

"Thank God," said Ed, "He seemed to believe you. And he's sending food. Good job, Dan. But how on earth can you speak like that?"

"Oh, because of my mum, I guess. She's a lecturer in English Language but she specialises in Medieval English."

"How is that even a thing? Why would anyone waste their life on that kind of stuff?" said Jim. Daniel was tempted to reply that some people enjoyed using language that consisted of more interesting words than 'thing,' 'stuff' and swear words. But he bit down his sarcasm and said,

"She got into it when she was a teenager through reading 'The Lords of the Rings,' and Tolkien's other books. He was a Professor of Medieval English at Oxford. It sparked her interest and became her dream, to teach at Oxford like him. I guess some of it must have rubbed off on me."

"No wonder you're so weird, with a mum like that," said Jim.

"I can see how it's weird to you. But it's what I grew up with so it's normal to me. And the stuff your parents are into would probably seem strange to me."

"Yeah, one person's normal is another person's weird. That makes sense," Ed said. "Anyway, thank God for Dan's weird mum. Otherwise we'd be screwed."

"So far so good, but we still need to be really careful," Daniel replied.

"How much further is it to the place that guy said we'd stop for the night?" said Natalie.

"I don't really know," said Daniel truthfully, though if he had known how far it was to Grantham, he wouldn't have told her. She and the others would freak out if they knew how far they'd be walking, not just today but every day until they reached London or managed to get back home.

Daniel wished there had been no mention of a horse. As far as he knew, Ed was the only one who could ride. But he was meant to be their groom, so unless there were enough horses to go round, he should definitely walk. He opened his mouth to discuss it with the others but promptly shut it again. Better to wait and see if the promised horse did actually materialise.

The others had brightened at the mention of food and for a few minutes, nobody complained. Daniel took the opportunity to look around and get his bearings. The baggage train spread out before them on the road as far as the eye could see. It was starting to ascend a steep incline. He was dying to get his map out of his pack but he knew he mustn't.

Jim and Natalie could not have imagined it was possible to feel so exhausted and yet keep putting one foot in front of the other. The dry bread rolls Lord Burnell had sent down had not made much of a dent in their hunger. They were oblivious to their surroundings and the gathering dusk that left them even colder. When the faint outline of buildings came into view, they managed to lift their heads to see a small church on their left and a castle on their right.

"This must be Grantham," said Natalie hoarsely, not knowing whether to laugh or cry.

"I don't care where it is as long as there's food and a warm bed," said Ed.

"What's that stink?" asked Jim.

"That's the smell of a town with no sewage system," Daniel replied. "I'm afraid it's another thing we'll have to get used to."

"Bloody hell. Just when I thought it couldn't get any worse," Jim said. Daniel didn't respond. In some ways, it was a relief to hear Jim speak, whatever he said. His sullen silences worried Daniel the most, leaving him trying to second-guess what was going on in Jim's head.

Chapter 43

4th December 1290, Grantham, Lincolnshire

The people of Grantham lined the road as the queen's bier approached. Some tossed tendrils of ivy or small bunches of mistletoe onto the ground ahead of the cortege. Some wept and all bowed their heads and made the sign of the cross. Whether their gestures were appreciated by the king none could tell. His regal visage was unchanged. He stared straight ahead. To strangers, he might appear aloof or haughty, but his close friend, Robert Burnell, riding just behind, understood that Edward dared not move a muscle lest his brittle mask should crack.

When they reached the lofty church, the bishop and his clerics turned aside to accompany the queen's bier to the altar, where her body would lay overnight. Brother Clément walked behind the king's party, keeping as close to his late mistress as his lowly position allowed. Trance-like with grief, he followed the other monks and priests. The king's eyes clouded with fresh pain as he watched churchmen file piously behind his wife's body. He cleared his throat but said nothing. His mind hurled darts of livid envy at them as they usurped him and prepared to keep his wife company through the hours of darkness. For thirty-six years she had laid beside him in the night, easing the lonely burden of monarchy. For thirty-six years she had followed him wherever he led, even to the beautiful parched earth of the Holy Land. Her love and companionship had strengthened him to face whatever challenges the next day would bring. But now she had gone ahead on the journey each person must make alone. One day, when God willed, he would follow, but not today, not for many a long, lonely day. And when at last he followed, would he find his Eleanor again in the next life or was she lost to him forever? This agonising question tortured him.

"My lord," Robert Burnell's sympathetic but insistent voice invaded his grim reverie. Perhaps Robert had been speaking for some time. Edward raised an eyebrow. "This way to the Angel, my lord. We sent messengers ahead so they should be ready for you. There is time to take refreshment before Vespers."

In the twilight, the king's household peeled off at The Angel Inn. Various other important-looking officials stopped at the castle. Those who were left headed across a market square towards an enclosure that housed several wooden buildings and a few unfinished stone ones. Daniel and his companions followed. Before they reached the gatehouse, the gate was thrown open by a friar in a grey habit,

"Welcome, honoured guests. Come within. We received notice of your coming and our guest hall awaits you." They filed through the gate to an open courtyard where another friar waited to lead the way. When everyone was assembled, he bustled away, talking all the while.

"Pray, forgive the simplicity of our accommodation. Our friary was founded only this year and there remains much work to do. We ourselves erected the wooden buildings while waiting for the stone ones to be built. But the workers have hit a brick wall, if you will pardon the jest. The labourers refuse to build according to the master mason's plans, saying that the church will fall on our heads. The master mason insists that his design is perfectly sound; he modelled it on a monastery he admired in France and what is more, he follows a tried and tested pattern from Euclid's geometry. Well, what can we do? We are in their hands. Euclid's geometry forsooth! It's all Greek to me – pardon my wit." Daniel and one or two others chuckled at the sight of the friar's shoulders pulsing up and down as he enjoyed his own gag, which was completely lost on his audience. Out of the blue, a wave of homesickness washed up from Daniel's empty stomach and stopped him in his tracks. The jolly friar's shaking shoulders were the image of his dad's, tickled by one of his own jokes. He stumbled and bumped into the woman in front, propelled by Ed crashing into his back.

"Hold steady there," the woman growled over her shoulder, not unkindly.

"Sorry, I lost my footing," Daniel said, reddening and blinking away the tears that had welled up.

"Keep up, Dan," said Ed. Ahead the jovial friar marched round a corner and was hidden from view. Daniel pulled himself together and trotted to catch up with Jim and Natalie. The friar chattered on, barely pausing for breath.

"The church falling on his head might be the only way to shut him up," sneered Jim. Daniel sniggered along with the others; again relieved to hear Jim speak, let alone crack a joke.

What passed that night for food, warmth and a bed would never before have been tolerated by Jim, Natalie and Ed. But beggars can't be choosers. The alternative to accepting rank stew and hard bread was to starve. The alternative to warming yourself by a smoky fire surrounded by smelly servants, was to remain numb with cold. The alternative to sleeping in a crowded room, on a wooden bench with a damp cloak around you, was to sleep outside in the snow. Natalie and Ed accepted what was offered with at least a show of good grace.

"I could stand it," Jim whinged, "I really could, if *Lord* Daniel was here slumming it with us. But where is he? Probably off socialising with the gentry. I bet he's eating proper food and sleeping in a proper bed."

"Let's just try to get some sleep. We probably have miles to walk again tomorrow," said Natalie.

"Fat chance of sleeping in this dump," retorted Jim, but fifteen minutes later the three friends were out for the count.

Chapter 44

4th December 1290, Grantham, Lincolnshire

At the shadowy rear of Saint Wulfram's church, Daniel sat shivering slightly on the stone floor with his back against a tombstone. He could hear the monks chanting prayers for the dead over the body of the queen as he turned their predicament over and over in his mind, trying to make some sense of it. Though their time travel appeared random, some instinct drove him to grope around for an Ariadne's thread that would lead them out of the labyrinth. It still seemed like a dream. He was a stone's throw from the recently deceased body of Queen Eleanor, whose 700-year-old tomb in Lincoln Cathedral had inspired his history essay. There must be a connection but it eluded him. The only facts that struck him as potentially significant were the place where it had happened, the site of the Eleanor cross, and the disappearance of his ammonite.

He had only noticed his fossil was missing when he changed his clothes at Aerlene's house. The pendant was gone, though the leather cord was still around his neck. It was possible that he had lost it back home, earlier in the day, but some inkling in his gut dismissed this perfectly reasonable thought. No, it must have disappeared when they slipped back in time, but why? Of all their belongings, this fossil was the only object that already existed in 1290, so why on earth should that alone vanish into some time travel vortex? Blimey, just thinking the words 'time travel' made his mind reel. He rubbed his temples. If anything was going to evaporate into thin air, surely it would be all their modern belongings that couldn't logically exist here. Suddenly he pictured that happening and he, Jim, Ed and Natalie arriving here stark naked. He cringed, then laughed; thank goodness for small mercies, as his dad would say.

Unlike all their other possessions, the ammonite pendant did already exist in this time. Daniel mulled this over. There were three possibilities: either it was just a fossil buried in a cliff somewhere, or it was already lying in that grave in Abbotsbury or it was hanging around the neck of some living person. And then it hit him, wherever it was right now, the same object couldn't exist in two places at the same time. That's why it disappeared. It probably had no other significance than that.

So, the only relevant factor was the link with Eleanor of Castile. Was it just some freaky connection in time? Because he happened to go and stand on the exact spot, on the exact day, at the exact time when the site had been selected? Didn't it say in his book that they set her coffin down on the chosen spot and said a prayer or something? Presumably, the same process would be repeated at each town where they stopped on the journey to London. Tomorrow he would watch carefully to see just what took place. But if it was merely a freak of 'right time, right place' for some weird time connection to form, their hopes of getting back were almost nothing. He couldn't possibly tell the others that. He had to keep their hope alive for now at least. All he could do was watch for clues in everything going on around them, and hope for the best.

He noticed that the chanting had stopped. The monks were filing out of the church, leaving only a few of their number to keep vigil over the queen's body throughout the night. Daniel stood up and made his way down the gloomy aisle towards the altar. When he reached it, he baulked; Queen Eleanor's body lay uncoffined, regally robed and crowned. A linen cloth covered her face but her wavy auburn hair cascaded onto the altar table. He could see the contours of her face, just like its stone image on her tomb at Lincoln, where her internal organs had been buried this morning. The enormity of their predicament shook Daniel afresh. He knelt behind the monks and prayed as he had never prayed before, for divine protection and guidance.

When he stood to leave, the light from the altar candle fell on the faces of some of the praying monks, to the left of the queen's body. One of them looked like the man Daniel had almost flattened when Jim tumbled onto him as they 'arrived' here this morning. The pallor of his face was matched by the white knuckles of his right hand, as he gripped something hanging around his neck - a crucifix, Daniel supposed. He felt he should apologise to the man, but he couldn't be absolutely sure it was the same person he had crushed. Besides, it didn't seem right to interrupt his prayers. He would look out for him tomorrow.

Chapter 45

5th December 1290, Lincolnshire

An arm shook Daniel's shoulder and a tentative voice said, "Wake up, my lord, we leave at first light. Wake your cousins." The words made no sense whatsoever to Daniel. Leave at first light? He didn't have any cousins. A stale sweat smell assaulted his nostrils and at the same instant, he became aware of a low hubbub. Last night as he sank into the fuzzy state between waking and sleeping, he had half wondered if he would wake up in his bed at school and find it had all been a weirdly long, drawn-out dream. Wishful thinking. He threw off the coarse blanket, sat up and leaned over,

"Jim, wake up. We have to get ready to leave." No response. He shook Jim gently. "Jim, I'm not kidding. Wake up." Still no response. "Jim!"

"Get lost."

"Suit yourself. You can spend the rest of your life in a Franciscan friary if you like, but I'm going to London. Bye."

Five minutes later a bleary-eyed Jim emerged into the dim courtyard and stood next to Daniel, stamping his feet and blowing clouds of steamy breath, just like everyone else. It struck Daniel how, apart from their different clothes, this group of people could just as easily be gathering on a frosty morning at a bus stop back home as in a medieval friary. He was trying to think of a way to say this when Jim spoke first,

"Where can we get breakfast? A hot drink? A shower?"

Daniel shrugged, "Makes life at school seem like luxury, doesn't it?"

"But what about breakfast?" insisted Jim, "I mean, I'm not expecting bacon and eggs but surely they have to eat something."

"I don't know, Jim. We have to go with the flow, okay? Where are Ed and Natalie?"

Natalie appeared at the door of the guest quarters, smoothing her hair with her hands. Daniel waved and she spotted them.

"Don't laugh at my fringe," she snapped, "It always sticks up in the morning. It only takes a minute to wet it and curl it under with a brush. But I can't find a mirror anywhere."

"You look fine," smiled Daniel. "Did you manage to sleep all right?"

"Eventually. The blanket set off my eczema so I had to choose between being warm and itchy or freezing cold."

Jim sniggered, "Which did you go for?"

"Warm and itchy."

On the other side of the courtyard, a door opened, releasing a delicious, warm waft of fresh bread. A small boy appeared; half hidden by the enormous tray he carried. Daniel watched him stagger into the centre of the gathering crowd, his little face beaming with pride at serving anyone connected with the king. The smell of new-baked bread and the young lad's shining face thawed the atmosphere in the courtyard as effectively as sunrise. Cold, groggy-looking faces broke into smiles and smiles warmed into cheery good mornings to neighbours. The boy began offering the guests what looked like bread rolls. Jim, Natalie and Daniel's hungry eyes followed the tray, willing it not to be empty by the time it reached them.

"Ooh, it's still warm," said Natalie as her fingers closed around a roll. Daniel watched Jim scoop up two.

"This one's for Ed," Jim said, a touch too defensively to be convincing.

"I had one before I saddled up," said Ed appearing behind them, making them all jump. He clapped Jim on the back, swiped the roll and said, "But good one, Jim," and stuffed it in his mouth. The rolls did not live up to their smell, but they filled a hole and no one complained.

"You stink, Ed," said Natalie.

"That's horses for you; I've been shovelling crap," he said grinning from ear to ear, with his mouth full of bread. Daniel could contain his anxiety no longer,

"How's it going with the other grooms? Do you think any of them are suspicious?"

"Chill, Dan, it's fine. I told you, I'm good with horses. And one of them was friendly; his name's Warin or something weird-sounding like that. He showed me where to find all the tack."

"What the hell's tack?" said Jim.

"Reins and stuff. I helped him with the feeding and grooming last night and just now he showed me how to grease the horses' hooves so they don't get balled up with snow and ice. That can make them slip. Speaking of horses—"

True to his word, Robert Burnell had procured not one but three horses for 'Lord' Daniel and his 'cousins.' Daniel had only been on a horse once, but at least he remembered roughly how to mount. He clambered up and, perched uncomfortably far from the ground, watched Natalie mount like a pro. Clearly, she had had lessons at some point. Jim, on the other hand, stood staring at the handsome chestnut towering over him. Ed came to the rescue, pretending he could see a loose strap under the horse's belly, buying time. Soon most of the other guests made their way across the friary courtyard to the gatehouse. Ed gestured for Daniel and Natalie to go on ahead, while he and Jim lagged behind for a crash course in basic horsemanship.

Until now Jim had not appreciated just how large a horse is up close; how difficult it is to propel oneself onto its back and how precariously high it feels in the saddle. But Ed was a good teacher and despite her size, Ruth was a slow, placid mare. Within half an hour Jim had loosened his cataleptic grip on the reins, relaxed his ear-level shoulders and even regained his habitual "look-at-me-and-your-dead" face.

Thankfully progress was achingly slow for the first half hour as the cortege assembled and crept forward, stopping and starting, stretching the length of Grantham High Street. Daniel watched with fascination, and wondered whose job it was to form the many riders, walkers and wagons into a coherent procession. As the front of the cortege finally left Grantham behind, Ed and Jim caught up. One look at Jim warned Natalie and Daniel not to comment on his horsemanship. Ed manoeuvred their mounts so that Daniel and Jim could ride side by side with himself in the middle, an unobtrusive hand on each horse's lead rein.

Ed virtually disappeared in the clouds of horse breath misting the frosty air. At least he's sheltered there, Daniel thought, and hopefully, he'll warm up as he walks. He tried to remember how far Ed would have to walk today to reach Stamford, the cortege's next overnight stop. But he couldn't recall the distance. Ed glanced up at him and grinned. Daniel smiled back, thankful it was Ed and not Jim who had experience with horses and could pass for a groom. Ed should be able to manage the walking and he wasn't a grumbler. Daniel's gaze passed from Ed's face to Jim's, which wore an unfamiliar look of total concentration. I'd better make the most of the peace and quiet, Daniel reflected; once he gets the hang of staying in the saddle, there will be nothing but moaning the rest of the way. And after riding all day as a total novice, tomorrow's saddle-soreness did not bear thinking about.

The good North Road led the party southwards through a gently undulating, snowy landscape, with the High Dike looming in the east. It was easy riding for those on horseback but challenging for the walkers, as every welcome descent led only to another uphill trudge. For Daniel and his little band, riding roughly halfway down the entourage, behind the middle-ranked officials, the first miles passed in uneasy silence, each of them lost in their own thoughts. Jim focused entirely on not falling off, trying to settle into a rhythm and move with and not against his horse, all the while attempting to mask his fear.

Natalie likewise was concentrating on not betraying her emotions. She felt tearful but determined not to let the others see how terrified she was at the thought of being stuck here, seven hundred years away from her family and everything else she knew and loved; everything she had taken entirely for granted until yesterday.

Daniel was musing on the bizarre events of the past twenty-four hours. And how his role in relation to the others had been transformed so swiftly from victim to unspoken leader. Yesterday he was intent on running away from them and now he felt responsible for their safety, no matter what threats arose in this unpredictable scenario. Moreover, it was down to him, somehow, to find a way back to their own time. What if Jim was right and they should have stayed in Lincoln? He rehearsed all yesterday's debates over again in his head and came to the same conclusion.

Eventually, Daniel shook himself out of the quagmire of doubts and anxieties in his mind and looked around. Beside him, Ed was strolling along with his usual steady composure. How does he manage that, he wondered? He has a knack of staying in the moment and taking things as they come. Daniel raised his eyes to the scenery. The road was starting to descend towards some woods but here the snowy fields on either side of the road were full of enormous sheep.

"Look at the size of those sheep!" he said. The others followed his pointing finger.

"Blimey, they're as big as pigs," said Natalie, "And their woolly coats are so long. Why don't they cut them? They must get filthy."

Ed peered over Daniel's horse's neck. He said, "Oh yeah, I remember seeing sheep like them at the university farm. They're a rare breed. What were they called? Lincoln something or other?" Ed studied them for a minute. "Lincoln Longwool, yeah that was it. Obvious when you look at them."

"What were you doing at the university farm?" asked Jim.

"It must have been when my uncle brought me back to school after the holidays. He's into farming and countryside stuff. He'd seen on social media that the university farm had recently got this new flock of sheep to study and breed. They were having an open day so we went along. It was good." Moments later the road entered woodland and the sheep were lost from view.

At midday, the cortege turned aside to a village for a short break from the saddle and a small meal. In the absence of a monastery or inn, the royal party made use of the parish church of St Mary. Everyone else had to brave the cold. Daniel and the others were stamping their feet and swinging their arms near the church door when the king emerged and swept by them, flanked by knights, bishops and advisors. Daniel's numb fingers and Ed's grumbling stomach were instantly forgotten.

"Whoa, that's my idea of a king," said Natalie, straightening up from a curtsey that took her back to ballet classes she hadn't thought of for years.

"Yes," agreed Daniel, following the king with his eyes, spellbound. Darkly and simply dressed, with no regal paraphernalia whatsoever, Edward stood head and shoulders over most of his companions and carried himself with quiet dignity. He strode away on his famous "long shanks" and mounted his huge horse with no more effort than we take to get into a car. For him it's the exact equivalent of getting into a car, Daniel reflected. How he wished he could take a photo. But he would have to content himself with a mental snapshot.

Daniel shut his eyes for a moment and tried to imprint the sight on his mind. The king's shoulder-length black wavy hair, lightly streaked with grey, surrounded a face with strong, even features. An image appeared unbidden in Daniel's mind of Edward's head and shoulders sculpted in marble – a "Roman emperor" face. The king was very like the images Daniel had seen of his statues and manuscript illustrations. And here he was in the flesh, larger than life, healthy and robust, but grim. He has just lost the love of his life, Daniel thought. I wonder how different he would have looked to us if Queen Eleanor was still alive.

Chapter 46

5th December 1290, Lincolnshire

Near the front of the procession, amongst the dignitaries, rode Princess Mary. She had inherited her mother's eager intelligence and alluring beauty in equal measure. In the convent school at Amesbury Abbey, her academic gift was admired and nurtured; her attractiveness was not. Yet what nature had bestowed could not be easily repressed. Mary was becoming aware of this as she approached the threshold of womanhood. Let loose from her cage for this sombre holiday, she was discovering that her nature was much like her unruly auburn hair – every day she modestly tamed and covered it, yet one irrepressible curl would inevitably break free.

Her grandmother, who was also her spiritual superior, as abbess at Amesbury, had allowed her to join the cortege on condition that she observe the offices of the church, when travel arrangements permitted. Within the cloister, Mary had always appeared devoted and dutiful. But in the last few days, she had been absent as often as she was present. And yet she always offered an exceptionally holy excuse – 'I was praying for my mother's soul' or 'I was nursing an injured owl.' This morning, however, she had been present for the office of Prime at St Wulfram's church and now she rode in solemn procession behind her father, King Edward, with her eldest sister, Eleanora, on one side and her watchful grandmother on the other. Mary's horse, Jasper, was skittish. Perhaps, like herself, he resented being held back; restrained to a walk when his restless energy urged him to run. He jerked his head, stamped his hoof on the frosty ground and snorted clouds of steamy breath into the cold air. Mary patted his neck and spoke soothingly to him,

"There, Jasper, there boy. Don't fret. Let's enjoy our freedom. Here we are out in the world, watching the snowy fields and lanes go by. Look at the oak tree there – clinging to its last bronzy leaves, as if it cannot quite trust in the hope of springtime." Suddenly a blackbird shot arrow-like from a nearby wood, crossed their path and disappeared into a hedgerow on the other side. A sparrowhawk darted in hot pursuit and crashed into the hedge, where it flailed around for a moment before emerging without its quarry. The ruckus startled horses and riders alike and Jasper reared, eyes rolling.

Not far behind the princess, Warin kept company with Brother Clément, partly out of concern that the exhausted monk would fall asleep and tumble from the saddle. Aroused by the commotion, he saw Mary's pony rear up. With unconscious speed, he was suddenly there to prevent her fall. Once she was secure in the saddle, he held Jasper's bridle and calmed him with strong hands and a soothing voice. Not once did their eyes meet, but never were two young people more acutely aware of each other. Warin's hands tingled as if he had touched an angel. And Mary's waist, which he had grabbed to steady her, throbbed as if his hands had been logs from the fire.

"Young man, unhand my granddaughter's mount," said the imperious voice beside him. Warin let go of the reins; instantly Jasper reared again. Mary lunged forward and clutched his mane. The king's mother instructed her elderly groom to control Mary's pony. Warin stepped aside to let them pass, following the princess with his eyes. Thus only he saw Mary subtly jab her heels into the pony's flanks to set him rearing again. Warin was summoned and commanded to keep Jasper calm.

And so, for two hours during which her eyes never appeared to stray from the road ahead, Mary applied her eager intelligence to study the breadth of his shoulders, the firm but light grip of the rein in his rough fingers and the way the winter sunlight ignited his unkempt, straw-coloured hair. For Warin, it was enough that he held the rein that held the pony that held her. And to savour the sweet anticipation of the moment when, as her groom, he would help her dismount.

Chapter 47

5th December 1290, Stamford, Lincolnshire

In the afternoon, the numbing cold, hours of concentrating on staying in the saddle and endless ups and downs of the route had such a hypnotic effect on Daniel and his companions that they were halfway down the long, gentle descent into Stamford before they realised the end was in sight. Dusk had fallen and the town ahead blinked with torchlight.

The weary procession came to a halt before they reached the town walls. Even Jim was too tired to complain, but Daniel dismounted and walked up closer to the front of the cortege to see what was going on. He hung back as he saw the queen's bier being removed from its carriage and borne with all dignity to a point where their road was met by another from the north. It was set down at the junction. The scene began to make sense to Daniel as he watched the king and important dignitaries gather sombrely around. A man who looked like a bishop, by his robes, stepped forward. He sprinkled water on the bier and the ground around it and raised his voice to intone a prayer in Latin.

"What are they doing?" Natalie whispered in his ear. Daniel jumped.

"Blimey Natalie," he whispered back. "Don't creep up on me like that. They're blessing the site where one of the Eleanor Crosses will be built, like the one that was in Lincoln."

"You mean where we came back in time? So this could be another portal thingy!" she muttered excitedly.

"Maybe, maybe not. Let me watch; I need to concentrate in case there are any clues." Natalie waited in silence beside Daniel but there was little more to see. The little group around the bier dispersed; the bier was replaced on the cart and the procession resumed.

"Well?" said Natalie, "Anything?"

"Not really; nothing that stood out. Only it's just dawned on me that when we were stopping and starting in Grantham this morning, this is probably what was happening. They must have been blessing the cross site there. They're going to do it at each place where the cortege stops for the night and later, at each one, a large stone cross will be built in the queen's memory."

"Right, the Eleanor Crosses you told us about. It's a nice idea, quite romantic really. But shouldn't we go and walk around there just in case it's a portal thing?" Natalie said.

"Not on our own, just in case it works. Let's get back to the others."

As they turned round, Brother Clément was approaching the site that had just been blessed.

"Hang on," Daniel said to Natalie. "That's the monk I saw yesterday when we first came through at Lincoln; he was lying on the ground. Jim bumped into me and I nearly squashed the guy. He frightened the life out of us, rising up like a ghost and charging off. I guess we must have scared him too."

"Are you sure it's the same bloke?"

"Fairly. I saw him again in the church last night. I feel like I should apologise to him."

"You're on your own then. I'm not going near him. He looks weird."

Daniel approached the monk, but before he reached him, Brother Clément stopped and knelt. As he leaned forward to lie on the ground, his snakestone pendant swung out from beneath his habit. Daniel's hand flew instinctively to his neck where his ammonite had hung; his fingers touched the bare cord.

By now Brother Clément was prostrate on the ground, arms outstretched, praying. I must have dropped my fossil at Lincoln, Daniel thought, and somehow this monk picked it up. Yet this didn't square with his memory of what had happened. He recalled the monk starting up from the ground in shock and fleeing the scene. There was no time for him to find the pendant. Unless it had got caught in the folds of his habit and he happened upon it later. That seemed unlikely, but Daniel could think of no other explanation. He wondered if the monk would let him have it back if he explained. But on reflection, it would be better not to draw any attention to what happened that day. He turned around and trotted back to Natalie.

"I can't do it now – he's praying. I'll have to look out for him later." He didn't mention the ammonite – that would have to be between him and the monk. "Let's find the others. Everyone's on the move again."

They headed back uphill, going against the flow of riders, walkers and wagons flowing down towards the welcome lights of the town. Ed was just helping Jim remount.

"Where have you two been? We thought we'd have to leave without you," said Jim tetchily. Despite his words, Daniel saw the relief on Jim's face and smiled inwardly.

Ed said, "Let's get going; we must be nearly there, wherever we're going to stop for the night and I'm starving."

"They've just blessed the site where the Eleanor Cross is going to be built. Natalie and I think we should go and walk around there, just in case it's another time portal like at Lincoln; so we'll have to lag behind a bit and then catch up. Okay, Jim? Ed?"

"Well, duh!" said Jim, his face lighting up. "Show us the place!" Fifteen minutes later, the hope in Jim's eyes had turned to anger and again the others had to drag him away from the spot on which he had pinned his hopes of getting home.

The sullen little band passed through Stamford's town wall via Saint Clément's Gate, proceeding downhill past a towering church, to catch up with the cortege. Thankfully the procession had halted in a spacious square where the townsfolk and their dignitaries had gathered to pay their respects. Men-at-arms held aloft blazing torches as the town sheriff, the constable of the castle and a Dominican friar stepped forward to greet the king and lead the procession towards the Dominican friary which would house most of them overnight. Silent well-wishers thronged the streets, slowing the cortege virtually to a halt. It wound its way through the centre of town, past fancy-looking merchants' dwellings standing cheek by jowl with peasants' hovels. In the shadow of another huge church, they turned right and descended steeply downhill.

"What the hell?" Jim muttered under his breath. Daniel was also confused. Before them lay the town wall. And now they were leaving through Bridge Gate.

"What's going on, Dan?" Natalie said nervously, "Aren't we meant to be stopping?"

"Yes, we're definitely stopping here in Stamford. Maybe the town has spread beyond the walls. I know it was growing like mad in the Middle Ages because of the wool trade. Remember those sheep. The wool trade was massive and towns around here did really well out of it. Stamford was a top player in the business."

Beyond the stone arch of the gate was a bridge over a river but they turned left before it and followed a track by the riverbank. Now there were fewer well-wishers by the side of the road, they quickened pace for a short while before abruptly coming to a stop. Daniel could barely make out the front of the procession but it seemed to him that they were turning off the path. Yes, now they began ambling forward again step by step. All the important officials at the front had turned aside and now most of the middle-ranking ones were following.

"About bloody time," said Jim. The horses caught the scent of stables and became restless but a few rows ahead of them the riders had halted again. Someone was directing them further along the road.

"Oh hell, what now?" Natalie whimpered. "I can't keep going any longer."

"If I can, you can, Nat," Ed said. "Come on, it won't be long now." They rode past the friary and left the town behind. It was almost completely dark, but the sky was clear and they could see well enough to ride at this slow pace. Daniel became increasingly anxious as they passed into the countryside again, but then he caught the darker silhouettes of buildings on the right rearing up out of the dimness. And at last, a monk came out to welcome them to Saint Leonard's Priory and they turned in at the gatehouse.

In the courtyard, grooms hurried out to meet them and lead the weary horses to the stables. Stiff and sore, and oblivious to their surroundings, they hobbled after the sub-prior who led them to the guest quarters. Light and warmth enveloped them, and they sank in thankful silence onto benches by the fire. An hour later they were warmer and full enough with some kind of vegetable stew; Jim resumed his complaints,

"What on earth is this piss?" he said, holding up his cup.

"It's ale, so we need to go steady or we'll all be drunk."

"Ale?" Natalie laughed. "Don't they know we're underage?" She pushed her cup away. "I want something else."

"No, we need to drink it. It's well watered down and the alcohol will help kill off germs."

"Alcohol kills off germs? Where did that come from?" Jim sneered. Daniel fought the urge to put Jim down for his ignorance.

"We still do it in our time. You know your hand sanitiser for covid, that contained alcohol."

"Yeah," agreed Ed, "My dad swears by whisky whenever he thinks he's coming down with a bug."

"So will every day be like this? Travelling all day in the freezing cold, staying in some grotty monastery and eating rank stew?" Jim said.

"Pretty much. It's tough for all of us, especially Ed, as he's walking all the way. But I can't see another way," Daniel said, as gently as he could. He was sure that after riding all day, Jim, like himself, must have aches in muscles he didn't know existed. Right then, walking seemed an attractive option. But on that point, he held his tongue.

"But the time-door-thingy is in Lincoln. I still don't get why we couldn't stay there and keep looking for it." The desperation in Jim's voice, along with the fact that Daniel had been having his own doubts, helped Daniel treat him with more patience than he felt. And so he reiterated the reasons yet again, ending with,

"The main thing we all have to do is try to stay healthy, keep alert and learn from everything that's going on around us. Ed's made a great start by making friends with Warin, the stable hand."

"I found out at lunchtime that he's not really a groom," Ed said. "Warin told me he's an apprentice goldsmith, but he prefers working with horses, so he bunks off to help in the stables whenever he can."

"Well, the point is, you now have someone to show you the ropes. We all need to follow Ed's lead. Anything we can learn about how things work here will be helpful."

"I'm not talking to any of them. For one thing, they stink." Jim said.

"We'll all stink in a day or two; I'm dying for a shower but that's not going to happen, is it?" Natalie piped up, running her fingers through her hair. "I don't even have a brush."

"If you see any of the women using a brush or comb you could ask to borrow it. It might be a way of making friends."

"Or getting nits," added Jim.

"It's probably already too late to avoid that," said Ed, scratching the back of his head.

"Uurgh," said Natalie. She started to scratch too, then Daniel, then Jim and suddenly they all burst out laughing. It was the first time they had had a good laugh together and for a moment they forgot their dilemma and anxiety.

"I suppose we should get to bed; we have another day's travelling tomorrow," Daniel suggested. This time there was no argument.

Chapter 48

6th December 1290, Lincolnshire

Again, Daniel was shaken awake in the dark and urged to rouse his cousin; that task was never going to get any easier. The morning followed a similar pattern to the day before. They gathered in the priory courtyard, this time in thick fog; a breakfast of bread and boiled eggs, while grooms led out the horses. They retraced their steps along the track towards the Dominican Priory where the king and his retainers had spent the night.

The king's party was ready to file out in front of them, maintaining the strict order of rank. Daniel tried to focus on the beauty of the crisp morning, to distract himself from his sore backside and thighs. He and Jim had already discovered that no amount of shifting in the saddle would make any difference. But at least the torrent of swear words from Jim had now subsided. They rode gently downhill alongside a river swathed in mist. Daniel strained to hear the sound of running water but could discern nothing beneath the jingling of harnesses and the horses' footfall. The wind blew right in their faces sending shivers down their necks. In no time at all their hands were lifeless shapes gripping the reins.

At the bridge, they turned left and crossed. The fog parted long enough for Daniel to notice that downstream the river split into two channels and at the edge of the island between, a heron stood motionless in the frosty air. Upstream he could see all kinds of moored boats, and men starting to load cargo, calling morning greetings to one another. Across the river their road began to climb again and churches and monastic-looking buildings hugged both sides of the street. As before, monks and working folk paused and bowed their heads as the queen's bier rolled past them. Near the top of the hill, a dark tower rose abruptly close beside the road, stark and sheer like a cliff. Daniel instinctively cowered as if it were falling on top of him. But they were soon past it and cresting the hill.

Daniel twisted in the saddle to take a last look at Stamford. Church towers, spires and the highest roofs and treetops floated above the lingering fog, looking strangely disembodied.

"How can one little town need all those churches?" said Natalie, counting the improbable number of spires.

"I guess a lot of people must be packed into those walls. And absolutely everyone goes to church."

"Look, a castle! Down there, across the river," said Ed, impressed. Daniel peered into the mist and just made out the stone keep on its grassy mound.

"Well spotted, Ed! A motte and bailey. Cool. I wish we could go and explore."

"Aaargh!" Suddenly Ed was down on the ice, almost under the horses' hooves.

"Whoa," said Dan and Jim together, reining the horses to a halt.

"You all right, Ed?" said Natalie, starting to dismount.

"Don't get down, Nat. It's so slippery; the snow's frozen over." Ed hauled himself up onto his feet again, brushing himself down, looking sheepish. "I'm all right. No bones broken."

They crested the hill; Stamford was gone and they rode ahead into snowy countryside. After a while, Natalie turned to Daniel and asked,

"Dan, last night when we were talking, you said we all had to try to stay healthy. Did you mean anything in particular by that?"

"Mainly that it won't be very nice if any of us get ill. And we'll just have to keep going, to stay under the protection of the cortege."

"Yeah. But do they have doctors and medicines?"

"Not that we would recognise. It's mainly herbal remedies and people skilled in using them."

"Well, just so you know, I have some paracetamol and migraine medicine stashed in my pockets."

"Good, we need to save anything like that for when we really need it, not just for headaches or colds that we can put up with."

Through the morning, most of their route lay in woodland which at least afforded some shelter from the biting wind. At midday, the brothers of Fineshade Priory served them generously with bread, cheese and ale.

"How come they have all this food ready? There must be three hundred people in the procession. Did they know we were coming?" Natalie asked.

"They must have done. I suppose they send scouts on ahead to warn them the king is coming. All the places we're stopping at must have been baking for days. And," he added after a moment's thought, "they're probably using up most of their stores so I hope the king is paying them well, otherwise they'll go hungry through the winter."

"Something I've been meaning to ask," said Ed, "is why some people in the funeral cortege are dressed in black and others in bright colours?"

Daniel looked round at their fellow travellers, seated near them at the trestle tables, tucking it to their lunch. "Yes, I noticed that too. I don't really know. The king and important people who ride at the front are all wearing black but the middle-ranking people and lower-ranking people aren't. My guess is that black clothes are more expensive, so only the rich can afford them, maybe?"

"I don't get it," said Ed. "Why would black clothes cost more than any other colour?"

"The cost of different dyes varied a lot in the past. So the colour of your clothes reflected your social status because it showed what you could afford. But, as well as that, lower class people weren't actually allowed to wear certain colours even if they could afford it. There were laws about it."

"Blimey. Fancy not being allowed a colour," Ed said.

Natalie tutted. "That's discrimination, that is," she said.

By mid-afternoon the light was failing. They rode on and on through dense woodland. A tawny owl hooted, and its mate quivered the air in response. Jim peered uneasily from side to side.

"What are you looking for, Jim?" asked Natalie.

"Nothing," he blushed. "It's just, it's a bit creepy, isn't it? There could be anything in those woods."

"Like what?"

"I dunno, bats? I hate bats. I hate anything that sucks your blood."

Daniel smiled inwardly, tempted to string him along but his better nature reasserted itself.

"In this cold weather, bats will all be hibernating. And anyway, it's only vampire bats that suck blood. We don't have them in Britain except in zoos. The rest is all horror film nonsense." He omitted to mention other wild animals which would be around in these woods. Wild boar he was sure of, but wolves? He had no idea when they became extinct in England.

Daniel's excitement mounted as they neared Geddington. At Lincoln, it had been impossible to go back and see the medieval city because they had to catch up with the cortege. But now he would see with his own eyes the medieval version of a place he had visited in his own time. A direct comparison. He wanted to spur his horse into a canter and ride ahead, but he satisfied himself with standing on his stirrups every couple of minutes and craning his neck to catch a first glimpse. Beneath him, his horse jerked his head and stepped sideways.

"Steady old boy," Dan said, patting his neck.

"It's you that needs steadying. For pity's sake, keep your bum in the saddle, Dan," said Ed.

"Sorry, I'm just interested to see the next place, Geddington."

"Oh yeah?" murmured Ed. "What's so special about Geddington?"

"Nothing really; it's just that I came here a couple of weeks ago with my mum. In our time it's a picturesque village with thatched houses, a big church and one of the three remaining Eleanor Crosses. Oh, and a medieval bridge."

"I quite like old bridges," said Ed. "Will it be there now, in this time – the same one?"

"Yes, I think so."

"Cool." They went on quietly for a few minutes until Ed said, "It's kind of comforting to know something is the same from this time to ours."

"Yeah, it is," agreed Dan. "There was a royal hunting lodge too. There are barely any traces of it left in our time but I reckon that's where we'll sleep tonight."

They began descending into a wooded valley. "Look, there's the church," said Daniel standing up again in his stirrups. His horse sidestepped and huffed.

"Dan!" said Ed, exasperated.

"Sorry. See the church? I'm sure it has a tall spire in our time but perhaps they haven't built that yet. We're almost there."

"Thank God," Ed said, "The fog's coming down again, and soon we won't be able to see the church at all, spire or no spire."

Chapter 49

6th December 1290, Geddington, Northamptonshire

Daniel had been exploring. A wind had whipped up and blown away the threatening fog. As he came back over the bridge, he was met by a knight he recognised.

"Lord Daniel," the knight said, inclining his head, "I am Otto de Grandisson. The Lord Chancellor sent me to invite you on a hunt tomorrow. The hunting hereabouts is rich. Coming from the Scottish Isles, you are accustomed to hunting deer, I make no doubt. Although meat is not permitted during the season of Advent, we need to victual the court for the Feast of the Nativity."

"Well, of course," stammered Daniel, thinking on his feet. "But has not the procession enough to carry without adding more?"

"The staff here at the palace will hang the pheasants and salt the meat and send them on to Westminster."

"I see," Dan replied non-committedly.

"Good, we have need of every able-bodied man. We muster at first light."

Daniel rushed back and found Ed. At least he knew now why they hadn't been given any meat. No need to tell the others. After all, stew was stew; they might not notice.

"Why the hell did you agree to go hunting? Ed said.

"I didn't! He just assumed I would; I have no choice. And it came across as a bit of a challenge – a test to see if I'm who I say I am. What am I going to do? I can barely ride a horse, let alone ride and simultaneously fire a weapon at a moving target!"

"Calm down, Dan. We'll just have to come up with a plan. Let's not mention it to the others until we've thought of something." They both sat brooding on the problem until Ed said, "You have to at least show up, in case it is some sort of test. Do you think I can come with you because I'm your groom?"

"Yes, I suppose so. That's something at least."

"Have you ever used any kind of weapon?" Ed asked.

Daniel groaned, "I had a go at archery at a summer camp once. I could barely hit the target with one arrow out of six by the end of the session."

"Do you at least remember how to hold the bow, for appearance's sake?"

"I guess so."

"Good. So, you can just about ride and you can hold a bow. That's something to work with. We can set out with them. You'll have to try to look comfortable and confident. Then we've got to come up with some way to get you out of needing to gallop or shoot."

"Maybe we slip away and say we got lost?" Dan suggested.

"Maybe they won't find any deer so the whole thing will be just be a long ride in the countryside," added Ed brightly.

"I doubt it. This is a royal hunting ground and it's against the law for anyone else to hunt here. So there should be plenty of game."

"If the worst comes to the worst, you'll have to pretend to fall off your horse."

"Who says I'll need to pretend?" said Daniel, laughing half-heartedly.

In the royal hunting lodge, later that evening, here and there members of the party began to settle down for the night. Daniel and Ed were still off somewhere trying to prepare for the next day's hunt. Natalie said to Jim,

"What shall we do while Daniel and Ed are away? I'll have to distract myself somehow, I'll be worried sick about them."

"Lord Daniel will be all right," said Jim with emphasis on Lord. "Geek's pretty good at winging it. It's us we need to worry about. I still think we never should've left Lincoln. The time door or portal is there. That's the only thing we know for sure. We should've stayed at the right spot and waited for the right moment. I don't know what the hell we're doing on this bloody funeral march."

"How many more times have we got to go through this, Jim? We can't just loiter around that spot on the road waiting for something to happen.

What would we eat? Where would we stay at night? At least joining the cortege has given us food, shelter and protection. And Daniel's figuring it out. He'll come up with a plan."

"What plan? By the time that hunting party comes back, he and Ed will probably have been arrested. We should get away while we can."

"I'm not going anywhere without the others," Natalie insisted, "and nor are you."

"Whatever."

∞

7th December 1290, Geddington churchyard

Daniel was digging a hole. He was in the churchyard just after midnight. He didn't dare use his phone as a torch as he knew there were priests in the church keeping vigil over the dead queen. But the sky was now clear and once his eyes adjusted, he could see well enough by the radiant starlight, undimmed by air pollution.

During the ride from Stamford to Geddington, Daniel had been turning over in his mind how to minimise the threats they faced. He was not at all convinced that their story was believed. Lord Burnell had appeared happy enough to tolerate their presence, whether or not he credited their tale. But the middle-ranking officials with whom they brushed shoulders were another matter. Their sidelong glances and offhand questions kept Daniel continually on his guard. And now this hunting party; he felt that a gauntlet had been thrown down and the odds were that he would lose the challenge.

What Daniel dreaded most was being searched. If their twenty-first century belongings were discovered they would be in grave danger. He knew he would never persuade the others to relinquish their phones so they would have to risk it with those. But his book about Queen Eleanor worried him the most. With its photographs and detailed accounts of recent and "future" events, it was a death sentence waiting to happen.

On their arrival at Geddington, Daniel had noticed a man digging a fresh grave in the churchyard. That set him thinking about burying his book. Ideally, he wanted to give himself half a chance of retrieving it later, though he knew that was a long shot. He had already discounted hiding it somewhere within the church; churches were always being altered - it would surely be found. Burying it in a grave was out of the question; they were re-excavated and reused every decade or two.

Before it was quite dark, he had come for a recce and to see if the sexton had left out his spade. There it was, leaning against the wall ready to fill in the earth after the next day's burial. He had cast his eyes around the churchyard mentally visualising the twenty-first century version he had visited with mum, to see what, if anything, remained unchanged. Could the spindly yew trees over near the east end of the church be the same trees in their infancy that he had seen as full-grown aged specimens? He knew that 700 years was no great age for a healthy yew. If he couldn't think of a better plan, he would bury his book under a tree.

So here he was in the dead of night, trying to break the frozen ground. Despite the sub-zero temperature, he broke into a sweat through fear and effort. Once he had pierced through the top layer of frosty ground, the soil gave more easily. He had wrapped the book in his plastic map case with the map he had retrieved from Ed. He tried it for size in the hole then scraped a little more earth from each edge and tried it again. Perfect. It cost him an effort to prise his hand away from the book and start burying it.

Any book was, to Daniel, something to be collected, not discarded. But this book was at the heart of their outlandish adventure. No matter how familiar he was with its contents, might there still be some nugget, a random snippet of information he had overlooked that would unlock the secret of why he was here and how to get home? Even so, the risk of keeping it outweighed that remote chance. From now on, he had to rely on his own powers of observation. What did he need with a book? He was absorbing information first-hand from real people and events in real-time. His own mind was now a historical source.

Suddenly Daniel's skin prickled with goosebumps. He spun round; the gloomy churchyard was still and silent but he sensed he was no longer alone. Here under the yew trees, he was shrouded in velvet darkness. No owl hooted, no twig snapped, but the feeling of being observed grew and intensified. Until a moment ago his mind had focused exclusively on the task in hand, scarcely acknowledging the potential horror of the whole graveyard-at-midnight scenario. Now his head teemed with terrors: zombies, vampires, witches and werewolves converged in a waking nightmare. Daniel turned back urgently to his task. He filled in the hole with three strokes of the spade, trod it down with his foot and turned and fled.

From the dim church doorway, a slight figure emerged, watchful and curious, walked briskly to the tree, and spotted the freshly dug soil. It moved easily after Daniel's hard labour, and the buried object was retrieved without difficulty.

Chapter 50

7th December 1290, Geddington, Northamptonshire

Ed and Daniel's horses blew clouds into the chill air as they led them from the stables to assemble in the courtyard with sleepy-looking knights, squires and grooms. Ed raised a hand in greeting to Warin, before giving Daniel a leg-up and mounting Ruth, on loan from Jim. Servants emerged from outbuildings offering warm bread, cheese and mulled wine to the riders before they departed.

"Do you think the king will be coming?" Ed asked, spraying crumbs from his mouth.

"I doubt it; he's in mourning."

"Yeah, I guess so. Shame."

Daniel tried to feel exhilarated at the prospect of taking part in a medieval hunt, but it was no good. For the first time, he felt like a fish out of water, and utterly vulnerable. It dawned on him that this was how the others had been feeling the whole time. If he got through this in one piece, he would try to be more patient with them. A horn sounded and the riders set out, thankfully at a walk. Dan tried to focus on the present moment and his physical senses - the creak of horses' hooves over compacted snow, the sparkle of branches glistening with frost under the high pale sky. Barely more than an arrow-shot from the palace enclosure, all the riders' heads turned at a distraught female voice behind them.

"Blimey, it's Natalie!" Ed said. She flew towards them, dishevelled hair streaming out behind her. "Nat, what's wrong?"

"It's Jim," she wailed, gasping for breath, "He's gone! I've looked everywhere. And last night he was trying to persuade me to run away with him, back to Lincoln!"

"What a plonker!" said Ed. Their exclamations were interrupted by the approach of a squire,

"Lord Daniel, Otto de Grandisson, sends me to enquire what is amiss, and to ask if he may be of service."

"I thank you, sir. My young cousin, James, has gone missing. We fear he may have foolishly set out alone for Lincoln to search for something he lost there. I fear I must abandon the hunt to look for him."

"Do you require men to aid the search?" the squire said. Daniel paused to weigh the pros and cons of enlisting help.

"My thanks but I believe we three will manage. He is on foot, and we are mounted. He can only have taken the road we came by. If we set out immediately, we must overtake him before too long. Please make my apologies to your master." The squire bowed his agreement, turned and rode away, leaving the young people to their search.

Natalie did not ride out with Daniel and Ed; someone needed to be at the hunting lodge in case Jim turned up. But she couldn't settle. Every half an hour she paced around looking into all the corners she had already searched. There was nowhere to hide in the great hall so she passed through the low, covered walkway into the busy kitchens and turned left through a cloister to the storerooms. Barrels and great jars were stacked high on all sides. Natalie peered into gaps between them and found nothing but rat traps. She dreaded finding one with a rat caught in it. She wasn't scared of rats; on the contrary, she'd always had gerbils or guinea pigs at home and her friend, Sam, kept rats. They were highly intelligent. What she dreaded, on spotting the traps, was finding a rat so seriously injured that she would have to put it out of its misery. She tilted her head towards a noise. It was coming from the far end of the room. Oh, there was a door she hadn't noticed before. And coming from beyond it, human sounds, though not talking; crying perhaps? She reached for the handle, pushed the door open and called,

"Jim, is that you?" There was a confusion of bare, flailing limbs and the door slammed in her face. Natalie ran from the room, her face scarlet and her heart thumping. Beyond the slammed door, Derian collapsed laughing onto the sacking spread out on the floor.

"You told me it was locked!" said Carlita, reaching for her bodice.

"Come, it was only a girl. She won't squeal. Come," he caught her hand and pulled.

"No, not now, not here." Carlita smoothed her hair, checked the coast was clear and left.

∞

Out on the road, Daniel and Ed rode up to the gatehouse at Fineshade Priory to ask after Jim.

"No, my lords, we have admitted no guests since we received the king's party yesterday. But will you come within to take refreshment and warm yourselves against the cold?"

"I thank you but we must press on to find our companion; if he did not seek shelter here, he may have been out all night in this freezing weather," Daniel said, but seeing Ed's crestfallen look, he added, "Yet if you can spare some bread for our journey, that would be most welcome. We left in haste and brought nothing with us." The monk bustled away, leaving the two boys in the shadow of the gatehouse, silently wondering whether Jim could have survived a night out of doors.

The good brother's reappearance was a welcome distraction from their gloomy thoughts. "Here is bread, cheese, a flask of ale and a blanket for your friend. And be assured of our prayers. God grant you find him whole and unharmed."

"Amen to that, brother, and my thanks," said Daniel. He stowed the provisions in his saddlebag; Ed gave him a leg up and they rode back to the highway.

"What if we don't find him?" said Ed, at last voicing the unspoken thought that plagued them both. "How much further will we go before giving up?"

"I don't know. How far he could feasibly have got if he left Geddington at say, midnight, and somehow just managed to keep walking all night? That's what we need to work out, so we know how far to go. I wish I still had my map. If he was still on the road this morning, I guess it's possible he's hitched a ride in a cart."

"Then we'll never catch up with him. He could be all the way back to Stamford by now. We should've let that Otto bloke send some of his men to help us. We'll never find him on our own."

It was unlike Ed to be so negative; Daniel wanted to snap at him but he knew it was just his anxiety talking. "I'm worried about him too, Ed. But to have the best chance of helping him, we need to stay calm and be logical. Walking in the dark, I don't think he could have gone faster than two miles an hour max. So if, by some miracle, he walked all night, he could have gone sixteen miles. We'll ride to Stamford and if we don't find him on the road, we'll ask around for him."

"And then what?"

"We'll cross that bridge if we come to it, Ed. But let's pray we don't."

∞

Back at Geddington, in a quiet bed-chamber, the Watcher of the previous night sat pouring over the wondrous book. Everything about it was strange: the parchment, the binding, the illustrations - exact representations of their subject, and the text, which was far too uniform for even the most gifted scribe to have copied. Though the words were presented very clearly, many were unfamiliar and the Watcher had yet to make sense of it. But there was no mistaking the title, Eleanor of Castile, the picture on the cover, sculptures of the King and the late Queen, and on almost the first page, their genealogies.

The Watcher longed to show the book to someone, but who? And surely then it would be taken out of their hands, given over to the king's guards and, as usual, the Watcher would be side-lined, left in the dark. Moreover, the poor terrified lad who had buried it would certainly be arrested and charged, with what - treason, witchcraft? The book surely held some devilry. But the boy had got rid of the book, not used it. The immediate question was what to do next; yet there seemed no clear way forward except to continue watching.

Elsewhere in the royal lodge, Natalie had just recovered her composure after stumbling upon the lovers, when she was accosted by an elderly man, tall and authoritative but leaning on a stick and looking at her with a friendly spark in his eye.

"Forgive me, my dear, but are you looking for someone?"

"Yes, my friend, I mean cousin. Have you seen him? I can't find him anywhere. I think he's run away but I keep searching the palace anyway in case he's just gone off in a sulk." Tears pricked in her eyes now she voiced it out loud. She said again, "Have you seen him?"

"Not this morning, but in the night. And I fear I may have startled him. He fled from me and I couldn't keep pace with him with this." He waved his stick. "But I am grieved to know he is missing. I thought he was just evading me. I did not imagine he would run clean away. And has no one seen him at all this morning? What does the porter say, at the gate?"

Of course! Why hadn't she thought of that? The porter was the person most in the know about all the comings and goings by day or night.

"Oh, thank you. I hadn't thought of that. I'll go straight away!" And once again the old man was left standing, outpaced by the young, leaning on his stick, and looking wistfully after Natalie.

She crossed the courtyard to the gatehouse and beside it, the porter's lodge. She knocked hesitantly and waited, wishing Daniel was there to do the talking. She needn't have worried. The door opened, the porter took one look at her, put his finger to his lips and opened the door wide, saying,

"Is this what you seek, my lady?" She looked beyond him into the small, neat room and saw Jim, asleep on a bench near the hearth.

He opened his eyes and squinted against the light from the open door, "Nat?" he said.

The sight of him enraged her. She pushed past the porter and as Jim tried to sit up, she shoved him back down, hard. "Ed and Dan are freezing their butts off riding to Stamford to search for you, you tosser, and you never even made it past the gate? What the hell were you playing at - letting us think you'd run away?"

"I did run away. I'm sorry; I know it was dumb. There were wolves - I was scared stiff. So I came back. And the porter said I could sleep here until it was light."

Chapter 51

7th December 1290, Geddington, Northamptonshire

Jim had not really intended to run away, at least not by night. It was the smell of freshly baked bread that began it. He was having a growth spurt at long last and he had the appetite to match it. There was no way he was going to starve himself out of growing. Though the food here was disgusting, he was getting used to it. He'd been trying to get to sleep for hours, and all the while the scent of freshly baked bread tormented him. Once he was sure he was the only person still awake, he got up, picked up his boots and bag, and picked his way gingerly through the sleepers, lying on benches or the rush-covered floor. In the chilly corridor, he slipped on his boots and wrapped his cloak around him for warmth. He followed the scent of the bread which soon brought him to the threshold of the kitchen.

It was lovely and warm with the ovens and fire still burning low. Near the enormous hearth, he could make out the shape of various servants fast asleep. On a large trestle table in the middle of the room lay the cooling bread rolls. He picked up one, then another, and another and put them in his bag.

"Helping ourselves are we, sir?" He spun round; there in the doorway towered a figure. If Jim had kept his cool, he could have brazened his way out of it. After all, he was Lord Daniel's cousin. But in the middle of the night, caught stealing by a tall stranger, his bravado deserted him leaving just a small, hungry, frightened boy. He looked around wildly, spotted another door, burst through it and fled out into the dark. The man pursued him for only a couple of minutes and then retreated back to the warmth. It took a few more minutes for Jim to realise this.

He stopped and leaned over, panting. What to do next? The sensible thing would be to eat his bread, thereby destroying evidence of his crime, then wait for a while before sneaking back, hoping his pursuer would not be waiting for him. But what if he was? Daniel had warned them about the hideous punishments for witchcraft. What would they do to a thief? Cut off a hand? Gruesome visions from his visit to the London Dungeon danced in his head. But what else could he do? He had failed to convince Natalie to run away with him back to Lincoln. She was determined to pin all her hopes on the Geek. But now here he was, away from the others, out in the open with food in his bag and adrenaline coursing through his veins. Maybe this was an opportunity, not a disaster.

All he had to do was retrace his steps first to Stamford, then Grantham, then Lincoln. Three days walking on his own as opposed to however many more, travelling all the way to London. How hard could it be? Now he knew that there were monasteries all over the place, offering free accommodation, finding food and a bed for the night shouldn't be a problem. In fact, hadn't they passed an abbey on the way to Geddington? How far back was it? He couldn't remember. Was it before or after they stopped for lunch? Jim wished he had paid more attention to his surroundings instead of letting them pass him by in a blur. If he could just make it to that abbey for the rest of the night, the monks would take him in and he could get a little sleep before setting out early in the morning.

When he had fled from the hunting lodge just minutes ago, his feet had automatically carried him back the way they had come on entering Geddington. The village lay behind him and he was halfway up the hill. He set his face to the task and began walking. Thankfully it was a clear night and there was enough moonlight, now his eyes had adjusted, to make out the road. The adrenaline was beginning to wear off; he started to feel the cold night air seeping in around his neck but walking uphill soon warmed him up. He would be all right if he kept moving.

Jim had never known such quiet. The only sound was from his own footsteps and breath. Silence had always unnerved him but right now, silence was good, silence meant there was nothing "out there" in the tangible darkness that lay at the edges of the track. But it couldn't last. Soon his ears attuned to the nighttime rustlings and scurryings, in the same way his eyes had attuned to the darkness. On either side of him, the woodland was alive. It was a royal hunting forest, Daniel had said. So Jim imagined the animals - mainly deer. Were they active at night? He didn't know. Foxes, rabbits, squirrels, owls, mice, what else? Bats? None of them were dangerous he told himself.

He wished he had a stick. Duh - he was walking through a forest. At the top of the hill, Jim stepped aside into the wood to try to find one. The change from dimness to utter inky darkness took his breath away, and he shot straight out again to the road. As he did so a large shadow stalked across the path, two bright eyes gleaming straight at him. He ran. Just a deer, just a stupid deer he told himself, as he pelted down the hill. His momentum carried him halfway up the next rise, where he slowed and bent over to get his breath back and started laughing. A deer, a bloody deer. I've got to pull myself together. It's people I need to worry about here, not freaking animals. But that was where he was wrong.

Jim had been walking for about an hour when his hunger resurfaced. He rummaged in his bag for the bread and ate one roll. It left him dry but he had nothing to drink. The road bent to the left and after about ten more minutes, a right turn led him into denser woodland. The trees almost met overhead, and even though they were bare, the road at his feet became almost invisible, so he felt like he was floating. And then he heard it, distant but distinct. A howl. Behind him and to his right. And then another. Bloody hell. It can't be wolves. There aren't any wolves in England. What else howls except wolves? The next howl set him running. If only he'd picked up a stick. What else could he use? He didn't have a flaming torch like in the movies. Torch!

He groped in his bag for his phone. Please God there's enough power for the torch. He mustn't put it on yet; he had to save the battery. And surely wolves would be chasing deer, not people, wouldn't they? On and on he ran. The howls came intermittently and he told himself they weren't getting any closer. He caught a glint of water as the road crossed a stream. He hesitated; he was dying for a drink but did he dare stop? Another howl, much closer. He ran on, his senses taut and alive to every sound and movement.

Chapter 52

7th December 1290, near Geddington, Northamptonshire

The next sound Jim's ear caught was not a howl but a human voice, singing, some way over to his left. A path led off the road in that direction and he plunged down it, drawn to the faint melody as to a siren's song. Jim's bag snagged on brambles and he stumbled over roots but his momentum somehow kept him on his feet. Please keep singing, please keep singing. She did. And at last, he came to a small clearing with two low buildings, both wonderfully glowing with candlelight. The singing came from a tiny chapel and he burst through the door without a care for what lay on the other side.

Despite her heavenly voice, she was not an angel. She lacked the dignity and also, at this precise moment, serenity, with her wide, green, startled eyes and her arms raised high, clutching a heavy candlestick against her would-be assailant.

"Oh!" they both said. Then also together, "I'm sorry." The woman replaced the candlestick on the small plain altar table and turned to face Jim. He saw with relief that she was relatively young, for he dreaded being alone with an old crone like Aerlene at Lincoln.

"Forgive me, I was startled. Welcome, all are welcome here, whatever brings them to my door. For you, it is the wolves, I make no doubt. How came you alone in the woods by night? But no, that business is your own. You may tell me if you wish. I am Judith."

"Jim, I mean James. I didn't mean to scare you. The wolves – I... I didn't even know there were wolves in England."

"King Edward has ordered that all wolves be killed in other parts further north and west than here. They are not so plentiful here but there are some."

"Do you live alone, out here in the woods? Aren't you scared?" Jim asked.

"Yes, I live alone. I am a hermit. And yes, despite my faith in God, I am subject to fear. It would be foolhardy not to respect the wolf. I was saying the midnight matins when the howling began. I confess that I feared to walk back across to my home and was singing to bolster my courage and my faith. Yet now I wonder if God's Spirit prompted me to sing, to guide you here to safety. Be that as it may, you are now safe, James, and what is more, I am too. There is comfort in company. Let us go across and I will warm you some broth."

Judith picked up a tiny oil lamp and Jim followed her dutifully out into the night. A few strides took them from one small building to the other. Unlike the bare chapel, the homestead was cluttered with pots and pans, tools and blankets, simple wooden furniture and a spinning wheel. The mess rendered it so homely that tears pricked his eyes. Judith flitted around making space, inviting him to sit, lighting little clay lamps and stirring up the fire. He perched on a stool by the fire and warmed his hands. He didn't know how to speak to a hermit; he didn't really know what a hermit was. But once Judith set him at his ease, he could have talked all night.

An hour before Prime, Judith lit a torch and accompanied Jim out into the morning darkness. They retraced Jim's path through the woods and back down towards the river and the royal palace of Geddington.

"You don't need to come in with me," said Jim, "Even if someone is waiting inside to report me for stealing the bread, I have to face it on my own."

"My prayers go with you, James, now and always. God has laid you on my heart as you are also on His. I believe you will find your way home, but if you do not, my door will always be open to you. God go with you. I will watch from here until you are within." Jim had no words to express the gratitude he felt and tears threatened, so he merely nodded and turned towards whatever lay ahead, before his newfound courage evaporated.

At the gatehouse, Jim told the porter his name and explained that he was part of the cortege but had lost his way. Telling this fib gave him an unfamiliar twinge of conscience. Yet, he realised that in a sense it was true. How long ago he had lost his way was a matter to come back to another time.

"Be that as it may, young sir, I cannot rightly let you go in without rousing someone who can vouch for you," said the guard, not unkindly.

"Oh. But I wouldn't want you to wake my cousin. Can we leave it until morning?"

"If you do not mind lodging here within for an hour or two, I will then go to seek your cousin." Jim agreed heartily, relieved beyond measure not to have to face his friends or his accuser until he had slept.

The porter showed him into the lodge and made him as comfortable as he could, on a bench by the fire. Within seconds Jim was asleep. The porter also nodded off until the horses of the hunting party clattered on the cobbles outside and he went to open the gates to let the huntsmen out.

When he returned, his charge showed no sign of waking, so he set off to enquire after Lord Daniel, whom the lad claimed as kin, only to discover that he had ridden out with the huntsmen. No harm in letting the lad sleep on.

Chapter 53

7th December 1290

Daniel and Ed set out again from Stamford in the fading light, wretchedly empty-handed. Each was lost in his own feelings. Ed was simply concerned for his friend but Daniel's anguish was a more complex blend of guilt, about being unable to hold his little band together, and anxiety over what to do next. Should they break away from the cortege to head back to Lincoln looking for Jim? Or plead for help in the search, possibly delaying the royal procession. He was no closer to deciding between these equally unappealing options when the gatehouse of the hunting lodge loomed out of the darkness and Natalie came running out with welcome news that made Daniel's decision unnecessary, since Jim was safe and well.

∞

8th December 1290, Northamptonshire

The following morning saw Daniel limping stiffly across the palace courtyard. Ed looked on, holding his horse.

"Rather you than me, mate," Ed said, giving him a bunk up, only too glad he didn't have to ride, since he was as saddle-sore himself. Daniel swore under his breath and shifted from cheek to cheek in the saddle, vainly trying to find a more comfortable position. He was so focussed on stifling the urge to wince and groan at each movement of the horse under him, that they passed the cross site before he was aware.

"Oh, that was the cross site; shall we get down and try it?" he said, turning to Jim.

"Only if you think it's worthwhile," Jim said.

"Yeah, let's give it a go. We've got nothing to lose, have we?"

Daniel turned his horse aside and dismounted with an involuntary gasp. Natalie shot Jim a filthy look and he turned away. "You hold the horses, Ed, but if we disappear, just let them go and follow us as quickly as you can." Ed nodded. The other three walked back and forth near to the spot, pretending to search for something they had dropped, as the wagons of the cortege rumbled towards the bridge. As the last cart passed them, they remounted and rode on, splashing through the ford, Daniel reflecting that they hadn't seen the monk who usually prayed on the ground at the cross site. The blessing of the spot was probably done yesterday, while he and Ed were away searching for Jim.

Only Daniel was sorry to leave Geddington behind; most of his time there had been absorbed in lurching from one crisis to the next leaving little energy or opportunity to explore the royal hunting lodge. Now he was riding away from it. The road wound up through the last straggly buildings of Geddington, through woods and back to the King's Highway where the snowy landscape fell away in giant ripples.

Daniel's eyes moved from the Christmas card scenery to his companions. Ed looked his usual self, plodding placidly, if somewhat stiffly, in his customary position between the two horses. But the other two appeared to have switched moods. Natalie was tetchy if spoken to and sullen if not. Jim, on the other hand, had got up this morning without grumbling, been polite to the servants who served breakfast and almost deferential towards Daniel. Whatever had happened to him during yesterday's escapade he seemed to have come through it unscathed and somehow, what was the word – chastened?

And indeed, in his mind's eye, Jim was back in Judith's hut and she was sloshing a second helping of delicious-smelling stew into a wooden bowl he held out; the first good food he had tasted since his last school breakfast - was it only 5 days ago? It felt like a month. His mouth watered at the thought of how its flavours had caressed his mouth like a warm blanket. But was it really any better than the other medieval food he'd been eating, or did he just appreciate it so much more, through sheer relief at being safe after the terror of the wolves? He thought about Judith herself: it was as if by looking at him she knew exactly what he needed. She had let him eat his fill and then sleep.

When he woke, he saw her watching over him like a young mother over her baby. And the whole story had poured out of him like a river through a broken dam; a haphazard tumble of anger, bewilderment and self-pity. How much she really understood he would never know. He suspected that his talk of the future passed her by. But she grasped the essence. She had listened, then contemplated, then said simply,

"You are afraid that you cannot get home."

"Yes."

"So home is good and here is bad?"

"Yes; no; not exactly. Home is what I'm used to; but there are things I don't like about it."

"So home is good and bad; good and bad that you know. And here is good and bad also. Bad that you know, and good that you do not yet know."

"Maybe."

"Only Heaven is purely good, only hell purely bad. Here on earth, we live with both, and at every moment we must choose which to follow. In this holy season of Advent, we look to Christ's coming, light into darkness; and now, in this darkest time of the year, we turn towards the light." Jim shifted uneasily in his seat but said nothing. Judith continued, "And your companions from home, Edward like the king, I remember but the other names I forget."

"Daniel and Natalie."

"Yes, Edward, Daniel and Natalie - they too are good and bad, like you and I. Do they want to get home as much as you?"

"Yes, I guess so."

"So you can trust them."

"I suppose."

"Can they trust you?" Judith added softly. Jim hung his head. "Come to the chapel and pray with me. Then we will see what is to be done." She rose and opened the door and what could Jim do but follow her? It was unlike any experience he'd had before - kneeling next to Judith on the chapel floor, ignoring the cold creeping into his legs and spreading through his body, and for once opening himself to some introspection. It wasn't pretty, what he saw when he looked inside himself, but somehow the faith-filled hope radiating from the bizarre young woman next to him shielded him from despair. In the darkness of the year, we turn to the light. It sounded so simple, but he knew it wouldn't be.

Jim surfaced from his reverie and looked round. His gaze fell first on Ed - stolidly leading his horse. Ed caught his gaze and grinned,

"Alright, Jim?" Jim nodded and smiled back, not trusting himself to speak. Judith's challenge came back to him. "Can your companions trust *you*?" Jim shifted his eyes to Daniel, who, as usual, was staring out at the landscape, looking for his precious birds. What possible reason could Daniel ever have to trust me, Jim asked himself? And if he was honest, Ed and Natalie had even less reason, because they knew him better. Based on past experience, none of these three had any cause whatsoever to trust him further than they could chuck him, yet so far in this weird adventure each of them had done their utmost to help him.

What else had Judith said about turning to the light? "We must open our eyes and look for it in each other." He thought about it. There was Ed, walking all these miles in the freezing cold and now he thought about it, Jim hadn't heard him moan once. And even Natalie, who was a whinger at the best of times, was putting it up with everything amazingly well. He didn't understand how they managed it. But he recognised he needed them, if he was ever to get home. And if they couldn't get home, he would need them even more. And maybe they needed him too. At any rate, they needed him not to be such a complete arsehole.

∞

At the front of the cortege, Robert Burnell rode beside the king. It pained Robert to witness Edward's zeal to leave Geddington, with all its memories of hunting trips spent there with Eleanor. During the last two days, he had only spoken to transact royal business. Counter to expectation Edward had joined his men for the hunt and driven his horse and himself so hard that Robert had worried for his safety. As they crossed the bridge by the ford, Robert cast around in his mind for something to say to distract the king,

"Your Grace, you recall the young Lord of Orkney I told you about?"

"The one whose party was robbed on the road?"

"Aye. He was to have joined the hunting party yesterday, but his young cousin had gone missing and he cried off to search for him."

"And they found him, I collect."

"Aye, my lord. Yet I cannot help but wonder if the so-called disappearance was a ruse to avoid the hunt."

"Why so, Robert? Do you think he is soft? Or a deceiver?"

"I cannot say, your Grace. He seems innocent enough; indeed, he seems an amiable lad, though young for his years. But I am not quite easy in my mind about his tale. To journey all the way from Orkney to London to pray seems unlikely, however devoted a man may be."

"Yet you say he seems innocent. Perhaps he just wanted to see some of the world before he takes up the mantle of lordship in his father's stead." The king adjusted his seat in the saddle, sore after yesterday's hunt. "Robert, I have it in mind to stay at the castle in Northampton instead of the abbey."

"Yes, your Grace, I will send a rider ahead at once to warn them." Robert peeled away to the right and trotted back along the procession to find the Clerk of the Marshalsea and add this change of plan to the poor man's burdens.

A little further back in the procession, the Watcher turned in the saddle and scanned the crowd behind, looking for the boy with the book, but could not pick him out. He must be too far back. It would have to wait.

Chapter 54

8th December 1290, Northampton

As the cortege passed Abington Abbey, a cacophony erupted in the skies above and Warin looked up, as did everyone else. He saw a skein of geese flying low, in an elongated arrow shape, across the darkening sky. Beneath the din of their honking, he heard a mellower rhythmic wheeze - their steady wing beats. Warin craned his neck to see their destination and caught his first glimpse of the river Nene, its marshy floodplains and pools gleaming faintly in the dying embers of the sun. After this first flock, more and more geese followed in their wake, their V shapes trailing in the dusk like ribbons.

"There must be hundreds of them!" Warin said.

"They are wise enough to seek the safety of numbers as they go to their rest. God grant that we too are nearing our night's shelter," said Brother Clément. "I for one am more than ready for a warm meal and a place to sleep."

"Amen to that, brother."

These two weary walkers kept companionable silence in the deepening dusk of the last leg of the journey. As they passed beneath the echoing gatehouse of the walled city of Northampton, a squire, whose face Warin recognised, approached him with a curt message from Lord Robert Burnell. Warin was summoned to the castle without delay, to appear before the Chancellor. Clément saw his friend blench; his eyes suddenly frantic. Without a word, he began to follow the squire as if walking to the scaffold.

"God go with you, my lad; I'm sure you have nothing to fear," Clément called after his young friend. He watched Warin trudge after the squire until they turned a corner. So I was right, he thought; all this time the poor boy has been harbouring some secret fear. And try as I might I could not coax it out of him. Lord Burnell has more persuasive methods, no doubt. I pray he may not need to use them.

∞

In the warm refectory of the convent of Saint Mary De la Pré, Jim sat quietly, attempting to find the right words. However he framed them in his head, they sounded lame or ridiculous, or both. In the end, he gave up trying to find the perfect formula and blurted out,

"Look, I'm sorry for running away. It was dumb; I see that now." He flushed crimson and, as if the blush was infectious, the others did too.

"No worries, mate," said Ed.

"You came back, that's the main thing," Daniel said. "To be honest, you got us out of the hunting party and who knows what would have happened if I'd tried to shoot anything." They chuckled and Jim looked at Natalie. He knew she was still angry with him; she had hardly spoken all day. There was an awkward silence as a wave of emotions that Jim couldn't interpret passed over her face. Then she said,

"It's over now and no harm done, Jim."

But there was harm done. After dinner, Jim started to shiver and went to lie down. His throat had started feeling sore mid-afternoon and by the time they reached Northampton, his head had begun to pound. But uncharacteristically, he had said nothing.

"Shall I give him some of my paracetamol?" Natalie asked Daniel.

"Only if he definitely has a temperature; otherwise, we need to save it. There should be an infirmary here. That's a kind of mini-hospital. The nuns will have herbal medicines; I'll go and see what I can find."

Daniel decided to go to Vespers to look around for someone approachable to help him. He arrived at the church too early and found it almost empty, apart from a young novice kneeling to polish a brass plaque on the floor.

"Good evening, sister," Daniel said. The girl stood up and made him an awkward reverence. "Oh, I don't mean to disturb your work," he continued, "My cousin is ill and I'm looking for the infirmary."

"I will show you, my lord, please follow me." Daniel followed her through the dimly lit cloister, across an alleyway and into a low building against the outer wall. She entered and approached a tall, middle-aged nun,

"Sister Benedicta, here is a young lord from the king's party whose cousin is ill." And before Daniel could thank her the novice was gone.

"What ails your cousin, my lord? I can wait upon him after Vespers, or now, if it is urgent."

"I believe it is only a common cold, but he is a little feverish. I wouldn't trouble you, only he must be fit to ride tomorrow when the cortege departs."

"If he has a fever, he will not be fit to ride; the king will have to do without him. Can he be spared and join you later?" Daniel caught more than a hint of irony in her tone.

"We are of no importance whatever to the king. His grace has allowed us to come under the protection of the cortege since we too are heading to Westminster. But for reasons of our own, it's essential that we keep our place in the procession."

"Bring him to me after Vespers and we shall see what can be done. And if he is too unwell to come here, send word and I will attend upon you in the guest quarters."

"Thank you, sister."

The nun turned back to her other charges. Daniel made his way back through the shadowy arches of the cloister. Though less grand, it reminded him of Lincoln. In the cloisters there, in his own time, there was a café. He thought of the hot chocolate and cupcakes and his mouth watered. A wave of homesickness washed over him, and he swallowed back the bile that pushed up his throat. One of the strangest elements of being here was that everyone treated him as an adult. At home, it irked him to be talked down to but right now he longed for someone to tell him what to do or, even better, take over completely and sort it all out. Perhaps being an adult wasn't all it was cracked up to be.

Chapter 55

8th December 1290, Northampton

At the castle keep, Warin was shown into a large, draughty room. Two sentries guarded the door which swung shut with a hollow clang, leaving him alone with the foremost official in the land. Warin made a gesture of obeisance to the Chancellor, lowering his head and staring at Burnell's fine leather boots, which made his pair look even shabbier.

"You are Warin of Fordingbridge, apprentice to the court goldsmith, Derian Scand?"

"Aye, my l-l-lord, I am at your s-s-service."

Burnell took in the lad's appearance. His clothes were somewhat threadbare for a member of the court, however lowly. He noted Warin's workmanlike hands wringing the edges of his tunic. Good, the poor lad's terrified, he thought; plenty of time later to put him at his ease if he tells me what I want to know. Burnell held silence a little longer, and adjusted his heavy fur-lined mantle.

"A report has reached me that you are in possession of sensitive information; information which may pertain to the demise of the late queen; information of a treasonous nature, which you have deliberately withheld," he said.

"My lord, I did not keep silent of my own accord," Warin's words tumbled out in a tremulous squeak. "The chaplain at Clipstone bade me keep my counsel and I have, though the awful secret has burned in my mind, night and day. Father David took it upon himself to decide not to inform the authorities and who am I to gainsay a priest? I could not speak out, though I swear I longed to with all my heart."

The Chancellor let out a non-committal sound and said, "That accords with Father David's letter. I see your predicament, though I do not excuse your secrecy. So, tell me your tale and I will decide what action, if any, will be taken against you." The Chancellor sat down at a desk, steepled his hands and listened attentively as Warin at last unburdened himself. At the close of Warin's account, Burnell took pity on the lad and beckoned him nearer the fire.

"Might you be in error about the words Master Scand muttered, this so-called curse?" he said.

"No, my lord. At first, I was so shocked that I thought I must be mistaken; so I listened until I was utterly sure. He repeated it over and over. And I was standing no further from him than I am from you, though his back was towards me."

Such details certainly made the lad's tale ring true, Burnell reflected.

"And what is your opinion of the effectiveness of this curse? Do you consider it to have contributed to the queen's death?"

"My lord, that question torments me but I do not know," Warin wailed. "All I know is what is commonly known, that she was suffering from her usual winter ailment but this time she did not rally."

"And what is your opinion of Master Scand's intention? Did he indeed mean to kill?"

"Of that I am in no doubt, my lord. He meant to kill."

"And no one else knows of this? Only yourself and the chaplain, Father—" he glanced down at the missive on the desk, "Father David."

"Aye, my lord."

"Then let it remain so. I will take no action against you on this occasion, since you obeyed the priest's instruction. But if, at any future time, information pertaining to royal security reaches your ears, you are to bring it directly to the authorities. If you do not, by all the saints, the full weight of the law will fall upon you."

"I will, my lord, upon my oath."

"Very well. Now come, sit down by the fire and take your ease," Burnell gestured to a stool on one side of the hearth. He watched Warin perch on it, and came and settled himself on a bench facing the boy.

"What more can you tell me about your master?" he said.

"He is my father's cousin, my lord, though until I became his apprentice, I had only seen him once, when I was a small boy."

Burnell already knew, from Father David's letter, of the kinship between Scand and his apprentice, but he was pleased Warin acknowledged it freely. It was another mark of the boy's trustworthiness. He gave Warin an encouraging smile and the lad continued.

"My family travelled to his wife Rebecca's burial. She died in childbirth, along with the child; I never saw her living but, by all accounts, she was a beauty."

"Before this curse, have you ever had reason to suspect your master of any evil or crime?" Burnell asked.

"No, my lord." Warin paused, thinking. "Though my father may know something to the purpose. When Master Derian came to offer to take me on, I am sure he confided something to my father. There was some secret between them." He paused again, staring over Burnell's shoulder. "And my mother was not easy in her mind about my being apprenticed. Father and Derian persuaded her. I overheard her saying to my father, 'Recall the rumours when Rebecca died. Why did Derian not send for the midwife, though the woman herself told me she was at home and could have come in a moment?'"

"Hmm. That is but hearsay. How does your master treat you, Warin?"

"Master Derian is somewhat free with his fists, my lord, but I dare say I often deserve it. I fear that I try his patience sorely. I do try to learn the craft, but I am not skilled at dainty work."

Here Burnell saw a potential question: the boy was clearly downtrodden, and often beaten.

"Warin, you must be aware that if Master Scand loses his place at court, you stand to lose yours too. How can I be sure you have not fabricated the tale about the curse to avoid serving out the long years of an apprenticeship which does not suit you?"

Warin gasped. "My lord, my father invested all he had for my training. I would not put it in jeopardy, not for all the world."

"Be at peace, Warin. I believe you. But if I pursue this matter, other men will have to be persuaded. Are you willing to testify against your master, whatever the consequences?"

"I will do whatever you think right, my lord."

"I have much to consider, Warin. I may summon you again." Warin departed, leaving behind him a grave and troubled Lord Chancellor. A steward entered the room bearing a goblet of wine on a tray. Burnell snatched it up and barked, "Fetch Otto de Grandisson."

Chapter 56

8th December 1290, Northampton

Daniel led Jim through the dim, draughty cloister to the infirmary. "Good evening, my lords, I have been expecting you. Please be seated here, by the lamp," said Sister Benedicta.

"This is my cousin, James, sister," Daniel said. Without ceremony, the infirmaress felt Jim's forehead, took his pulse and held up the lamp to examine the back of his throat.

"Yes, a mild fever and a sore throat. Not too troublesome for a fit young man. Only the elderly, such as my charges here, need fear a chill such as this. I will make up a tincture of herbs and honey for you to gargle. And a sleeping draught if you wish?" She swept away into a small anteroom.

"I feel like death," groaned Jim. "She doesn't know what she's talking about; let's go before she comes back." He had hoped the infirmaress would be like Judith but she was more like a strident teacher.

"You stay put, Jim. We have to take what help we can get to give you the best chance of sleeping off this cold and feeling better in the morning."

"Yeah, right. Like some medieval herbs are gonna cure this overnight. I've got flu or something worse." Dan was spared from answering this by the return of the sister.

First, she handed Jim a warm, opaque bottle stoppered with a cork, "Gargle with half of this before retiring and the rest in the morning." Then she gave him a tiny clay jar that sat snugly in the palm of his hand. "This smaller vial is a sleeping draught." She looked him up and down as if mentally measuring him, "Take only a few drops in a small drink of ale or mead, otherwise you will be too drowsy to ride in the morning."

"We thank you, sister, and bid you good night," Daniel said, nudging Jim who caught the hint and mumbled his thanks.

The infirmary door creaked shut behind them. Daniel steered Jim towards the lavatorium in the cloister as he knew of no other sink they could use.

"Try the gargle here, Jim, by the sink thing, if the liquid's not too hot still." Jim uncorked the bottle, sniffed it cautiously, then took a sip.

"Urrrgh!" he yelled, spraying it everywhere. "I'm not drinking that! It's gross!"

"You're not meant to drink it, idiot; it's a gargle. You gargle it."

"What's a bloody gargle?"

Daniel was momentarily stunned. "Well it's ... it's ... surely you know how to gargle."

"You don't know either!" said Jim.

"I do. I've done it loads of times, usually with salt water or mouthwash. But it's hard to put into words. Hang on a minute. Don't go anywhere, I'm coming straight back."

He trotted away with Jim trailing after him, croaking,

"I'm not staying there on my own. It's freaking creepy." Daniel found the others and swiped Ed's drink.

"Oi, I was enjoying that."

"Sorry, I need it for a gargling demo!" Daniel said and turned on his heels back to the cloister.

Ed and Natalie followed, intrigued.

Daniel stood at the sink, "Right, Jim, to gargle, you take a mouthful of the liquid without swallowing; then tip your head back and kind of blow through your throat, so the stuff bubbles around at the back of your throat. Then spit it out. He took a swig of Ed's ale, tipped his head back, gargled, then spat.

"Gross," said Natalie.

"Go on, Jim. Give it a go," Ed said with a grin.

Jim scowled, "It's all right for you, doing it with beer. This stuff is disgusting!" He waved the little bottle in Daniel's face. But he took the cork out anyway, stepped up to the sink and took a mouthful. He tilted his head back started to gargle, spluttered and spurted the liquid into the air. The others tried to stifle their laughter but failed. Jim coughed, wincing at his sore throat.

"Get lost, you lot," Jim said. "I'll get the hang of it if I can do it on my own." They backed off. Jim smiled to himself as they walked away. He could see the funny side and for once, he didn't mind being the butt of the joke.

"I'll wait for you on the other side of this door," Daniel called, remembering Jim's fear, a few minutes ago, at being left alone in the cloister. Jim gave him a thumbs up.

∞

A weary Warin followed the squire through the dark cobbled streets of Northampton to the convent. By the time he stepped through the wicket of the gate, his teeth were chattering wildly, from a mixture of shock, relief and the gnawing cold. Clément, pacing in the courtyard, released a long breath and rushed to meet his young friend, rejoicing to see him whole and unscathed. Warin's blue eyes lit up at the warmth of his welcome, but he raised a warning hand,

"Do not question me, brother. I am not permitted to speak of what has passed."

"It is enough for me to see you free and well, lad, albeit chilled to the marrow. Come within and we will soon have you warm and fed."

Chapter 57

9ᵗʰ December 1290, Northamptonshire

The next morning in the priory courtyard, the extraordinary sweetness of the nuns' morning praises stilled the hubbub of the gathering cortege. Servants tiptoed about their business, dry bread rolls became a holy feast and even the horses, sensing the atmosphere, stepped softly from the stables over the chill, compacted earth.

The blessing of the cross site, almost opposite the convent gatehouse, followed its customary format. Daniel recalled that this would be one of the three crosses still standing in their own time. He and his companions had, by tacit consent, dropped the practice of pacing round the spot hoping to find a time portal. For one thing, they couldn't pretend day after day to be looking for something they had lost. But as they rode past the site, Daniel once again noticed the monk lying prostrate in prayer. When he turned his attention back to the road ahead, he saw the king and his immediate entourage riding ahead at a faster pace than the rest of the procession. They soon disappeared from view.

By the time they halted at Towcester for a midday break, the early cloud cover had thinned and dissipated, brightening the day and cooling the air. All through the chilly afternoon, the cortege followed the arrow-straight course of Watling Street, heading southeast.

Towards dusk, the road became a causeway above the surrounding boggy landscape.

"I wonder where we're stopping tonight?" Ed said to Jim.

"Google it," Jim replied, tossing his head at Daniel, "We have our very own walking Wikipedia, remember?"

"Thank you, Jim; I'll take that as a compliment. I think the next place is called Stony Stratford. I've never been there but apparently it's the main place for crossing a big river, the Ouse. We must be getting close - look at the reeds, this is marshy land." As he spoke, the sky over their heads darkened with birds and the shushing of a thousand wing beats.

"What the hell?" squealed Natalie instinctively ducking and cowering.

"Chill, Nats, they're just starlings," said Ed. The entire royal procession faltered and fell quiet as the birds streamed over their heads towards the marshes. And as they watched, the vast and still-growing flock coalesced and began wheeling and arcing en masse, undulating like waves in a restless aerial ocean.

"Whoa! It's like a dance! How do they do that?" said Natalie.

"I've no idea. Awesome, isn't it?" Daniel said. "I think it's called a murmuration; a form of self-defence to confuse predators. I've seen it on television but never in real life."

"Look! Is that an eagle?" said Ed. They followed Ed's finger pointing towards an elegant, long-winged bird of prey soaring on the fringes of the murmuration, its russet wings backlit by the dying sun.

"A marsh harrier, maybe?" said Daniel. Up and down the royal cortege, king and bishop, lords and servants stood in silent awe, as the gigantic flock of birds spiralled and flowed, painting shadow pictures in the sky, until abruptly they descended and vanished into the reedbed. A collective sigh issued from the onlookers. Gradually movement and sound began again along the royal train, though for long minutes everyone spoke softly and moved reverently, as if in church.

The bridge over the Great Ouse carried Watling Street from the upper to the lower part of the settlement of Stony Stratford. The cortege passed by the respectful inhabitants, and at the southern end of the town, it was met by a delegation of monks. Robert of Ramsay stepped forward and welcomed them in the name of the brothers of the Priory of St Mary at Bradwell. The queen's bier was again lowered at the side of the road and the site blessed by Bishop Oliver and Prior Robert. The last part of the journey lagged achingly; the riders were obliged to keep in step with the monks, who saw fit to match their pace to the great dignity of the occasion rather than the needs of their cold and weary guests.

Later in the evening two of those guests had managed to find a private corner of Bradwell Priory. Derian and Carlita were so engrossed in each other that they failed to hear the heavy tread of soldiers approaching the door. Three of the king's guards burst in and filled the room. The foremost one, boomed,

"Derian Scand, in the name of King Edward, I arrest you on suspicion of treason." Derian whirled about; his eyes skittered this way and that for an escape route but he was hemmed in. His frantic glare locked on Carlita. As if on cue, her head rolled back, her knees buckled and she sank languidly to the floor. In the ensuing moment of confusion, Derian sprang forward, limbs flailing in all directions to ward off the guards' lunging hands. He launched himself directly at the soldier nearest the door, toppling and trampling him. He erupted into the passageway and hurtled down the stairs, blundering straight into the crossed pikes of the guards posted at the exit. Stunned for only a moment, Derian found his feet and surged up with inhuman strength. But they were ready for him. A blow to his head knocked him senseless.

The three guards from upstairs emerged, shamefaced before their more successful colleagues. They bound his hands and feet while he was still unconscious and dragged him unceremoniously to the priory penitentiary cells to await Robert Burnell's pleasure.

∞

"Did you see the king and his guards at all this evening?" said Daniel. Jim shrugged, Ed and Natalie shook their heads, intent on mopping up the dregs of their stew with some bread.

"Maybe he's staying somewhere else, a castle or something like he did at Northampton?" suggested Ed.

"Yeah, it's not exactly five-star accommodation here, is it?" said Natalie.

"Mmm. I have a vague idea that the king left the cortege part way through and re-joined later, nearer London. I wish I still had my book, so I could check."

"What difference does it make to us?" asked Jim, slurping his ale.

"None really. I just want to be in the know about what's going on around us. So there's less stuff that could take us by surprise."

"I could ask Warin when I see him at the stables. He might know. But I don't know what I'll get out of him - he was a bit weird in Northampton, not himself."

"Yeah, good idea Ed, no harm in asking, as my dad would say." They fell silent, each thinking of homes, parents, siblings and the thousand other ties that the mention of 'dad' evoked.

∞

King Edward was in fact at Saint Alban's, closeted in the abbot's parlour with Master Richard Crundall, who was saying,

"If I understand correctly, your Grace, this twelfth cross is to be erected somewhere between the Dominican Priory here," pointing at the roughly sketched map spread on the table before them, "and the palace and abbey of Westminster."

"Yes; in fact I already have a particular spot in mind, though I will not make the final decision until the cortege reaches the place. My cousin was an anchorite, walled up in her cell in a little place called Charing, here on this bend on the river," the king said, pointing. "She was a renowned holy woman and people came from miles around to seek her counsel. My late wife herself visited her after the death of our son, Alfonso, and was much comforted. It would please me to know that people would pray for Eleanor's soul in a place where she herself found consolation."

"Most fitting indeed, your Grace," said Crundall, surprised and somewhat flattered that the king should be so frank. He rummaged among the papers on the table and placed a sketch on top of the map. "And to come back to the cross itself: I envisage a number of steps for elevation, an octagonal conical pillar housing eight statues of the late queen, topped with a gilded wooden cross."

"Yes, and the very finest marble. Though it will stand beyond the city wall, in a spot less visited than some of the other eleven crosses, I am in no doubt that London will grow in the coming decades and encroach on these outlying villages."

"Yet does the Fleet River not obstruct the city's spread in that direction, your Grace?"

The king waved his arm dismissively. "You astonish me, Crundall. You must know a river can be diverted or even directed underground by way of a system of culverts. The Fleet is but a small river; no barrier to today's master builders."

"It is indeed marvellous what can be achieved, your Grace," the mason said, chastened.

The king continued, "I have no doubt London will expand greatly, perhaps even as far as Westminster itself. This twelfth cross will commemorate my wife to future generations in our great city. No expense is to be spared, you understand?"

"I understand perfectly. I will submit my final designs by the feast of the Nativity. Now, with your Grace's permission, I will take my leave." The king inclined his head; Crundall gathered his papers, rose and bowed.

Chapter 58

10th December 1290, Bradwell Priory, Stony Stratford, Buckinghamshire - Midnight

On one side of the hastily arranged impromptu courtroom sat twelve important men, six representatives each of church and state. On the other side, the defendant, Derian Scand. Chancellor Burnell stood up, tall, authoritative, dignified.

"My lords, please pardon the lateness of the hour. A matter has arisen of the gravest nature, which can only be dealt with by night, since we spend each day travelling. The queen's cortege must not be delayed." Turning to Scand, he continued, "Derian Scand, you are charged with High Treason, namely that you did wilfully attempt the assassination of the late Queen, Eleanor, Consort of His Grace, King Edward. How do you plead?"

Scand rose and eyed Burnell across the chamber, "My lord, I decline to plead," he stated in a tone oozing derision, "for I do not recognise the validity of this court. Before me sit twelve great men, that I do not deny, but among them I see neither serjeant-at-law, nor sheriff, neither justice of the king's bench nor any other person authorised to hear my case. If I am to plead, I demand fair trial before a judge and in daylight." He sat down, still holding Burnell's gaze.

A clamour of voices erupted in the room.

"Silence!" roared Burnell. He paused to regain his composure. "Allow me to name the twelve great men, as you call them, whose legal authority you do not deign to recognise. Nay, better, I call on them to introduce themselves." He gestured to the nearest, who stood up.

"Henry de Lacy, Earl of Lincoln, Baron of Pontefract, Baron of Halton, Constable of Chester, Lord of Denbigh, Councillor to his Grace, the king." As he sat down, his neighbour stood up.

"William de Leyburn, Constable of Pevensey."

"Otto de Grandisson, Knight of Savoy."

"Walter Langton, Keeper of the King's Wardrobe."

"John de Weston, Steward to Queen Eleanor."

"Hugh of Cressingham, also Steward to the Queen."

"Oliver, Bishop of Lincoln."

"William de Rybus, Prior of Saint Leonard's Priory, Stamford."

"Robert of Ramsey, Prior of Bradwell."

"Galf de Gropes, Priest of Saint Mary Magdalene's, Geddington."

"William of Hakburn, priest of Saint Wulfram's, Grantham."

"Nicholas de Culham, Abbot of Saint Mary's Abbey, Abington."

Lord Burnell rose again, "Robert Burnell, Lord Chancellor of England, Bishop of Bath and Wells." With these lengthy and somewhat unnecessary introductions (for Scand knew very well who most of them were and had made jewellery for several of them), Burnell had bought himself time to formulate a response to Derian's unforeseen objection. He continued,

"Master Scand, be aware that the unconventional nature of this court arises purely from my concern not to add to the king's burdens at this sad time. We have no reason to avoid due legal process. If these arrangements offend your delicate sense of justice, we shall put aside our scruples and summon the king. Then we may proceed in the open. What say you? I am at your disposal. Is it your wish that we send for his grace?"

A flicker of fear disturbed Derian's mask of scorn, but he mastered it. His calculating mind rapidly sifted the options. His life was forfeit, that much was clear. He could either submit quietly to a clandestine trial and summary execution or he could assert his rights and cause the greatest harm on his path to death. The latter course appealed to him, for he despised their so-called authority, and the outcome was the same for him, surely. But, if the king were to hear of his treachery, might not his death come with prolonged agony at the hands of a vengeful monarch half-mad with grief, rather than a swift knife thrust? He stood up and cleared his throat.

"My lord, I have never in my life wished harm to the king and I honour your intention to spare his grace any further pain." He spread his hands and inclined his head. "I submit to your court in all humility."

"And how do you plead?" said Burnell.

"Not guilty, my lord. And since I have no idea of the details of my alleged crime, I beg your lordship to enlighten me."

"The charge is as follows: that on the night of September sixteenth, you did knowingly lay a curse upon a pendant which you were preparing for Eleanor, the late queen. Moreover, that you did curse also the twin of the said pendant, which you gave to Bother Clément, also with intent to kill. And that within days of receiving and donning these pendants, both the queen and her scribe fell ill with identical symptoms. Fortunately, knowledge of the curses came to light and the pendants were removed, whereupon Brother Clément recovered, presumably due to his youth and robust health. Sadly the queen did not. This is how you stand accused. Do you wish to change your plea?"

A moment's hesitation, then Scand said, "I do not, my lord. I find the charges preposterous. Who thus accuses me? Where is their proof? I defy you to bring before this so-called court any evidence of this shocking and wholly unfounded accusation. What possible benefit could accrue to me by murdering the royal patron in whose service I have laboured faithfully these dozen years? I respectfully suggest that your lordships have been taken in by some person who imagines me his enemy. Otherwise, I cannot account for it."

Scand masked his satisfaction at the disconcerted looks on the faces of the men opposite. Clearly, they had not expected this reasoned argument. They were merely here to lend their weight to a decision already taken by the Lord Chancellor. Burnell addressed a boy at the door,

"Summon Master Warin."

Warin entered the room, gawky, trembling and shrinking under the gaze of the magnates he saw there.

"Be at ease, young Warin," said Burnell kindly. "You have nothing to fear here. All that is required of you is that you introduce yourself and give a true statement, in the presence of these men, of the events of the sixteenth day of September." Warin stood transfixed. "In your own time, if you please, Master Warin."

"N...now, my lord?"

"If you please."

Warin attempted to clear his throat, hiccoughed, reddened and gripped the sides of his tunic.

"My name is W...Warin Scand. I am apprenticed to Derian Scand, the Court Goldsmith, my father's cousin." He had turned his back on his master but as he spoke, he could sense Derian's anger rising like a spring tide and rolling towards him with an unstoppable force. He was suffocating; could...not...breathe...

"Master Warin? Pray continue," soothed Robert Burnell's voice.

Warin gasped and tried to inhale the easy confidence emanating from the steady figure before him. He took a deep breath.

"On the day mentioned by Lord Burnell," he began, "I was out running errands for Master Derian at Newstead Priory. It was between the hours of Vespers and Compline. When I returned, for once I remembered to enter softly. I have often been beaten for bursting in and disturbing my master at his work. Any marks you see on my body are his doing," he stated matter-of-factly, "I do not deny that sometimes I deserve them, but often they are at his whim. So I entered quietly and was surprised to hear my master speaking in a low murmur as he worked. Master Derian always works in silence. He is a fine craftsman and great concentration is needed for such work. I paused there on the threshold, uncertain whether to go in. And as I hesitated, listening, I realised Master Derian was repeating the same words over and over in a kind of chant. I had never known him do such a thing before. So I stood and listened."

"Can you repeat the exact words you heard, Warin?"

"Yes, because he said them over and over, so eventually I made it all out,

'Cursed be this mysterious stone
And cursed the neck on which it hangs;
Cursed the queen who wears the crown,
Beguiles the king and steals our land.
Let this stone bring her nought
But sickness, pain and death!'"

The twelve seated men exchanged looks of consternation, several crossed themselves, muttering prayers for protection against such evil.

"And you are sure, Master Warin, that these words were spoken by your master as he held the pendant which he was fashioning for the queen?" said Robert Burnell gravely.

"I would stake my life on it."

"You better had, you worthless, treacherous runt," spat Derian.

"Keep silence there," ordered Burnell, "You will be given opportunity to respond in due course."

"Pray continue, Master Warin. Tell us what you did when you heard the alleged curse."

"At first, I could not believe my ears. I thought I must be mistaken. So I listened some more to make absolutely sure."

"And then?"

"I ... I am not proud of what follows, my lord. I realise now that I should have acted to prevent. I should have sought the advice of someone more learned in these matters. But I panicked. So many thoughts rushed headlong into my brain and argued with each other. I knew I had a duty to report what I had heard but I also felt a kind of double duty towards Derian, being first my kinsman and also my master. I could not obey both these duties. I have been raised to injure no one. But now whatever path I chose led to harm."

"Your error was grave but understandable."

"My lord, I am willing to bear whatever punishment this court sees fit to place upon me. But to my dying day, I will be haunted by my failure to protect her grace. And though I pray daily for God's forgiveness, I will never forgive myself."

Robert Burnell said, "Be that as it may, this night we consider only the case against Derian Scand. Go on with your tale."

"I panicked and I ran from the priory, I ran where my legs carried me. When I could run no more, I lay down and let weariness take me. I awoke before dawn and walked until I came to a homestead where I asked for directions back to Newstead. On the way, it came to me that if I stole the pendant before it reached the queen, I could prevent harm to her grace without injuring my master. So I planned to steal it at the first opportunity."

"And did you carry out this plan?"

"No!" Warin wailed. "Events overtook me and, God forgive me, I baulked. The moment I returned, my master bad me to inform Brother Clément that the pendant was ready to be collected. I left, pondering how to contrive to steal it before he came. But he met me in the courtyard, already on his way. Time was against me. Brother Clément collected the pendant and went straight to the queen's lodging to present it to her. O God, God, forgive my weakness; I did nothing and the queen is dead!" Warin hung his head and let the tears come.

Burnell eyed him tolerantly, gave him time to recover himself and said, "Have you anything to add, Warin?"

Warin gulped, wiped his eyes on his sleeve and said, "Only that I hoped and prayed that the queen would not wear the necklace. But I soon learned from Brother Clément that she did. Next, I hoped and prayed that Derian's curse would have no power. And every day, many times a day, I enquired about the queen's health. I thought I would run mad with care and shame. And some days later, my worst fear was realised. Her grace the queen fell ill and soon after, so did Brother Clément, who wore the pendant's twin. Finally, I acted. I myself cut the pendant from Clément's neck. I was seen and taken for a thief. And only then did I tell what I have repeated here this night to Father David, the chaplain. He ensured that the queen's pendant was removed and told me to keep silent about the curse. He would report it to the authorities if he deemed it necessary." Robert Burnell thanked Warin and a guard led him from the room.

Chapter 59

10th December 1290, Bradwell Priory, Stony Stratford, Buckinghamshire - After Midnight

"You have heard how you are accused, Master Goldsmith, what have you to say in your defence?"

Derian stood and locked his gaze on the twelve important men seated before him. "Firstly, my lords, I wonder that experienced men of the world such as yourselves should give any credence to the cock and bull story of a mere apprentice. At best, this Warin is an unpractised, unworldly youth, given to foolish fancies. At worst, he is an ungrateful, resentful, devious schemer."

Burnell interjected, "Clearly he cannot be both; which is he, in your opinion?"

"I am here to defend myself, not to accuse my kinsman. But if you press me, my lord, I suspect the former. Not long ago, his world and his expectations in life went no further than his father's small farmstead, near Winchester. But when I visited my cousin there, he pleaded with me to give his boy the chance to better himself. I could see that the lad was an unpromising oaf, and that he himself did not wish to come with me. But for his father's sake, I agreed to give him his chance. And not a day has gone by when I have not regretted my decision for his sake as well as my own. He is clumsy with his hands and idle, to boot."

Derian's gaze swept the bench before him, making eye contact with each of the men in turn. "I am a patient man; my craft demands it. Several of your lordships have purchased work from me, for yourselves or your wives or sweethearts. And which of you has found fault with my workmanship? None. For there was no fault to find. My work is the finest in the land, as my position in the royal household proves. I say again, I am a patient man, yet I freely admit that on occasion, this lad has driven me to blows. He knows as well as I that he has neither the skill nor the temperament to train in my art. But as you know, gentlemen, an apprenticeship is a contract. He must serve his full seven years. His family expects it. Neither he nor I have an honourable way out. Unless," he said in a wry tone, "anything should happen to me.

"I will let God be the judge of Warin's motives in this matter - whether he hates me for the occasional knock I have dealt him; whether he saw a chance to free himself from the apprenticeship in which he knows he will disappoint his father, or whether the extreme change from farm life to life at court has unsettled his mind. Whatever the reason, he has concocted this tale to discredit me; I urge your lordships to consider whose word is to be trusted – his or mine?"

He left a long pause and then locked eyes with Robert Burnell, "It has been my honour to serve their graces, King Edward and Queen Eleanor these twelve years, first as assistant court goldsmith, then as Master Jeweller. In all these years has ever a complaint come to your ears, my lord, about either my work or my character?" The Chancellor declined to comment, but inwardly he reflected on the suspicion Warin had confided about the death of Scand's wife, and other unsavoury rumours he had heard from time to time.

Derian continued, "My loyal service is as tried and tested as the gold I fashion for the king and his late beloved wife. What reason could I possibly have to harm the queen, in whose service I am employed? Do I not injure myself if I injure her?" He paused again to let the weight of this argument sink in.

Some of the courtiers, knights and clerics who had been deprived of their beds to hear this case began to look askance at the Chancellor. Derian's defence certainly sounded plausible.

The jeweller turned his attention back to the twelve seated men. "The only undeniable facts are that I fashioned a pendant for her grace the queen, and soon afterwards she became ill and died. There is no connection between the pendant and the illness apart from unfortunate timing. I am not privy to the personal affairs of the king and queen, but it was my understanding from what was voiced abroad in the court that she was suffering from her usual winter ailment. I expected her to rally and recover as she has numerous times. I was as shocked as any man here when she succumbed. Never in my wildest dreams did I suspect foul play and nor, I imagine, did any of you, my lords, until you were summoned in the dead of night to this mockery of a trial."

Derian was warming to the task in hand, which did not feel as hopeless now as it had half an hour ago. He sensed the balance shifting in his favour. "Since I myself have become the unwitting suspect, I ask that the queen's physician be called upon to give an account of her demise. Surely if anyone had cause to harbour doubts as to the origin of her illness, it would be him. I call upon you, my lords, in the name of justice, to summon him."

Lord Burnell inclined his head in reluctant agreement. "Have you done, Master Scand?"

"No, my lord; if I may I beg your indulgence a few moments more, I have one further point to make. Even if the court physician should testify that it may not have been the queen's regular illness, I ask you to consider this. The pendant in question, which I beg you will produce for examination, is of unknown origin. In all my years of experience of gems and precious metals, I have never seen its like. It was brought to me by the queen's scribe, one Brother Clément." Here Scand let his guard slip slightly and could not quite keep his loathing of Clément from his voice. "I believe he found it on the shore in some remote place on the south coast. If anything untoward did in fact afflict her grace as a consequence of wearing the pendant, then perhaps the stone itself should be considered. Not everything in nature is harmless.

"Consider the well-known examples of poisonous plants. It may be that this highly unusual stone possessed some natural qualities detrimental to health. My lords, look to the stone and to Brother Clément, who was responsible for giving it to the queen. I make no allegations of foul play upon the scribe. I know him to be most devoted to the queen, but may there not have been some oversight, some negligence on his part in offering her grace a gift whose qualities were at best unknown?" He sat down abruptly, satisfied that he had done all he could to lift suspicion from his own shoulders and cast its shadow elsewhere. If the unofficial jury found that natural causes were to blame, that was enough, but if blame settled upon Clément, so much the better.

Robert Burnell was all too aware that the mood in the room had changed considerably. He nodded to the guard to take Scand away. As soon as the door closed, voices were raised, but they gave way to the quiet authority of Bishop Oliver,

"My Lord Chancellor, the matter in question is not as straightforward as we were led to believe."

"No, Lord Bishop, I concede that Scand has mounted a robust defence."

"Nevertheless," said Otto di Grandisson, coming to his friend's aid, "if either of the men whose witness we have heard this night were to be, in Scand's words, a devious schemer, it is Derian himself. There is no malice in Warin. He is either telling the truth or innocently mistaken." This drew a general murmur of assent.

"I think that we cannot in all conscience reach a judgment this night," Burnell said, "And I must let you good men go to your rest. I believe we need to hear testimony from the late queen's physician and possibly Brother Clément. The scribe, I know, keeps company with the cortege and may be summoned at any moment but the physician's present whereabouts are unknown to me. I will make enquiries. I thank you for your patience."

He rose and quit the room, closely followed by De Grandisson and De Lacy.

Chapter 60

10th December 1290, Buckinghamshire

"Did you find anything out from Warin about the king?" Daniel said to Ed as he appeared leading two horses. Natalie and Jim looked up, still munching their bread and honey.

"Yeah, he said the king rode ahead to Saint Albans and the rest of us will catch up with him there."

"Why should we trust any info we get from Warin? He's only a groom or apprentice or whatever," said Jim.

"Yeah, but he picks up the chatter from the servants and stuff." Ed's eyes scrolled right as he tried to remember, "Warin said he got it from a cook, who had it from Carlita, a lady-in-waiting, who had it from the Lord Chancellor himself apparently."

"It sounds legitimate. The king's not with us anymore, at least that much is probably reliable," said Daniel. "Give us a bunk up, Ed." He mounted his horse and groaned, vainly shifting in the saddle trying to get comfortable. Behind him, a robin burst into song on a brick wall before swooping to the ground to chase a rival. The monks of Bradwell gathered to pay their respects to the queen's bier and the assembled cortege began to amble off through the gatehouse.

Immediately Jim and Natalie began complaining about the ongoing icy weather. But Daniel reflected that, if it were to warm up and a thaw set in, their riding conditions would become much more difficult. He kept this to himself. Please God, let it not rain, he thought. The prospect of travelling with the other three all day in pouring rain did not bear thinking about.

By mid-morning, Daniel noticed that the saplings were shifting in the mounting breeze on the verge of the road, still Watling Street. Most of their way led through woods and by the time they halted at noon, the bare trees were bristling with jackdaws hunkered down, head to wind, in the billowing branches. It was a dismal lunch break, in the hamlet of Bletchley, with lords and servants alike sheltering from the icy wind as best they could, mostly in the lee of the resting horses, as they chomped oats from their nosebags.

"Where are we stopping tonight, Dan?" asked Natalie as they rode on in the early afternoon.

"Woburn Abbey, if I remember the order correctly," Daniel replied.

"What, as in Woburn Safari Park? We went there once for my sister's birthday."

"Yes, but I don't think there'll be any tigers on this visit."

"I guess not." After a pause, Natalie continued, "Dan, what do you miss most about home?"

"I know I should say my parents, and I do miss them; but right now, a hot cup of tea. And toast!"

"Tea? Uurghh! Mine's hot chocolate. Or any chocolate to be honest. And I never thought I'd be dying for a drink of water but I am - good clean water." Natalie's horse veered towards the verge and nibbled some leaves in the hedgerow. With some difficulty she urged her back, saying, "I reckon she knows we're talking about food and drink."

Daniel laughed and said, "When we're at school, I miss my dog most."

"I'd love to have a dog. What's he called?"

"Hadrian, as in the Roman emperor."

Natalie laughed. "Typical Dan."

"But you should see him, he's a pointer and he looks, well, kind of regal. You know," Daniel stretched to his full height in the saddle, stuck his chest out and raised his chin, "Like this!"

"That is absolutely nothing like either a Roman Emperor or a dog!" giggled Natalie.

"What are you two laughing about?" said Jim, stirring from his chilly stupor.

"Dan's dog. Apparently, he looks like a Roman emperor," Natalie said, "Have you got pictures of him on your phone, Dan?"

"Yeah, loads. I wish I could show you. But we can't risk it. And anyway, we've got to save the battery for emergencies, even if it's only to use the torch. I don't even know if there's any power left. It would be stupid to turn it on just to see."

"Yeah, but if you did want to know about the power, you could switch it on later and quickly show me some photos of Hadrian?"

"Maybe," said Daniel. Natalie interpreted this as an indirect no; the way her mum would say "maybe" instead of "no." But she was wrong.

Several hours later, after dark but before supper, she and Daniel snuck out of Woburn Abbey and into the edge of the woods. Once they were out of the sight line of the gatehouse, Daniel extracted his mobile from the lining of his leather scrip and switched it on.

"Thirty percent power, not too bad, considering," he said, scrolling through his gallery. "Here's Hadrian, with my dad." Natalie peered at the screen to see a handsome, tall, slim dog – white with black spots and splodges.

"Oh, he's gorgeous! I see what you mean. He is pretty emperor-like. Cool. What's that building in the background?"

"St. Catherine's Chapel. I can see it from my bathroom window at home."

"It looks really old."

"Yeah, 14th century. Flip, that means that right now, it's not even built yet. Weird. But the abbey would be there; I can see its ruins from my bedroom window. That's much older. It goes right back to before William the Conqueror." Daniel leant back on a tree trunk.

"No wonder you're such a history nerd, with all that on your doorstep."

"Yeah, it's pretty cool. There's much older stuff as well - Bronze Age burial barrows and an Iron Age hillfort. So, living in Abbotsbury, I just sort of fell into the history thing."

"Yeah, I guess if you're surrounded by it, it starts to mean something. I could never get a handle on all those terms: *Bronze Age, Iron Age,* even *medieval* was just a word until all this." She waved her arm round vaguely. Natalie looked back at the picture on Dan's phone. "I wish I had a dog," she said, "but my mum's allergic; at least, that's her excuse. Your dad looks nice."

"Yeah, he's all right. He takes Hadrian for loads of walks when I'm at school. He works really long hours but his schedule's flexible because he's a vicar. And he usually takes Hadrian with him when he's visiting people. It cheers them up and breaks the ice, having a dog. Well, usually."

"And what about your mum? Does she walk him too?"

Daniel noticed Natalie shiver. "You're getting cold, let's keep moving," he said. He switched his phone off and they were plunged into darkness. "Flip, we'll wait a minute for our eyes to adjust and then walk. Um, what was it you asked me just now?"

"If your mum walks Hadrian."

"No, not really. To be honest, she's not around much. In term time, Monday to Thursday she lives in London, with my grandpa, partly to look after him. She's a lecturer at King's College, London. Then she goes back down to Abbotsbury to spend the weekends with dad."

"Sounds like a good arrangement."

"I suppose it makes sense but I sometimes wonder..." he trailed off. "Can you see alright now?"

"Just about," Natalie said. They started moving, lifting their feet overly high to clear the tree roots.

Daniel said, "Talking of my mum - was it you that returned her letter, the one that was supposedly shredded?"

"Yeah, that was me."

"At first I thought it must have been Ed, but he would have just put it back in my room, not sneaked it into a parcel in the pigeonholes."

"It was fun, managing that without getting caught." Natalie paused, then said, "The thing is, I read the letter." Natalie saw Daniel grimace and carried on, "I'm sorry to have invaded your privacy and all that. I nearly shredded it like Jim wanted, but that was because I was so jealous. My mum has never written to me. No-one has. A real handwritten letter. In the end, it was just too precious to shred."

"Well, thanks," said Daniel.

There was a slightly awkward silence until Natalie remembered what they had been talking about before the letter. She said,

"So, you're worried that your mum likes living apart from your dad some of the time, right?"

"Yes. I don't know if Grandpa is more of an excuse than a reason. And I wonder whether in a few years when I've left home, she'll move to London permanently even if he's not around anymore."

"Don't worry about it. My parents split up when I was in Year Five. It was horrible at the time but it's better now really. No more rows, well only over the phone. I guess it might be awkward though with your dad being a vicar."

"That's probably the main issue, to be honest. Dad wasn't a vicar when she married him. And I think she feels people have expectations of what a vicar's wife should be like; you know - baking cakes, visiting the sick. She's not cut out for that stuff. She's an academic."

"Why should she have to play the vicar's wife? She's obviously brainy like you, and she's got her own career."

"Yeah, weekend vicar's wife is about as much as she can take. And dad doesn't blame her."

"If this part-time arrangement suits her, and your dad's okay with it, maybe they'll just keep it like that permanently. Especially if it works. You'll just have to wait and see."

"Yeah, I guess so." They reached the main path to the abbey and from its relative safety, listened more placidly to the squeaks and rustlings from the undergrowth, as nocturnal creatures stirred to their night's business.

Daniel was thinking how he wished he could travel home to Abbotsbury now and see the abbey in its glory; see the familiar ruins come to life, with monks going about their daily business, as they did here at Woburn Abbey. They walked back through the wicket of the gatehouse and nodded to the gatekeeper, whose pale hooded cowl gleamed yellow in the torchlight.

"I don't know which monks I find the creepiest, the ones all in black or these guys, with lighter, dirty-looking robes!" muttered Natalie.

"I suppose I've got used to it now," Daniel said. "And I asked someone about the difference. These are Cistercians - that's their order. They're sometimes called white monks, even though their robes aren't really white. They're just natural, undyed wool. The ones all in black are Benedictines, like at Bradwell Priory last night. And back home at Abbotsbury, the monastery there used to be Benedictine as well."

"Like him," said Natalie jerking her head to a black-habited monk making his way from the church to the refectory for his supper. He had stopped dead, six feet in front of them. Seeing the youngsters staring at him, he lowered his startled face and scurried away. Daniel said,

"Oh, that's him again; the one I fell on when we arrived at Lincoln." Daniel said, "I meant to find him again and apologise, but I completely forgot. Let's try and catch up with him. I expect he's on his way to supper." Daniel sped up but Natalie hung back.

"I'll leave you to it; he looks like a right nutjob!" she said.

Daniel reached the refectory, and stood still amongst the stream of people jostling to find a seat at one of the long trestle tables. He scanned the seated figures, looking for the dark monk among all the lighter habits.

Natalie appeared behind him and said, "There's Ed and Jim. Well, you can search for your mad monk if you like, but I'm going to get my dinner." Daniel carried on looking half-heartedly, but Brother Clément was nowhere to be seen and hunger conquered his good intentions. He squeezed onto a bench next to the others and tucked into a meagre bowl of pottage.

"Is it just me, or is this stew worse than normal?" said Jim. The others grumbled their agreement. The portions were smaller, the bread coarser and the flavour more bland than usual. Daniel wondered if the Cistercians had a stricter interpretation of their monastic vows and rules. It would account for their meagre meal. He kept this thought to himself, however, as he mopped up the last dribbles of stew with his bread.

Chapter 61

10th December 1290, Woburn Abbey, Bedfordshire

Peering through the refectory window, a hooded figure contemplated Lord Daniel and his friends, and mentally reviewed all they had witnessed this past hour and more. The young lord had shown his female companion a small object that emitted light, with no discernible flame. As well as light, it contained pictures, as if it were some kind of illuminated manuscript, lit from within. Like the strange book retrieved at Geddington, it was either a marvel to behold or a work of the devil. These young people were harbouring secrets, that much was certain. But rather than plotting some mischief against the royal party, they seemed somewhat lost and scared themselves. The Watcher was perplexed.

On the other side of the refectory, in the dark, empty cloister, Brother Clément sat on a bench under a stone arch, fretting. What was it about that lad? Each time he caught sight of him he had a queer feeling, like an inward nudge, as if the boy held some significance. And now he had overheard him clearly saying the name Abbotsbury. It made no sense. He resolved to lay the conundrum before the Lord in prayer at tonight's vigil. His stomach complained with a loud growl that he was missing another meal.

Another inward nudge, this time not from hunger, reminded him that he had seen Warin speaking with one of their party; though not the one who had mentioned Abbotsbury. It would be worth finding out what, if anything, Warin knew about them. Clément might see him shortly at Vespers.

Clément had noted with approval that in the last few days the lad suddenly appeared to be much more devoted to the services of the church, not only Vespers but even the early morning office of Prime. What is more, for the first time in their acquaintance, Warin presented himself so carefully washed and brushed that Clément couldn't help wondering if some maid among the servants had caught his eye.

This evening, Warin came early to Vespers. He watched, with unfeigned admiration, the arrival of the royal household; then he followed them into the church and carefully positioned himself with the best vantage point to observe the choir monks chanting their prayers. And if Princess Mary of Amesbury happened also to be in his line of sight, who would notice?

If Warin ever recollected the times he had enjoyed Derian's scorn at Clément's besotted devotion to the queen, he gladly ate his words now. For he had fallen under the spell of Eleanor's daughter. So far, he had worked out that she was but an inch or two shorter than he and that she looked much of an age with his fifteen years. He knew these precious facts to be irrelevant; she was given to the church; married, as it were, to Christ. And even if she were not, she was a princess. But he was smitten and could not help himself. As long as the cortege lasted, he would cross paths with her as often as possible. And so their acquaintance grew, with never a word spoken and hardly a glance exchanged.

Chapter 62

11th December 1290, Woburn Abbey, Bedfordshire - Midnight

"Gentlemen," Robert Burnell began, "I beg forgiveness for disturbing your rest on a second night, but we all understand the necessity. Our host," he gestured to the Prior of Woburn, seated on his right, "has been apprised of the case so far. The hour is late; so without further ado I summon the defendant and the witness."

The squire at the door slipped out and returned immediately with Derian Scand, followed by Peter of Portugal. Derian cast a respectful yet defiant look along the row of stern faces. Peter's eyes flickered nervously this way and that.

"Be seated, Master Scand," said Burnell. "And sir," he beckoned towards the court physician, "if you would be so good as to stand here." The Lord Chancellor cleared his throat and said, "Please state your name and occupation to the men gathered here." He did so.

"As you have been informed," Burnell said, "we are making certain inquiries into the circumstances surrounding the demise of the late queen. Be easy in your mind; no suspicion whatsoever attaches to you or your treatment of her grace." The physician attempted to relax, but failed. He stood rigid and alert, on his guard. The Chancellor continued, "We would like you to give a succinct account of the queen's final illness from its onset until her grace's death on the twenty-eighth day of November. We are aware that she had suffered from a recurring winter ailment in previous years, so we would be obliged if you could pay particular attention to any differences there may have been in the progression of the illness on this occasion." He gave Peter an encouraging smile and sat down.

"My lords, I have consulted my records and will do my utmost to assist your inquiry. I was summoned to attend her grace on the nineteenth day of September. She had been unwell for several days, with a fever and cough. I prescribed complete rest and a course of bleeding as well as syrups for the cough. At this stage certainly, it seemed to be the usual complaint and Queen Eleanor bore it with her usual defiant composure. As you know, my lords, the late queen was a lady of remarkable ability and it irked her extremely to keep to her bed; all the more so when it prevented her from accompanying his grace. The fever abated and she rallied for a while but not with her accustomed vigour.

"What marked the course of the last illness was that each time the symptoms lessened, she was unable to recover her previous strength. There was a gradual deterioration, which is easier to discern with hindsight than it was at the time. In this, I do reproach myself, my lords. How often I have turned those days over and over in my mind. And yet, I do believe all was done that could be done, not only by myself but by all who attended her."

"Indeed, Master Peter," Burnell said, slightly vexed, "we doubt neither your ability nor your intentions. But were there any symptoms not seen previously, any differences, however slight? That is what we seek to learn from you. It is of the gravest importance."

"My lord, the difference lay not in the symptoms, but in the severity of the attacks, their quick succession and Queen Eleanor's inability to recover between them." He glanced down at his notes, "On the thirteenth day of November, I urged the king to accompany his wife as far as Lincoln, where she could be cared for in greater comfort. But just before we reached Lincoln, the queen suffered a fatal attack, at Harby."

In the corner of the room, Derian Scand listened with increasing confidence. The physician's testimony was bolstering his defence, not undermining it. He had been right all along. Nothing could be proved. And for all that he disliked Robert Burnell, he believed him to be just. If he had wanted to do away with him in secret, what would have prevented? No, although this 'court' was unorthodox, Burnell would not harm him without due regard for justice. He leaned back on the wall behind him and allowed his mind to wander to the moment he would lay hands on Warin. His pale eyes blazed.

The Chancellor noticed an expression pass fleetingly over Derian Scand's usually inscrutable face, not the relief of someone about to be acquitted of a crime he did not commit, but the triumph of a man about to get away with murder.

"My lords," he said, rising, "we will withdraw." And he left the room closely followed by Otto De Grandisson.

"I fear it is by no means certain that our makeshift jury will condemn Scand," said Burnell. "My gut tells me he is guilty despite the insufficient evidence. How do you read the situation, as it now stands?"

"I am of the same mind, Robert."

"We must find another solution, and quickly, before we rejoin the king at Saint Albans."

"We could just let him go, providing he quits his post and leaves the royal court," Otto suggested.

"Yes, but he is a proud man. Can we depend upon him to leave quietly? I am by no means certain that he might not prefer to remain, to rub our noses in what he would see as his victory over us."

"He is not to be trusted in any way, of that much we can be sure." Otto gave a huge yawn, "Forgive me, Robert."

Burnell patted his shoulder, caught the yawn and said laughing, 'We both need our rest. Let us speak again in the morning.' And they headed towards the abbot's lodging.

Chapter 63

11th December 1290, Bedfordshire

In the pale grey predawn light, as the cortege assembled just beyond the walls of Woburn Abbey, the air filled with chirps, clicks and twittering calls and responses. Daniel was captivated. The sounds brought his dad vividly to mind; he loved birds and would occasionally drag Daniel out of bed for a trip to hear the dawn chorus. Today's birdsong was louder, sweeter, shriller, and more intense than he had ever heard. Dad would be in seventh heaven. Suddenly Daniel's heart ached so keenly for family, home and safety that his chest felt like a punch bag being pummelled over and over. His legs wobbled and he realised he might collapse. He slipped away to the edge of the group and sidled into the trees.

Leaning on a massive trunk he let the stinging tears come. He had told the others so often that they would get home he almost believed it himself. But in the rare moments of solitude, and even rarer ones when he dared to be honest with himself, he knew the chances were wafer-thin. And although his passion for history buoyed him up some of the time, he had a gnawing apprehension that if he let his guard down, anxiety, dread and the weird strangeness yet familiarity of everything would overwhelm him like an incoming tide.

His tears subsided, he wiped his cheeks and nose with his sleeve and took some deep breaths. He looked directly up along the oak trunk he was leaning on, still clinging tenaciously to some orange-brown leaves in its upper branches. The colour stood vivid against the whitish-grey sky. It was immense and many of its bare branches were the size of thick trunks. It might be five hundred years old, he thought, born in the dark ages, or at the very least from before 1066. Such an ordinary thing, a tree, living out its life cycle season by season, weathering the storms, whatever era of history it happened to grow in. He mused on this for a while.

Were human lives really so different in different periods of history? He was beginning to suspect that, beneath the glaringly obvious differences between the lives of the people here in 1290 and his own time, there were lots of similarities. Maybe there were essential elements of being human, wherever and whenever you lived. He tried to draw these impressions together in his mind. The people here grew up in a family, like him; they had some kind of education, probably at home whereas his was mainly at school; and as young adults, they had to learn to earn a living, as he would; most of them married and had their own families, as he assumed he would one day though he'd never really thought about it. They experienced the turning of the seasons in the natural environment; they marked the progress of time with special occasions – saints' days and bigger festivals like Christmas and Easter. And God, if he exists, thought Daniel, is the continuing thread through all of history.

All the things that seem so different about life here in 1290 are the trappings of life, not life itself. If we are to be stuck here, once we've adapted to the superficial differences, the only true loss will be our family. An enormous loss, but one which some people have to endure anyway, whenever they live. And it can be done. Even if we are stuck here, as well as danger there is beauty, kindness, friendship, hope. He took one more deep breath and pushed himself away from the solid trunk. He began to trot back to the cortege party with a small spring in his step. He had looked the worst-case scenario in the eye and found it bearable.

"Is it just me or does it feel warmer to you?" said Natalie, with something approaching cheerfulness. The boys agreed with her but Daniel eyed Ed's footwear and kept his fears to himself.

A couple of hours later Ed's sodden feet squelched with every step and he tightened his grip on the horses' lead reins to steady his slithering footsteps. Jim and Dan sniggered at lumps of melting snow sliding off branches and landing on the heads of travellers in front, until it was their turn to be dumped on. To Daniel's surprise, not far beyond Woburn they turned off Watling Street and headed in a more easterly direction.

"Whoa, look at that castle!" said Natalie. Ed looked up from the slushy track and brightened; glad to be distracted from his freezing, wet feet.

"Cool," he said.

"Please let this be our lunch break," said Jim, "I'm starving."

They entered the modest town of Toddington, guarded by a wooden fortress looming over them from an improbably high mound. They reached a manor house where the local lord waited, looking somewhat nervous, to offer hospitality to the Lord Chancellor and other exalted dignitaries at the head of the cortege. The rest of the procession crossed the spacious market square and the queen's body was carried to the church where townsfolk had gathered to pay their respects.

Daniel grinned at Ed as the remaining party made for the motte and bailey castle.

"Cool," said Ed again. The kids were enchanted by the textbook medieval fortification. They chomped their bread rolls while skirting the perimeter, admiring it from every angle. On the north face, some children were sledding down the motte on the last of the melting snow. Daniel and the others hovered, watching for a while until one of the town lads gestured them over and held out his homemade sled.

"Cheers, mate," said Ed, jogging over to take it from the slightly bemused boy. He climbed to the top of the slope, jumped on and careered down, whooping all the way to the bottom of the deep ditch. Everyone roared with laughter and there was a general scramble to share in the fun. Twenty minutes later, Daniel and his companions were exhausted as much from laughing as sledging.

"We'd better go and make sure they don't leave without us," Daniel said, shaking his arms and legs to knock off some melting slush. "My thanks," he said simply and waved to their tobogganing friends, who were yet again squelching up the slope which was fast turning into a mudslide. They tramped off to join the cortege, giddy, drenched but lighter-hearted than they had been for many days.

On the road, in the afternoon, the kids tried not to regret the fun they had had in the lunch break, as their sodden clothes clung frigidly to their limbs. Weak winter sunlight threw dappled shadows across their muddy path through undulating woods. Not a trace of snow was now left, even in the densest shade. All through the relatively mild afternoon, every step in the slithering mud threatened to topple Ed. He bore with Jim and

Natalie's smirks and giggles at his slipping and sliding until his left foot sank completely in the gloopy sludge.

"Wait! Stop, I'm stuck." He yanked and yanked at his foot to no avail. Daniel began to dismount.

"No, don't," Ed said. "You'll get stuck as well if you get down here." His voice trembled and Dan noticed Ed was breaking out into a sweat. Panic was starting to take hold.

"It's all right, Ed, we'll use the horses to pull you out. Give me a minute to work out how." His mind's eye conjured up, from somewhere, a tractor towing a car out of a ditch. But the car was tied on by a rope. They couldn't really drag Ed out by a rope, even if they could get hold of one. "Jim, do you think you can lean down and link your arm under Ed's armpit without falling off your horse?"

"Er," stammered Jim.

"No matter; you swap places with Natalie, then, and we'll try it." Daniel and Natalie each leaned over in the saddle, gripped Ed under the armpits and then spurred their horses into a gentle walk. They felt the resistance as the horses picked up the slack; Ed didn't budge; Dan and Natalie were leaning as far back in the saddle as they could and still nothing. All three of them were groaning and grimacing, clinging on tenaciously. Any moment now, we'll have to let go or we'll dislocate our arms, thought Dan. With a squelchy slurp, the mud released the captive and out came the foot – bare.

"My shoe!" wailed Ed. "We have to get my shoe!"

"We'll never get it out, Ed. We have to leave it."

"But, we can't, he can't," began Natalie, shocked. Dan pulled his foot out of the stirrup and said,

"Take mine, Ed. I can ride without it and I don't think we're too far from our overnight stop."

Ed hesitated. "Go on, Ed. It's the only solution. You've got to walk. I'll be fine."

Ed unlaced Daniel's boot, limped to the side of the road and pulled it over his frozen, mud-caked foot. He was pale and grave. It was the first time the others had seen him really shaken. Soon dusk began to fall and they joined a larger road, Watling Street again, Daniel assumed. The roofscape of a considerable town took shape in the gloom and they entered Dunstable.

It could have been Disneyland or the moon for all Jim, Ed and Natalie cared. All they wanted was to get indoors, thaw out and dry their clothes in front of a good fire. But yet again the cortege slowed to a halt to be greeted by the town dignitaries so Queen Eleanor's bier could be led in solemn procession to the priory church. Though it was growing dark, Daniel could see well enough to be impressed by the town and its fine, ornate buildings. There seemed to be a priory on each side of the High Street.

Chapter 64

11th December 1290, Dunstable, Bedfordshire

Ed was rubbing down Daniel's horse when Warin came along with some fresh hay. "These are massive stables, aren't they, Warin, even for a large priory?" he said.

"Aye, I said as much to an old groom who's worked here for many a year. He told me this used to be part of a royal palace that was given over to the priory. But that's not all." Warin leaned in and said confidentially, "You should hear the other tale he told me. The people of Dunstable are none too keen on the king, it seems."

"Why? Did something happen here?"

Warin made as if to spill his secret, thought better of it and disappeared. Moments later he reappeared with an elderly man limping along behind. "You can hear it from the horse's mouth!" Warin said with a flourish. "Master Toby, I beg you to tell your tale over again for my friend.

"But are you not another of the king's grooms? I don't want no trouble," he glanced nervously from one to the other.

"Oh, I'm nothing to do with the royal party," said Ed. "My master joined the cortege for protection after we were robbed on the road. Please tell me your story."

"It goes no further than you two, mind."

"Understood," said Ed.

As the old stable hand settled himself on a hay bale to tell his story, the Watcher slipped into the stall next door, fed the pony there some hay to quiet it and, between the slats of the stable wall, found a gap to peer through. The old man began,

"Folks round here are right glad that the king is not with the cortege, because they have not forgotten the troubles. Above ten years ago a royal party stayed here, though the king was not among them. An argument arose between the king's falconers and the chaplain and others from the priory. The substance of it I do not recall, if indeed I ever knew. But," he leaned forward, warming to his tale, "the quarrel got out of hand and the falconers turned nasty. They rampaged through the town and beat the chaplain so badly he was mortally injured. And what is more, when the gatekeeper refused to let them back into the priory, they beat him too and went on the rampage here, within this holy place!"

He let these words hang in the air but his dramatic pause was somewhat lost on Ed, who was struggling to follow the gist. The old boy continued, "The brothers had to ring the bells to bring the townsfolk running to help. And even then, it was a struggle to restore order. Such goings-on as we have never seen before nor since! And would you credit it, the falconers went complaining to the king that *they* had been mistreated, even naming Father Prior?"

Another pause. "Well, the case came before the local justice, and a dozen witnesses swore that the falconers were at fault. The justice ruled in favour of the prior and the town, as well he might. But was the king content?" The groom looked from one to the other of his spellbound audience of two. "He was not! He would come in person and would hear the evidence told over again in his presence. But this time, not one but three dozen men testified that the prior, the brothers and the town were perfectly innocent and what is more," the old man snorted and slapped his thigh as if telling the punchline of a joke, "they insisted that the culprits responsible for the chaplain's death should be held accountable and duly punished."

He grunted, "We never heard of any such punishment being meted out. So, you can see why here in Dunstable we are not sorry that the king is absent from the party." He scratched his ear and sniffed, "Though, on reflection, it may be his way of making amends, honouring the town with this visit; resting the queen's body here overnight on her last pilgrimage."

"And have you heard that in each town from Lincoln to London where the queen lies overnight, a great stone cross will be erected in her memory?" Warin said.

"Aye, I did hear something to the purpose, but I am glad to have it confirmed. And I will say this for King Edward – never was a man more devoted to his wife. And she to him, God rest her." And he crossed himself.

The Watcher stroked the pony in the next stall once more and slipped away. What did this add? One of Lord Daniel's party had listened to the disloyal tittle-tattle of an old man. It was hardly treason. And it explained nothing of who they were and the origin of their strange possessions.

∞

Just after midnight, while the brothers were singing the office of matins, Carlita made her way to the penitentiary cell of Dunstable Priory. The candle flickered in her trembling hand as she inserted the key in the lock and turned it slowly. The grating sound roused the prisoner. Scand was instantly on his guard. So they had come for him after all.

"You?" he said, astonished. "What are you doing here, Carlita? How on earth did you come by that key?"

"It's not difficult to watch the comings and goings at the porter's lodge. Never mind that now. The brothers are at Matins and you must fly, now. You will not be missed till morning. You can get clean away. Go north, or better, west into Wales."

"But I don't understand. They have no evidence against me, only hearsay. And though Burnell is the king's lackey, he is known to be a fair man. I do not think he will have me quietly shuffled off."

"You cannot know that. I believe he is capable of anything. You must go!"

"No, I will not run. I have my reputation to think of, not to mention my plans for that squealer, Warin."

"Please, Derian. I have risked much to help you."

"What have you heard?"

"There is no time to go into it all now. Trust me; I know. You must flee now, while you have the chance. Here," she said, picking up a pack she had left at the door of the cell, "Here is food for the next few days."

"I can go nowhere without the tools of my trade," Scand protested.

"They are within here," she shook the bag – the metallic jangle echoed in the bare cell. "I took them in the confusion when you were arrested, before the guards could come back to confiscate them." She snatched up the blanket from his cot and roughly stuffed it in. "Here is warmth, food, your tools, your purse and the pieces of jewellery you gave me. Enough to set you a good way on your journey. Head away from London and start afresh. A new life."

Derian's lingering doubts were dispelled by the urgency of Carlita's voice and her pleading eyes. He took the proffered pack, squeezed her hand by way of thanks and stole out of the cell.

Carlita accompanied Scand to the gatehouse, let him out at the wicket and closed it behind him. She leant back on the gate and took a deep breath of the cold night air. Then she made her way to the abbot's lodging. She knocked quietly and was let in by Robert Burnell himself.

"Is it done?" he asked.

"It is done, my lord."

"Good, come within. The abbott will soon return from Matins." Carlita followed him to an inner chamber.

"Did he go willingly or did you have to persuade him?"

"I did have to bring him around. He said that you had no evidence against him. He would not have gone without his tools."

"Yes, that was a good idea, Carlita. You have a sharp mind. It was wise to give him his instruments. A man must have his living."

"And did he trust that you were acting on your own, purely to aid him? It is imperative that he believes it's a genuine escape."

"Yes, my lord, I believe so. But did he truly conspire against the queen, my lord?"

"I am convinced he did. But it was hard to prove. It is good to be rid of him. I thank you for your service, which must remain confidential." He walked to a desk and beckoned her to follow. "I would like you to put your name to this document, if you please, which states that you will never disclose the actions you have performed this night. And in return, I will help you to a new position; that is, if you wish to remain in England." Carlita's face brightened.

"I do, sir, most heartily; there is nothing for me back in Castile." She leaned over the table, dipped the quill in the inkwell and signed her name.

"Good. Would a position attending on my children please you? My household is nothing akin to the royal court, of course; but I have a sizeable estate in Shropshire, several other manors and a house in London. And, of course, the bishop's palace at Wells, which is very fine.

My wife prefers Shropshire, so she and the children live mainly there, but there would be some travel."

"My lord, that would suit me very well, I thank you."

"Good. That much can be easily settled. Sign your name here and go to your well-earned rest."

Chapter 65

12th December 1290, Bedfordshire

The grassy verge of the king's highway began to show green in the lifting light as Otto de Grandisson rode up to the front of the cortege. He reined in his mount to fall into step alongside his friend, Burnell, who said,

"Well, Otto, Carlita has done her part and I trust you have done yours?"

"Yes, two of my men shadowed Scand out of Dunstable, heading west. One has reported back to me as arranged, leaving his fellow to maintain the tail. He has orders not to return until Scand is fifty miles clear of us."

"Good. Let us hope that is the last we will see or hear of the goldsmith and his wretched curse."

"Was there much fuss when the empty cell was discovered?" Otto enquired.

Burnell chuckled, "The poor porter, he was in state, poor fellow," he said, recalling the man's trembling voice and wringing hands. "He thought I was going to string him up. It was all I could do to keep my countenance and feign a little vexation." Otto grinned. Burnell continued, "Of course I had to send a search party after Scand, to maintain the deception. And over breakfast, I informed our twelve unofficial magistrates that they may look forward to a full night's sleep instead of being rudely awakened and summoned to hear more evidence."

"And how did they take it?"

"Mostly with consternation and relief in equal measure. But Bishop Oliver is a shrewd one; he gave me a particularly penetrating look and said that it seemed the best possible outcome for all concerned - 'rather convenient, in fact,'" Burnell said, imitating the bishop's churchy intonation. Otto laughed and said,
"Is that all? He didn't suspect foul play?"
"He did. So I took him into our confidence; I did not want him thinking we had quietly slit Scand's throat."
"It certainly was tempting," Otto said, raising one eyebrow.
"Indeed," his friend agreed.

The day was colder than yesterday but not chilly enough to refreeze the ground. Towards the rear of the procession, Ed slithered along in the slush. He had managed to borrow a spare pair of boots from Warin. Apparently, they belonged to his master but for some reason, he would not miss them for now. They were rather fine, so Daniel wore them to keep them out of the mud and Ed had Daniel's pair. But the pointed toes pinched and irritated Daniel's itchy chilblains. So the ride was more than usually uncomfortable and he was relieved when they turned aside to the Benedictine nunnery of Holy Trinity in the Wood. The sisters fed them generously with the ubiquitous pottage and ample hunks of bread to dip into it.

"This isn't bad," said Jim, tucking in. "Not as nice the stew at Judith's though. That was delicious." Daniel raised his eyebrows, swallowed a barbed comment, and agreed heartily. "You haven't even tasted it yet!"
"Well, no, but just the smell is making my mouth water. It must be flavoured with herbs."
"You a chef now as well?" Jim laughed.
"I like cooking if that's what you mean."
"Me too," said Ed; Jim and Natalie rolled their eyes. Ed wriggled his toes closer to the fire, which the nuns had fed to a blazing pitch to warm their honoured guests. He had taken off his boots and stood them on the hearth to dry in front of the fire.
"Don't get too close, Ed. You'll get chilblains. Mine are itching like hell," said Daniel.
"Is that what the itchy feet thing is? I thought I had fleas!" said Natalie.
"You've probably got fleas as well, but yeah, the red, swollen itchy toe thing is chilblains. Haven't you had them before?
"I've never heard of them. Can you even get them in our time?" said Jim.

Daniel snorted. "Of course you can. I've had them a few times. You get them if your feet get really cold. And when they warm up afterwards, they itch like hell. I have to walk the dog whatever the weather, so I've probably been outdoors in the cold a lot more than you. And I don't mind it as long as I can warm up afterwards."

"I bet the nuns have something for the chill-foot thingies. Loads of people in the cortege must have them," Ed said.

"Good thinking, Ed." Daniel said, standing up. "I'll go and ask now, before we get underway." He returned looking chuffed, with a little clay jar stoppered with a rag. "Witch hazel ointment," he said, handing the jar to Natalie.

So their toes at least were more comfortable as they rode down the straight Roman road in the afternoon.

"Have any of you ever been to Saint Albans?" said Daniel.

"Is that where we're headed, Dan?" said Natalie, trying to settle her horse, who was unusually skittish this afternoon.

"Yes."

"I don't think I've been there," said Ed.

"Me neither," said the others.

"I went with my dad," Daniel said. "He had to go to some service for vicars at the abbey. And I went to the Roman museum. In Roman times the city was called Verulamium. Oh no!" He exclaimed and stopped.

"What? What's wrong, Dan?" Natalie said urgently.

"I just realised; there probably won't be any Roman ruins visible in this time."

"Dan," Natalie said, thumping his arm, "don't do that! I thought something was wrong!"

"Huh?" said Ed, "What do you mean, no Roman ruins? The Romans came before the Middle Ages, didn't they?"

"Duh! Of course they did. Even Jim knows that!" said Natalie. There was a sudden tense silence and the others glanced at Jim. Making him the butt of a joke was new territory.

"Yeah, even I know that, numbskull!" Jim said, leaning forward in the saddle and rapping his knuckles on Ed's head. They all laughed, mainly from relief.

Daniel said, "What I meant was, at this point I think most of the Roman remains will be buried under the medieval stuff. Nobody's dug it up yet."

"This time stuff is doing my head," groaned Ed and they laughed again.

"I suppose there might be some Roman buildings that haven't fallen down yet," Daniel said brightening. "But the really well-preserved remains were underground. There are some great mosaic floors and a perfectly preserved hypocaust."

"Hyper what?"

"Hypocaust - Roman underfloor central heating," Daniel said enthusiastically. Natalie groaned. But Ed said,

"My dad's got underfloor heating at his new house. It makes sense because heat rises. So the Romans invented that, did they?" In a posh accent, Jim piped in,

"How absolutely fascinating, Professor Dan; do tell us how it worked." Then in his own voice, "Not."

Daniel wished he'd thought of something cooler to mention. Roman weapons from the museum maybe or skeletons? It was difficult for him to work out what other kids might think was cool. Especially about history - to him, it was all cool. "Okay, I get it; no more Romans relics," he said.

They rode on in silence till they came to a river, running slack and heavy with the thaw and followed it south.

"Look, the ducks are shooting the rapids," Jim said, pointing and laughing.

"They're having fun," Dan replied, enjoying the fact that it was Jim, not he, who noticed the birds. "Hey, this must be the river in the story I heard about when I came here before. It supposedly dried up so Alban could cross on the way to his execution." Ed craned his neck but couldn't see the river, wedged as he was between the two horses. Soon afterwards the Abbey of Saint Alban rose above them solid and impressive, stamping its authority on the landscape.

∞

Derian Scand stretched and shook the hay out of his hair. After travelling west under cover of darkness, he had slept most of the day in a hayloft near Aylesbury, not daring to venture out in daylight. A mounted search party would have been sent out as soon as his escape was discovered. Hopefully, they would have already overtaken his position. He wriggled in the itchy straw, trying to find a more comfortable position. Inside it was already getting dark but he needed to wait for full darkness before he set out.

He thought about his destination. Wales was wild terrain to navigate in mid-winter, but once he was across the border, he could use main roads and travel by day. There were fine gold mines; a skilled craftsman such as himself would be highly valued. And hopefully, too, someone compelled to flee the English royal court would be sure of a welcome. Edward must be hated there, in the aftermath of his defeat of Prince Llewellyn.

Yes, the Welsh would welcome him with open arms. A wry smile lit Derian's sharp eyes as he imagined holding a Welsh audience spellbound with the tale of his crime, sham trial and escape. He would be hailed a hero.

As to making a living, did the Welsh lords retain enough wealth to pay for fine jewellery, he wondered? Or would he have to cow-tow to the English Marcher lords? Perhaps he could manage to court both the esteem of the Welsh and the riches of the English? That thought pleased him and his smile broadened. He peered again through the slats of the hayloft. Still an hour or so until he could re-join Akeman Street. How many nights' walk would it take to reach Wales? Four, or maybe five? He could not cover as much ground in the dark. But the nights were long and the days short.

Brooding, he ran over the events of the past day again in his mind. The chance to escape had arisen so suddenly, it had given him no time to think it through. Some misgiving gnawed at a corner of his mind. It astonished him that Carlita should put herself in danger for his sake: he had always taken her for a rather scheming wench. Perhaps he had misjudged her. But risking so much for him? Somehow it didn't quite ring true. He had never known her to do anything without some advantage to herself. But what could she gain from his escape?

Could anyone else benefit from his being out of the way? The face of Robert Burnell rose in his mind: a face no longer confident, on the second night of the clandestine trial, that he could secure a conviction against Derian. There was insufficient evidence to prove he had placed a curse on the queen. But having arrested him, Burnell would want him out of the way before the king returned.

This reading of the situation made more sense to Derian. The Chancellor did not have the gall to slit Derian's throat; he would rather employ a woman to facilitate a so-called escape. So, Carlita was in the pay of Burnell, the treacherous hussy. He cleared his throat and spat into the hay. He ruminated on these suspicions for a while. If I were Burnell, he thought, I would have the 'escapee' quietly tailed until he was well clear. I can test my theory: if I am being followed by a lone man, I will know the escape was a set-up.

Chapter 66

12th December 1290, Saint Albans, Hertfordshire

By the time the rear of the cortege entered the grateful warmth of the abbey, the Lord Chancellor was already installed on one side of a roaring blaze and King Edward, opposite him, was saying,

"Has all proceeded quietly in the cortege in my absence?"

"Yes, your Grace, on the whole. The steward has been fussing like an old maid over the arrangements, of course," he said, smiling. "Oh, and the jeweller fellow, Scand, seems to have fallen out with someone or other and taken to his heels."

"No great loss there," said the king. "Still, I'm surprised at him being the one to run. He did not strike me as the kind to back down."

"True; he's a shifty fellow and, to my mind, we are well rid of him. And what of the matters that required your presence here, your Grace? I hear that John of Berkhamsted was elected the new abbot. What of that land dispute you told me of?"

"Yes, that was resolved." The two men stared at the fire, neither broaching the subject that hung in the air. In the end, Burnell said, as delicately as he could,

"And the final arrangements for Blackfriars and Westminster, your Grace?"

The king cleared his throat and said, "A few details remain that I will discuss with Bishop Oliver this evening or tomorrow at Waltham."

"We are still to make the detour to Waltham then, your Grace?"

"Yes, I see what you're getting at, Robert. But the Westminster tomb is not quite complete so we have a day or two in hand. We could stay here but Eleanor and I both have a fondness for Waltham." Edward cleared his throat again. "My family has a long association with the abbey and I wish a vigil to be kept there. Moreover, I do not think the memorial crosses should number eleven. Twelve will be much better. But I do realise it will be somewhat arduous for the servants, all the more so now the thaw has set in. And I am sorry for it."

"Aye, the land around Waltham is full of rivers and channels, all swollen after the thaw."

"We will head northeast from here on Stone Street, join Ermine Street above Ware and approach Waltham from the north. It is all good high road." The king sipped his wine.

"It will be above twenty miles, your Grace."

"We will require an earlier start then," the king said, in a tone that brooked further resistance.

"I will have a word with the steward." Robert raised a hand towards a servant standing by.

Warm and fed, Daniel entered the abbey church through the west door. The others trailed behind him, for the huge solidity of the building had impressed even Jim. They walked up the improbably long, empty nave. Dim candlelight threw strange shadows on the vivid crucifixion murals on the pillars. The queen's bier lay on the high altar and in front of it knelt the monks who would keep vigil later after the evening offices of Vespers and Compline.

"Look at all these paintings!" said Natalie, admiring the colourful frescoes on the pillars "I thought churches were plain and boring."

"They all used to be decorated like this, but the paintings were all scrubbed off in the reformation – you know, Henry VIII?"

"I wish they weren't all of the crucifixion. It's a bit freaky, isn't it, when you think about it?" said Ed.

Daniel walked round to the other side of the pillar. "These ones are different," he said, "Oh, I think this is Saint Alban – the one who dried up the river."

"Yeah, why was he being executed anyway?" asked Jim.

"Um, my dad told me the story when we came here. I think I can remember it. So, there was this guy, Alban, living in the 200s AD or a bit later, when the Romans ruled Britain. At the time, the religion was a kind of blend of Roman and Celtic paganism, but there were a few Christians and they were being persecuted." Daniel paused and looked around. Blank expressions on all their faces. "They blamed Christians for anything that went wrong, and hunted them down and punished them," he explained. "Anyway, Alban lived here in Verulamium. And he came across a Christian priest running away from Roman soldiers. He let the man hide out in his house. The priest's name," Daniel pointed to the other man in the painting, "was Amphibalus. In Alban's house, he kept watch and prayed night and day. Alban admired his faith and holiness so much that he became a Christian himself. Eventually, someone grassed them up and soldiers came to search the house. So Alban swapped clothes with Amphibolus and gave himself up, so the priest would get away."

"Oh, come on," said Jim. "He'd only just met the bloke. And anyway, who would really do that for anyone?"

"Someone who follows Christ, I guess." Daniel tried to recall the words, "Didn't Jesus say something like 'There's no greater love than to give up your life for your friends.' And that's what He did, at least, that's what Christians believe."

"Like Harry Potter letting Voldemort kill him in the Deathly Hallows, you mean, to save everyone else?" said Ed.

"Yeah; I get that it happens in stories," Jim said, staring at the paintings of Alban and Amphibalus, "like the Bible and Harry Potter and this Alban bloke. But real people wouldn't do that, would they? Don't they look after number one?" Behind Jim, Natalie rolled her eyes.

"Getting back to the story; what happened, Dan?" Ed asked, "Did the priest escape or did they catch him as well?"

"He escaped that time but I'll come back to him. Alban was whipped to try to make him give up Christianity and go back to being pagan, but he refused. So he was sentenced to be beheaded. When the execution day came, so many people came to watch that when they came to the river, the one where Jim saw ducks shooting the rapids, remember?" They nodded, "Well, when they got there, the bridge was overcrowded and Alban and the soldiers couldn't get across. The story goes that Alban looked up to heaven, the river dried up and Alban and the soldiers walked across."

"What? If he could do that, why didn't he escape instead? What an idiot," said Jim.

"Maybe because he was following Christ?"

"I don't get it," said Ed. "Do you mean like, if Jesus didn't do some miracle to get out of being crucified, then Alban shouldn't either?"

"Something like that. Anyhow, the executioner was so impressed that he threw his sword down, fell at Alban's feet and prayed. Then they carried on walking to the top of a hill for the execution. When they got there, Alban was thirsty so he prayed for water and a spring sprang up at his feet."

"Whoa, did they still kill him? After two miracles?" said Natalie.

"Yeah, another soldier chopped off his head and the head of the first executioner, the one who wouldn't kill Alban. But as Alban's head rolled away, the eyes of the second executioner popped out of his head and dropped to the ground. There's a great drawing of that bit in a medieval manuscript. I googled it after dad told me the story."

"Awesome!" said Jim. "I didn't realise they had things like that in old books."

"Oh, yeah, medieval texts are full of monsters and torture and gruesome stuff. I guess it was their version of horror films."

"When you think about it, the crucifixion's pretty gross; it's just that we're used to seeing pictures of it," Natalie said, looking around at the other murals.

"Is that the end of the story then, the bloke's eyes popping out?" Ed asked.

"Not quite," said Daniel. "The authorities eventually caught and killed the priest, Amphibalus, who'd escaped. He was also made a saint. And eventually, Verulamium was called Saint Albans after Alban, the first British Christian martyr. They're both buried here in the abbey and pilgrims come to visit their shrines to pray."

"What, like we're supposedly going to pray at the shrine of Edward the Confessor?" said Natalie.

"Exactly," said Dan.

"That just weirds me out," Ed said, "praying to bones."

"Yeah, me too," Dan agreed. "But I guess because Christians believe these saints are in heaven and," he gestured speech marks in the air, "'close to God,' it's a bit like, um, like us at school going to one of the more approachable teachers to ask them to ask the headmaster something."

"Oh, right. That makes more sense," said Ed.

"But this is what I don't get," said Natalie. "They believe in some wonderful all-loving God, right?" The others agreed, and Jim went on, "And they believe they can pray to him, right?" Again, agreement all round. "So why pray to the saints? Isn't that like the headmaster being the nicest, most approachable teacher but going to Miss Hetherington instead?" They all laughed.

"You're right!" said Daniel. "It makes no sense to me either, but we'd best keep that thought to ourselves otherwise we'll blow our own cover." By this time, at the other end of the long nave, the monks were preparing to perform the office of Vespers; local people were filtering in through the great west door. Members of the cortege, pilgrims and other abbey guests entered via the cloister. Jim, Ed and Natalie waded against this tide of incoming people and left the abbey church but Daniel chose to stay. He stood among the worshippers, wondering what troubles in their lives drew them here to pray this evening. And he prayed for light and help in his own plight.

∞

Derian Scand ventured from his hiding place at twilight and headed west as expected. He wanted to check if he was being tailed by one of Burnell's men. He soon detected a soldier some yards behind him. Derian squatted down, pretending to adjust his shoe, to see if the man would go past. He didn't; he disappeared into the trees. So, the 'escape' was a ruse to get him out of the way, scurrying off to Wales, never to be seen again, Derian concluded. His disappearance would be a small mystery that fuelled the chatter of the royal court for a month or two. And then he would be forgotten. His reasoning mind urged him to fall in with the Chancellor's plan. Yet the thought of yielding to Burnell's manipulations irked him beyond reason. He was still squatting on the ground, but now his stance stiffened. The pretence of adjusting his shoe fell away; he became a crouching beast with hackles raised, poised to spring.

It gave Derian little trouble to duck into the woods, double back round and come at the soldier from behind. With one hand he grabbed his face and with the other, he slit his throat. The man dropped like a stone and Derian stood aside as his lifeblood gushed out and pooled on the ground. He waited for the convulsions and twitching to cease, then dragged the corpse by the feet to avoid the blood. He hauled it further from the road and searched the body for valuables. Next, he stripped it down to the blood-soaked shirt; this was the hardest part of the whole business, for he took great pains not to bloody his own garments. He may well fall suspect of this crime, but there must be no evidence. Everyone knew it was dangerous to travel alone by night: there was always a risk of masterless men who might lie in wait, ready to kill for the clothes on your back as well as the money in your purse.

Finally, Derian hauled the corpse deeper into the woods and rolled it clumsily into a ditch. He went back for the clothes and valuables. The coins he pocketed himself but the clothes and more identifiable goods he had to discard. He searched for a hollow tree and found one a good distance from the body. Derian wiped his hands on the cold grass and made his way back to the road, sweating and flushed with exertion and exhilaration. He stood on the highway verge. Which way should he go? West to Wales or southeast towards London?

Chapter 67

12th December 1290, Saint Albans, Hertfordshire

In the abbey church at St Albans, the monks were singing evening prayers. To Daniel's ear, the style was very different to his choir in the cathedral back home, but it had a gothic yearning beauty; serene and eerie in the candle glow. Already age-old in this ancient setting, the familiar, hallowed atmosphere of divine worship sharpened Daniel's homesickness. Eventually, the brothers fell silent and filed out. Amongst them, Daniel again spotted the monk he had collapsed upon at Lincoln. He went to intercept him,

"Excuse me, brother, may I speak with you?" Clément, startled, jerked slightly and his snakestone pendant lurched outside his habit. Daniel tried not to stare but his hand unconsciously went to his neck, where his ammonite used to hang.

"I am at your service, my lord. Shall we go into the cloister?" responded Clément. They walked out to the arched quadrangle and sat on a stone bench, each confused and aware of some confusion in the other.

"I am Daniel of Orkney."

The monk inclined his head to acknowledge Daniel's higher social position and said, "And I am Clément. Clément of *Abbotsbury*," he added with a slight emphasis. "I doubt you have heard of the place, since you hail from the far north, as I understand." The unexpected mention of home gave Daniel another visible shock, as Clément intended, but he recovered well, saying,

"As a matter of fact, I have heard of Abbotsbury. It is on the southwest coast, I believe."

"Yes, my lord. And how may I serve you?"

"I owe you a long-overdue apology, Brother Clément. When my party came upon the cortege at Lincoln, I fear I may have accidentally trodden on you; I certainly stepped on your habit. You were praying in the snow and in my haste, I did not see you."

"Ah," said Clément, casting his mind back. "I recall being startled but not how or by whom. As you see, no harm was done, my lord. But I thank you for your apology." There was an awkward silence, which Daniel eventually broke.

"I couldn't help noticing the unusual pendant you wear. May I ask how you came by it?" Now that he knew the monk was from Abbotsbury, an idea was forming in his mind.

Clément grasped the snakestone and let out a strange, muted groan. "Forgive me; it has painful associations," he said.

"I am sorry to distress you, brother. I am curious but do not speak of it if it pains you."

Clément stared beyond Daniel for a few moments and then said, "I will tell you, but let us go somewhere warmer. You are shivering, my lord."

They walked across the dark courtyard to the monks' warming room. Brother Clément sat on a bench opposite Daniel and with one hand unconsciously on the pendant, he said,

"I am – no, I was – scribe to the late queen. Some months ago, in the summer, my mistress commissioned me to visit my own abbey at Abbotsbury, to copy a manuscript in the library. While there, I found this strange stone on the beach after a storm. One of the brothers had found other such stones and he showed me how they could be split in half and polished as you see this one is. So I brought it back as a gift for the queen." Here, Brother Clément inexplicably broke down in tears.

Daniel didn't know what to do. Trying to offer comfort, he said, "I'm sure she appreciated the gift, Brother Clément."

The monk let out a strangled moan. "She did but it killed her!" he wailed. "I killed her! She might still be alive if not for that evil stone. But it won't kill me! Why won't it take me too?"

Daniel turned crimson and looked around to make sure they were alone. He felt torn between changing the subject to distract Brother Clément from his distress and pressing him for further explanation.

"Calm yourself, brother. I am afraid I do not follow you. What connection could your stone possibly have to Queen Eleanor's death? Surely she died of natural causes. Why would you think otherwise?"

"I had the stone polished and mounted by the queen's jeweller. It pleased her greatly and she wore it. And I wore the other half." The sympathetic frankness of the young stranger overcame Clément's better judgement, and the whole story tumbled from his lips. "Soon afterwards we both fell ill with identical symptoms. Someone realised there might be a connection between the illness and the pendants and they were removed. I quickly recovered but the queen did not. I loved her. I would have died for her a thousand times over; but instead, I have been her death."

"But you did not know, Brother Clément. You are not to blame, even if there was something amiss with the pendant; but I do not think there was. Had not the queen suffered with the same symptoms before?"

"Yes, it often affected her in winter," Clément admitted. "It was not so bad in warmer climes, but with this year's cold, damp weather, once the cough started, she could not rally."

"There, you see, it was not the pendant; it was a sickness she already had. Take heart, brother, and do not be so hard on yourself. I'm sure Queen Eleanor would not wish it."

But Clément was not listening, "She always recovered before and this time she could not. Now she lies cold and it seems as if the sun itself has lost its warmth and all colour has drained out of the world." Clément visibly sagged, his head in his hands.

Daniel let him grieve for a few minutes and then said, "Brother Clément, when did you last sleep?"

"I know not."

"I have seen you at night, keeping vigil by the queen. Have you done so every night?"

"Yes, it is my penance. And the only way I can now serve her."

"Surely this is a duty to share with others, brother, not a burden for you alone. Last night the friars of Dunstable Priory kept vigil; this night the monks of Saint Albans will do so. So many prayers are being offered for the queen's soul. Take comfort. You are no more to blame for Queen Eleanor's death than I. You must sleep, but first let us find you a bite to eat." Daniel got up and took Brother Clément's arm. As he felt the monk's bony elbow, he shuddered slightly at the thought that this was probably the arm of the skeleton he had seen on the dig at home. He dismissed the grisly thought and said, "And you must tell me more about your abbey of Abbotsbury."

The travellers were woken well before dawn and ushered sleepily into the guest dining hall to snatch a hasty, hot breakfast. The brothers were serving a kind of porridge; Dan was so hungry that anything was welcome and this wasn't bad, though he would have loved to add a few spoons of sugar. In between mouthfuls, he told Clément's story to Jim, Ed and Natalie, and then summarised,

"Clément comes from the abbey at Abbotsbury where I'm from. The fossil pendant he is wearing is identical to the one I found in the tomb there at half-term. I'm sure of it; so it must have been his grave."

"You mean you've been talking to a guy that you've seen as a skeleton?" Jim said.

"Yes; but keep your voice down," said Daniel, lowering his still further. "When you think about it, all these people are long dead in our time," he made a vague gesture to those around them tucking into their porridge. "Anyway, the point is - Clément is from Abbotsbury, like me; wearing a fossil pendant. Mine disappeared when we arrived here. I thought I'd just lost it somewhere but now I'm not so sure. I've spent half the night trying to puzzle out whether these weird connections between us mean something or are just coincidences. I don't understand it, but my gut tells me that monk must be something to do with why we're here."

"He sounds like a right nutter," said Jim.

"True," admitted Daniel. "But I think it's mainly that he's out of his mind with grief. He can't be like that normally otherwise he wouldn't have been the queen's scribe in the first place, would he?"

"Yeah," said Natalie. "It's worth following up, Dan. Find out as much about him as you can."

"I'll try," Daniel replied.

Ed shovelled one more spoonful of porridge into his mouth and then sprayed half of it around as he said, "I have a feeling Warin knows this Clément. I've seen him with a monk a few times. I'll ask him. I've got to go and get your horses now anyway."

Others around them were also stirring and readying themselves to leave.

"Here we go again," said Jim. "Surely we must be getting to London today. I can't believe how many days it's taking us when it's only a few hours by car or train."

Chapter 68

13th December 1290, Hertfordshire

The cortege rumbled slowly through the grand brick gatehouse and departed the abbey precinct. In the washed-out light before dawn, the party made its way slowly uphill to the marketplace, the broad street lined with dutiful townsfolk paying their last respects. There, with the usual ceremony, the site of the future memorial cross was chosen by King Edward and his advisors.ABbot John offered a final prayer and the procession moved eastward towards the rising sun and the town and abbey of Waltham.

Daniel vaguely recalled that this leg of the journey was the longest, an unnecessary detour, but he kept this to himself. He settled himself into the saddle for a long ride as the shrill morning songs of robins pierced the air. Jim and Ed were a little way behind and being so early, he thought Natalie would be too grumpy to chat but he was wrong.

"So your dad's a vicar; you kept that quiet," she said.

"I'm not stupid. It's bad enough being a choir boy without you lot knowing my dad's a vicar too."

"Oh, um, yeah; look Dan," Natalie paused, reaching for the right words.

"I know," Daniel said, to let her off the hook, "You don't need to explain or anything."

"But I want to. I'm sorry about everything. The way we treated you before; it was out of order. It seems like another life now; it must've been awful for you."

"It wasn't the best. But it's okay."

"How come you don't hate us? I would if I were you."

"I did hate you, a bit. And when we ended up here, I guess I was tempted, you know, to get my own back. All of a sudden everything switched and I had the power because I'm clued up about history. You and Ed changed almost immediately and anyway, I always knew you only sided with Jim to prevent him picking on you. But Jim was still being such a pain, blaming me for everything, moaning all the time, arguing against every suggestion, putting us all in danger."

"Yeah, until he came back after running away, he was a complete pain in the butt," Natalie agreed.

"There was this one time, on the way to Stamford, I think; Jim wandered off for a pee. He went quite a way to find some bushes and I followed for a bit to keep an eye out for him. When he came back to the track, he went in completely the wrong direction."

"The plonker," laughed Natalie.

"But this is the point; I was tempted just to let him keep going in the wrong direction. For a few minutes, a voice in my head was saying, 'This is the chance you've been waiting for. Teach the so-and-so a lesson. He's had it coming to him.'"

"So why didn't you?" asked Natalie.

"I suppose my dad would say I resisted temptation. The light inside me overcame the dark. But what it felt like at the time was trying to see the bigger picture. If Jim had really got lost, how would I feel? I mean, we know that now because he ran away at Geddington. And on that long ride to look for him I had a lot of time to really think about him. Why he acts like he does."

"Because he's a prick?"

"We both know it's more complicated than that. If he was happy and confident in himself, he wouldn't feel the need to big himself up all the time or put other kids down, would he?"

"I suppose not."

"The thing is, he's small, he's not particularly bright in the way that helps you pass exams at school. He doesn't want to be laughed at and to avoid that, his strategy was to act tough and laugh at everyone else. I thought that maybe if I could stand up to him, but at the same time show him respect, he'd have a chance to find another way to deal with it."

"And do you think he's finding another way?"

Daniel shrugged, "I guess the jury's still out on that one. He's definitely been different since he ran away. My dad says it's never too late to start again, and that we should give people as many chances as it takes to change. He describes it as waves on the beach, washing away all the footprints and stuff. However many times we mess up, God always has another wave to wipe the slate clean. In the Bible, it's called grace."

"I'd like to meet your dad sometime."

"When we get back you can come and stay. After all, you're my cousin now!"

Blue wrinkles were cracking the cloudy face of the brightening sky. Jim and Ed had caught up and as they passed through woodland again, even Jim heard the escalation of birdsong and noticed flashes of colour as birds flittered through the bare branches. They rode in silence for a while enjoying the soundscape.

The cortege came to a ford. The horses up ahead sloshed through warily. Ed did not relish the thought of walking the rest of the way with wet feet.

"Skooch forward in the saddle, Jim," he said. He hoiked himself up unceremoniously and reached around Jim to take the reins from his friend's hands.

"Oi, there's no room for your big butt!" Jim said, more as a protest he was expected to make than one he genuinely felt. He was nervous of navigating fords and now he could sit back and let Ed guide the placid mare. They splashed across and Ed slid down and handed back the reins, grinning. At the next ford, twenty minutes later, Jim shimmied up in the saddle without being asked.

On and on they rode through the grey cold; stomachs were grumbling and tempers frayed by the time they turned aside at Rowney Priory for a much-needed break. The Benedictine nuns had done their best but the hot meal they served was the worst Daniel and his friends had yet tasted. At least there was plenty of bread to wash it down.

"That was disgusting," said Jim, mopping up the last of his pottage from his bowl nonetheless.

"Yes, this priory seems pretty shabby compared to the others we've been to. I think the sisters are actually living by their vow of poverty, either through choice or necessity. I imagine they can ill afford to feed all of us. They're probably using up half their winter stores. I hope the king gives them some compensation."

He did; for a similar conversation had taken place in the prioress' lodging where the distinguished guests had fared only a little better with their meal. In no time the steward and his minions were rounding everyone up and they were underway again.

Ed had an excited look on his face as he stopped to give Daniel a bunk up to mount his horse.

"I've spoken to Warin," he said, "and he told me this Brother Clément has been very kind to him; took him under his wing a bit when he was being bullied by his old master. He confirmed what you said, Dan; Clément's been devastated by the queen's death, and has gone a bit crazy, staying up every night to pray for her soul. This was weird though, Warin said Clément feels partly to blame for the queen's death, but that if anyone was to blame, it was him - Warin. But then he completely clammed up, I couldn't get any more out of him. So I've no idea what that was about." The others digested this information quietly as the cortege filed slowly through the priory gate.

Before long the procession came to a junction and turned south onto Ermine Street. Up ahead, Warin said to Clément, "At last we are heading in the right direction." Clément noticed he was gnawing his lip. In fact his friend was fretting over having said too much to Ed. He had vowed to the Lord Chancellor not to breathe a word about the cursed stone to a living soul. What he said could not have made any sense to Ed but it might make him curious and prompt further questions. He must be more guarded in future. And why was Ed asking questions about Brother Clément in the first place? He glanced over to his friend, plodding along on his faithful old mule. Should he tell him? No; why bother him with it? It must have been idle curiosity and though Ed was a stranger, he seemed a good-hearted fellow. There was no harm in him, surely?

Chapter 69

13th December 1290, Hertfordshire

The party proceeded south all through that gloomy December afternoon, passing through the town of Ware, lined with respectful locals. Once they were through the town, Natalie said,
"Is it boring, your dad being a vicar, Dan?"
"Sometimes, but everyone's life is boring sometimes, isn't it? And vicars aren't necessarily goodie goodies. There have been lots of vicars at Abbotsbury who weren't very good at all. In the 1540s there was an abbot of the monastery who was a thief and kept a harem."
"What's a harem?" Ed asked.
Daniel blushed. "Um, a place where you keep lots of women as your concubines."
"Oooh! A naughty vicar!" said Jim, getting interested.
"Yeah; and in the 1700s practically everybody in the village, including the vicar, was involved in smuggling."
"What did they smuggle?" Natalie asked.
"Mainly brandy, tobacco and tea, I think."
The others burst out laughing and Natalie said, "Tea! Why on earth would anybody smuggle tea?"
"There was a really high tax on it in those days. I admit it doesn't sound very cool. But smuggling was illegal and they always ran the risk of being caught by the coast guard."
"So what does your dad get up to being a vicar nowadays?" Natalie said. "I presume he doesn't have a harem or run some drug smuggling ring?"

"Nah," Dan smiled. "Just the usual stuff - preaching on Sundays, weddings, funerals, visiting people when they're sick, helping people who are struggling with different issues."

"Not as cool as smuggling then, but pretty cool I suppose, helping people and stuff."

"Yeah, I guess. For me it's just normal life. The only thing that sometimes bugs me is that it's pretty relentless. He's always on call, day and night, seven days a week. And of, course, Christmas and Easter, when I'm home for the holidays, are his busiest times of the year. That's probably why I miss Hadrian more because I spend more time with my dog than with my parents."

"And it must be a bit lonely, being an only child," Natalie said.

"Sometimes, but being the vicar's son in a small community means everyone knows me. If I'm bored, I can knock on anyone's door and have a drink and a chat. And cake - there's always homemade cake. The old folk, especially, love to chat and they tell me loads of stories about the past. I guess that's also so fed my love of history - hearing their stories."

"Sounds boring as hell, listening to a load of old people droning on about the good old days," said Jim.

"I wish I could have a dog," said Natalie. "My mum's allergic to practically everything with fur. I sometimes get to play with my neighbour's dog, Rolo. He's a golden Lab - a guide dog that flunked the training so he's really obedient but not much fun. You don't even get to tell him what to do because he just does it anyway. In the holidays I sometimes take him for walks, so they don't have to do it when they come home from work."

"That's nice of you," Daniel said.

"They pay me for it, otherwise I wouldn't bother," Natalie said. But then she grinned, poked him in the ribs and said, "Just kidding. I'd do it anyway. I love being with animals. But when I get home after walking Rolo, I have to get straight in the shower and put all my clothes in the washing machine otherwise mum would have an allergic reaction to me!"

"No way!" Ed said, amazed and relieved no one in his family had fur allergies.

"Yeah, it's a pain in the butt."

"Worse for your mum than for you though," Daniel said.

"Worse how?"

"Because she can't go anywhere near animals. Does it bother her?"

"Oh, I don't know. I've always assumed she doesn't like animals, but maybe she'd love to have a dog or a cat or something. Now I think of it, she loves TV programmes about animals. And she's pretty good at looking after my poxy goldfish. When we get back home, I'll ask her."

"Good idea," Daniel said, hoping desperately that Natalie would have the opportunity to ask her mum that question. They settled into a silence that Daniel noticed was quite comfortable, even though each was lost in their own thoughts of home, tinged with concern over getting back there.

To the east of the Roman road, the land became increasingly marshy while in the west the light of the sinking sun hardly penetrated the gathering clouds. It began to spit with rain as darkness fell. In the villages of Emmewell and Broxbourne, respectful mourners bowed their heads in the gentle drizzle as the queen's bier passed by them. The sound of flowing water to their left, as well as the softly falling rain, gave Dan the sense of an all-pervading dampness. The friends hunkered down in their cloaks and rode on in miserable silence. At last, they came to Waltham-on-the-Street and turned westward.

Chapter 70

13th December 1290, Waltham-on-the-Street, Essex

Presently three stone bridges carried the horsemen at the front of the cortege over channels of the river Lea with the long procession straggling behind them. By the time the last wagons rolled over the bridge, the abbey of Waltham rose up, blacker than the surrounding darkness, ahead of the bishop carrying the cross in front of the queen's bier, which lay in a covered carriage, due to the rain.

Robert of Elenton, the abbot of Waltham, noted the wet, bedraggled appearance of the bishop, and cut short the welcome speech he had prepared. He greeted the king and the royal party and offered the briefest of prayers over the queen's bier. Then he and his charges led the procession into the torchlit abbey precincts. Some yards behind, Warin said to Brother Clément walking beside him,

"So, this is Waltham Abbey and therein lies the holy cross you told me about."

"Yes, my lad. And you will see it this very evening if you attend at Vespers."

"I will, and I pray that this night's vigil may speed the queen's passage to heaven as she lies before the miraculous cross."

Further to the rear, Daniel and his three companions trudged in weary silence to their overnight rest. As they passed through the abbey gatehouse, Daniel shuddered. It was their last stop before London; his mind reeled with excitement and anxiety. In a day or two he would see the medieval capital with his own eyes. But if, as he hoped, the queen's cortege held the answer to their conundrum, the time window to find their way back home was rapidly shrinking.

The altar candles cast a glow aslant the queen's body while the rest of the abbey church fled away into dark recesses, beyond the hefty pillars. Clément took a place behind the choir monks keeping vigil. The closer the cortege drew to Queen Eleanor's final resting place, the more he yearned to be alone with her. But by day she was surrounded by the royal procession and at night by dutiful monks. All night long these brothers would fend off sleep and ignore the seeping cold to pray for her soul's repose. He owed them his thanks, but he felt only a churlish, sullen anger.

Once again Clément reminded himself, Eleanor never was and never would be his. In death, she belonged to God. In life, she had belonged to the king, to her children, to the royal court and to the people. And I resent them all, God forgive me, he thought, crossing himself. Yet on night after night of his voluntary vigil, he had been astonished at the kindness of God. The Lord had blessed him with insights, with visions and with a peace that sat alongside his ungovernable rage and grief. He had been drawn deeper into the heart of prayer, the baring of the soul before God's loving gaze.

So now, alongside the good brothers whose company he so begrudged, he opened his heart once more to God: his longing that Eleanor be remembered; that the monument to be built here at Waltham would endure throughout the generations. It rose up before his mind's eye - tall, slender and beautiful like the queen it commemorated; he saw people passing by, stopping to look, to admire and remember. How strangely dressed they were. And among the crowd were four young people whose faces he recognised. Clément jerked into consciousness. The same faces again, now in his waking dream as well as his sleep. The young lord Daniel, 'from the north' with his three followers. Something about this boy both unnerved and yet comforted him; as if they had met before these recent events, though he knew for a certainty they had not.

After he heard the lad mention Abbotsbury, Clément had made discreet inquiries. Lord Daniel was a pilgrim, so he said, en route to Westminster to pray for the souls of his parents. He had come, so he said, from the islands north of Scotland. Last night, at Saint Albans, the boy had stopped him, ostensibly to apologise, and then questioned him closely about his pendant. Clément regretted his imprudent response; he had been caught off guard. In his years of travel with the queen's entourage, Clément had met many from much farther-flung parts, but this Lord Daniel struck him as somehow more foreign, more outlandish. Nonetheless, the lad also struck a chord of familiarity that lent him a significance Clément did not yet understand. It nagged at his mind like the matins bell penetrating his midnight slumber to call him to prayer.

As he knelt there, he fixed his gaze on the miraculous cross - the ancient crucifix, discovered centuries ago, after God-given dreams. He recalled the story and marvelled at how the guiding hand of God, interpreted by one devout servant, had led, by such a mysterious path, to the foundation of this abbey; Waltham was now one of the most prestigious religious houses in the land. One man's dream, the source of all this - the worship of the brothers that expressed itself in prayer by day and night, and through the daily ministry of hospitality to travellers, treatment for the sick and education for the young.

All this, Clément mused, began with an inspired dream - one that recurred until the dreamer understood and acted. And what if I am now an inspired dreamer, he asked himself. How am I to interpret and act? His eyes were still locked on the figure of Christ upon the cross, its polished gold concealing the original black cross beneath, which had been buried in the ground for unknown years until the dream revealed it. Clément's dream dwelt not on a buried cross but on a boy. The divine hand had not yet revealed to Clément the nature of the lad's significance but surely if God wanted Clément to act, further revelation would follow. With this thought, Clément prayerfully put his own hand into the divine one and allowed himself to be led wherever God saw fit, which at this moment, was to his bed.

Chapter 71

14th December 1290, Waltham Abbey, Essex

Well before first light, Robert Burnell sent for Otto di Grandisson. He spoke in a low tone so as not to be overheard by a bleary-eyed servant who stoked and fed the embers of yesterday's fire and gathered up the late evening wine cups.

"Forgive me for waking you to receive unwelcome news, Otto. The search party has returned, but on the way back they heard tell of a murdered man, discovered on Akeman Street between Aylesbury and Alcester. They went to investigate and I grieve to tell you it was your fellow, Thomas, who was tailing Scand; his throat was cut."

"God's blood! He was a good man; may he rest in peace." Otto made the sign of the cross. He studied his friend's grim face and said, "You believe it was Scand?"

Burnell nodded. "He is more dangerous than we thought."

"Thomas was no fool, yet Scand bested him," Otto said. "So, he is on to our ruse; but why not just comply? We gave him his freedom and the wherewithal to ply his trade in a new place. We could not prove him a murderer before, so why make himself a murderer now?"

"To send us a message perhaps? I agree it makes little sense. But I fear Scand may prove to be a vengeful man," Burnell said.

His friend agreed. "Aye, do you recall the deadly looks he cast at poor Warin during the trial, in the rare moments when his self-possession lapsed?"

"Indeed; and we now have no idea of his whereabouts."

"He would have to be mad as well as bitter to venture back to London."

"Yes, that is true," Burnell said, rubbing his stubbly chin. "If he does show his face, we will arrest him for Thomas' death, though I fear that crime would likely be as hard to prove as the other. But I cannot spare the men to chase him down. I am sorry, Otto."

"I understand. With your leave, Robert, I will go and write a letter to Thomas' wife, now widow. And make her what recompense I can." Burnell nodded gravely and they parted.

∞

Daniel mounted his horse in the abbey forecourt with the cortege party gathering around him. He sensed in his fellows a mood of anticipation mixed with relief that mirrored his own feeling at embarking on this last leg of the gruelling journey to London. For the majority of the travellers, from the highest members of the royal family down to the servants and baggage carriers, the queen's funeral would lead to a return to normal life. For Daniel, it would signal the success or failure of his quest to find a way back home. He drew his cloak more tightly around his neck, unconsciously gnawing his lip.

The procession re-crossed the three bridges over the Lea, the sound of rushing water reaching them from the river below, unseen in the darkness. At a place where the road widened, the cortege halted for the blessing of the cross site.

"This place will change its name once the cross is built," Daniel said to Natalie once they were underway again. "Now it's called Waltham-on-the-Street but it will become Waltham Cross."

"Oh, right," Natalie said sleepily.

And Charing will become Charing Cross, Daniel mused, thinking ahead to that last cross site they would reach in a couple of days' time. And what then?

∞

Today Princess Mary's grandmother had opted to ride in a coach, somewhat fatigued by the recent incessant travel. So Mary rode beside her sisters. Her eldest and favourite sister, Eleanora, was daydreaming, perhaps of her husband, Alphonso, who had been absent even from their wedding some months ago. Her situation was peculiar. The marriage ceremony was performed with a substitute bridegroom and even now, Eleanora had not yet been united with her new husband, the King of Aragon.

On Mary's other side, Joan and Margaret were reminiscing about their weddings earlier in the year. Mary had never seen anything as stunning as Margaret on her wedding day; her head held high, her golden headdress flashing with rubies and pearls. The aura of romance had so swept Mary up that it almost eradicated the inordinate rush and strained tempers of the preceding days. Recalling the royal wedding now, she found herself both bewitched and repelled by its extravagance. Am I growing ascetic, she wondered, so influenced by the relative simplicity of convent life that I baulk at the lavish celebration of my sister's wedding? The contrast between the dual aspects of her life was a perpetual source of unease. Back at Amesbury, she spent months on end within the convent walls participating in the ceaseless daily round of worship, which alternately delighted or bored her. Then a summons from her father would transplant her into the luxurious, itinerant life of the royal court. Whenever she started to settle in one style of life, she was uprooted and dropped into the other. It was disorientating. Navigating these two extremes was emerging as a chief pattern of her life.

Jasper shook his mane and jerked his head round, bumping her foot and knocking it out of the stirrup. A groom ran up to assist her but she waved him away, preferring to release the other foot too and stretch both legs for a while. Beside her, Joan and Margaret suddenly snorted with laughter.

"Shush, Mary's probably eavesdropping," said Margaret. Mary surmised that their conversation had moved from weddings to wedding nights.

"Stopper your ears, Mary," Joan said, confirming her suspicion. "Eleanora may listen because one day, perhaps, Alphonso will finally appear and bed her. But you will only ever be married to Christ."

Mary disregarded her sister's barb. She was not ignorant about relations between men and women. The novices sometimes indulged in whispered tête-à-têtes about spying on their parents or servants wriggling under the blankets. She had pieced together these titbits of information into a fairly coherent whole. And since her monthly bleeding had started a few months ago, her own body was instructing her as to the rest.

Moreover, one of the effects of her separation from her family was that in subsequent visits she was more keenly aware than her siblings of the joy of her parents' union. Tears smarted in her eyes; whether from the loss of her mother or the loss of experiences she would never enjoy, she could not tell. She was called to put aside the desires of the flesh. Time marched inexorably towards the day she would take her final vows and then she would be married to Christ, as her sister reminded her. This fact was a knot she could not untie, but that did not stop her tugging at it repeatedly.

The cortege progressed south on The Great North Road, built long ago by the Romans to connect London to Lincoln. Beyond its grassy verge, slender birch trunks gleamed in the lambent light of pre-dawn. The sky gradually gained its blue and the day broke cold and clear. In the morning they passed through the villages of Enfield and Toteham and crossed the Moswell Brook, on its way to join the Lea, just audible beyond the trees. On the far side of the river, rose the ridge of the great Forest of Essex. Daniel's stomach growled as the road began to climb steeply. But all thoughts of hunger were forgotten as they gained the top of Sandford Hill and there below them, a few miles ahead, lay the medieval city of London.

Even though he knew roughly what to expect, the sight fairly took Daniel's breath away. Its massive, crenellated city walls, punctuated by imposing gatehouses, gave him the impression of a vast, sprawling fortress, which indeed it was. Jim, Ed and Natalie were speechless. This was an utterly different London to the one subconsciously imprinted on their brains, with its skyscrapers topped by the Shard; yet this London was every bit as impressive. All they could do was gawp in wonder.

With the end in sight, the queen's cortege pressed on down the gentler southern slope of Sandford Hill and crossed the ford of Hackney Brook. The dead straight road to the capital cut through the hamlet of Newington. In the already fading light, the cityscape conjured in Daniel's mind a monstrous creature, porcupine-like, with its multitude of church spires bristling above the walls. They were approaching this weird man-made beast at its flank, but over to the west reared its huge head – old Saint Paul's Cathedral, with its horn-like central spire rising to an astonishing height.

Part III

The Twelfth Cross

PART III LONDON

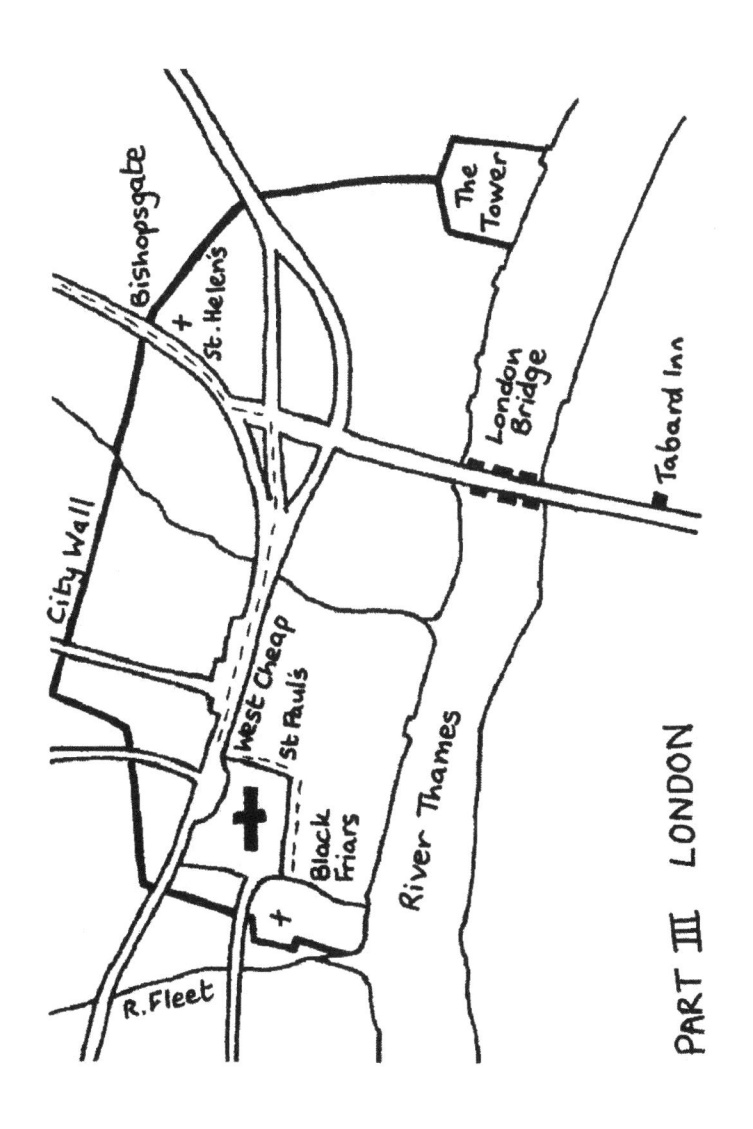

PART III

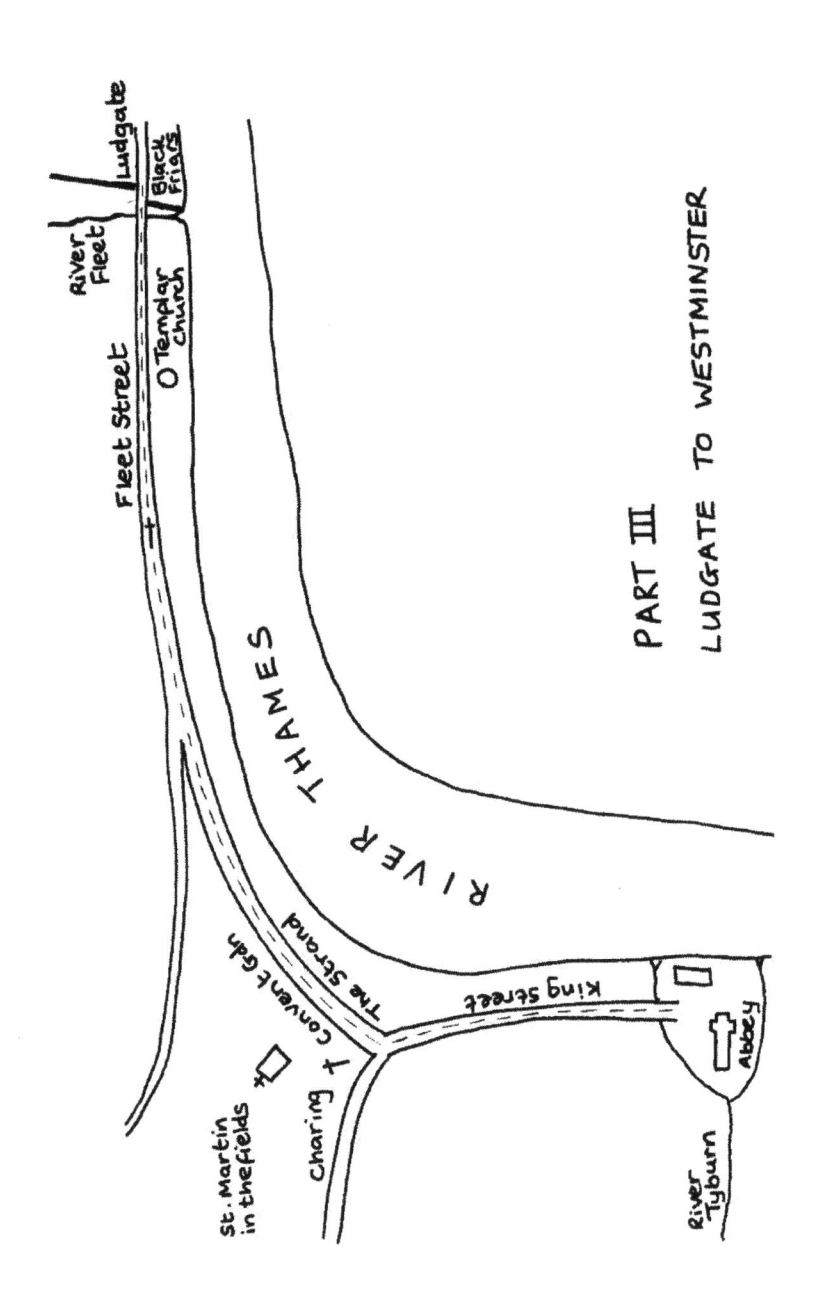

LUDGATE TO WESTMINSTER

Chapter 72

14th December 1290, London

The dignitaries of London filed in solemn procession outside the city walls to meet the royal cortege, but before these worthy men reached them, the travellers were greeted by the stench of the capital. Though by now acclimatised to the raw-sewage-rotting-garbage stink of medieval towns, Daniel visibly recoiled and his friends actually gagged when it hit their nostrils.

"Crap," Jim said, "I can't go any closer." He covered his nose and mouth with his sleeve. Natalie and Ed did the same.

But Daniel said, "We have to. Breathe through your mouth; it helps a bit. And take your hands away from your faces before anybody notices."

Carlita, further ahead in the cortege, also baulked slightly at the familiar smell. She was passing the brothers and sisters of St Mary's Hospital, who lined the road as the procession approached the city walls. She urged her pony forward under the tall, pointed arch of Bishopsgate, with its two sturdy towers. Beyond the city gate, the street was thronged with Londoners waiting to pay their respects to the late queen.

Carlita's gentle palfrey was growing nervous at the onslaught of sights and sounds. She reached forward to pat her neck. A man's hand shot out and grabbed her wrist; the pony reared, its movement jerking her free. She spurred the pony on and twisted in the saddle to see her would-be assailant. A tall figure withdrew his hood sufficiently for her wide, startled eyes to meet the defiant gaze of Derian Scand. He smiled and made a cut-throat gesture at his own neck, before pulling up his hood and melting into the crowd. Carlita rode on, her heart thumping in her chest, her thoughts frantic. She must tell Lord Burnell.

The solemn nature of the procession had muted the usual raucous bustle of the city, nevertheless by the time Daniel and his friends rode, marvelling, under the grand gate in the towering wall, the crowds thronging the street of Bishopgate were growing restive. Daniel's eyes ranged avidly over people of every walk of life, whose clothing expressed their social status, from the jewel-studded velvets and satins of noblemen and women in shades of fashionable red, green and blue, down to the drab homespun of peasants. He was surprised to see that at the head of the cortege, the bishops of London and Lincoln were leading the procession aside through a humble gatehouse into a priory. The queen's bier was carried with due solemnity into the priory church to lie in state upon the high altar, while the nuns chanted prayers. King Edward and his immediate followers proceeded to the prioress' lodging while the rest of the party, having dismounted, were led gratefully towards the refectory.

Daniel was slightly disappointed at this unexpected stop. Though ravenous, he badly wanted to see London. There was little daylight left and he knew it would not be safe for him to venture out after dark. If he remembered correctly, tonight's overnight stop would be at Blackfriars, somewhere over in the west of the city he thought vaguely. By the time they had eaten, it would be dark for the final stage of the journey. From his place in the queue for the refectory, he watched another queue forming at the parish door of the church, as members of the public waited to view the late queen lying in state and to offer prayers for her soul. Despite the number of people making up these two groups, a reverent hush pervaded the priory courtyard.

In the quiet, Natalie's stomach growled suddenly like a bear. The others stifled their laughter.

"Yeah, I'm starving too," whispered Ed and they shuffled forward towards the aroma of stew wafting from the open doorway ahead. By the time they entered the dining hall, it was so packed with guests that they couldn't find four spaces together. Warin had saved a space for Brother Clément, but he, of course, was praying alongside the nuns in the priory church. He beckoned to Ed, who squeezed onto the bench next to him, reached for a bowl of pottage and a hunk of bread and tucked in.

"Thank you, Warin," he said, liberally spraying his mouthful of stew. He wiped his mouth on his sleeve, swallowed and repeated, "Thanks, it's rammed in here."

"Edward, do you know why we have broken our journey here at the Priory of Saint Helen?" Warin said.

"To eat, I presume," said Ed, reaching for another chunk of bread and mopping up the last vestiges of stew with it.

"Well, yes; I suppose that is also a factor. But the main reason is that the church contains a most holy relic – a piece of the true cross of our Lord!"

"No way!" said Ed, not believing a word of it.

"I had it from Brother Clément as we turned in at the gatehouse. Five years ago, King Edward came here on foot in a holy procession to present a relic of the true cross to the sisters."

Ed was clueless how to respond to this. "Goodness," he said lamely, "But I don't quite see the connection; what does it have to do with us stopping here?"

"For Queen Eleanor, of course. She is at this moment lying on the high altar of the church beside the sacred relic where prayers are being said for the repose of her soul. What higher honour could there be?"

Again Ed was a bit flummoxed; he wished Daniel was there. It seemed safest to agree heartily, "Yes, what an honour."

Just then a knight approached them. Ed recognised him from Geddington, the one who had invited Daniel to the hunt. To his relief, it was Warin he wanted. He spoke in Warin's ear and the lad rose and left with him. Moments later the young man reappeared, as pale as a night owl, and sat down heavily. Otto de Grandisson's message had shocked him deeply. Derian Scand was at large in London.

"You all right, mate? You look like you've seen a ghost," Ed said.

"I have seen a ghost, in a manner of speaking. Or, at least, I am about to. But, forgive me, I am not at liberty to speak of it." He took a big slug of ale from his pewter mug.

Chapter 73

14ᵗʰ December 1290, London

In the prioress' lodging, drinking wine from a silver goblet and eating a fine meal, Princess Mary sat, for once, by her father, her brother Prince Edward and her sister Joan. The royal family was joined, as usual, by various top-ranking clerics and officials. The king was seated opposite the prioress of Saint Helen's, whom he now addressed,

"How have you fared here since I saw you last, Sister Felicia?"

"Much better, your Grace, I thank you, since your generous gift. A steady stream of pilgrims comes, especially in the summer months, to pray before the relic of the true cross. Our coffers are now full enough to fund our ministries and the upkeep of our buildings."

"I am glad to hear it. And I thank you for your hospitality to our large party today. I will see that you are recompensed." The prioress inclined her head in grateful acknowledgement.

The king turned his attention to his mother, also a prioress, of a far more affluent convent.

"Will you be taking Mary straight back to Amesbury after..." The word funeral hung unspoken in the air, "afterwards, Mama? Or do you give her leave to remain a little longer at court among her family?"

"I must set out straight away; there are many matters for me to attend to. But if it is your wish, Edward, perhaps Mary may remain a few days longer, if you will grant her safe escort back." The look on the former queen's face belied her compliant words. It was clear that, in her opinion, Mary had been out amongst the temptations of the world for long enough and should be delivered as soon as possible back to the safe confines of the cloister.

Prioress Eleanor of Amesbury had lived long enough in the royal court to tire of its endless power struggles, danger and restless travel, and even of its wealth and comfort. Her beloved King Henry had clung to the throne largely by the efforts of their son, Edward, who was altogether more suited to wielding the sceptre. When Henry died, she retired to the convent and become queen of a smaller, more spiritual realm. But though Prioress Eleanor held complete sway over her granddaughter's life in the convent, she could not gainsay the wishes of the king.

"What of you, Mary?" Edward asked his daughter with a twinkle in his eye, "Can you countenance staying among us a little longer or do you long to hasten back to your sisters?"

"I think I can bear the separation, Father," she replied, her face lighting up like a beacon. Her thoughts flew to Warin and she felt her colour rise, prickling, from the base of her neck right up to her temples. Her grandmother glared at her as if she could read her mind but Mary held her gaze defiantly, in spite of the blush.

The candles on the table flickered in the draught as a door opened and one of the priory sisters entered. She made a deep reverence to the king and then spoke quietly with her prioress, who said,

"Your Grace, our brothers of Holy Trinity have arrived."

"Good," said the king, rising. Everyone at the table followed his lead, as he continued, "Once again we thank you, Sister Felicia, for your hospitality. If you would be so good as to assemble your sisters; we will be on our way."

∞

Ed emerged from the refectory into a priory courtyard ablaze with flaming torchlight.

"What's going on?" he asked.

Warin had fallen into step close beside him. "Ah, yes, Lord Otto made mention of this: the torchbearers are friars of Holy Trinity, Aldgate. They have come en masse to light the procession to the Friary of the Dominicans, where we are to stay for the night." As he spoke, he scanned the crowded courtyard for Derian Scand. He also looked for

Brother Clément. Lord Burnell's message, communicated by Otto, had given him leave to warn Clément of the potential danger.

Poor Brother Clément. Hitherto it had been agreed to keep him in ignorance of Scand's curse on the snakestone since he was already so distressed about having given the pendant to the queen. But now for his own safety, he must be told. And the task fell to Warin. At least he had stowed in his scrip some bread for the scribe and he would see him eat it before imparting the unwelcome news. Warin's eyes continued to flit back and forth over the disparate groups being herded into order by the king's steward. He was so intent on his search that Ed's voice startled him when he said,

"Are you looking for someone, Warin?"

"Huh? Oh, yes, for Brother Clément. I will go and see if he is still in the church. But if I might be so bold, perhaps you could ask Lord Daniel if I might join your little party and walk with you to Blackfriars?"

"Yes, of course. If you can find us!" said Ed, blundering through the throng towards Daniel.

∞

Derian Scand stopped by a street vendor on London Bridge and bought a hot meat pie. A light rain began to fall but it hardly reached the ground, so crowded was the space between the shops perched on either side of the bridge, their rear ends jutting out bravely over the Thames. Scand was licking the last pastry crumbs from his fingers as he passed the chapel of St Thomas, midway across the bridge. He came to a standstill and then was even driven backwards; the tide of human traffic was flowing against him. He made his way to the side of the street and with head down and elbows out, barged his way through the oncoming crowd. Word has got out that the cortege is passing through the city, he thought; so much the better for my purposes.

He crossed the lowered drawbridge at the southern end of London Bridge and made his way past the docks and down the High Street, putting the sacred part of Borough behind him as he passed the Priory of Saint Mary Overie. It was many years since he had frequented this seedier part of town, thinking it beneath him once he became goldsmith to the royal court. But the sight of the street girls and the familiar reek of the taverns brought to mind many a pleasurable, raucous night spent here in his youth.

At last, he reached the Tabard Inn and found it agreeably quiet. The pilgrims, who gathered here virtually any day of the year before setting out to Canterbury, had all gone up to the city to view the royal procession and only the regular batch of drunkards, drabs and criminals were left. He went through to the courtyard to see if any cockfighting or bearbaiting were to be had. But the reach of royal mourning had put a dampener on entertainment even here.

Derian bought a mug of ale. The landlord put down his change on the bar but Scand slid it back saying,

"Have one for yourself, friend," he said, "and tell me, might I meet hereabouts a man called Tom Armourer, who used to work for the king until he fell into bad ways?"

"Yes, I know Tom; he is one of my regulars. I have not yet seen him this day but he may be in by and by." Derian settled himself in a corner and sat drinking his ale, waving away the attentions of the girls who approached every now and then. He was on his third mug of ale and still no sign of Tom. He fished in his purse for another coin, laid it on the table in front of him and contemplated the king's head. He quaffed the last of his ale, returned to the bar, pushed the coin the barman's way and said,

"When Tom is not here, where might I find him?" The barman gave him directions and Derian headed back out into the chilly December air. An hour later he re-crossed London Bridge with a small crossbow stowed under his cloak. His face wore a smug look; he was enjoying the irony of paying for the weapon with the jewels Carlita had returned to him on the night of his sham escape.

Chapter 74

14ᵗʰ December 1290, London

Carlita was at that moment on her knees by the bier of her late mistress before the relic of the true cross, praying, "Lord God of Heaven, I confess my wrongdoing – I gave myself to a man for pleasure and trinkets. I knew he was not a good man; it was against my conscience but I allowed myself to be led astray. Christ, my Saviour, forgive me." She looked up at the cross, "I implore you, merciful God, to save me from Derian Scand. And I vow, on this holy relic, to dedicate my life to serving you, if you rescue me from peril at the hands of that man."

Her prayers were interrupted by the arrival of the prioress, who bowed before the cross, lifted it from its place at the high altar and carried it in procession down the aisle of the church, followed by nuns who had been keeping vigil over the late queen. Carlita rose from her knees. Clearly the cortege was preparing to depart. She followed the queen's bier down the aisle and out into the priory courtyard, blinking in the unexpected light of dozens of blazing torches.

Fifteen minutes later, she was riding in the torchlit procession, flanked by two of Lord Burnell's officers for her protection; nevertheless, she cast her eyes this way and that at every hooded man in the crowd. Ahead, she could see the more formal part of the cortege. At the very front, Sister Felicia, bearing the relic of the true cross, walked in between the bishops of London and Lincoln, who also carried great crosses. Behind them was the queen's bier, draped now with two vivid flags; the quartered standard of Eleanor's royal house of Castille and Leon with its gold castles and purple leaping lions and the royal banner of England, its three golden lions every now and then coming alive in the flickering torchlight. Behind the bier rode King Edward, towering over everyone on his tall black charger, and behind him his mother, riding alongside six-year-old Prince Edward. Next came the prince's sisters, Joan and Margaret with their husbands, superseding the elder Eleanora, who brought up the rear of the royal family with the younger princesses, Mary and Elizabeth. Apart from Mary and her grandmother, who wore the simple black and white of their order, the royal party wore rich black cloaks, edged with ermine, and crusted with jewels that scintillated in the torchlight.

At the very back of the procession, Daniel was saying, "King Edward knows how to put on a show."

"Yes," Natalie agreed. "Whoever's in charge has a great sense of theatre."

"Perhaps the stop at Saint Helen's was at least partly to allow darkness to fall."

"Yeah, probably. But all this is kind of freaking me out," Natalie confided. "Do you remember watching the funeral procession of Queen Elizabeth on TV? Now we're taking part in a procession from 700 years before; for the funeral of our queen's great, great, however-many-greats grandmother. Or were they not actually related?"

"I'm not sure about that. Yeah, it's uncanny; I had a flashback to Queen Elizabeth's funeral procession when I saw the flags."

"Do you think we'll be allowed to go to Queen Eleanor's funeral or will it just be VIPs?"

"I have no idea, to be honest, Natalie. But we will have to go to the abbey, to keep up our cover story; that we're pilgrims going to pray at the shrine of Edward the Confessor. Have you ever been there? In our time, I mean?"

"I've seen it from the outside but never been in. I mean, it's just a big, fancy church, isn't it?"

Daniel winced at such colossal ignorance. But on reflection, he recognised a core of truth in what Natalie said; at its heart, the abbey was actually a big, fancy building for the worship of God.

"Yes, you're right. But if we see it here and then visit it again when we get home, you'll be able to see how it's become a kind of monument to a thousand years of British history."

"Where exactly are we now, does anybody know?" Natalie asked. The cortege was going so slowly that Daniel was able to lean over and ask someone in the crowd what street this was,

"Why, Cornhill, a'course, my lord," a middle-aged woman replied, "and beyond the junction here is Stock. You will see the signs, though the animals have been cleared away for the queen, a'course, God rest her." She made the sign of the cross and without pausing for breath, went on, "And beyond Stock lies Poultry, and then Cheap." Her neighbour, presumably her husband, elbowed her in the ribs and she stopped abruptly. The man rolled his eyes and said,

"Forgive my wife's prattle, my lord, it is kindly meant but she forgets herself."

Daniel smiled and said, "On the contrary, friends, we are strangers from the far north, visiting your city for the first time. I thank you for your information." He nodded his goodbye and nudged his horse to walk on, for the procession was on the move again. Cornhill, Stock, Poultry, Cheap; he tried to picture what these broad streets would look like on an ordinary day, bustling with traders selling cereals, animals and every other product a medieval Londoner could desire. But, apart from the whiff of livestock in the air, the area had been so thoroughly cleared and cleansed in honour of the royal occasion that it was hard to imagine. He did notice the signs above their heads, however, as they passed into Stock. Some were iron, displaying finely-wrought curved rams' horns, others showed simply-painted animals on wooden placards.

"Did she say Cornhill? My dad works near there," said Jim. "I think we must be just approaching where Mansion House and Bank station will be in our time. Bloody hell."

"What are you three muttering about?" Ed asked.

"Just about the London streets; how they're not what we're used to back home," Daniel responded, jerking his head slightly at Warin, walking the other side of Ed. "In Orkney."

"Huh? Oh, yeah, in Orkney," Ed said, catching on slowly, "We've never seen streets like this, not to mention the crowds; it's amazing."

They came to a junction where Cornhill met with Threadneedle Street on their right and Lombard Street on their left, and the three roads merged into Stock. Jim gazed around, then leant over to Ed, walking beside him and murmured,

"I was right, this is where Mansion House will be, and Bank Station. The road layout hasn't changed in all these years. And bloody hell, that must be Saint Paul's."

At the end of the long, straight street before them, directly ahead was a huge church, its spire towering over everything around it.

"Nah, Saint Paul's has a dome, not a steeple. I've been there," Ed said.
"This Saint Paul's burnt down in the fire of London, you numbskull. And then the one with the dome was built," Natalie said, enjoying a rare opportunity to flaunt her basic general knowledge.

"Keep your voices down," Daniel urged. "Just because we've got this far doesn't mean we're not still in danger."

They rode on in silence, gawping in wonder at the utterly different London, which every now and then, gave them a glimpse of the city it would become. With old Saint Paul's looming even larger before them, the cortege came to a halt. Daniel and his friends could not see what was happening up ahead, but Daniel guessed it was the blessing of the eleventh cross site, at West Cheap. The ceremony cannot have taken long for they soon ambled forward again but the torches remained static up ahead. Once they caught up with them, Daniel worked out what was happening. The royal party and other members of the cortege were proceeding past the abbey precincts of Saint Paul's while the queen's bier remained at Cheapside for a public vigil, surrounded by the torch-bearing brothers of Holy Trinity.

They rode on around the high stone wall of the Abbey of Saint Paul's towards the west end of the city. As they neared Ludgate, the black friars came out to greet the king, a long-standing friend to their house. Daniel and his friends rode under the gatehouse into a scene of mildly chaotic bustle as horses were led to the stables and the large party was welcomed into the copious friary buildings. They entered the guest hall, eyes smarting slightly at the welcome fire inside. Before she was led away to the women's quarters, Natalie gave a huge yawn which spread like a rash between them. The gamut of sights, sounds and experiences of the day suddenly overtook them, and with hardly a word, Jim and Ed found a spot to lie down, wrapped themselves in their cloaks and fell fast asleep.

Daniel too was dog-tired but his growing anxiety left him restless. Their journey was almost at an end and he felt no closer to finding a way home. Above the general hubbub of folks settling down for the night, he heard the church bell tolling the hour for Compline. As if it were a summons, he got up and followed the Dominican brothers to evening prayer. Daniel let the chanting of the monks bathe him in a warm glow that soothed his conscious mind, but at the end of the service, he felt no closer to solving their conundrum. There was nothing to do but go to bed.

Chapter 75

14th **December 1290, London**

The threat that Warin faced from Derian rendered him fearful yet paradoxically bold and reckless. He lingered in the friary stables long after dark, enjoying the musky, sweet, horse-hay scent, after the stink of the city. He hoped that Princess Mary would bring an apple or carrot for her pony, Jasper, as she sometimes did. Eventually, his patience was rewarded. A lantern bobbed towards him in the dimness and as it drew closer, its shadowy bearer resolved into her form. He cleared his throat and intercepted her.

"Forgive me, your Grace, may I make so bold as to speak with you?"

Mary raised the lantern to see whose face the voice belonged to and the two youngsters, long fascinated by each other, found themselves eye to eye.

"You may speak," she said.

"You probably do not remember me, but I was called upon when Jasper here was skittish near Stamford." Mary recalled him very well. Warin's earnest cornflower-blue eyes flickered in the lamplight and her colour mounted but she said nothing. Warin continued, "Since that moment when your pony reared and I held you to prevent you falling, I have thought of little but you."

She held up her hand to stall him. "You must not speak to me in this way, young man. And however much I might wish to, I must not listen. I am given to God, as well you know. And in any case, I am but twelve years old."

"Forgive me; I would not have dared but I have reason to believe that my life is in danger. I could not bear to think of going to my death without having spoken. I seek nothing from you. Only that you should go through life knowing that there was one who admired you more than words could express."

"Your life in danger - this cannot be! Who threatens it? I will call down my father's knights upon his head." Mary said, aghast.

"I am not permitted to speak of it, my lady. The Lord Chancellor forbade it."

"Oh, what can be done?" Mary wailed.

"Nothing, my lady. I will take what care I can and perhaps the threat may come to nothing. I will leave you now." He made her a deep reverence and turned to leave.

"Please, may I know your name?"

The lad spun round, exultant. "Warin, my lady, at your service, always." He bowed again.

"God be with you, Warin, as will my prayers. Farewell."

∞

15th December 1290, 2.30am, Blackfriars Church, London

Late in the evening when the royal family departed for Westminster, Mary fabricated an excuse to remain at Blackfriars so that she could stay close to Warin. She was near the high altar, keeping vigil near her mother's bier, when she heard a loud gasp as Brother Clément awoke from a vision.

The sound also roused Carlita, who had taken refuge in the church for fear of Derian. She had found a hidden corner and settled herself for a less than comfortable night's sleep. She was none too pleased to be disturbed, but Clément's waking mutterings and movements were so comical that she forgot her displeasure as she watched. He tried to leap up from his knees but fell straight back down because his legs had gone to sleep. Undeterred, he began crawling on all fours in the direction of the cloister, murmuring, "I must find him. He must be warned." Diverted and intrigued, Carlita followed.

When Clément reached the end of the quire, he stood up tentatively to try his legs again. Finding they could now support him, he broke into a trot. Carlita scurried after him. As Clément reached the south door he suddenly checked and looked back. Carlita flung herself behind a pillar. Clément came back towards her, glided past and, moments later, reappeared carrying a candle. With one hand shielding the flame, he moved steadily in the direction of the guest hall.

Clément moved among the sleeping visitors, peering into each face as the candlelight fell across it. Carlita followed, watching and wondering. At last, he found the one he was looking for. He set the candle down, covered the sleeper's mouth with his hand and gently shook him by the shoulder. Daniel woke abruptly and knocked the hand away from his face.

"Hush, don't fret Master Daniel, I mean you no harm," whispered Clément. "I must have some talk with you. Come."

Daniel rubbed his eyes and got up in a daze. He wrapped his cloak tightly around him and followed Clément, shivering, out into the December night. The cold took his breath away but cleared his mind.

"Brother Clément, what is this all about? Why have you woken me and where are we going?"

"We need to talk."

"Can't it wait until morning? Why do you suddenly need to talk now?"

"I will tell you in the church." Clément pushed open the heavy wooden door of the abbey church and held it open for Daniel. Once again Carlita shrank back into the shadows.

They walked to the front of the nave, near the quire where the queen's bier was laid at the high altar. The black friars were keeping vigil beside her.

Clément whispered, "Let us kneel. If any come, they will see that we are praying and leave us alone." They knelt side by side, noticing neither the dark-hooded figure who skulked behind a pillar nearby, nor Carlita, who crept into the back of the quire just within earshot. Though Daniel and the monk spoke quietly, their voices carried in the heavy night-time stillness of the great church.

Chapter 76

15th December 1290, Blackfriars Church, London

"Who are you?" demanded Clément.

"You know who I am; Daniel of Orkney."

"And I am the Pope," said the monk, raising an eyebrow. "I have had a vision this night, as I kept vigil by the queen. I was taken back in my mind to Lincoln, when I first beheld you. At the time I was out of my wits with grief. I cared not who or what I saw. It happened in a moment, then I fled and thought of it no more. But in my vision, God took me back. I saw it all again, as if I were watching from a distance, and as if time had slowed down. I saw your strange clothes. I saw the smaller boy appear out of thin air. I heard your strange speech."

He reached into his habit and drew out his pendant. "Next in my vision, I was transported back to the road by Stamford, where we halted for the blessing of the site of the future cross. I saw you observe my snakestone with a look of recognition. Your face showed surprise and confusion. You raised your hand to your own neck. Now I ask you again, who are you?"

Daniel let out a deep sigh. All this time he had been concealing his true identity, weaving a delicate web of lies, weighing every word he spoke in case it gave him away. The effort had been immense – it had built up tension in every part of his body. As Clément watched him, his brow uncreased and his shoulders dropped. "You must not tell anyone, Brother Clément."

"I will not."

"You must swear. Swear on something holy - the Bible." Clément reached into his habit once more and drew out a large silver cross on a chain.

"I swear on the cross of Christ." His grey eyes bored into Daniel's and Daniel knew he could entrust his secret to Clément.

Daniel told his story. Clément listened in wonder and incredulity but without interrupting. When he had finished, Daniel looked into Clément's eyes. "Do you believe me?"

"I know not what to think. It sounds impossible but how or why would anyone invent such a tale? What use could it serve? And then there is my vision."

"I swear to you, I have come from seven hundred years in the future. I don't understand how or why. And I don't know how to get back to my own time. If only I had not hidden my book about Queen Eleanor. It had pictures of the crosses which the king plans to build in her memory; well, pictures of the three that are still standing in my time."

Clément gasped. "Only three left standing? Three of twelve! How can this be? They are to be made of stone, which endures. I have been praying night and day since the queen went to her rest, that her name and memory will last forever." Clément broke off suddenly and placed his forefingers on his temples while his mind caught up a new idea and ran with it. "You!" he burst out, and clapped Daniel on the shoulder. "You are the answer to my prayer! Now it all fits." Seeing the puzzled look on Daniel's face, he continued. "It was through me that the idea for the memorial crosses was sown in the king's mind, and I have been praying day and night for the queen's name and fame to endure through all generations. Now you have told me that in your day, seven hundred years hence, only three crosses still stand. You must be the answer to my prayer. God has brought you to me."

The monk paused and pondered the enormity of the idea. Daniel too was silent, his mind reeling.

Clément continued, "Is not God eternal? All ages are as one to Him. In your time, you were already interested in Queen Eleanor, that much you have told me. You visited her tomb in Lincoln Cathedral, you wrote about her in school, you visited the site of the Lincoln Cross and then you were transported here. It has fallen to you to reawaken her memory in your own time."

Daniel was silent for a long moment. "Even if what you say is true, how can I reawaken her memory in my own time if I'm stuck here in your time?"

"Ah, yes. That is a fair question. Therein lies our problem. Clearly you are not meant to remain here. You are meant to witness the outpouring of grief at the queen's passing and then, surely, to return. If the Lord brought you here, He must intend to send you back. For our part, we must ensure that we are heedful of any signs He gives us."

He paused and looked at the altar for a few minutes. Then he said, "Let us spend some time in prayer and reflection."

Daniel clasped his hands, bowed his head and closed his eyes. He was used to praying, being a vicar's son; at times he was sure there was Someone listening but at other times, he felt as if he was just talking to himself. Right now, his brain was so boggled by Brother Clément's fantastical ideas, he didn't really know where to start. Dad always told him to speak to God respectfully but also just as if He was sitting next to you and having a conversation. In his mind, he said, "God, this all seems completely far-fetched, but far-fetched is pretty average at the moment. If I have been sent here for a purpose, as Brother Clément thinks, then please show me how to get back. And if I do get back, I promise to do what I can to resurrect the memory of Queen Eleanor."

Daniel stole a look at Brother Clément. His lips were moving but no sound came out. At that moment, the absurdity of the situation struck him so forcibly that he didn't know whether to laugh or cry. Here he was, stuck in the year 1290, at goodness knows what time of the night, in a medieval friary kneeling on the freezing cold floor next to a slightly unhinged, sleep-deprived monk. It was beyond belief, but it was true. Then a new thought struck him. In one sense he and Clément were worlds apart, and yet they had a lot in common, as he had already noticed. One of those things was prayer. The God they both prayed to was above and beyond time and history. He visualised their prayers rising up, passing beyond our dimensions of space and time and into the eternal presence of God.

Daniel tried to picture God, looking down on human history as if it were a timeline. If God was separate and superior to time, was it really so hard to believe that, in response to prayer, He could reach down into the timeline of history, pick someone up from one time and put them into another. Although it seemed mad, there was a kind of logic to it.

Come to think of it, he had heard about minuscule particles that appeared to travel faster than the speed of light, which used to be thought impossible. The way scientists rationalized this, was to say that the particles must have gone into another dimension or parallel universe, and then back into ours. If top scientists could believe that kind of stuff, Clément's suggestion must be at least worth taking seriously.

As he pondered all this, a memory rose vividly in his mind - of the time he spotted the ammonite pendant in the grave at Abbotsbury. He thought about the fossil - how the seven hundred odd years between 1290 and his own time were just the blink of an eye compared to the time since the creature had died and its shell had fossilised in the rock. To the eternal God, those years must be even less substantial.

Another idea came to him; if prayer lay behind all this, maybe resurrecting the memory of Queen Eleanor was not the only purpose God had in mind. What had he been praying or longing for just before he came back in time? The only thing on Daniel's mind then had been what to do about Jim. That all seemed strangely irrelevant now. By now the four of them had more or less learned to work as a team, especially since Jim ran away. His prayer had been answered. And if they could get back to their own time, Clément's prayer could be answered too.

Chapter 77

15th December 1290, Blackfriars Church, London

In the choir stalls, the bench creaked and groaned under Carlita as she shifted to ease her stiff limbs. She froze. Her eyes darted back to Brother Clément and the young lord, but they remained as oblivious to her presence as she was to the hooded figure watching all three of them. Carlita could make no sense of what she had overheard. She had taken refuge in the priory church to hide from Derian, only to stumble upon this secret conference, incomprehensible and therefore dangerous.

At last Brother Clément broke the silence. "Daniel, I did not tell you the rest of my vision. Now its meaning begins to take shape in my mind. In the vision, the queen's bier was resting in the street somewhere nearby - probably on the site of the last cross. You and your companions approached as the bishop blessed the spot and consecrated it with holy water. The pallbearers raised the bier and moved away. I saw myself praying there on the ground. Now, cast your mind back to Lincoln. I was praying on the ground on which the bier had lain. When you appeared, you trod on my habit because you appeared at that very spot, the first cross site."

"Yes, and I appeared there because that's exactly where I was standing in my own time. I stayed still and the surroundings changed. What shifted was the time, not the place."

"It begins to make sense. In answer to my prayer, you were brought to the first cross site. I believe you may be able to get back to your own time by being at the final cross site, just after its consecration, as you were at the first. You see, my vision ended with two of your companions reaching the consecrated spot and disappearing into thin air."

"Only two of us? What happened to the other two?" Daniel said, dismayed.

"Someone else obscured my view of you as the vision faded. I'm sure you reached the spot and disappeared too; I just could not quite see it." He omitted to tell Daniel about Derian Scand aiming a crossbow in their direction and firing. The last moment of the vision showed the crossbow bolt hurtling through the air. "You and your companions must reach the location of the twelfth cross site just as the bier has been lifted from it. Make haste. Rouse your companions and prepare yourselves. But beware of a man called Scand."

"I don't know anyone called Scand. How can I avoid him if I don't know who he is?" Daniel said.

"He is above the middle height, with dark hair and countenance, and pale eyes. I do not understand why, but he may mean you harm."

"But you will be there, brother, will you not?" He saw the monk hesitate. "What is it? There is something you're not telling me." Clément rubbed his stubbly tonsure, he must get it shaved before the funeral, he thought randomly.

"Very well. The man I spoke of, Scand; it is me he wishes to harm. He has taken against me; I know not why." And he told Daniel the whole story of Derian cursing the stone pendants, as Warin had told him the evening before. "Perhaps I should stay away from the cross site lest I put you and your companions in danger."

Daniel knelt there still, thinking. "Brother Clément, you were there at the beginning of our adventure. If what we have discussed is the truth, it is because of you and your prayers that we are here. My gut tells me you must be there at the end. And besides, if this vision is truly from God, must we not let events unfold as you have seen, regardless of the danger?"

"I salute your faith, young Daniel, and you may be right. It may be that we must let the vision come to pass, entrusting ourselves into God's care. I will ponder on it and seek God's will."

They sat companionably for a few moments, enjoying the safety of the here and now, whatever danger lay ahead.

Then Daniel said, "We have a few hours until first light. I'll let the others sleep a bit longer. I'd like to explain why I reacted at the sight of your ammonite pendant. But please can we get off our knees? Mine are killing me." He rose and rubbed his stiff, cold legs. Clément did the same. Once they could both move again, they walked around for a few minutes to stretch their limbs. The two fascinated eavesdroppers shrank deeper into the shadows to remain unobserved.

"Ammonite pendant?" said the monk. "Is that what you called it? What does ammonite mean?"

"Oh, it's a kind of fossil."

"And what is a fossil?"

"Right; I suppose that hasn't been worked out yet either. What is your name for it?" Daniel asked.

"I have heard it called a snakestone. When I first found the strange stone at Abbotsbury, Brother Anselm told me what he had read in ancient works about such stones. Xenophon speculated that long ago the shells and bodies of dead creatures rotted and disappeared and that the space they had occupied was filled in with particles that gradually solidified into stone. I do not know if this is true."

"Wow," replied Daniel. "Who's Xenophon?"

"I believe he was a Greek philosopher from the time before our Lord's birth."

"No way! Well, he was right. In my time we call them fossils. Millions of them have been discovered. This kind is called an ammonite after the creature that lived in the shell that became this fossil. It was a sea creature."

"I see. It makes good sense."

Daniel reflected for a moment and then said, "What I'm going to tell you next is kind of weird, so promise me you won't freak out."

Clément smiled and stretched his legs. "I can guess by your tone what you mean by "freak out." I don't imagine that anything you tell me can be stranger than you coming here from seven hundred years in the future."

"Well, it's on the same scale but a lot more personal to you." Clément raised his eyebrows but said nothing. Daniel continued, "Although I go to school in Lincoln, I actually come from Abbotsbury, where you found the stone. And my dad is a priest at the parish church there, next to the site where the abbey church used to stand."

"Used to stand? What happened to the abbey?"

"That's a long story; maybe another time." Or not, Daniel thought. Telling him that all monasteries were destroyed by Henry VIII is probably a bit more than he can cope with. He carried on. "A couple of months ago, some archaeologists - do you know what that means?"

Clément shook his head. "Um, they're people interested in the past, who dig in the ground to search for stuff like fossils and old relics," Daniel explained. "They were digging at the site of the old abbey church and they found the grave of one of the abbots. There was nothing much in the grave except a large silver cross around the skeleton's neck and a ring on his finger. So, the archaeologists took those away to clean up and examine.

"I was there helping them and after they went, I noticed something else, a fossil pendant. It was dirty and had no chain; it must have been on a leather one like yours, that would have rotted away. I took it home and cleaned it up. I threaded it onto an old shoelace and started to wear it around my neck. The thing is, brother," Daniel had been looking down and twiddling his fingers nervously but now he looked Clément in the eye. "I think it may have been your grave."

"You ransacked my grave? And stole my pendant?" he crossed himself.

"Forgive me, Brother Clément. I meant no harm. But do you not see what it means? You will become abbot one day! And when your life is over, you will be buried at Abbotsbury, still wearing the ammonite pendant which reminds you of the queen. When I fell into your time, my one disappeared because it couldn't be in two places at once: around my neck as well as yours."

They sat in silence for a few minutes and then Clément said, "If what you say is true, then God has brought you here for another purpose too - to show me my future path. I have been wishing myself dead like my queen. But if God wills that I return to my abbey to live and serve Him there, so be it."

"You will be abbot one day; I'm sure of it." Daniel shivered and rose to leave.

They walked down the length of the chill, dark church and out into the cloisters where a biting wind rattled the windows in the stone arches.

"Suppose your theory is right," Daniel said to Clément as they walked, "and I am to resurrect the memory of Queen Eleanor; in my time, there are records about her life in the royal archives and history books. In fact, I had a whole book about her which I wish I could show you. But by and large she is overshadowed, firstly by King Edward and also by other queens in history who took a more active role in politics. But from you, I can gain a unique insight into her character. How do you think she should be remembered? What was it about her that excited such devotion in you?"

Clément's eyes took on a dreamy, far-away look. Though painful and personal, Daniel's question could not be more welcome. The scribe was accustomed to adopting a certain reticence in speaking of the late queen, stifling his admiration, lest it be misinterpreted or mocked. But now, where to start? He sat down on a stone bench and pondered a while, until the sight of Daniel shivering roused him and they walked briskly to fend off the cold, making circuits of the cloister.

"Before I left my monastery to join the royal household, I was unused to the company of women. I came early to the cloistered life and grew up surrounded by men, many of whom had the same kind of male nurture as I. I have come to be ashamed of the way I used to view women. When I joined the royal household, I discovered from my dealings with the queen that, if given the same advantages of education afforded to a man, an intelligent woman may hold her own in disputes of all kinds, be they theological, legal, philosophical or political. Indeed, Queen Eleanor not only held her own, but bested me many times. I am reasonably well educated and I do not deny that I have a rare talent for copying texts, but I am not ashamed to admit that I was not her intellectual equal."

Daniel chuckled despite the chattering of his teeth, and said, "I go to a school for both boys and girls and I am also well used to being outsmarted by girls."

"A mixed school? I am gratified to hear it. In your time, do all abbeys receive girls as well as boys to be educated?"

"Yes; most schools have both boys and girls." Daniel answered tactfully.

Clément was thrilled. "Queen Eleanor would have been delighted to know that. As well as having a quick wit and an enquiring mind of her own, the queen was a great patron of learning, supporting the black friars here, for instance." Clément's eyes took on the dreamy look again, "But above all, I believe that Queen Eleanor herself would wish to be remembered for her devotion to the king. Although I am a monk, I am aware that many marriages are not happy, especially amongst the nobility and royalty where, sadly, marriage is used to forge alliances and bolster fortunes. But never was there a couple more devoted than King Edward and Queen Eleanor. And it was not for outward show; time and again I have witnessed and even envied the intimate glances that passed between them. They loved each other passionately, to the end."

They had reached the threshold of the guest hall. "One thing more before we part," Clément said. "While we were praying earlier, I began to doubt whether it could really be in answer to my prayer that you were brought here. Not the possibility, since the Immortal and All-Powerful God can do such miracles if He so chooses; I doubted the likelihood of His choosing to act in this way. From all that we see in Holy Scripture and in our everyday lives, He seems to prefer to operate in ways that are within our comprehension most of the time. But then I was reminded of the event of the Transfiguration of our Lord in the Gospels. There, in front of Peter, James and John, Jesus met and talked with Moses and Elijah. God allowed Moses and Elijah to appear in a completely different era of time. So, even in the Bible, this kind of event is not unheard of."

"Brother Clément! I'm just a boy, confused and far from home, desperate to return to my normal life. Please don't compare me to Moses or Elijah!" But even as he said these words, Daniel knew they were not entirely true. Confused and far from home he certainly was, but by coming back in time, he had discovered strengths and skills he did not know he possessed. Normal life would never be the same again for he was not the same person, and nor were the others. In as few words as possible, he communicated this to Brother Clément.

The monk contemplated the information for several minutes and then said, "Your coming here has given both of us new hope. God does indeed work in mysterious ways." They were startled by the loud creaking of a door behind them. The brothers were filing down the night stairs towards the church to sing the office of Prime. As Daniel turned to watch them, out of the corner of his eye he noticed someone creeping away from them; a lady, in fine clothes.

"Clément, quick, who is that?" Clément turned and glimpsed her as she reached the far end of the cloister and disappeared back into the church. "Oh no!" cried Daniel. "What if we've been overheard? We have to find out who that was and stop her from telling anyone."

"Leave that part to me," said Clément, picking up the skirts of his habit and setting off after her at a trot. He called over his shoulder, "Wake your companions and stay close to the queen's bier. Whatever happens this day, you must be there when the twelfth cross site is blessed. Make haste!"

Chapter 78

15th December 1290, Blackfriars, London and Westminster

Daniel caught the first strains of the monks chanting Prime in the church behind him, before he opened the guest hall door. He was surprised to see that most people were already starting to get up, moving stiffly and trying to shake off sleep. Of course, the burial of Queen Eleanor's heart was to take place today. It would be a busy day for most of the guests. He found Ed and Jim still fast asleep, rolled up in their cloaks. He knelt between them and nudged them both at once.

"Jim, Ed, wake up. I think I know how we can get home, but it has to be this morning. Come on, get up." No response. He shook their shoulders. Ed groaned and sat up but Jim just rolled over, turning his back on Daniel. "Jim, come on; this might be our only chance. You've got to get up and come with us. We can't wait around for you." Jim turned over and studied Daniel's face, trying to work out if this was merely a ruse to get him out of bed. But Daniel's earnest expression was one he had to take seriously.

"Okay, okay," he said and got up.

While the other two were getting ready, Daniel said, "There's no time to explain it all now. Basically, we have to stay with the queen's bier and go with the royal party towards Westminster. We must be at Charing when the last cross site is blessed. But we could be in danger; someone overheard me talking about it. So try to keep a low profile. I'll go and find Natalie and we'll meet you in the church."

"All right," said Ed, "We'll try to get some breakfast, then go to the church and wait."

"I'll be there as soon as I can. Try to blend in. Kneel down and pretend to be praying or something."

Daniel made his way to the women's guest quarters and knocked at a heavy wooden door. It was opened by a fresh-faced young woman who greeted him with a warm, sheepish smile.

"Good day, my lord, how may I serve you?"

"Good morning. I'm looking for my cousin, Lady Natalie. I need to speak with her urgently."

"I remember the lady. Please wait here while I fetch her." Daniel tried to remain calm while he waited but the minutes ticked by and he began to fidget.

At last, the young woman returned, alone. "My lord, I am afraid she is not here at present. She has gone out, perhaps for a walk? I made inquiries and another guest saw her leave by this door about half an hour ago." She saw the concern on Daniel's face. "If you wish, I will remain here to watch for her. I will give her whatever message you entrust to me."

Daniel felt that she could be trusted. "Yes. Um, I would be grateful. Please tell her to go directly to the church. It is most important."

"I will keep watch here and convey your message, lord," she said.

Daniel headed to find Jim and Ed. "Natalie's not there. She's gone for a walk or something."

"Typical," said Jim.

"She didn't know we needed her. I'm going to look for her and I'll meet you back here. There's going to be a service, to bury the queen's heart. but I don't know what time or how long it will last. If the procession moves off, follow it but keep your distance. I'll find Natalie and catch up with you."

"And what if you don't?" said Jim.

"Right, this is all you need to know. When the final cross site has been blessed—"

"What," Ed interrupted, "you mean when they sprinkle the holy water and stuff?"

"Yes, that bit. As soon as they pick up the bier and start carrying it away, go and stand on the exact spot where it was laid, like we used to at the earlier cross sites. Whatever happens, make sure you do that."

"We gave up trying that because nothing happened. What makes you think it'll work this time?" said Jim, raising an eyebrow.

"I'll explain later. Please just trust me and do it."

"Okay," said Ed.

Daniel was already jogging away. He retraced his steps to the women's guest hall. The young attendant was waiting by the door; when she spotted Daniel, she shook her head. Daniel stood on the stone threshold of the guest hall, looking outwards. He stared for a moment in each direction. *If I were Natalie, which way would I go?* An unexpected tap on his shoulder made Daniel jump and spin around. It was the young woman.

"If you wish to know whether your cousin left the precinct, my lord, you should enquire of the porter."

"Of course, thank you." He set off at a trot for the gatehouse.

"Yes, my lord," said the porter straight away. "She asked the way to the Abbey of St Peter at Westminster, so I told her to cross the Fleet river and follow Fleet Street, then the Strand, and finally bear left for Thorney Island."

Daniel made a mental note of the directions, then said, "And where is the Fleet River?"

"Why, just beyond our wall here, to the west." Daniel jogged away in the direction of his pointing finger, chasing his own shadow, elongated by the rising sun behind him. *Thorney Island?* It rang a vague bell from his Eleanor research, but he couldn't place it.

With a twinge of frustration, Daniel left London behind, contained within its great wall, and headed for Westminster, a town in its own right. He had hoped to have a chance to explore today, at least Saint Paul's and London Bridge. He had seen so little of the medieval city, and that mostly in the dark. But, if Brother Clément's vision was to be trusted, he must seize the opportunity to get his friends safely home.

He crossed the River Fleet flowing south to join the mighty Thames. He hurried past another priory and spotted the circular church of the Knights Templar. He remembered visiting it once with his mum, taking photos of stone effigies of knights on their tombs, set in the floor. At this point, some of those knights still be alive. Maybe they would even be here for Queen Eleanor's funeral.

Next, he skirted a church in the middle of the street; beyond it, the road broadened out into a well-to-do thoroughfare. This must be the Strand, he thought, looking at grand houses on the left as far as the eye could see, their gardens backing onto the river. Eventually, the road forked and he bore left, following the Thames, already alive with boats of all shapes and sizes.

Ahead Westminster Hall and Abbey came into view, looking strangely familiar and yet different. He wondered if the king had slept here last night or at his palace in the Tower of London. He hurried past a particularly fine house. And now he saw why it was called Thorney Island. A smaller river, over to his right, split into two channels and flowed around the abbey to join the Thames, encircling Westminster in a natural moat.

On the stone bridge over to the 'Isle of Westminster,' Daniel paused, panting, and watched his breath making clouds in the cold air. He had jogged most of the way and was surprised not to have overtaken Natalie by now. She must have entered the abbey already, via the gatehouse directly ahead. He set off again, The gate was closed so he knocked and waited. A plump, ruddy-faced young monk opened the wicket and said,

"Good morning, my lord. How may I serve you?"

"Good day, brother. I am looking for my cousin, who came this way, probably only minutes ago. May I enter?"

"Come in and welcome, my lord; but I assure you, none other has entered this full half hour, so I doubt your cousin is within. What is his name?"

"Her name is Lady Natalie," Daniel said, starting to feel uneasy. "Perhaps you do not remember her. She is about my age, slightly shorter than me with long, dark hair."

The porter bristled slightly. "I recall everyone who enters through the wicket; but even if I did not, this being a monastery and only men within, a young maid could hardly pass unnoticed. I fear it is you that must be mistaken, my lord."

"But I know she asked for directions to Westminster. And I would have overtaken her on the way if she had not yet arrived."

"Are you of the royal party? And did the young lady leave the friary without an escort?" His deferential tone did not quite disguise the hint of criticism.

"I fear she did, brother, and I share your concern. We are unfamiliar with London and the south. In our travels thus far she has never ventured out alone and I had no reason to think she would. So I failed to warn her of the dangers she might face."

"Dear me, cutpurses are ten-a-penny, even in daylight, and—" he cut himself short, perceiving Daniel's distress. "Though I dare say Westminster is a good deal safer than the city itself. Even so, you must find her, my lord, and quickly. Here within we are busy preparing for the queen's funeral, God rest her. But I am sure we can spare a couple of scullions or lay brothers to aid you in your search."

"Thank you, but I will not trouble you further. Is this the only gate?"

"Why no, my lord. This is the north gate but there is a western gate too. If the lady came from the Strand, it would be strange to pass by this gate and enter the other, but of course, you must check. Come within and we will walk together across the cemetery. It is quicker than going by the road outside."

Daniel stepped through the gate in the monastery wall and there in front of him rose the north side of the abbey church. The porter secured the gate behind him and strode off diagonally across a wide, open space, between a bell tower and a cemetery. They skirted the west end of the abbey, which looked different to how Daniel remembered it.

"Brother Porter," called the first porter to his colleague.

An older monk appeared, eyebrows raised, from his lodge beside the gate. "Aye, brother, what's amiss?"

"This young lord is seeking his cousin, a maid of his own age, who set off from the Black Friary earlier this morning intending to visit us. She has not entered by the north gate. Have you seen her?"

"I am sorry to be of no help, lord," he said, addressing Daniel. "But no maid has asked entry here today."

"No. We thought as much, but it was worth a try." The two porters exchanged a glance and then the older one continued, "You look weary to the bone, young sir. Have you breakfasted this day?"

"No," said Daniel, distractedly, "Nor slept last night, but that matters not. It is imperative that I find my cousin but I don't know where to start." Tears welled up and one spilled down Daniel's cheek; he brushed it away impatiently.

The younger monk lowered his eyes, embarrassed, but the older man reached out and took Daniel by the arm. "Come now, you will be of more use to your cousin if you take ten minutes to rest and have a morsel to revive you." And he led him gently towards his lodge.

Chapter 79

15th December 1290, Blackfriars Church, London

After Clément parted from Daniel, he lay in wait for the lady who had been eavesdropping. He had no idea how much of their conversation she may have heard, but if she reported them, she might add to the peril facing Daniel and his friends. Who could resist the temptation to pass on such gossip? People travelling from another time – it would certainly be put down to devilry.

Clément secreted himself in a nook with a view of the courtyard, which was dimly lit by torches in sconces on the wall. He waited for the woman in the green cloak to re-emerge from the priory church. He shivered in the chill, damp air and pulled his cowl closer around his head and neck. An early morning mist was rising from the nearby Thames. Minutes later the woman appeared and walked purposefully towards the guest hall.

He hurried to catch her; when he was within earshot he called, "My lady, wait. May I speak with you? I fear you are troubled by what you heard, but I can explain."

At first, she quickened her pace, but then she stopped abruptly, turned on her heel and confronted him, "Stay back!" She caught sight of the snakestone pendant at his neck and added, "Queen Killer."

Clément stopped dead in his tracks through utter shock. His hand shot instinctively to the pendant around his neck.

"Come one step closer wearing that murderous stone and I'll raise enough noise to wake the whole priory," Carlita said. "How can you still wear it? How can you even bear to touch it?"

Clément saw that she was, in her own way, as grief-stricken as himself. He recognised her - the youngest of the late queen's ladies-in-waiting, a distant cousin he believed. He could not recall her name at that moment. She too had loved the queen and she was now set adrift in the world with no patroness, no position and an uncertain future.

"My lady," he said with utter conviction, "I would have died a thousand times over before causing harm to her grace. I was devoted to her. I still wear the stone, yes, but you misunderstand my intent. I confess that I put it back on in the hope that it might kill me too. But I am hale and well, as you see." He touched the pendant again and added confidingly, "Wearing the stone makes me feel close to her. But my lady, regarding what you overheard in the abbey, I beg of you to hear me out. I can explain. Please do not act rashly and add more sorrows to those we already share." Clément saw that this appeal momentarily reached her. Her resolve wavered, but then her eyes hardened again.

In a tone devoid of warmth, she said, "Stay away from me." She turned her back on him and pushed open the heavy door. Within, the guest hall bristled with all manner of servants and stewards going swiftly about their business, carrying out the orders their master or mistress had given them in preparation for the funeral. She intercepted a steward who greeted her somewhat distractedly.

"Good morrow, my lady," he said with a slight bow. "May I assist you? As you see, you find us in a state of busyness."

"I wish to speak to whoever is in charge here," she stated as confidently as she could.

"That is out of the question, I fear. We are preparing for the arrival of the royal family for the funeral service here."

"I have information, confidential information, bearing on security. I must speak with someone of rank."

The steward stiffened at the implication that he was not someone of rank, and said curtly, "If it concerns the security of the cortege, I can send your message to the captain of the guard."

"It is complicated. I need to speak to him myself."

"He may not be here yet."

"Please find out."

"As you wish. And if he is here, who shall I say wishes to speak with him?"

"Lady Carlita of Castile, the late queen's lady-in-waiting."

"Wait here, if you please."

Carlita stood waiting and watching the bustle of the royal household. A nun approached and greeted her. "Good morning, Sister," she replied before looking up at the face framed by its wimple. "Oh, forgive me! I did not realise, your Grace." She lowered her eyes and curtsied.

"I must have some talk with you," said Princess Mary, "on an urgent matter in which we may be able to serve one another." The two young women withdrew to a quiet corner.

Clément stood outside the guest hall and pondered how to proceed. Carlita's name drifted up unbidden from his memory. He hoped and prayed that whoever she spoke to inside would not take her seriously. But in his heart, he knew they would.

All Clément could do was watch and wait. With one eye on the guest hall door, he stood shivering in the lightening winter morning and contemplated the revelations of the past few hours. As the sun rose, its full impact dawned on him: the awesome power of the One who had given him the vision, the One who, in answer to his prayer, had sent Daniel from the years to come. A blackbird trilled his mellow song nearby. Clément turned as it took to the air and flew over the priory wall and out of sight. He imagined his prayers like a bird, rising higher and higher on wings of grace, until they passed beyond this world into that greater reality where God dwells and love flows unbounded between Creator and creature. Prayer - that was his task in all this mystery. Someone else might wield a crossbow but prayer too was a powerful weapon. Watch and pray; were they not the very words of our Saviour to his disciples? So he watched and he prayed.

No one came or went via the guest hall door for an interminable age. But presently from the other direction, members of the royal household arrived started arriving at the priory, lesser dignitaries at first, robed in black and looking solemn. The funeral of the queen's heart! It had almost slipped his mind. How much longer should he remain watching the door?

Suddenly it opened. Here was Princess Mary, looking paler than usual against the white of her wimple. He pitied the child, grieving for the mother she had rarely seen. Walking next to her was Carlita. Seeing the two young ladies side by side, Clément was utterly astonished. He knew Carlita to be a cousin to his late mistress and that Queen Eleanor had a special fondness for her because of her likeness to Mary. But until now Clément had never seen them together and the resemblance between Mary and Carlita struck him with unexpected force. They were even of similar height, though the princess was several years younger. "They could be twins," he said aloud.

He tried to attract Carlita's attention but she looked straight through him and set off surrounded by members of the royal party. There was nothing more he could do here. The king's steward was trying to marshal the large group into due order to proceed into the church. Clément sidled past as inconspicuously as he could. At least he could try to warn Daniel and his friends of the potential danger if Carlita had confided what she overheard last night to anyone in the king's household.

In the friary church, a verger was lighting the last candles. Clément's eyes ranged over the spacious building, looking for Daniel. He was nowhere to be seen, but the monk spotted his two friends, kneeling in an obscure corner.

He knelt beside them and murmured, "Young sirs, where is your friend, Lord Daniel?" Ed and Jim looked at each other.

"He's not here. He's looking for Natalie." Ed said.

"Why do you want him?" added Jim.

"I bring a warning. I believe you are in danger. I will remain nearby. As soon as he returns, tell him I must speak with him before he leaves here."

"All right," said Ed.

"But in case I do not see him, please give him this. He will understand." Brother Clément handed him a small leather pouch and withdrew. Jim opened the pouch and peered inside. It contained a gold chain strung with a large pendant.

"Why's he giving Dan a necklace?"

"How do I know?" said Ed. "Just keep it safe."

Behind them, the 'twins' entered the church, each young woman contemplating the outrageous plan they had concocted, following a frank discussion of what had been overheard during the night. Both Carlita and Princess Mary were staggered at their own audacity. If their scheme worked, it would deliver longed-for security for one and unimaginable danger for the other. And if it did not work, the consequences for both young ladies did not bear thinking about. Princess Mary cast her eyes modestly downwards, doing all she could to avoid attracting the attention of her ever-watchful grandmother.

Chapter 80

15th December 1290, Blackfriars, London

Natalie had woken early, by now acclimatised to being roused before dawn. For a few minutes she tried to enjoy a snooze, but her eczema was driving her mad. She got up, scratching, and went to have a wash in the sort of running water she had discovered the evening before. The guest hall was quiet and there was no sign of breakfast, so she picked up her cloak and let herself out into the chill morning air. She walked in circles around the friary courtyard for a few minutes, stretching out her legs, still stiff from riding. She was soon bored of that; the restlessness inside her swelled into that pent-up feeling she often had at school – confined to the structure, the timetable, the rules. There she got some release by playing hockey or carrying out some of Jim's dubious demands or skipping a class or two just for the sake of it.

On their adventure here so far, it had been relatively easy to comply – everything was new and strange and every day they were travelling. The danger they were in, though scary, felt exciting. But by now, she had grown used to that too. She was always hemmed in by walls; priory walls, town walls and now London wall. But all the walls had gates.

∞

Derian Scand had spent a cold night in a ramshackle shelter in woodland west of the city. Since first light, he had been at target practice amongst the trees. He had a good eye and soon found his aim. The knack of reloading the crossbow bolts at speed was challenging, but he had persevered and mastered it. Now he was heading back to the unassuming chapel of Saint Martin-in-the-Fields. He hoped its squat tower might afford him the vantage point he was looking for. He reached the settlement of Charing, slipped inside the gate to the convent garden and paused to reconnoitre.

One or two brothers were at the far end of the field, tending to their winter crop. He waited until their backs were turned and made his way across to the church. He ducked his head under the wooden porch and paused again, listening. No sound came from within but there could be monks inside, praying or resting in this, their chapel-of-ease. Derian turned the hefty doorknob and the door swung creakily inwards. A figure kneeling at the altar rose in a fluid movement and turned to greet him.

"Good day, sir. Come in and welcome," the lanky, young brother beamed, opening his arms wide in a gesture of friendship. "Use our little chapel as your own."

Derian nodded his acknowledgement and entered. He smiled, darkly amused by the youth's trustful innocence, considering the "use" he planned to make of their sacred space.

The young monk baulked, arrested by the disparity between Derian's s smile and his cold eye. He said, "I will leave you to your prayers; it is time I returned to my work." The skirts of his habit disturbed the still air as he swept past the stranger and beat a hasty retreat.

The door opened and closed and Derian was left alone. He approached the altar planning to kneel there for a while in case the monk returned, but his feet would not carry him towards the cross. Instead, they took him to a little door to the tower and up a narrow winding staircase. At the top, he pushed open a trap door and climbed through it onto a small landing.

Light filtered into the empty space through narrow slits on three sides. But on the fourth, a wooden shutter covered a larger window hole. Derian released the catch, opened the shutter a little and peered through the crack. There was no one below so he opened it wide and leaned out. Yes; this was perfect; before him lay the broad junction between The Strand, to his left, and King Street, leading down to Thorney Island. He had a clear view of the bell tower of the monastery of Westminster in the distance and everything that lay between. His stomach growled low and long. He refastened the shutter, unslung the pack from his back and knelt on the wooden floor.

He took out the crossbow and his supply of bolts, laid them down carefully and reached again into the bag. He pulled out his leather flask and a cloth parcel, containing a second pie he had purchased on London Bridge last night. It was not as tasty served cold but it filled a hole. He ate it wolfishly, slaked his thirst and wiped his mouth on his sleeve. Then he sat back against the stone wall, stretched out his legs and settled himself to wait.

∞

A mile away, Ed and Jim stood near the back of the church in the Dominican Friary and observed the funeral of the heart of Queen Eleanor, understanding nothing of the Latin liturgy.

"That's a big coffin for just a heart," Ed whispered.

"Urgh. Don't remind me; it's gross," said Jim. "And anyway, why is her heart being buried separately from the rest of her?"

"Dan told me it's because this was a special place for her and one of her sons was buried here. He died when he was a kid."

"Oh, that kind of makes sense then. What on earth can Dan be doing?" said Jim. "How long can it take to find someone who's gone for a walk?"

"Me and Dan spent a whole day looking for you when you went AWOL at Geddington."

"That was different," said Jim. Ed didn't push it; he knew Jim was just anxious. He too was starting to feel concerned, but he said,

"They'll be here. There's plenty of time. The service will probably go on for hours."

The service did not go on for hours, however. The church fell silent. Queen Eleanor's heart had been laid to rest and now the pallbearers lifted from the high altar the bier, bearing her body. With due solemnity, the bishop led the procession down the aisle, followed by King Edward. The rest of the congregation filtered in behind them in order of rank and everyone filed out of the church.

As he passed them, Brother Clément looked in Jim and Ed's direction, his eyes still full of grief for his queen. He raised his eyebrows questioningly. Ed gave a slight shake of his head. Brother Clément attempted a smile to encourage them, and motioned with his head that they should fall into line close behind him.

The solemn hush of the church persisted, as the procession took shape in the great court of the priory. More grandees of the church and nobility had joined the cortege. It made an impressive sight leaving the priory for the final stage of a journey that had begun two hundred miles away in Lincoln. They left the city of London via Ludgate, crossed the River Fleet and proceeded westwards, following the route taken earlier by Daniel, and before him, Natalie, and before either of them, Derian Scand. But the quiet street of earlier was entirely transformed.

While the heart burial was being conducted, crowds had flowed into Fleet Street and the Strand, squeezing into every available space to stand, jostling for a prime view. On the right-hand side of the street high and low-born folk stood cheek by jowl and children squeezed to the front or peered from behind their mothers' skirts. On the left, the white-clad Carmelite friars lined the boundary of their convent. And beyond them, the red crosses on the surcoats of the Knights Templar blazed out in the pale winter sunshine. A hush fell on the crowds as they caught sight of the carriage bearing the bier draped in flags; Queen Eleanor on her final journey.

Chapter 81

15th December 1290, Charing, near London

After a ten-minute break in the porter's lodge, and feeling slightly refreshed by some bread and ale, Daniel left the abbey of Westminster by the wicket in the west gate and crossed the river Tyburn. He had no choice but to retrace his steps to the Dominican friary in the hope that Natalie had returned. Fighting against his dejection of spirits, he propelled his weary limbs into a jog once more. Before he reached the first junction, the sky suddenly darkened, an icy wind blew up and in spite of running, Daniel began to shiver. Something hard flicked his forehead, then his hand; hailstones. His heart sank even further.

Moments later the hail shower ended as abruptly as it began. He slowed down, shook the melting ice from his hair and took in his bearings. Immediately ahead lay the road junction and it dawned on him that this must be Charing, the site of the final Eleanor cross. He turned right and stopped dead. The Strand, deserted an hour ago, was now full to bursting. He could see marshals here and there trying to cut a swathe through the crowd to create space down the middle for the procession. He was watching their attempts to impose order on the chaos when a gate opened on his left and out walked Natalie.

"Where on earth have you been?" he snapped. Natalie was taken aback. She had never seen Daniel lose his cool. "I went for a walk. That's not against the law, is it?"

"No, but it's risky. Anyway, you're safe, thank God; I've been searching for you. Come on, we need to find the others." He picked up the pace again. "Where were you just then?" Daniel jerked his head in the direction of the gate.

"I don't know. I looked for somewhere to take cover from the hail and saw that church, so I ducked in there for a minute until it stopped." Natalie broke into a jog to keep up with Daniel. "Slow down, Dan. What's so urgent? Blimey, where did all these people come from?"

"They've come to watch the funeral procession. We've got to get through them and find Jim and Ed. I think I know how to get home; we have to be ready at the blessing of the site of the twelfth cross."

"We've tried that loads of times already."

"I know, but I had a long talk last night with Brother Clément, you know, the strange monk who prays at all the cross sites. Between us we worked something out that makes a kind of sense of why all this has happened, at least I thought it did last night." The anticipation of saying it out loud to Natalie was making the whole thing seem more and more far-fetched in Daniel's mind. But it was all they had to go on. "I think the cross site will be back there, where we met just now."

"How can that be Charing Cross? This is almost countryside," Natalie said, looking over the fields to their left, on the other side of the broad street to the grand houses whose grounds backed onto the Thames.

"It wasn't called Charing Cross until the Eleanor Cross was built here; so at the moment it's just plain Charing."

Soon they were elbowing their way against the tide of bodies flowing out of the city towards Westminster. They made their way to the edge of the street where the oncoming throng looked slightly less dense. No one wanted to be at the back. Over the heads of the crowd, they could see London Wall, the buildings of the black friars and towering above them, the spire of Saint Paul's.

They spotted Jim and Ed, walking near the rear of the cortege and joined them. Now that they formed part of the procession and were going with the flow, not against it, walking was much easier and they could talk discreetly. Ed produced a couple of squashed bread rolls from his pocket that he had filched from the breakfast table for Daniel and Natalie.

"We can't eat them here, with the crowd watching us," Daniel said, tucking his one away in his scrip.

"Speak for yourself, I'm starving. I'll be subtle," said Natalie.

They walked mainly in silence, as befitted the occasion, each wondering what lay ahead. And neither Jim nor Ed remembered Brother Clément's message for Daniel.

Brother Clément, at that moment, was passing the Carmelite Friary as a young brother came out at the gatehouse supporting an elderly monk on his arm. It was an unremarkable, everyday sight but it moved Clément and the tender scene stirred a yearning for the quiet simplicity of brotherly life. He thought of his desk in the scriptorium at Abbotsbury with his inkwell and quill upon it, and suddenly he longed to be there again with his brothers, plying the tools of his trade.

Half a mile ahead, Derian Scand picked up one of the tools of his trade and used it to jam shut the trapdoor of the church tower, so no one could enter and disturb him. He loaded a bolt into the crossbow, laid it carefully on the floor again and opened the shutter. Hawk-like, he surveyed the scene below. It was utterly different from the last time he had looked; the whole of Charing was now thronged with people. Craning his neck to look up The Strand, he saw the front of the royal procession approaching at a stately pace. From this distance, he could not yet pick out the faces of his prey.

He picked up the bow, placed it gently on the window ledge and amused himself by aiming, without firing, at sundry members of the crowd. Presently he trained his weapon on the bishop who led the procession, as it reached the spacious junction at Charing, a stone's throw from Derian's hideout. Behind the bishop, the pallbearers carefully set down the queen's bier. Derian watched the bishop walk ceremoniously around the casket sprinkling holy water on the ground around it. He handed the salver to an assistant, raised his arms and intoned a prayer. Derian caught the mumbled "Amen" of the onlookers, many of whom crossed themselves. The pallbearers once again shouldered the queen's bier and resumed their slow march towards her final resting place, Westminster Abbey.

As the royal party proceeded westwards, Scand caught sight of his quarry. Brother Clément stepped aside from the cortege. Derian guessed what he was about; waiting until the cortege had passed before abasing himself on the ground in his usual grovelling posture. A few onlookers were hanging around near the scribe but they were inconsequential. The next person, however, he certainly recognised; Carlita – what luck! Two of the three persons he sought, right here in his sights. He laughed aloud as Warin also appeared on the scene.

The front of the cortege reached the gatehouse of Westminster Abbey and passed out of sight as the rear of the procession cleared the settlement of Charing. The spectacle was over. Most of the crowd began to disperse and head back towards the city, though some stood and gazed as the last members of the cortege faded from view. Derian turned back to his task. He raised his crossbow and aimed at Brother Clément as he made his way to the spot recently vacated by the queen's bier. Staring down the shaft of the weapon, Derian's keen eyes saw the snakestone pendant dangle from Clément's neck as the monk laid down on the ground, with arms outstretched, to pray.

Derian smirked, "You want to meet God? Let me speed you on your way." As he made to fire the bolt, two young people, a boy and a girl, ran from somewhere on his left, heading directly towards Clément. The moment they reached the monk, they vanished into thin air. Derian jerked; the bolt shot out but missed its mark. He leaned out of the tower window and scanned his field of view from side to side, searching for a place they could have hidden, but there was none. His mind could make no sense of what he had seen; the two youngsters were lost to sight as if they had stepped through a hidden doorway. Nonplussed, he returned to his task and reloaded his weapon.

By now Brother Clément had leapt to his feet and was searching the ground. Derian watched him stoop to pick up the crossbow bolt that had clattered on the cobbles. Then the monk looked up in the direction from which it must have been fired. Derian ducked out of sight as Clément's eyes alighted on the tower. Moments later he peered out again. The monk's attention had been drawn away and he was beckoning to someone Derian could not yet see. He watched as two boys, raced into view. Clément turned towards the tower, opened his arms wide, making himself a target, and stood still perfectly still.

Derian trained his crossbow on the monk, watching the lads out of the corner of his eye. The second boy tripped over, yelling as he hit the ground. The smaller boy, in front, span round and looked at his companion, sprawled on the cobbles. He hesitated, looked back at the monk, then relented and rushed to help the other boy up. Together they hurtled towards Brother Clément and just before the moment of impact, they disappeared, leaving only the dust of their footsteps swirling in the air.

Derian stared, bewildered, with the crossbow dangling from his arm. Another figure moved into his line of sight - a young nun. Was it Princess Mary? He could not be sure. She circumvented Brother Clément, followed the monk's gaze and locked eyes with Derian.

Shielding her brother monk, she too opened her arms wide, forming the shape of the cross and called towards the tower,

"Do you dare threaten my life also?"

Now that his view of Clément was blocked, Derian turned his attention to his other prey. His eyes found Warin, at the sidelines, and he raised the crossbow. With the apprentice in his sights, he saw Carlita grab him by the hand and pull him towards the nun. Derian took aim once more, as they too reached the unearthly spot and vanished. Derian Scand dropped his weapon and fled.

Chapter 82

15th December Current Year, South of Trafalgar Square, London

Mary's eyes blazed with exaltation. She had done it; escaped the convent life she had never chosen. But instantly her senses were bombarded: a stale, choking smell, terrifying alien sounds and strange carts blurring past her at unimaginable speed. She stood paralysed with horror, the colour draining from her face. Then she threw herself into Warin's arms, sobbing. The others stood dumbfounded. Warin too was speechless, cradling the girl in his arms, smoothing her green velvet cloak with his fingers.

"What the hell are they doing here?" said Jim.

"I have no idea," said Daniel.

"Warin!" said Ed. "What are you doing here? You have to get back!"

"No. I stay where the princess stays. And I believe she knew what she was doing, following you."

"Princess! Bloody hell," said Jim. "Do you mean this girl is King Edward's daughter?"

"She is. This is Princess Mary."

"She can't be," said Daniel. "Mary is a nun."

"It is Mary. She exchanged clothes with someone else in order to follow you here." Warin held Mary close, stunned by the otherworldly sights and sounds around him, and even more by the fact that he held a princess in his arms. He tried to stem the tide of possibilities that began coursing through his mind. In her decision to come here, had Mary abandoned her royal status and her nun's vows? If so, she herself would have to embrace that change. And nothing would ever alter the fact that she had been born a princess and he a peasant. He must hold back. He would be her liege man in this strange new world, and hope to become more to her in time. With Mary in his arms, Warin stood awed, mute, content and ready to face whatever befell.

For some moments they all stood and gaped like idiots at 21st century London. Everything was noise and motion: traffic flowed incessantly past them: cars, lorries, black cabs, white vans, red buses. Horns blared, a siren wailed in the distance. On the pavement, people jostled past them, chatting and calling in a hubbub of languages and accents. Then their little group instinctively turned to Daniel for a lead. He looked around to get his bearings. One glance showed him Nelson's column and another, a huge Christmas tree. At least there was no doubt about their location. They were standing on a traffic island below Trafalgar Square, next to a large plinth. Daniel glanced up at the statue above their heads. A man on a horse, Charles I perhaps, he wondered vaguely in the back of his mind. The first step at least was clear; to get to a safer place.

"Right, we have two roads to cross. Stay together, everyone, but if we do get split up, we'll meet at the bottom of Nelson's column by the nearest lion." They all swivelled, following his pointing finger.

"Do you understand?" he said to Warin. Warin nodded.

"I'll stick close to Warin," said Ed.

"And he's looking after Mary." Daniel pressed the button on the pedestrian crossing and said, "Wait for the green man."

As they waited at the second road, Daniel said quietly to Jim, "Thanks for helping me back there, when I tripped."

"No worries," Jim replied.

"I thought for a moment you were going to leave me behind," Daniel added.

"So did I." After an awkward silence, Jim said, "Oh, I forgot; that crazy monk gave me some necklace for you." Jim fumbled in his pocket, drew out the leather pouch and handed it to Daniel. The green man lit up and they jostled their way across the road.

Moments later, they stood by the immense black lion. While Warin and Mary gazed up at Nelson looming high above them, Daniel undid the pouch and tipped the necklace into the palm of his hand. An ammonite pendant on an intricate gold chain. He stopped breathing – Queen Eleanor had worn this, the twin of the one he had found in Brother Clément's grave. He inwardly thanked Brother Clément as his fingers closed around the precious gift.

"It worked, Dan! You did it - we're back," Natalie said, beaming. They stood awkwardly for a moment, unsure how to celebrate, then Natalie threw caution to the wind and hugged Daniel and then the others. Another awkward silence fell, broken by Ed,

"What now?" he said, addressing Daniel. Daniel looked at Jim and hesitated.

Jim's dormant angst sputtered into life. If he wanted to regain control of this unlikely little gang, now was his moment. He should reassert himself and cow the others into submission. It would be so easy to slip back into his old ways. He looked at Ed and Natalie. In their adventures they had become his friends rather than his followers. Even Daniel had become a friend instead of - well, he didn't really want to admit to himself what Daniel had been before. Jim snuffed out the flicker of resentment, grinned at Daniel and said,

"Well, Geek, you're the man with a plan. What do you think we should do? Change out of these ridiculous clothes?"

"Yep. I reckon that's a good place to start, so we need to find some shops. Anyone got any money?"

"I have," said a voice behind them.

Daniel spun round at the sound, "Miss Hetherington! What are you doing here?"

"Looking for you four; following a ridiculous hunch," the history teacher said. She turned to a smartly dressed man beside her, gave him an *I told you so* look, and continued, smiling, "Not so ridiculous after all, it seems. So, the first and last Eleanor Cross sites were some kind of time portal? I presume you discovered this by accident, Daniel."

"Yes, Miss."

"And have these two also just discovered it by accident?" she said, gesturing to Mary and Warin, standing behind the others, holding hands.

"I'm not sure, to be honest. We didn't tell them anything but I think Mary somehow worked it out."

"Well, we can talk about all this later. Right now our priority is to inform your parents that you're safe and sound."

"I'll see to that," said the stranger, stepping forward. "I'm Simon Penrose; I work for the government. Welcome back," he said, smiling. "You can probably imagine the search that's been going on for you four since you disappeared. We'll get on to your parents straightaway but I'm afraid before you see them, we will need a full debrief. And you all need to be checked over medically. But first, let's get you off the street before you're recognised. The last thing we need is for photos of you in those clothes to pop up all over social media."

From here on, Simon Penrose called the shots. Colleagues appeared from nowhere and ushered them into two cars. Daniel went with Warin, Mary and Miss Hethington. He sank into the cushioned back seat of the car, unable to speak for the lump in his throat; relieved beyond measure that the burden of responsibility he had been carrying twenty-four hours a day was finally lifted. To keep from going to pieces he focussed on poor Warin and Mary. Perched on the faux leather seat as if it might burn them, they clung to each other while Miss Hetherington fussed around them trying to explain how to fasten the seat belt. She might as well have been speaking Chinese. The driver became restless and threatened to fasten them himself. Daniel roused himself from his comfortable stupor, undid his own seat belt and said,

"This is a cart without horses; it travels very fast. This girdle," he gestured to his own belt, "keeps us safe." He demonstrated in slow motion how to put it on. After several attempts, Warin managed his and, grinning at his success, reached over to help Mary, but she had beaten him to it.

Miss Hetherington instructed the driver in a firm undertone to drive slowly. He gave her a defiant look but complied; the car inched away. Mary gripped the door with one hand and Warin's arm with the other. They stared at the buses, vans and cars whizzing past them on all sides and gasped whenever another vehicle came close. Daniel suppressed an urge to laugh. After all, it had been terrifying enough for him and the others going back seven hundred years. But at least once they worked out what had happened, they had a rough idea of what to expect. Warin and Mary had none whatsoever. They might as well have landed on a different planet. Eventually, they would discover some deeper aspects of continuity between their own time and the present, as Daniel had. But for now, even he could barely imagine what they were going through.

Chapter 83

15th December Current Year, London

They drove to a nondescript apartment where more government people, including a doctor, were also arriving. Two of them were tasked with buying new clothes for the young people. They visually sized them up and then left, but not before Miss Hetherington collared them in the hall to give them some unasked-for advice. Next the doctor, Penny, introduced herself and explained what was involved in the medical examination they needed to have. Miss Hetherington physically barred her way to her students until she was fully satisfied that consent had been given over the phone by their parents. All this was completely lost on Warin and Mary. Daniel interpreted.

"This lady is a physician. We do not feel sick but she will check that we have no illness. She can examine me first and you can watch."

The doctor did the works on Daniel: temperature, blood pressure, heart rate and blood tests and gave him a clean bill of health, pending blood test results. Natalie, Ed and Jim went next and also allowed Mary and Warin to watch, which they did mutely, though the doctor chatted away to them explaining what she was doing. At length, Warin and Mary were asked to give their consent. Warin did so readily, bewildered but willing to go with the flow. But once the doctor's attention was focussed on Mary, she began to tremble.

"She's going into shock," said Penny, approaching. But the teacher intercepted her.

"This girl is a minor, she cannot give consent. I take responsibility for her and I withhold my consent."

"With the greatest respect, madam, she is by default a ward of the state. She may be a threat to the health of the nation. She has come from the Middle Ages and may be carrying the plague or other infections. She must be examined and her blood must be screened."

"I understand that," said Miss Hetherington, "and I appreciate that you're just doing your job but I am also doing mine. This child is distressed and bewildered. It is inappropriate to subject her to an intrusive medical examination at this moment in time; though I understand that it must be done."

"And sooner rather than later. Everyone who has had contact with them will have to stay in quarantine until the blood results come back. The longer it takes for that to happen, the longer the other kids will have to wait to be reunited with their families."

"I'm sorry for that, of course," Miss Hetherington said, turning to the others, "truly I am, but we need to give Mary time." They had reached a stalemate.

Daniel had been watching Mary while all this was going on, "She's getting worse, Miss," he said.

"Clear the room! Everyone except Warin and Daniel," Miss Hetherington boomed, and though she had no official power, nobody could withstand her moral authority.

Warin had his arm around Mary and said, "She's cold." Miss Hetherington strode to the door and called after the others,

"Bring a blanket, sweet tea and chocolate."

The teacher knelt down in front of Mary and said gently, "You've had a terrible shock, my dear. Everything is strange and unfamiliar to you. But we will look after you. You are safe with us, I promise." The blanket arrived, along with chocolate biscuits and tea. Miss Hetherington tipped half a cup away into a plant pot and left it to cool, saying, "She's shaking too much to hold it steady. And I imagine she's unused to hot drinks."

"Yes," Daniel said, "apart from mulled wine." They tucked into tea and biscuits, Mary and Warin grimaced initially at the strange taste of the tea but there was no such reaction to the chocolate biscuits. Warin ate five, clearing the plate and then asked if there were any more. Everyone laughed, including Mary. The blanket, sugar and caffeine began working a quiet miracle.

"I've been thinking," Daniel said. "It was different for us. When we were flung back to the year 1290 we didn't know what had happened, so the first hours were taken up with working that out and trying to get back.

Mary chose to come with us and does kind of understand what has happened. But everything is much stranger than she could have anticipated."

"You look as if you have an idea, Daniel," said Miss Hetherington.

"Yes, well, it's just that Mary was a nun, used to life in a religious setting. And she was on her way to Westminster Abbey for her mother's funeral. What if we were to take her there, to see her mother's tomb?"

"That might give her some continuity," said the teacher, "and closure. The government lot won't like it, not unless we can persuade her to have the blood test first. But it's worth a try."

"And we'll need to change out of these," Daniel said, brushing his hand over his tunic and leggings.

Daniel's plan was conveyed to Simon Penrose, who reluctantly agreed, if it would get them past the impasse over Mary's medical. It did. The opportunity to visit her mother's final resting place brought Mary out of herself. She submitted to the medical examination. While they waited for blood test results, the boys were ushered into one en-suite bedroom, and Mary and Natalie to another, to change. Miss Hetherington went to accompany the girls but Natalie said,

"We'll be fine, thank you, Miss," and shut the door in her teacher's face. Natalie left Mary investigating the strange clothes, and headed straight for the bathroom, saying,

"I'll help you with those after my shower."

She emerged ten minutes later, wrapped in a towel, her dark hair dripping.

"That was the best shower I've ever had!" she said, beaming.

"Shower?" said Mary. She sniffed the air, stepped towards Natalie and sniffed again. "You smell lovely."

"You've never had a shower, have you? Come on," she grabbed Mary by the hand and led her to the bathroom. Mary stood in front of the glass cubicle none the wiser. Natalie laughed and got back in, still wrapped in the towel. She showed Mary how it worked, soaking herself in the process, which reduced them both to giggles.

Moments later, Mary was left alone in the bathroom; alone for the first time in this new alien world. First she used the privy, amazed by its flush. Next she took one of the small bottles, unscrewed the cap and sniffed it. This was what Natalie's hair smelled of. She removed her clothes and stepped into the cubicle. The force of the water shocked her extremely. It was like being out in a heavy downpour but with the water warm. Once she grew used to it, she relaxed, closed her eyes and basked in the feeling of the water running over her hair and down to her feet. Eventually, she squeezed some of the creamy liquid onto her palm and rubbed it into her hair, which transformed into a bubbly mass. She guessed that she needed to rinse it. She let the water run over her hair as before and the bubbles ran down her face and over her body.

"Ooh! Ow! Help!" Natalie rushed in and saw Mary rubbing her eyes. She grabbed a hand towel and passed it into the shower.

"Close your eyes and wipe them gently with this. I'm so sorry. I forgot to warn you not to get soap in your eyes."

A few minutes later, a slightly red-eyed Mary appeared, looking sheepish, wrapped in her towel.

"Why do you wear a man's garments?" she said.

Natalie laughed. "Girls can wear trousers too now. They're much more practical when it's cold. I hate wearing tights."

"What are tights?"

"Right," said Natalie, turning towards the array of clothes on the bed, and picking up a pair of knickers, "Let's start with the basics."

Soon afterwards, Mary followed Natalie to rejoin the others, wearing a long-sleeved floral maxi-dress and a cardigan. With her unveiled chestnut hair cascading onto her shoulders, she felt both exposed and liberated. Her eyes sought Warin's. He was staring at her, open-mouthed, clearly moonstruck. Mary looked self-conscious and fiddled with her hair.

"Are we all ready?" said Miss Hetherington, smiling. She was glad she had insisted there should be something modest for Mary to wear if she chose. She was, after all, used to a nun's habit. But looking at her now, the teacher imagined that Mary would shrug off convent life with hardly a backward glance.

Chapter 84

15th December Present day, Westminster Abbey

They entered through the west door of the abbey. Mary paused to look at the Tomb of the Unknown Soldier, then crossed herself and said a prayer. The nave was very much longer than the church she was used to in 1290 but otherwise, structurally the building was much the same.

"Where are the paintings?" she asked.

Now was no time to go into the Reformation. Miss Hetherington merely said, "I'm afraid religious tastes have changed, my dear, and you will find churches much plainer nowadays." At the end of the nave, they turned left towards the Shrine of Edward the Confessor which was far less ornate than the one Mary was used to, with its many golden statues.

Mary approached her mother's tomb and laid her hand on it. "All these years and she is still here," she whispered. And after a long pause, "Is my father here also?"

"Yes," Daniel said gently, "over there."

"Everyone I know is gone," Mary said, weeping soundlessly.

"Yes, but they lived out their lives after you left. Your father lived another twenty years."

"I should like to be alone awhile," she said. They all withdrew except Simon Penrose, who had insisted on accompanying them to the abbey, along with a couple of other government agents, in case Warin and Mary made a dash for it. Daniel thought that running away from the only people they knew in this alien world was the very last thing they would do. But there was no point arguing with the authority of the state.

Minutes later Mary re-joined the others and Simon Penrose led the little party out towards the cloisters, through a narrow wooden door on the right and up a spiral staircase to the abbey library, which had been cleared for their use. In this hallowed setting, Mary was as comfortable as she could be, surrounded by row upon row of ancient leather-bound books on wooden shelves. Miss Hetherington smiled as Mary paused to look at a medieval illuminated manuscript in a glass case. The teacher gave Simon Penrose a look and nodded her approval. He was finally at liberty to question the young princess. He gestured to them all to find seats around a large wooden table and asked Mary to tell her story.

Mary took a deep breath and said, firstly to Daniel, "I have to confess to spying on you, Lord Daniel."

"I'm just plain Daniel here," he said.

"At first it was purely by chance. I was in the church at Geddington, on the night of our arrival there, keeping vigil; I became sleepy and stepped out into the cold air to rouse myself. And there you were, digging in the churchyard in the middle of the night. So I watched, and after you had gone, I retrieved the book you had buried there."

"I felt someone was watching me," said Daniel.

Mary continued, "Many words in your book were strange to me, but a little study of it soon gave me to understand that it was about my mother. And that it was written many years after her death and burial. I was afraid. Somehow you had come here from the years to come. I didn't understand how this could be, except through witchcraft. Yet instinct told me that there was no harm in you. I felt it my duty to warn my father, and yet I knew that his first responsibility was the safety of his kingdom. He would have you arrested, tried and executed. Indeed, in his position I would do the same. But, as I said, you seemed to pose no threat, so I delayed and determined to watch you at every opportunity." Mary blushed at her own confession. Her little audience was charmed.

"I saw nothing more to arouse my suspicion until Woburn. I followed you and Natalie into the woods and you showed her pictures on something like a small book that emitted light. An otherworldly object. Yet my spying hitherto had convinced me you were no more witches than I. You were bewildered and afraid, though most of the time you hid it well. I tried to imagine myself in your place. I didn't know what your world was like, but I supposed that you and your companions would wish to rejoin your families there, unless you had come here to escape some terrible fate that awaited you in your own time. As I watched you and pondered your predicament, another possibility awoke in my mind. If you were able to visit another time, why could not I? From then on, I observed you for my own purposes, without any wish to betray your secret.

"Last night I was in the friary church praying for Warin here, because he confided in me that his life was in danger. And when I noticed you enter with Brother Clément, I crept closer to listen. What I heard utterly amazed me, and confirmed my suspicion that you had come from the future. Later I found Carlita, one of my mother's ladies-in-waiting, who had also overheard your conversation. Before then I had avoided her, harbouring a petty jealousy, for I knew we shared similar looks and my mother kept her close to remind her of me. Last night I confessed my resentment; it was no fault of hers that I was sent away and she had taken my place. We joined forces and dreamt up a plan." A grin spread over Mary's face and her eyes sparkled. "It was outrageous and very risky but if it worked, it had the potential to deliver me from the cloistered life and save Carlita and Warin from peril at the hands of Derian Scand. We agreed to change places and right then and there, she dressed in my clothes and I in hers."

"Like Saint Alban and that other bloke, the priest!" Natalie exclaimed.

Mary smiled, "Saint Amphibalus. I had not thought of it, but yes, there is a similarity to the story." Her face clouded and she sighed, "How I hope Carlita will not share their fate."

"Please go on with your own story," said Simon Penrose, with slight impatience. He had no idea when it came to saints, but under no circumstances would he admit to ignorance.

Mary continued, "This morning we left together for the procession, in trepidation that my father or grandmother might find us out at any moment. But all their attention was on the funeral of my mother's heart. I advised Carlita to remain as silent as possible for, being Spanish, her accent might give her away."

Jim interrupted, "But didn't your plan save this Carlita girl from one danger by dropping her into another? She'll be been in terrible trouble once it comes out. They might even think she murdered you in order to take your place!" Daniel rolled his eyes. He shared Jim's concern but had more tact than to voice it.

"We thought of that," Mary replied. "Carlita intends to confide in my grandmother and the king and tell them the whole story this evening."

"They'll never believe her," said Ed, before he could help himself.

"I gave her Daniel's book as evidence."

"Hmm, the book is pretty convincing," said Daniel. "They may believe her and what then?"

Simon Penrose said, "They'll hush it up; just like we will. Whatever era they belong to, the authorities can't afford to have information about time travel getting out into the public domain. Think of the panic it would cause if people thought that they might fall through a time portal anytime they walk down the street."

Daniel had the distinct impression this was not the first time an experience like theirs had been hushed up. He held his tongue on that issue, however, and said,

"Yes, but that's not how it worked. We didn't just happen to fall through a time portal by walking down the street."

"That's pretty much what it felt like to me," said Jim with a shrug.

"Yes, I know that's how it felt, but it's not what actually happened."

"I take it you have some kind of explanation," said Penrose.

"Brother Clément came up with a theory that made sense to me last night, when Mary overheard us talking. But it's going to sound completely demented to you,"

"What explanation? said Miss Hetherington, leaning forward.

The anticipation of saying it out loud in front of all these people made the concept seem more and more far-fetched in Daniel's head. He took a deep breath. "That the sites of the first and last Eleanor crosses acted as portals but the time travel itself was powered by prayer."

"Holy crap," said Jim. "That's weirder than it happening by chance!"

Daniel continued, "Just humour me for a minute and try to keep an open mind. If God exists, He is outside of time, right? Brother Clément was praying night and day for Queen Eleanor to be remembered through the centuries; but here, in our time, she's pretty much forgotten. I became interested in her because of my essay. Then I *happened* to go searching for the Lincoln cross site, the exact spot where Brother Clément was praying, at the exact time, on the exact day. What are the odds?" He looked around at the others, gesturing with open hands. "And now, through our time travel experience, we've taken part in the two-hundred-mile procession in the queen's memory."

"The greatest funeral procession ever held in this country," Miss Hetherington chipped in.

Mary said, "The idea that the time travel was empowered by Brother Clément's prayer makes sense to me. Daniel and his friends are now eyewitnesses to where all the memorial crosses were to be erected. Besides, if the cross site was a time portal that anyone could fall through, why are Brother Clément and Carlita not here too? They stood on the same spot." Daniel had not thought of this angle. He was so glad Mary had taken over the explanation, for she expressed it with utter conviction.

Mary continued, "Carlita and the monk have remained there because God's purpose for their lives will best be fulfilled there." She cast her eyes over Daniel and his friends. "You four have a part to play in resurrecting my mother's memory, in answer to Clément's prayers; and now that I am here, I will help."

"As will I," Warin echoed. It was clear to everyone that he would champion any cause Mary supported. Daniel hoped that one day he would feel like that about someone. Without conscious thought, his eyes found Natalie, who was also looking at him. Each abruptly turned their attention back to Mary, who added,

"I only hope Carlita is safe; I would not want her to suffer on my account."

"I can offer you some assurance about that, my dear," Miss Hetherington said. "History tells us that you lived into your fifties and died at the convent in Amesbury. I think we can conclude that the "Mary" whom history records is actually Carlita." She looked over at Daniel and said, "You're no longer the only Queen Eleanor expert around here, you know. I've done a lot of research about her since you four disappeared."

The teacher turned to Mary, "Do you have any regrets, now that you have had a small taste of the world you have come to?"

"No. Life in the convent is a good life for those who choose it, but I did not. By coming here, I have chosen to love and serve God outside the confines of its walls. I have chosen a new life in a new world and I will accept what comes, for good or ill." She spoke passionately but at the same time serenely, at peace with herself. She was a tall girl in any case but at this moment, she appeared taller, and despite being set adrift in this brave new world, she spoke with earnest authority.

Daniel and the others were silent, mesmerised by this vision of regal medieval beauty hurled headlong into a future utterly alien to her. She was strong - one glance showed them that. Her mother, Eleanor, had followed King Edward on crusade to the Holy Land. That same spirit had brought Mary to a different adventure. Now that she had overcome the initial shock, she would cope. But what were they to do with her?

Where should they start? How could someone appear like a rabbit from a hat and begin a new life in twenty-first-century Britain?

Chapter 85

The Following Spring, Lincoln

Daniel was sitting in the nave of Lincoln Cathedral next to Warin, Jim, Natalie and Ed, listening to the choir. His voice had begun to break and was currently too scratchy for singing. He looked at the tenors and basses and wondered which section he would join once his voice had settled. He glanced at Warin beside him. Warin's gaze was fixed on Mary, singing with the sopranos, looking perfectly at home in her choir robes and her surroundings. Joining the choir had been a godsend for Mary; singing at the daily service of evensong gave her a thread of continuity with her old life and a refuge from the bizarre new life she was adjusting to.

In this process, she and Warin were being championed by Miss Hetherington who had taken them under her wing. The pair were lodging in her home where she tutored them each morning and set them homework and chores to occupy each afternoon, while she taught at the school. Mary had the advantage of a sound medieval convent education and a quick, eager mind. She excelled and would soon be able to join Lincoln Minster School. Warin preferred chores to lessons and he had far more to catching up to do, since he was only now learning to read. Miss Hetherington persevered and encouraged him but when she discussed him with the headmaster, they agreed that it might be better to home-educate him until he was competent enough to pursue a vocational course, possibly training to work with horses, which he clearly loved.

Along with Daniel and his friends' parents, the headmaster was the only other person who had been let into Mary and Warin's secret. All of them had been obliged to sign the official secrets act and declare that they would never divulge the story of Mary and Warin's background and, in the case of the four young people, their own experience of time travel.

On weekends, sometimes Daniel and the others joined Miss Hetherington, Mary and Warin for trips, when they learned to use our money, buses and trains, shops and cafes. They tried their hand at bowling, which Mary hated but Warin loved. In ice skating, Mary had ended the session gliding elegantly round and round the rink, feeling euphoric, while Warin tottered and fell every time he let go of the side. As for their first trip to the cinema, Mary and Warin were equally overwhelmed by the sensory onslaught of the big screen experience, though they loved watching television at home.

Daniel had not forgotten his promise to Brother Clément. He had set up a social media channel about Eleanor of Castile, with a lot of technical assistance from Jim. He appreciated Jim's help, not just practically, but because it cemented their new relationship. They would probably never be best mates, but they got along fairly well. Their joint project included a crowd-funding initiative to raise money to set up information boards at the sites of the lost Eleanor Crosses, starting with Lincoln. These were a good first step but would commemorate little more than Eleanor's name.

Daniel loved books and for him, there was no better way to resurrect a person's memory than to write their story. He devoted most of his spare time to writing a memoir of Queen Eleanor, and his long discussions with his living sources gave Warin and Mary welcome opportunities to speak of the life they had left behind. What he could never divulge in his book, however, was the most significant legacy of his time travelling experience – Mary herself. Eleanor's daughter, reflecting her mother's keen intelligence and loving nature, was learning to thrive in 21st century Britain - a living, breathing monument to Queen Eleanor of Castile.

And now, here they were at the last evensong service before the Easter holidays, which Mary and Warin were going to spend in Abbotsbury with Daniel. He looked again at Mary. She was wearing her mother's fossil pendant; Brother Clément's parting gift to him. Because of the so-called curse, Daniel had sought Warin's advice before giving it to her, and Warin had told him how Father David had lifted the curse and replaced it with a blessing. With the age-old ammonite at her neck, Mary sang the words of today's Psalm, "My time is in thy hand." Daniel watched her face light up exultantly. He smiled. Yes, he thought, from the Jurassic era, when ammonites swam in the oceans, to the year 1290, to now, our times are in God's hands.

Epilogue

Easter 1315, Abbotsbury, Dorsetshire

A traveller, walking eastwards along a ridgeway near the coast, crested a hill and stopped to admire the view. He squinted and raised a hand to shield his eyes. Southwards, to his right, the land fell away to the sea, which blinked in the glare of the morning sun. But between the land and the sea lay a curiously long, narrow bank and, behind it, a long, narrow lagoon, stretching away and away eastwards towards an island. In his long, itinerant life, the traveller had never seen a view like it. He filled his lungs with cool air and moved onwards, seeking a path down towards the settlement. Presently he arrived at the gatehouse of the Abbey of Saint Peter at Abbotsbury. He stooped to enter through the wicket in the gate and greeted the porter cordially.

"My business is with one Brother Clément, if he is still in residence here. He would be above fifty years of age by now."

"Yes, he is still with us; but he is now called Father Clément. He has been our Abbott these five years past," said the porter, his eyes glinting with the pleasure of imparting unexpected tidings.

"Abbot Clément, is it? Why, that is fine news. I should like to see him, if he is at leisure."

"He passed this way not half an hour ago and walked downhill towards the shore. He goes there to pray when his mind is much occupied. Will you come within and wait, sir?"

"I thank you, no. I will follow him down to the beach. Good day." The stranger began to walk away.

"Good day, sir. I did not catch your name."

"Scand, Derian Scand," the man called over his shoulder.

Derian's tension mounted as the track to the shore led him downhill. He stopped to roll his shoulders, and dislodged the heavy leather pack on his back. The tools of his trade emitted a distinct metallic clang. He set the pack straight, rubbed his temples and pursued his path through a wooded gully and across a stream. He skirted the edge of a hillock where sheep grazed on lush grass, sprouting from strangely reddish earth. Derian shuddered at a memory it stirred, of blood-drenched soil beneath the body of a guard. His hand moved to the pommel of the slender knife hanging from his belt. He quickened his step.

Ahead lay a longer, flatter stretch of track with water meadows on his left and beyond them a dense reedbed. That must be the end of the lagoon I could see from the ridge, he thought. I have to pass beyond it to reach the shore. At last, he arrived at the stony bank, the final hurdle of his arduous journey to find his quarry. He paused for breath, recalling how he had last seen Brother Clément, five and twenty years ago, down the shaft of his crossbow.

Derian scrambled up and over the steep bank of stones and spotted the monk. He was standing by the water's edge, staring out to sea. Derian called to him but his voice was drowned by the crash of the surf and the crunch as the ebbing wave dragged the shingle away. Derian approached and tapped the monk on the shoulder. Clément spun round.

"Forgive me, Abbott Clément, I did not mean to startle you. You may not remember me," he began.

"Yours is a face I am unlikely to forget, Master Scand. What brings you to Abbotsbury?"

"You do, Father. My purpose is two-fold; firstly, to beg forgiveness for the wrong I did you. And also, to seek an explanation for those strange goings-on at Charing. Even after all these years, I find that my curiosity will not lie down and sleep. And I suspect that you understood what passed there a good deal better than I."

"Your coming gladdens me more than I can say, Master Scand. My forgiveness you have had these many years, but it does my heart good to tell you of it face to face. And how have you fared all this time?"

"There were some wilderness years after we parted," Derian admitted. "I fled to Wales and plied my trade among the princes there under a different name, but I was forever looking over my shoulder and I no longer took satisfaction in my work. Moreover, no matter how many hours I brooded on what I had witnessed that day, its meaning eluded me. Gradually I came to be thankful that my bolt missed its mark and your life was not on my head. But the mystery of the disappearing children – all I can say is that at last I came to accept that there are things in the universe beyond mortal comprehension. This humbled me. Little by little my contempt of the world and my fellow man diminished until finally I was able to repent."

"God be praised! How happy I am to hear it. On the matter of the queen's death, I think you may rest easy in your conscience. I have long since come to believe that your curse was ineffectual and she died of natural causes."

"Be that as it may, brother, my intent was to kill. And I did murder the guard sent to follow me from Dunstable. Though Christ's mercy absolves me of divine wrath, I still had to answer to human justice. I turned myself in to Lord Burnell. But there too, by God's grace, I found mercy. Lord Burnell did not wish to bring to light the matter of the curse. He saw that I had reformed my life and asked of me only that I make amends as best I could to the widow of the murdered man. Nothing can atone for the taking of a human life, but I sought her out and gifted her enough fine silver candlesticks that she might provide for her family and live out her days in comfort."

"Then you were free to live your life as you chose," observed Clément.

"Aye, I thought of following you into the cloister, brother. But God showed me a better way to serve him. When I cursed that stone, I defiled the skill God had granted me. Now I wished to turn my gift to his glory. For a dozen years now, I have plied my trade among the monasteries of Wales and England, gilding statues and undertaking whatever ornate commissions the monks request. For payment, I seek only the cost of materials and my board and lodging. But fashioning crosses is what pleases me most. For then I can contemplate Christ, who paid the penalty for my grievous sin. And whereas once I placed a curse on that jewel long ago, intending harm to yourself and the queen, nowadays I place a blessing on each cross I make, and pray for God's grace on whomsoever may wear or use it."

Listening to Derian's tale, a broad, serene smile had spread over Clément's face. "I thank God for bringing you here and giving me the privilege of witnessing a life so transformed."

"Father Abbott, I have travelled the length and breadth of the land and heard many strange tales and legends, but none that could shed any light on the question of the vanishing children."

Clément took Derian's arm and said, "Let us walk along the shore and I will show you where, on this very beach, it all began. For this is where I found the snakestone, in September of the year my beloved Queen Eleanor died." And, reaching into the neck of his habit, he drew out his fossil pendant into the light of day.

Author's Note

Queen Eleanor had two scribes in her entourage but Brother Clément is a fictional character, as are Derian Scand, Warin, Carlita, Aerlene and Aldred. All other named characters in the medieval part of the story are based on historical figures.

Bishop Robert Burnell served as Edward's Lord Chancellor from 1274 until his death in 1292. The ruins of his family manor can be seen at Acton Burnell in Shropshire.

Otto de Grandisson was the king's closest friend and right-hand man. He left England after Edward's death, remained unmarried and lived until 1328.

All the present-day characters are fictional.

Queen Eleanor died of natural causes on 28th November 1290; the structure of the plot follows the historical narrative that led up to her death and then to her burial in Westminster Abbey on 17th December.

Three of the Eleanor crosses are still standing: Geddington, Hardingstone (Northampton) and Waltham. The cross at Charing Cross Station is a replica. The original was located approximately 300 metres to the west, on the south of what is now Trafalgar Square. A statue of Charles I, mounted, stands there now. The other crosses either fell into disrepair or were deliberately destroyed during the Civil War period.

The Legend of the Miraculous Cross of Waltham was written by a canon of Waltham in the 12th century. The cross appears to have remained an object of pilgrimage until the abbey was dissolved in 1540, when it was lost.

In writing historical fiction, a compromise over language is inevitable. The reader would not be served by zealous use of archaic language. That said, in the dialogue of the medieval parts, I have endeavoured to use only words that were in existence in their old English form in the medieval period. I hope I have given a flavour of the language of 1290.

The issue of language is even more pertinent in a timeslip novel, where present-day characters must communicate with people in the past. In a nod towards authenticity, my main character, Daniel, is a self-confessed history nerd whose mother is an academic specialising in medieval English. He naturally assumes the role of spokesperson. I realise that this is merely a gesture, since at the time the medieval Royal Court used Old French not Old English.

I began research for this book in 2010, before the publication of Sara Cockerill's excellent 'Eleanor of Castile, The Shadow Queen.' My main secondary source has been the earlier 'Eleanor of Castile,' by Jean Powrie. For dates and locations, I have largely accepted Powrie's version, which is entirely plausible.

Where historical sources differ, I have chosen whichever version best suits my artistic purpose. One such example is when Queen Eleanor entreats Otto de Grandisson to pray for her soul in the Holy Land. There is a much-faded painting of this scene on Eleanor's tomb in Westminster Abbey. But other sources state that Otto had already set out to prepare for the proposed crusade, discussed at the Clipstone Parliament. I opted for the painting's version of events since it is more romantic and because I wanted to keep Otto in the story throughout, as he was such a key character in the king's inner circle.

King Edward lived another 17 years after Eleanor's death and in 1299, he married Margaret of France. With her, he fathered two more sons and one daughter, whom he named Eleanor.

In addition to the 12 crosses, Edward established and set up funding for many other elaborate commemorations of his beloved Eleanor. Throughout the first year after her death, he distributed alms in her memory every Tuesday. On the first anniversary of her death, such spectacular memorial services were held in Westminster Abey and the Black friars' priory church that 3000 pounds of wax candles were burned and the clergy were reportedly exhausted. After this, a lavish annual memorial at Westminster was instated, and carried out until the dissolution of the monasteries.

On January 3rd 1291 Edward wrote to the Abbot of Cluny, asking that the monastery pray for "our consort whom in life we loved dearly and dead we do not cease to love."

Glossary of Terms

Bier - a framework on which a coffin or corpse is laid before burial.

Brazier - a freestanding heater consisting of a stand and a pan for holding lighted coals.

Cloister - a place of religious seclusion, such as a monastery or convent; covered walk around an open court.

Cot - a simple bed.

Divine Office - the regular cycle of worship services recurring at various times during the day and night, also called the Offices of the Church or Divine Hours. The services were as follows: Matins just after midnight; Lauds at dawn (Matins and Lauds were sometimes combined); Prime at 6am; Terce at 9am; Sext at noon; None at 3pm; Vespers at sunset; Compline before bedtime.

Girdle - belt.

Infirmarer - one who tends the sick in an infirmary.

Infirmary - a sick bay in a monastery.

Lavatorium - a washbasin.

Mantle - sleeveless cloak.

Motte and bailey castle - a fortification made up of a mound (motte), a keep (bailey) and a courtyard.

Obeisance - a bow or gesture of respectful submission.

Oratory - small chapel.

Phial – a small bottle.

Pommel – ornamental knob at the end of the handle of a sword hilt or the grip of a dagger.

Prie-dieu – prayer kneeler or prayer desk.

Sconce – a candlestick or small lantern, or the metal bracket fixing a candlestick or lantern to a wall.

Scrip – small bag.

Solar – living room on an upper storey.

Tonsure – the shaved top back part of a monk's head.

A Note from the Author

I write my stories in Essex near Epping Forest, where I walk as often as possible, preferring trees and birds to streets and buildings. I also love all things oceanic, hence the mermaid tales. I'm slightly envious of my daughters who live at the coast, where land borders the sea. I live with my husband, David, on the border of Essex and London; I manage life on the borders of health and ill health; in writing, I enjoy exploring the border of reality and imagination.

I'm available to visit book clubs in my local area or on Zoom. And for author events.

To find out more, visit melaniehodges.com

Contact me – mel16.hodges@gmail.com

Also by Melanie Hodges

Sirenna's Song - a heartwarming story of friendship, determination and bravery against the odds. When Lizzie and her brother Tom discover Sirenna's magical secret, will they be in time to save her? For ages 8 - 12 years and the young at heart.

Sirenna's Secret - Sequel to Sirenna's Song, a story where the sea meets the land, the past enters the present, and the mystical invades the mundane. When Lizzie and her brother Tom encounter Sirenna again, can they help her exchange loss and loneliness for hope and companionship?

Patience for Patients – A gentle devotional written from Melanie's experience of managing fibromyalgia syndrome alongside work and family life. She applies her understanding of God's love and purposes to the spiritual challenges faced by Christians living with long covid and other chronic health issues.

Printed in Great Britain
by Amazon